S
Smith

Smith, Mitchell,
1935-

Kingdom River.

DATE			

KINGDOM RIVER

BOOK TWO OF THE SNOWFALL TRILOGY

MITCHELL SMITH

A TOM DOHERTY ASSOCIATES BOOK

NEW YORK

KINGDOM RIVER: BOOK TWO OF THE SNOWFALL TRILOGY

Copyright © 2003 by Mitchell Smith

This book is printed on acid-free paper.

A Forge Book
Published by Tom Doherty Associates, LLC
175 Fifth Avenue
New York, NY 10010

www.tor.com

Forge® is a registered trademark of Tom Doherty Associates, LLC.

Library of Congress Cataloging-in-Publication Data

Smith, Mitchell, 1935-
    Kingdom River / Mitchell Smith.—1st ed.
        p. cm.—(Book two of the Snowfall trilogy)
    "A Forge book"—T.p. verso.
    ISBN: 0-765-30008-7
    1. Mexico—Fiction.   2. Glacial epoch—Fiction.   3. Kings and rulers—
Fiction.   4. Wilderness survival—Fiction.   5. Regression (Civilization)—
Fiction.   I. Title.

PS3569.M537834K56 2003
813'.54—dc21

                                                            2002043946

First Edition: May 2003

Printed in the United States of America

0 9 8 7 6 5 4 3 2 1

To absent friends,
Arthur Williams . . . Milburn Smith

Concern has been expressed by the National Science Foundation that possible alterations of Jupiter's orbit, following successive major cometary impacts, may affect the earth's orbit—slightly, but still decisively—and so change the annual patterns of our planetary weather.

ASSOCIATED PRESS, MAY 16, 2006
Article in Bloomington Times-Tribune
Bloomington, Indiana, May 17, 2006

Had this latest—and most severe—ice-age taken an age to arrive, instead of only decades, enough preparation might have been possible to spare those hundreds of millions who froze in the north . . . those hundreds of millions who starved in the south. Might have spared us, as well, four—now almost five—barbaric centuries, with what remains of civilization learned, like our language, from those relatively few books surviving.

EDWARD CABOT-LODGE, ADJUNCT
New Harvard Yard, Cambridge,
Massachusetts. *Commentaries*

To the Kipchak Prince and Khan Evgeny Toghrul, Lord of Grass, Ruler Perfect of the Bering Strait Traversed, the Map-Pacific Coast, Map-California—and, lately, Conqueror of Map-Texas to the Guadalupe River and beyond.

Greetings from Neckless Peter, old man and librarian, who years ago, having been taken captive from my Gardens Town by naked savages—Border Roamers serving with your father's subsidiary forces—was privileged to tutor a brilliant boy in what we know of Warm-times gone, and their wisdom.

This boy has become you, my lord—and I, your recently assigned ambassador and agent to North Map-Mexico, take this opportunity to tell you that I quit.

'I quit.' Is it any wonder we get not only our written and spoken language from the books of centuries past, but even its casual slang—so neat, so pointed, so appropriate?

I am, of course, aware that your strangler's bowstring awaits any who disappoint you, and can only hope that a thousand miles of distance—and perhaps some slight regard you might still hold for your elderly tutor—will prevent a determined attempt at murder.

In any case, I can now say what I felt it unwise to mention to you before—so as not to increase an already understandable arrogance—which is that you were by far the most extraordinary intelligence I had ever encountered or ever expected to encounter, and as such were a joy to teach. I have not forgotten and will never forget sitting by the Meadow Fountain at Caravanserai with a quiet, slender boy whose eyes, black, glossy, steady as a spider's and slightly slanted beneath the folds of their lids, drank from the pages of every copybook I presented to him.

Your first question to me: What had happened to the countless thousands of Warm-time books now lost to us? You'd asked, and been saddened by my answer: "Burned, libraries of them, almost all those not eaten by centuries of winters. Burned with all knowledge of their miracles of learning—perfect medicines, the making of black bang-powder, the secrets of flying machines and laboring machines and thoughtful machines, as well as endless wonderful intricate tales. . . . Almost all the books burned for warmth as their peoples' world collapsed beneath weather, and they and their children froze."

Yours proved to be a genius clear and encompassing as flowing water. And now, of course, driven by a ferocity that impressed even your late and quite ferocious father, that intelligence is causing our ice-weighted world to tremble, so only Middle Kingdom, and of course New England, might stand against you.

Do you remember the afternoon we read of Ancient-Alexander's life and conquests? We read it together in a spectacular copybook, a treasure copied from an original found in the ruins of Los Angeles. (—I trust, by the way, that the library at Caravanserai is being cared for. Over eight hundred copybooks. No moisture. There must be no moisture—and copying and recopying continuous. The books are all we have of Warmtimes and civilization.) Do you remember how we yearned for an encyclopedia, that dreamed-of miracle of answers? Never found, alas; too wonderful as kindling.

We read of Ancient-Alexander, and you diagramed his battles with squid ink on wide sheets of the court's perfect paper. You refought those conflicts in your mind, your quill moving here and there . . . and finally decided how the Persian center might have been more suitably arrayed.

"Clumsy forces," you said of the Persians and their Greek allies, but gathered them together on your paper, set them in odd echelon . . . then waited for Ancient-Alexander and his Companions to make the inevitable charge.

"He would have beaten me at the Granicus," you said, "but at Issus, I would have destroyed him. There would have been no Gaugamela." And satisfied, you let the white sheets of paper, swarming with the inked lines and arrows of battles never to be fought, slip from your lap to the grass.

I will not forget those afternoons, lord, nor your love of Warm-time poetry—particularly the New England lady's. *I could not stop for Death, so he kindly stopped for me* . . . (How sad that those Map-Boston people have fallen to growing beasts in women's bellies.)

Remembering our rich days, why then do I quit you? And for the service of an upstart Captain-General of North Map-Mexico, Small-Sam Monroe, to whose camp you sent me as ambassador and spy?

First, I leave your service for his because I loved his Second-mother, Catania Olsen, as a friend, and because Small-Sam was born at Gardens, my home, when it was still tree green and full of families and fine weaving, all under the rule of the last great Garden Lady, Mary Bongiorno. So, I choose my future in honor of my past.

Second, I leave your service for his because while Small-Sam Monroe is a war-captain, and successful at it, I think he will not be *only* a war-captain, determined as you are to devour all our cold-struck continent, and so cause a barbarous age to become even more so.

You will be interested to hear that when I mentioned my intention to Monroe—to leave your service for his—he insisted I first complete the task for which you sent me, and forward to you a complete history, description, and report of the current essential military and economic matters of his overlordship. This report to be carried sealed and unread by him or any man of his, and delivered along with his personal apology for depriving you of an amusing servant. . . . I'm not sure why 'amusing.'

He also refused to accept any report I might have made to him concerning you or the Khanate.

I believe you would like Sam Monroe—the 'Small-Sam,' I understand, has gone out of usage since his victories. He is a very interesting young man—your age, as it happens, within a year or two. He possesses a sort of informed, stony common sense, an interesting contrast to your brilliance.

I will miss you, my lord. You were an incomparable student . . . though I have felt more and more that I failed you as a teacher, to have left you with nothing but the determination to enforce your will across our world.

Once your servant, but no longer such . . .

Neckless Peter Wilson

KINGDOM RIVER

The ravens had come to This'll Do.

Sam Monroe, Captain-General of North Map-Mexico—and commander of the army that, before this, had been called Never-Defeated—frightened birds here and there as he walked among the dead.

A messenger-pigeon had reached Better-Weather, and he'd come, down with headquarters' Heavy Cavalry, come quickly, but still arriving two days too late. Troopers of the Second Regiment of Light Cavalry lay scattered through high grass for almost a Warm-time mile down the valley from Please Pass.

Sam Monroe walked through tall brown stems still brittle from last night's frost. Death had come in Patchy-fool Autumn, the eight-week summer ended two weeks before. Dead troopers lay here and there, almost hidden in the grass except where low mounds of the slain showed—Light Cavalry's hide-and-chainmail hauberks hacked by the imperial cataphracts' battle axes.

More than three hundred dead within sight of his encampment on the near hill, and dozens more lying out of sight to the east, where the village stood, ridden down as they'd spurred away. It seemed to Sam Monroe there would certainly be at least four hundred dead, when totaled.

Though the villagers had been spared the empire's usual rapes and murders, valuable squash and pumpkin fields had been trampled, their last harvest destroyed. Farms had been burned or battered—pine-plank buildings feathered with the cataphracts' arrows, doors smashed in, the furnishings axed for campfires.

The valley fields were quiet now, excepting only a raven's occasional croaking, only the dawn wind's murmuring through the grass. A cold wind, almost freezing, with Daughter Summer dead. Sam's soldiers believed Lady Weather would be weeping sleety tears for her, as Lord Winter came walking south from the Wall.

The imperials' commander had already recovered his killed and wounded, taken them back south through the pass, heading farther south of the *Sierra Oriental* to what would certainly be a triumph in Mexico City for the Empire's first victory against the North.

Not a great battle—only a clash of cavalry along a mountain border. But Sam Monroe's army had lost it. The charm of always winning was broken.

The Heavy Cavalrymen not digging john-trench, tending horses, or guying tents, were watching from the hill as he walked through the grass from corpse to corpse; Sam could feel them watching. . . . He knew so many of the dead. A small army was full of familiar faces—even though the chill afternoons had still been warm enough to spoil these, begin to swell them with rot in the army's brown wool and leather.

He knew a number of these troopers—and all the officers, of course. He'd saluted them in battle many times as they'd poured past him to trumpet calls in a flood of fast horses, shining steel, and banners.

Sam walked through the grass, visiting this one . . . then another. The women were the worst. If it hadn't been for the women, he would not be weeping. They lay, slender bones broken, soft skin sliced, faces—some still beautiful—astonished at their deaths. Where bright helmets had been beaten away, gleaming drifts of long hair, black, red, and golden, lay in broken grass.

He visited the dead for a Warm-time hour, then went back up the hill as the picks and shovels were brought down to bury them.

Two Heavy Cavalry corporals were posted as guards just beyond ear-shot of his tent (wonderful Warm-time phrase, 'ear-shot'). They saluted as he passed. Sam saw Margaret had brought his breakfast to a camp table by the tent's entrance.

"Sir, please eat." She stood watching him. "Done is done." A favorite saying of hers.

"The wounded?"

"Mercies found the last of them, eleven WT miles east. They've started bringing them in." She saw the question in his face. "Fifty-three, sir. And Ned Flores. He lost a hand . . . left hand."

Sam sat at the table. The breakfast was scrambled chicken eggs, goat sausage, and *tortillas*—almost a Warm-time breakfast out of the old copybooks, except the sausage would have been pig, the *tortillas* toasted bread with spotted-cow butter.

"You have to eat."

He took a sip of hot chocolate. "Thank you, Margaret."

Margaret turned and marched away, her boots crunching on the last of morning's frost, her rapier's length swinging at her side.

Margaret Mosten, old enough to be an older sister, always served his breakfasts. Always served every meal. She would come riding up to his horse, on campaign, with jerk-goat or crab apples for his lunch. Boiled water, safe from tiny bad-things, for his leather bottle. No food came to him, but from Oswald-cook by her hand.

Her predecessor, Elder Mosten, smelling something odd in chili, had tasted Sam's dinner once along the northern border by Renosa, then convulsed and died.

"To you—only through me," his eldest daughter, Margaret, had said, then resigned her captaincy in Light Infantry, and come to Sam's camp to take charge of it with a much harder hand than her father's had been.

Though that fatal chili's cook had hung, Margaret had ridden back to Renosa, inquired more strictly, and left four more hanging in the square—the cook's wife for shared guilt, and three others for carelessness in preparation and service.

"That many," Sam had said to her when she returned, "and no more."

"The cook and his wife were for that dinner;" Margaret Mosten had answered him, "the others were for our dessert."

So, as with many of his followers, the burden of her loyalty leaned against Sam Monroe, weighed upon him, and tended to make him a short-tempered young man, everywhere but the battlefield.

He could take bites of the breakfast *tortilla*, but the sausage and eggs were impossible. He must not—could not—vomit by his tent for the army to see.

"Too young," they'd say. "What is Sam, twenty-six, twenty-seven? Too young, after all, for a grown man's work. All that winning must have been luck."

And Sam Monroe would have agreed it *had* been luck—the good fortune of having the Empire's old, incompetent generals for enemies; the good fortune of having fine soldiers to fight for him; and what had seemed the good fortune of being born with battle-sense.

But battle-sense had led to victories; victories had led to ruling. And ruling had proved a crueler field than any battleground, and weightier duty.

It seemed to Sam, as he tried to eat a bite of eggs, that his will, which he had so far managed to extend to any necessary situation—as if a much older, grimmer, and absolutely competent person stood within him—that his will, his purposes, had turned him *into* that someone else, a man he would never have liked and didn't like now.

The proof lay beneath the hill, in dead grass.

But even that grim and forceful person had not come forth this morning to eat goat sausage and eggs.

Margaret came back, her sturdy bootsteps quieter; the light frost was melting under the morning sun.

"Sir. . . ." With official business, "sir" was all the Captain-General required. Sam had early decided that honorifics promoted pride and stupidity; he had the south's imperial examples.

"The brothers," Margaret Mosten said.

"Lord Jesus." He ate a bite of sausage to show he could, then took deep breaths to quiet his belly. The Rascobs had to be spoken with, but a little later would have been better. "Will they wait?"

"No," Margaret said. "And it would hurt them to be told to."

That was it for the sausage. Sam took another deep breath and put down his two-tine fork—silver, a spoil from God-Help-Us. "I'll see them."

"You should finish your eggs."

"Margaret, I don't want to finish the eggs. Now, send them up." Odd, when he thought about it. Why 'send them *up*'? The camp was on high ground, but level. His tent was only 'up' because he gave the orders.

Different bootsteps, stomping. The Rascobs appeared side by side and saluted—a fashion that had settled in the army after the early days in the *Sierra*. It was something all soldiers apparently loved to do.

The brigadiers, Jaime and Elvin Rascob, were twins, scarred and elderly at fifty-eight—both tall, gray-haired, gray-eyed, baked brown and eroded by weather. Elvin was dying of tuberculosis, caused by poison plants too small to see, so he wore a blue bandanna over mouth and nose as if he were still a young mountain bandit and sheep-stealer.

"We just rode in." Jaime Rascob's face was flushed with rage. "And saw what comes of sending Light Cavalry where infantry should have gone."

"Told you, Sam," Elvin said, the south's blue cotton fluttering at his mouth. "Heavy Infantry to hold the pass—Light Infantry to come down the hills on them. Would have trapped those imperials, maybe killed them all. *Told* you." Dying, Elvin was losing courtesy.

"Ned thought he could deal with them." Sam stuck his fork in the eggs and left it there.

"Ned Flores is a fool kid-goat—a Light-Cavalry colonel! What the fuck does he know about infantry situations?" Courtesy lost entirely.

"It was your fault, sir." Jaime's face still red as a rooster's comb.

"Yes, it was my fault." Sam looked up at two angry old men—angry, and dear to him. "Scouts reported only a few hundred imperials, and from the careful way they came, with no great force behind them. So, it seemed to me that Light Cavalry, with room to run east if they had to, could handle their heavies without our infantry to lever against. I was wrong."

"Three hundred dead," Jaime Rascob said.

"That's incorrect. It will be nearly four hundred."

"Goodness to Godness Agnes . . ." Elvin, through his bandanna—certainly a Warm-time copybook phrase. "Almost three out of every four troopers dead. And we *told* you!"

"Elvin—"

"Jaime, I'm just saying what everybody knows." A statement definite, and with the weight of years as well, since he and his brother were each old enough to have been their commander's grandfather.

Squinting in morning sunlight, Sam pushed his breakfast plate a little away. The smell was troubling.

A mistake. He noticed the colonels noticing; an exchange of glances. He picked up his fork, ate a bite of eggs, then another. Took a sip of chocolate. "Do we know the cataphracts' commander?"

"Voss says it was likely one of the new ones, probably Rodriguez." Jaime didn't sound convinced, though the Empire, slow at everything, had begun to allow promising younger officers commands. Michi Rodriguez was one of those 'Jaguars.'

"Whoever," Jaime said, "he whipped Flores with just six hundred heavy horse."

"Less."

"*Not* less, Elvin," his brother said. "Three squadrons, at least."

Elvin didn't argue. Any argument with Jaime Rascob ended only after a long while.

"Still a damn shame." Elvin cleared his throat behind the bandanna. "We could have bottled them in Please Pass, maybe killed them all."

Sam chewed a bite of sausage and managed to swallow it. "*My* decision to let them come through. *My* decision to send only Light Cavalry down to deal with them. *My* fault." The breakfast was hopeless—one more bite and he *would* be sick for all the camp to see. The young Captain-General, who'd never failed, vomiting his breakfast while troopers rotted in the mountain grass.

"You got too big for your bitches," Elvin said, certainly not the correct Warm-time phrase. The old man took little care with them, rarely got them right.

"It's a mistake I won't make again." Sam took a sip of chocolate. A smell of spoiling was rising from the valley.

"We can't win every fight, Elvin." Jaime gave his brother a shut-up look.

"For sure not campaigning like this!" Elvin coughed a spatter of blood into his kerchief, turned, and marched away into the camp. His brother sighed, and followed him.

Sam turned on his camp stool to watch them go. Two tough old men. Both wore heavy double-edged broadswords scabbarded aslant down their backs, the swords' long grips wound with silver wire. Elvin stumbled slightly on the uneven ground.

Half a year ago, Portia-doctor had reported he was dying. She'd heard bad sounds in his lungs when she'd thumped him.

It had been a difficult examination. Elvin had thumped her in return, then attempted a kiss.

"He's just a boy," she'd said to Sam, "in an old man's body."

"Then he's younger than I am, Doctor."

"Yes, sir. In many ways younger than you are."

Portia-doctor had apprenticed in medicine under Catania Olsen, which said everything in North Map-Mexico—and south in the Empire as well. Portia had learned as much as that dear physician, four Warm-time medical copybooks, and seven years of hard experience could teach.

She'd been pretty those years ago, a sturdy young woman with dark brown hair and eyes to match. Now, the army work and civilian work had worn her. And losing Catania to plague at Los Palominos had worn her more.

Howell Voss, commanding the Heavy Cavalry, called her "the noble Portia," looked for her in any group or meeting, and was thought by a thoughtful few to have been in love with her for some time.

"Why doesn't he just tell her so?" Sam had once asked his Second-mother, after an officers' evening *asado*.

"Because," Catania Olsen had said, tightening her mare's saddle girth, "because Howell has lost an eye, and fears being blind and a burden. And because he believes that Portia is very fine and good, and that he is not."

. . . Sam sat and watched the Rascob brothers walk away down the tent lines. The other, grimmer Sam Monroe inside him began to consider inevitable replacements for the two of them, certainly following Elvin's death. Jaime's replacement, then, would of course destroy him.

'Fools do top with crowns, and so bid friends farewell.' A copied Warm-time line, and very old.

The Captain-General of North Map-Mexico pushed his breakfast plate a little farther away, took a deep breath to calm his stomach, and sat at his camp table with his eyes closed, not caring to watch the *Sierra's* shadows—lying across a wide, meadowed valley lightly salted with flocks of sheep—slowly shorten as the sun rose higher.

Bootsteps. No one in the army seemed to walk lightly. "You didn't finish your eggs."

"No. I've had enough, Margaret."

"Oswald-cook goes to some trouble with your eggs. Herbs."

"Oh, for Weather's *sake*." The Captain-General picked up his fork, reached over, and took another bite of eggs.

"Sir, there's no winning forever. You don't have to be perfect." It was a burden-sharing she often practiced. At first, it had annoyed him.

Margaret stood in bright, chill morning light, watching him eat two more bites of egg. "They had room to run."

"Yes—*if* they'd run, instead of fighting." Sam put his fork down a little more than firmly. Margaret took the plate, and went away.

It was a great relief; he was tired of people talking to him. He stood to go into his tent . . . get away from distant murmurs and the troops' eyes, their unspoken concern—concern for him, as if he were the party injured. They were wearing him away like constant running water. Wearing that lucky youngster, Small-Sam, away—and so revealing more and more of the present Sam Monroe. Someday, they might be sorry. . . .

He pulled the tent flap back—then let it fall, turned, and walked out into the camp, stepping on his morning shadow as he went.

The mercy-tent was the largest the army raised—but not large enough, now. Wounded lay in a row by the entrance— silent as was the army's pride, though Sam saw some mouths open for cries unvoiced. He went to those first, and knelt by stained raw-wool blankets. He knew many.

He spoke to them in turn, and most—those in least agony—could listen, even make reassuring faces to comfort him. Two of them tried to make jokes.

". . . Sir, didn't think it was possible for a trooper to outrun her horse. But by Mountain Jesus, I was scared enough and did it."

"Mavis, you were just charging to the rear." That oldest of cavalry witticisms.

Trooper Mavis Drew had been cut across the belly. The wound was bandaged tight to keep things in.

Sam kissed her on the forehead, and went on down the line. Those who could see, seemed glad to see him.

"Where's Colonel Flores?"

The mercy-medic, a bearded older man, and tired, pointed to the tent entrance. "Inside, down to the left."

"He'll live?"

"Live one-handed," the medic said.

The tent was filled with sunshine glow through canvas woven of the Empire's southern cotton, filled with that light and a soft, multiple hum of agony, the army's silence-in-suffering fallen away. Portia-doctor was with someone, bent over, doing something that made the person's breath catch and catch again.

Sam went down the narrow aisle to the left, and saw, at the end of a row, Ned Flores lying slight on a folding cot. His left arm was out on the blanket, the wrist a fat wad of white bandage spotted with red.

The man in the cot beside his was snoring softly, unconscious.

"Sorry, Sam. Not quite as planned." Barely Ned's voice, rusty as an old man's, and from what seemed an aged face—no longer a young hawk's, handsome, high-beaked, and cruel. His youth had gone with his wound, and losing.

Monroe knelt beside the cot. "No, not quite as planned, Ned.

At least three hundred more dead and wounded than planned." He kept his voice low. "I sent you down here to lose a battle—to lose maybe forty or fifty of our people, then break off and run."

"Right . . . right."

"That was only between us, Ned. I thought you understood why it was necessary to lose at least a skirmish."

"I know. Necessary . . ."

"Our army's always won—never lost—and that's become dangerous. Even more so, now, with the Khan moving on Middle Kingdom. I didn't want him to think us a serious threat, and I didn't want the shock of our first lost battle, my first lost battle, to occur when we couldn't *afford* it. I thought you understood that."

"Yes." A long pause, eyes closed. "Like cow-sore vaccination against the pops."

"Then"—careful to speak softly—"then why the *fuck* didn't you order the regiment disengaged after the first melee? Behind you was all the room in the world to run!"

"Well . . . tell you, Sam. Seemed to me . . . we had a chance to beat the bastards." Apparently great effort required to get that said.

"Ned, you did *not* have a chance to beat them—almost seven hundred imperial cataphracts met in a pass at such close quarters? And you weren't sent *down* here to beat them!"

"My fault." Flores seemed to doze, then woke with a start.

Sam stood. "Yes. And my fault for trusting you to obey orders."

"I know . . . I lost all those people."

"Yes, and deserved to lose more than a hand, Ned. You deserved to lose your head."

"You . . . can have it."

Sam bent over him. "Ned, we've been friends since we were boys on the mountain. But if that order to lose, lose and run, hadn't been only between us—and have to *remain* only between us—I would have you tried and hanged for disobedience."

"Don't doubt it, Sam," Ned Flores said. "And what a relief . . . that would be."

2

To the Great Khan and Lord of Grass:
Neckless Peter Wilson, elderly and once your servant and ambassador, submits and conveys this report of information concerning the history, winning, and holding of North Map-Mexico by the young Captain-General Small-Sam Monroe—by whose order this is forwarded sealed from all eyes but yours, Great Lord.

Twenty-seven years ago, a band of fugitive Trappers—driven south from the mountains and ice-wall of Map-Colorado by the Cree—stopped to rest at Gardens, the town in forest and of forest.

Their notable persons were Jack Monroe, that mythic fighting man; Catania Olsen, a physician; Joan Richardson, an Amazon; and Tattooed Newton, to be revealed errant third son to the ruler of Middle Kingdom.

Within the year, Jack Monroe was dead—in tales, murdered by a bear jealous of his strength. Within this time also, Newton, with Dangerous-Joan Richardson, returned to the Boxcars' Middle Kingdom, where he came in time to his inheritance. On his death, years later—while arranging a reasonable agreement in Map-Kentucky—Dangerous-Joan was left to rule as Dowager Queen, and remains so today, aged, but no less dangerous.

As these storied ones met their fates, so Catania Olsen, caring for an orphaned Trapper baby, Small-Sam Monroe, traveled down to North Map-Mexico, and into the *Sierra Oriental.*

In the *Sierra,* after killing two men—one having attempted rape, the other having tried to steal her goat—Catania Olsen became physician to the savages and bandits of the mountains, and came to be loved by them.

Her adopted son, Small-Sam, grew to manhood in those

harsh and freezing altitudes—a world largely peopled, as all North Map-Mexico had been, by North Americans driven south centuries before, as the cold came down. So their language was and is book-English, their ways also informed by those surviving copies of Warm-time books.

The original, the Beautiful Language, now is only spoken in the Empire of Map South-Mexico and Guatemala—and, one assumes, in the continent of wilderness below.

Twenty-two years passed after Doctor Olsen's arrival. Then, the Empire's Duke Alphonso da Carvahal attempted a reconquest of their lost northern territories. This went badly.

In a series of attacks along the western flank of the *Sierra Oriental,* Carvahal lost battle after battle—never, as the Warmtime saying had it, 'getting his ducks in a row.'

In these battles, the men and women of North Map-Mexico lost two leaders slain. A third, a very young man, was elected for lack of better. This was Small-Sam Monroe, and at the town God-Help-Us, he attacked the imperial forces by night, and defeated them. Then he sent all the common-soldier prisoners south, alive and whole, at the plea of his Second-mother, Catania Olsen, whose name is still praised as a saint's for mercy in South Map-Mexico and Guatemala.

The duke and his officers were disemboweled.

So successful as a war leader that no man cared to stand against him in rule, young Small-Sam found himself acclaimed Captain-General of all the provinces of North Map-Mexico—as they still are named in the Beautiful Language, *Baja California Norte, Sonora, Chihuahua, Coahuila,* and *Nuevo Leon,* now united.

He was urged to invade the south as the south had invaded the north, and so destroy the Empire. He refused, on consideration of that ancient stability better left preserved.

Now twenty-seven years old—though looking older—Sam

Monroe rules south from the Bravo down into both *Sierras*, and east from the Gulf of California and Ocean Pacific to the Great Gulf Entire.

He enforces lightly in rule and taxes—but holds the towns, villages, mountains and fields of these fractious and turbulent people as with a fine noose, which lies slack unless tugged against.

He is respected and popular, but treated with caution, since his reasons for violence are often not anticipated by ordinary men.

Small-Sam Monroe—'Sam' to his friends and near-equals, 'Sir' to all others—is stocky, sandy-haired, and exceptionally powerful and active. It is said in his army that few can match him with the sword. He carries what is called a 'bastard'—that is, a weapon a little lighter than a two-handed sword, with a grip called a 'hand and a half.' This weapon, I understand, is a rain-pattern blade, forged and folded many times from the empire's rare 'wootz' steel. And—which I think of some interest—though the important fighting men and women of this country follow the barbarian tradition of naming their swords, Monroe hasn't done so. A modesty availing not, since his officers and men christened the weapon 'Nameless.' So the great, in small ways as in large, are defined by those they rule.

Monroe's face, square and harsh-featured, is marked by weather, war, and cares of state. His eyes are very clear, a dark hazel, his lashes almost long as a girl's. Commanding an army whose men are often mustached and bearded, he shaves his face clean—as do most of his senior officers and administrators, likely in imitation.

The Captain-General's intelligence, like his vision, is clear, direct, devouring of subjects of interest, and dismissive of others. He is alert, profoundly practical, and unafraid. He works harder than any of his servants, though all, whether soldiers or administrators, are hard and constant workers.

Finally—and this may be unimportant, may simply reflect the pressures of great power on a young man less than hungry for it—finally, it seems to me that Small-Sam Monroe is not happy.

Important administrators: Charles Ketch—an exceptionally tall, stooped man in his fifties, once a prosperous valley farmer, then first Chief of Supply . . . and now Chief Executive, North Map-Mexico. What Monroe commands, Charles Ketch effects— and stands, it seems, somewhat in the role of father to the much younger man.

Eric Lauder—current Chief of Supply, a man in his thirties, squat, bearded, bald, lively and humorous. Lauder, besides commanding the army's supply train, is also the edge of the secret civil sword . . . collecting information, dispensing any necessary covert deaths. (He has informed me, in the pleasantest way, that he considers my resignation from your service likely a clumsy ruse, and that I remain under his eye.)

Margaret Mosten, Secretary. Mosten, an officer's widow— and herself an ex-officer of Light Infantry—administers Monroe's quarters and camps, and commands his personal guard. A sturdy blonde in her thirties, apparently easygoing and amiable, Mosten is both more efficient and more formidable than she appears. (I was told by a muleteer that on one occasion she personally escorted two drunken armed trespassers—found in the camp at night—to the perimeter guard post, where she cut their throats. A warning as well, apparently, to the guards who had not discovered and prevented them.)

Margaret Mosten decides who sees the Captain-General, but doesn't appear to abuse her position. Her relationship to Monroe seems to have always been that of a friend, not a lover.

Military Commanders: Almost elderly, and ranked brigadiers in the old Warm-time style, Jaime and Elvin Rascob have functioned as Monroe's senior commanders. These brothers, often in disagreement with each other—and occasionally with Monroe as well—nevertheless have a strikingly successful record in war. Their staff, field officers, and subordinate commanders hold these old men in great esteem. My impression is that the two brothers, together, have made one very formidable general. It may prove important, therefore, that Elvin Rascob is ill of tiny plants in his lungs—certainly the Warm-time TB—and is dying.

Ned Flores, Colonel, commands the Light Cavalry regiments. A restless young man—violent and charming—Flores is a childhood friend of Monroe's, his closest friend. Though apparently only the image of a perfect dashing commander of light horse, this officer, as many of Monroe's people, reveals more depth on examination. He is responsible, more than any other, for reviving the game of chess in this territory—where checkers had been the board game of choice—and more often than not beats Monroe at it. He more often than not beats me as well, and crows like a child at his triumphs.

Howell Voss, Colonel, commands the Heavy Cavalry. Colonel Voss, like Eric Lauder, is often amusing. He is also large and handsome—though missing his left eye—and is a favorite with women. (The eye was lost in a duel with an angry husband.) Howell Voss is occasionally subdued, 'blue' as Warmtimes had it, and then stays alone in his tent. He plays the banjar very well indeed . . . and is said to be suicidally brave in battle.

Phillip Butler, Colonel, commands the Heavy Infantry. An older man, gray-bearded, small, silent, and eccentric—he always has tiny dogs about him; he puts them in his jacket pockets—Colonel Butler was the mayor of Tijuana-City before the South invaded. It's said by Monroe's people, certainly an exaggeration, that Butler has never made a tactical mistake on a battlefield. He is regarded as an extraordinary soldier, having become, as it were, a Regular among inspired amateurs. His pikemen and crossbowmen love him, though he can be a harsh commander; they treat him like an irritable old uncle.

Charmian Loomis, Colonel, commands the Light Infantry. A tall, thin, awkward-seeming young woman, with light blue eyes and a bony—and, it seems to me, quite plain—face, she commands the elite of Monroe's army. ('Elite,' lord, may be found in Copy-Webster's. Bottom shelf on the right as you enter the library. I believe the word may have been Warm-time Canadian in origin.) . . . This officer, a woman with no family, quite silent, and who appears to offer little in any social situation—I've met her several times—is by reputation a demonic figure in battle, with quite extraordinary skill in controlling a force designed after all to be mobile, occasionally fragmented, and self-directing to a considerable degree. Monroe occasionally calls her 'Joan,' I suspect in reference to some Warm-time figure he has read of. All others call her 'Colonel.'

In summary, it is my civilian impression that these officers, and those they command, represent considerable military talent—experienced, highly disciplined, confident, and aggressive. I believe you would enjoy their company, if matters were otherwise, and would certainly then find them useful to employ.

As to Sam Monroe. His Second-mother's death—while fighting an outbreak of flea-plague in the township of Los Palominos three years ago—has left him with no family. (I must add that I mourn that most tender of physicians still, and deeply regret not seeing her again.)

The Captain-General's occasional women are companions as well as lovers and, I understand, come and go as tasks and places come and go. He is very generous to them, and to his close friends and officers—but only once. An important gift is given—a prosperous farm, or wide sheepland, or large herd of fine riding-horses—but after that, nothing ever but army wages. So men and women who continue to serve him, do so because they wish to, expecting no further reward.

His army is relatively small, but as I understand it is a 'balanced force,' composed of five fairly equal elements: Supply; Light Cavalry; Heavy Cavalry; Light Infantry; Heavy Infantry. Monroe has stated, in my hearing, that his Light Cavalry, while very good, is not quite a match for the Khanate's, that his Heavy Cavalry, while excellent, is not quite as formidable as the Empire's best, and that his Heavy Infantry, though solid, is not quite the instrument that Middle Kingdom fields. His Light Infantry, however—men and women of the *Sierra*—Monroe believes to be the finest of our world.

It is the *balance* of these forces he considers crucial. That, and the strategy and tactics of their use. I'm told he has said, 'These are the edged tools for fashioning victory, as a carpenter fettles a table.' (For 'fettle,' Great Khan, see my monograph on Warm-time Words Unusual.)

The Captain-General's sigil—and, by adoption, the army's banner—is a black scorpion on a field of gold. Though a far-south creature, it is appropriately ominous. While the enlisted men among their prisoners are very well treated, captured enemy officers are invariably beheaded—or, if they are senior, disemboweled. This, apparently, a brutal remainder of these people's desperate days of revolt against the Empire.

FORCES, IF AT FULL ESTABLISHMENT:

Supply: Two thousand men and women. Five hundred draft horses. Five hundred pack mules. Wheeled wagons. Drays. Sledges.

Light Cavalry: Two regiments—each, one thousand men and women. Remounts.

Heavy Cavalry: Two regiments—each, one thousand men and a small number of women. Remounts.

Light Infantry: Two regiments—each one thousand men and women.

Heavy Infantry: Two regiments—each one thousand men and a small number of women.

The fighting formations above are to some extent based on Warm-time copybook models. (See that most valuable *Kipling, Rudy.* Back shelves, Great Lord, and perfectly alphabetical.) All the army is uniformed in plain dark-brown wool or leather, black cloaks, and black boots—high-topped in the cavalry, cut low for the infantry.

In each cavalry regiment, one hundred persons serve as farriers, armorers, remount herders and fodderers. The nine hundred fighting men and women are divided into three squadrons, first, second, and third. Each squadron then divided further into three troops of one hundred, A, B, and C.

The infantry regiments are each made up of two battalions of four hundred men and women, the battalions then being divided into four companies. The two extra companies in each regiment are assigned special duty as engineer-laborers, assault formations, headquarters detachment, scouts, and cooks.

It should be noted that while the other units often consist of both full-time paid regulars and veteran reservists serving annual duty, Supply is always fully maintained. And noted also, that the structure of 'Supply' includes the army's intelligence, police, and security functions as well as its field medical personnel.

Originally organized by Catania Olsen, the army's medical service is also available to any citizens nearby and in need, a useful component of Monroe's administration, which still tends to be a government-in-the-saddle, to be found alongside units of the army as often as in their capital, the undistinguished small town of Better-Weather, south of Chihuahua City.

Finally, I understand there exists a competent volunteer militia of well-armed men and women organized in each of the five states—and in each, numbering approximately a thousand—

intended as the cadre around which a much greater force of irregulars would be organized at need. Since almost all men, and many women, go habitually armed in this country, with weapons play and archery their habit, this irregular force would likely prove formidable.

Military History: Elements of the army have fought five major battles, seventeen to nineteen minor battles and skirmishes. They have, until very recently, never been defeated. This single loss—and only two days ago—has been of more than three hundred Light Cavalry from a regiment unwisely sent down unsupported to meet a weightier imperial force venturing north. An extremely unusual misjudgment by Monroe, and something of a shock to his army, perhaps more disturbing than the casualties resulting from it. In this battle, Ned Flores lost his left hand, but is expected to survive.

A note of interest: Monroe's army is required to submit payment vouchers for any food, fodder, or materiel requisitioned, and the soldiers' behavior on maneuver or campaign is strictly governed. By this, the army's popularity with the people—and Monroe's popularity as well—is preserved.

The army is known for fighting in silence. No cheers, shouts, or battle cries. No sounds but infantry bugles or cavalry trumpets, then the clash of arms when the enemy is met.

And no crying out after, not even by the wounded, a custom apparently descending from the silence and sudden ambushes of mountain banditry, once a principal occupation here.

Commerce: North Map-Mexico is an agricultural and stock-raising area. With a seven-week summer so far south of the icewall, they grow cabbage, kale, broccoli, and onions . . . and trade with the Empire for the tomatoes, planted potatoes, yams, cotton-wool, tobacco and corn grown farther south.

Livestock are sheep, goats, chicken-birds, and to a lesser extent, pigs and spotted cattle.

For trade, as well as convenience, the Empire's silver *peso* and copper penny are allowed to circulate as North Map-Mexico's currency.

Intentions: Sam Monroe's probable long-term intention: a reasonable and well-administered peace—with local officials now elected every five years by those locals they rule. Territorial defense being sustained by a compact, capable, and veteran army, with the east and west *Sierras* flanking any invading force.

My Opinion: If placed under sufficient pressure—as for instance by the Khanate—Monroe will certainly seek alliance with either the Empire or Middle Kingdom . . . and more likely the latter. All New Englanders are despised here, perhaps in some cases unfairly, because of those ruling few who use their minds' rare talents—for warming themselves, and walking-in-the-air—also to make monsters in women's wombs. On occasion, people of this territory have galloped after the few fliers that appear—chasing those individuals by relays for many Warm-time miles—until the New Englander wearies or loses attention, and descends or falls . . . to be seized and burned alive.

Monroe has put an end to that rough sport.

Finally, my lord Khan, a personal note. I had thought that Trapper cooking was shocking, and Caravanserai's little better—mutton, mare's milk, and more mutton. I did not know when I was well-off. Broccoli and goat-gut sausage . . . I'll say no more.

To you by my hand only—and otherwise unseen.

Neckless Peter Wilson

3

Dieter Mayaguez, nine years old, heard singing in the sky. The sun dazzled him when he looked up. His sheep shifted to left and right down the steep hill pasture as a shadow that might have been an eagle's came out of the sun and raced up along the grass.

Dieter saw, a sling's throw high in the air, a girl wrapped in a long dark-blue coat, singing as she sailed along the rise of the hill's slope. She flew sitting upright, yellow-booted legs crossed beneath her. A curl-brimmed, blue hat was secured with black ribbons tied in a bow under her chin.

She held something across her lap, and flew slowly, steadily over him and away, her coat's cloth ruffling as she went higher . . . then higher, to cross the ridge.

Dieter could still hear her singing. It was a song he didn't know. '*Mairzy doats . . . dozy doats . . .*'

Excited, he did a little dance in frost-browned grass.—Certainly a Boston person! He would tell everybody, though only his mother would believe him. People were always saying they saw Boston people, and usually were lying. Now he really had seen one, but only his mother would say it must be true.

The sheep—so stupid—baaa'd and began to scatter. Dieter yelled, ran to circle them and hold the ram. If his father had given him the dogs for high pasture, he wouldn't have to be running after the fools.

A shadow came out of the sun—and he thought for a moment it was the singing girl come back. But this was a much bigger shadow. . . .

Patience Nearly-Lodge Riley, her song ended, settled into herself and Walked-in-air over the hills—that 'pushing the ground away and behind' that fools called flying, as if fine-family New Englanders were birds with wings.

True wings, an occa's, were following her, carrying her strapped baggage-packs and Webster's basket. An occa stupid as all of them, but still an impressive result of mind-work on some debtor woman's fetus. Cambridge-made in Cambridge Laboratory, Harvard Yard . . .

Patience closed her eyes a moment to better feel the slopes and outcroppings a hundred or so Warm-time feet beneath her. She felt them rumble and bump, rough as she went over. But so much soldier, so much better than the Gulf's shifting surface had been, its waves wobbling below her as she went. That had been uneasy traveling—as had the whole several weeks of air-walking south from Boston Town, when sailing a packet down and around and up into the Gulf would have been easier.

"Safer, too," her Uncle Niles had said. "But you will go the difficult way, and air-walk—or, by Frozen Jesus, ground-walk—every mile south. It'll be good for you, Patience, knock some of the Lodge-Riley hoity-toity out of you."

Her Uncle Niles loved her, just the same. She was his favorite niece.

And it *had* been good for her, those weeks of air-walking. The first weeks were on the ice-sheet, then off it and down over warmer snowfields and sedge willow, past caribou ranches and little towns. Air-walking, and when her mind grew tired, ground-walking. Then, the occa, too baggage-burdened for her to ride, had circled overhead, hooting and honking as she strode along.

She'd hunted for herself and the occa when the smoked seal was eaten up, swooping—while remaining mindful of the ground she kept away—to snip the heads off wild turkeys or ptarmigan with her scimitar, to hack the necks of deer. Then landing, settling into snowy woods, she'd gathered dry branches for her fire, started it with her flint and steel . . . then butchered the meat out while the occa landed, loomed beside her, hobbling on knees—and what would have been elbows, otherwise—and poked at her with its long jaw, whining for bird or venison bones and bowels.

In all those weeks, Patience had been troubled only three times. An ice-fisher had refused to exchange her smallest silver coin for a meal, so she'd had to take two char from him—but only sliced him lightly, so as not to cripple, since property rights were sacred.

Later, while ground-walking through lower Map-Pennsylvania, well south of the ice-wall, she'd been chased up a tree by a hungry black bear. Too startled, too suddenly set upon, to push the ground away for rising in the air, she'd risen from the tree limbs soon enough and left the bear snuffling, clinging halfway up its climb to reach her.

Patience had been troubled those two times, and one time more. Deep in Map-Alabama, almost to the Gulf, she'd fluttered down to kill a woman who'd thrown a stone and almost struck her as she sailed over a hedge of holly.

. . . The hill ridge thumped beneath her in her mind, and Patience thought-stepped . . . thought-stepped down the western slope, the wind chilly at her hat's brim, lightly buffeting her face. Her face, charming, absolutely pretty by the judgment of everyone who knew her, was reddened, roughened by the weather of travel. But the inherited bit in the brain, that with training allowed a talented few New Englanders—and the very rare exceptions from other places—to air-walk and also keep warm on the ice, was no use in smoothing one's complexion. It seemed unfair.

Before her, across a wide valley to the west, rose mountains harsher than the Map-Smokies had been. The *Sierra*. A cold wind flowed down from them, and Patience thought *heat* and caused it to warm her ears, her gloved fingers . . . the tip of her nose.

She sailed on, out over the valley—sitting properly upright, her sheathed scimitar held across her lap. It was her joy, a present from her mother on her sixteenth birthday—two years ago, now—and a true Peabody of a thousand doublings and hammerings. She called it 'Merriment,' since it had antic curling patterns flowing in the surface of its steel, and also a modest, amusing style of slicing. She'd killed Teresa Bondi with it in a duel, and Tessie's parents had never forgiven her, said she was cruel, a spoiled brat, and bad.

Patience looked back and saw the occa laboring far behind. It appeared to be holding something in its long jaw.

She stopped in the air—a difficult thing to do—and sat waiting for it, rocking slightly in the mountains' breeze. The occa shied and swung on great leathery wings, with the foot-long toothed jaw and bald knob of its idiot head turned away as if not to see her. It did have something in its mouth.

Patience, impatient, whistled it over, and it slowly sidled toward her through the air, its long bat arms and long bat fingers—supporting a skin-membrane's wingspan of almost thirty Warm-time feet—fiddling with wind currents as it came.

Patience whistled again, made a furious face—and the creature came swiftly flapping through the air to her, wind-burned and whining, its wings buffeting alongside. Her baggage duffels and Webster's basket were strapped to its humped back. A sheep's leg hung bleeding from its jaws.

Patience leaned to rap it sharply on the head with her scabbarded sword, and dipped a sudden few feet as her concentration faltered, so she had to recover. "Drop! . . . *Drop!*" The creature was getting too fat for good flying as it was.

The occa muttered what was almost a word.

"*Drop it!*"

The sheep's leg fell away through the air. The occa bent its awkward head to watch it go.

"Now," Patience said, "you fucking *fly*. And keep up!"

* * *

"Signals say company's coming!" Margaret Mosten's round pleasant face appeared beside the tent flap. "From the Say-so mirror, far south slope."

Sam sat up. "What sort of company?"

"Wings." Margaret seemed not to notice the leather vodka flask lying on the floor beside the cot, the squeezed rind of lime from far south. "Some Boston flier, presumably. With winged item following."

"From McAllen."

"Likely; they've been wanting to send someone down." Margaret watched him with concern. She'd never mentioned his drinking, never would. But twice—when traveling, not on campaign—he'd drunk from his saddle-flask to find the vodka and lime juice gone, replaced with water.

Sam swung off the cot. "What a pain in the ass." It was a Warm-time phrase out of copied books almost five hundred years old, a phrase that had become popular in the army. Too popular, so rankers were now forbidden to use it in reference to orders.

Sam stooped to pick up his sword belt . . . and had to steady himself, which Margaret appeared not to notice. "Where?"

"Michael Sergeant-Major is waving the thing in to the football pitch."

"All right." Looping the belted sword over his right shoulder to rest aslant down his back, he followed Margaret out into an afternoon he found too bright for comfort, and cold with Lady Weather's commencing fall into Lord Winter's arms.

The camp was seething like cooking Brunswick at the flier's coming, but soldiers settled down along Sam's way, sensitive as girls to their commander's mood—many recalling duty elsewhere.

Football, the army's sport even in marching camps of war—

though some said it was old Warm-time rugby, really—had been marked to be played just south of horse-lines on a stretch of meadow softened by cold-killed grass. The field, already enclosed by dismounted heavy cavalry, had been cleared of all except Michael Sergeant-Major, Margaret Mosten's man, who stood in the center of it waving a troop banner for a landing mark.

Sam saw a formed file of the Heavies' horse-archer squadron had arrows to their longbows. The bows, their lower arms curved short for horseback shooting, were half-raised, arrows nocked. He nodded that way. "Whose orders?"

"Mine," Margaret Mosten said.

"Quiver those arrows." He walked out onto the football field, looked up, and saw a figure high against the blaze of the sun. *Didn't have to come out of the sun. Making an entrance.*

"The thing's above." Margaret had come out to him. She was carrying one of the Heavy Infantry's crossbows, wound, cocked, and quarreled. "My privilege, sir," she said, as he noticed it. "Look there. . . ."

High above the small human figure sailing down to them in silhouette—perhaps a woman, perhaps not—a larger thing wheeled and flapped.

Soldiers murmured at the edges of the field.

"Silence!"

Their commander's mood confirmed, murmuring ceased.

In that quiet, the soft sound of cloth breezing could be heard. In dark-blue greatcoat and dark-blue hat, the Boston person—certainly a woman—sailed down, sailed down . . . and settled with no stumble on the ground. She held, sheathed in her right hand, a slender curved scimitar, and was smiling.

"Mountain Jesus," Margaret Mosten said. "She's a baby."

"Clever." Sam smiled to match the visitor's, and went to meet her. He was still drunk, and would have to be careful.

The woman—the girl—had a white face, wind-roughened

but beautiful, oval as an egg. Black hair was drawn tightly back under the blue curl-brimmed hat, and her eyes were also black, dark as licorice chews. Sam noticed her gloved hands were fine, but what could be seen of a slender wrist was corded with sword-practice muscle.

The girl was smiling at him as if they were old friends— apparently knew him from description. "I thought I had another day or two to walk to Better-Weather, but then I saw your camp, and said to myself, 'Ah—there's been fighting! So surely there the Captain-General will be.' " She made a little curtsy as a lady might have done south, in the Emperor's court, then took a fold of heavy white parchment from her coat, and handed it to him.

"I'm instructed to serve the Lord Small-Sam Monroe as the voice of New England, at his pleasure of course. *Ambassadress.*" The girl dwelt on the final *s*'s and made a sudden face of glee.

"From McAllen?"

"No, lord. Second-cousin Louis is superseded. I come down from Harvard Yard directly to you. . . . Poor old Cousin Louis; he'll be furious." She spoke a very elegant book-English.

"I see."

There was a spatter of dried blood down her long blue coat.

She saw him notice it. "Travel stains of the travel weary—I walked all the way down."

Walked, Sam thought, *and walked in the air.* . . . Still, from Boston-in-the-Ice to North Map-Mexico—alone and in however many weeks—was remarkable. And New England's first mistake, to let him know she was remarkable. They should have sent her by ship.

He read—in black squid ink on fine-scraped hide—the submission of Patience Nearly-Lodge Riley's service as go-between (and Voice of the Cambridge Faculty and Town Meeting) to 'the person Small-Sam Monroe, presently Captain-General of North Map-Mexico'. . . . The 'presently' being a good touch.

"Am I accepted?" She had a girl's fluting voice, as free of vibration as a child's.

"For the present." 'The present' being a good touch.

"Then, my baggage?" the ambassadress pointed up into the air. "So, soon I will be out of my stained coat."

"Call the thing down," Sam said, and raised his voice to the troops. "Stand still, and keep silent!" The shouting hurt his head.

The girl looked up, put two fingers into her mouth, and whistled as loud as he'd ever heard it done. That hurt his head, too.

From high . . . high above, came a distant hooting, a mournful, uneasy sound. The troops shifted in the sunshine, and sergeants called them to order. They were looking up at what slowly circled down, sweep by sweep on great wings, making its low worried noises.

Sam didn't look up. Margaret Mosten watched the Boston girl.

Slow sweeps, slow descending, so the girl put her head back and whistled again. Sam's head throbbed. *Fucking vodka—and the wrong day to have drunk it.*

Then the thing came swooping in, wings sighing . . . the sighs turning to thumps of air as it beat the hilltop's wind to slow . . . hang almost stationary over their heads in heavy flappings, and finally—as the girl stamped her booted foot and pointed at the ground—come down in a collapse and folding of great bat's wings. It folded them once, then again, so it fell forward on what should have been elbows, and crouched huge, hunched, and puffing from exertion or uneasiness. Its body was pale and freckled—smooth skin, no fur—its neck long, wattled, and odd. But it was the head made the troops murmur, no matter what the sergeants ordered.

Sam stayed standing close by an effort, and looked at a toothed thin-lipped jaw almost long as a man's arm, a round bare bulge of skull with human ears, and eyes a suffering woman's tragic and beautiful blue. A pair of little shrunken breasts dangled from the creature's chest.

The Boston girl went to the thing, made soothing *puh-puh* noises to it, and began to unbuckle its heavy harness. The wide leather straps were difficult to deal with, stiff with wetting and drying.

Sam stepped beside her—heard Margaret grunt behind him— and leaned against the thing's flank, warm and massive as a charger's, to work a big buckle free. The creature smelled of human sweat, its skin smooth from crease to crease, and damp with the effort of flying.

"What have you done?" he said, not a question he would have asked without the vodka.

But the girl understood him.

"Oh"—she patted its hide—"we make these . . . Persons from beginning babies, inside tribeswomen, or New England ladies who won't be responsible, fall into bad habits, and don't pay their debts." She tugged a second strap loose, then stepped aside so Sam could lift two heavy duffels and a shrouded wicker basket down from the thing's hunched back.

Something rustled in the basket.

"Weather be kind . . ." Michael Sergeant-Major came and shouldered Sam aside, bent to pick up the baggage. "Sir, where do you want these?" There was sweat on the sergeant-major's forehead.

"Set a tent for the lady. East camp, beside Neckless Peter's, I think. Tent and marquee, camp furniture."

"Canvased tub-bath," Margaret said. "Canvased toilet pit."

Sam turned away, and the Boston girl came with him in quick little steps alongside, the long blue coat whispering. She smelled of nothing but the stone and ice of the high mountain air she'd walked through.

"How are we to keep that sad thing, lady?"

"Call me *Patience*, please, Lord Monroe; since we'll be camp-mates. I don't keep her; I send her home."

"Home . . . And it goes all that distance back?"

"Oh, yes. Its mother is there. It will wander a few weeks . . . but get to home hutch at last."

"Its mother?"

"Occas always rest in their mothers' care."

"Nailed Jesus . . ."

"May I change the subject—and ask, are you always so sad at your soldiers' dying?"

Sam stopped. "What did you say?"

The girl smiled up at him, her right hand resting at her side, casually on the grip of her scimitar. "I thought you must be sad for the soldiers I saw being buried below me, to be drunk so early in the day. It proves a tender heart."

Margaret had come up behind them. "You mind your fucking manners," she said to the Boston girl, "or we'll kick your ass right out of here. Who are you to dare—"

"Let it go, Margaret," Sam said. Then, to the girl:

"Still, not a bad idea to mind your manners, Patience . . . or I *will* kick your ass right out of here."

"Oh, dear. I apologize." The girl curtsied first to him, then to Margaret. "It will take us a while to learn to know each other better." She snapped her fingers at Michael Sergeant-Major, and he led her away, bent beneath the weight of her baggage and basket.

When she was a distance gone, Sam began to laugh. It hurt his head, but was worth it for the pleasure of first laughter since coming down to This'll Do.

"Nothing funny there," Margaret Mosten said.

"Wouldn't want her for a daughter, Margaret?"

"Sir, I would take a quirt to her if she were."

"Mmm . . . It's interesting that the New England people sent us such a distraction. I wonder, to distract us from what?"

"If necessary," Margaret said, " 'distractions' can have regrettable accidents. And that blood on the coat—'travel stains.' "

"Yes . . . See that people are careful with her. She carries to fight left-handed or with both hands. And there're parry-marks on the hilt of that scimitar—but no scars on her face, no scars on her sword arm when she reached up to undo the thing's harness." Salutes from the two cavalrymen guarding his tent. One of them had eased the chain catches on his breastplate slightly.

"Johnson Fass."

"Sir!" A more rigid attention by Corporal Fass.

"Getting too fat for that cuirass?"

"No, sir." Hurried fumbling to tighten the catches.

"If we had a sudden alarm, Corporal, and you mounted to fight with that steel hanging loose on your chest, then one good cut across it with a saber or battle-ax would break your ribs like pick-up sticks."

"Won't happen again, sir."

Sam walked on. The young commander had spoken—unheard, of course, by the hundreds of dead buried beneath the hill. He wondered how many such disasters it would take, before the corporals stopped saluting. . . .

"About our guest, Margaret; I want people mindful that if she kills someone, I can only send her away. And if someone kills *her*, it means difficulty with Boston. So, no attempted lovemaking, no insults exchanged, no discourtesies, no duels on duty *or* on leave. Let the officers know that's an order."

"Too bad," Margaret said, "because it's going to be a temptation. What the fuck do those New Englanders have in mind, sending us a girl like that?"

Sam stopped by his tent's entrance. "What they first had in mind, was to make us wonder what they had in mind."

"Right."

"And Margaret, I thank you for not mentioning it was a bad beginning, for her to find me drunk. . . . Now, I need some sleep. And Lady Weather keep the Second Regiment's dead from visiting my dreams."

He put back the tent's entrance flap, and ducked in.

Margaret started to say, "They would never—they loved you," but Sam was gone inside. *And just as well,* she thought. *My foolish mouth would have hurt him more.*

* * *

No lost cavalry troopers came to his dreaming.

Sam dreamed of being a boy again in their mountain hut . . . and his Second-mother, Catania, was reading to him from an old copybook traded out of the south for twenty sheep hides. She read to him often, fearing he might take to the mountains' signs and tribe-talk instead of book-English.

" ' . . . *There were a few foreign families come to the prairie, Germans, Balts, Hungarians. But they were not felt as foreign as they might have been in cities or small farming towns, since all of us had come to the prairie as foreigners to it, so in Western-accented English or Eastern English or Southern English—or in English hardly English at all—we made do together, and were Americans.*

In time, we were to master the rough grasses, the black earth beneath, though it cost us all our lives to do it. The sky we never mastered. We were too small, too low. We were beneath its notice.

. . . One Sunday, we took the wagon the long, rutted road to church, and in church, in the last row of benches, I saw for the first time a sturdy, small, blond little girl, her hair in braids. She was wearing a flour-sack dress with little blue blossoms on

it—not as nice a dress as my sister's—and she was to become my friend.' "

His Second-mother stopped reading then, and put the top-sewn copybook away. Her eyes, in the dream, were the gray he remembered; the scar down her cheek as savage; her hair was white as winter.

"What happens?" Sam asked her.

"Sweetheart, always the same things happen," his Second-mother said. "Happiness is found . . . then it is lost . . . then perhaps found again. And the finding, the losing, and the perhaps, is the story."

. . . Sam woke, saying, *"Wait!"* aloud—though for what, he wasn't certain.

A voice from outside and a courteous distance said, "Sir . . . ?"

Sounded like Corporal Fass.

Sam called, "Just a dream, Corporal," and got up off his cot.

There was no more time for mourning, for considering his stupidity in sending a man like Ned Flores to lose a fight. No time for more vodka. The young Captain-General, that *almost-never-defeated* commander, must get back to work.

Ned wouldn't much mind the missing hand. He'd have a bright steel hook made, to wear and flourish with a piratical air, like the corsairs in that most wonderful of children's Warmtime copybooks.

Sam stepped outside the tent. Afternoon, and the morning wasted. "Fass!" *What in hell was the other man's name?*

"Sir?"

"Colonel Voss to report to me."

"Sir."

"The Rascobs as well."

"Sir—the brigadiers rode out of camp a while ago. Rode north."

And no good-byes. The old men were still angry. And were about to be made much angrier.

4

"Chancellor Razumov, have you read this?" The Lord of Grass, at ease on a window couch in the Saffron Room of Lesser Audience, shook sheets of poor paper gently, the slight breeze disturbing the prairie hawk that perched on his other forearm.

"Yes, my lord." The chancellor, very fat, still made an easy half-bow of continued attention. Tiny bells tinkled down the closure of his yellow robe.

"And your opinion of our fugitive librarian's report?"

"Accurate, from what we know otherwise. It describes minor—though formidable—rule, ruler, and ruled. Certainly to be taken into account as they lie along the Khanate's southern flank, and might disturb your movement against Middle Kingdom. Still . . . perhaps not so formidable, lord, since the librarian writes they've lost a skirmish to the Empire, apparently just before his message left their camp. A Light-Cavalry matter, but still a loss."

"Yes . . . Perhaps a loss, perhaps not." The Lord of Grass exchanged glances with his hawk. The open window's autumn sunlight, dappled through figured fine-cotton curtains, seemed to stir across them in a chill breeze.

"Certainly a defeat, my lord, according to accounts, according to the Boston people as well."

"A defeat, but perhaps not a *loss*. Tell me, Razumov, how best does one prepare winners to continue winning?"

"By the victories themselves, lord."

"Oh, no. Victory's lessons are few—but defeat's are many. Something we might well keep in mind. . . . I believe our commonsensical Captain-General of North Map-Mexico has deliberately made a false demonstration to us of his apparent limitations in command . . . *and* at the same time has taught a hard lesson to his army, particularly his Light Cavalry—our principal arm, by no coincidence. He has taught them a painful first lesson in the uncertainties of war."

"An expensive lesson, surely. We understand there were heavy losses."

"And so, all the more effective." The hawk shifted on the Grass Lord's arm. "Though, since the loss *was* so heavy, I suspect it will be quickly followed by a triumph in revenge."

"But lord, is the young man that clever?"

"Perhaps not, Razumov. Perhaps only that sensible. . . . This damned bird has shit on my sleeve."

* * *

An Entry. . . . As I have been appointed the role of historian, librarian, and informational to the young Captain-General, I feel it behooves me—what a Warm-time word! 'Behoove.' Its dictionary definition, of course—but also perhaps as in shoeing a horse, preparing for an action, a journey? So much we will never know. . . .

Still, as occasional historian of Lord Monroe's rule, it behooves me to make my entries on our army's inferior paper, then bind the note-books myself. Clumsy. Clumsy work.

There came a scratching at my tent-flap fairly soon after the New Englander's descent—a sight (seen over the ranks of uneasy soldiers) to remember. It was all childhood's horror stories come to life, though concluding as only a small girl swaggering with a sword. Her huge Made-beast left there, crouched and moaning, apparently resting from its long flight.

A scratching at my tent-flap, as if a kept cat wished in—then the Boston girl's quite pretty face peeping past the canvas cloth. She had set her large blue hat aside.

"Are you doing something private?" she said. "Something you wouldn't want anyone to see?"

"Not that private," I told her. "Come in."

She ducked inside, very small in a voluminous coat—a coat freshly unpacked, by the even creases in it, and made of dark-blue woolen cloth, finely woven and heavy, though not the equal of what Gardens used to weave. I've seen no cloth of *that* quality anywhere else.

The young woman sat on the edge of my cot—perched there, her booted, blue-trousered legs crossed like a boy's—and settled her scimitar across her lap as if it were a pet.

"Neckless Peter. Is that correct?"

"Peter Wilson—but yes, my friends call me Neckless Peter. 'Neckless' since my neck is short—though originally 'Neck-lace' because I wore the gold necklace of Librarian in Gardens. The nick-name was given me by a friend; I keep it in her memory."

"I know 'nick-names'; we called a friend Piss-poor Penelope, just for the three *p*'s in a row. And you're the intelligent person here, aren't you? Little and old, but intelligent?"

"I suppose that's true."

"Isn't it wonderful?" She made a child's face of wonder. "I'm little and intelligent, too! Though I'm not old. So we can be friends, and find out things from each other. Try to hide things . . . then find them out."

"I don't doubt it, though I'm not told North Map-Mexico's secrets."

"Oh, you and I will discover them." She gave me that steady fresh regard—knowledgeable and innocent at once—that children bestow on their elders. And I saw that she was dangerous, certainly—would not have been sent, otherwise—but also, that she might be mad.

"You're thinking something about me."

"Yes."

"You think I'm very strange. Perhaps with a bird in my head?"

"Yes."

"And has it occurred to you, small, old, and intelligent one, that I might *not* be strange? That's it's you people of the warmer places, you who haven't learned to live in ice without being swaddled and farting in furs, who haven't learned to do even simple things with your thoughts, that you are the sad and strange ones?"

"Yes, it has occurred to me."

"Then let me confirm it—it's the fact."

"Perhaps."

" 'Perhaps.' 'Perhaps' is the curse of intelligence."

". . . Perhaps."

She'd spoken like a clever child, but now laughed like a woman, richly, and in deeper voice. She laughed, then recovered in near hiccups. "Now"—she settled herself comfortably—"is the young Monroe, our Captain-General, a war-lord perfect, despite his losses here?"

"No."

"The Kipchak Khan, Toghrul, whom you *betrayed*—is that a painful word?"

"Only a little."

"He is believed in Boston to be a war-lord perfect, and almost certain to win, moving against Middle Kingdom."

"Mmmm."

"You don't believe that?"

"I believe that war is too imperfect for a perfect master."

Again that steady regard. She ran a small white finger slowly back and forth along her saber's sheath, thinking. Then she nodded. "You are intelligent—but are you cruel? You wouldn't hurt me, would you? Use intelligence against me, who am only a girl, and pretty?"

"I think . . . you would be difficult to injure."

She grinned, was up off my cot, bent and kissed my forehead, then sat back down again. She'd smelled of cool air, and nothing else.

"Let's tell our stories—but only the truth; it's too early for lies. Yes? May I call you NP? Short for Neckless Peter?"

"I suppose so. And I suppose I must call you . . . *Im*patience."

"I like that. My Uncle Niles would agree it was just."

"Your Uncle Niles . . . ?"

"Ah, you want my story first."

"Why not?"

"Hmmm." She sat at ease, thinking . . . her smooth, oval, nearly childish face changing in swift reflection of the memories she was choosing. Her face seemed to me not an ambassador's— an ambassadress's—but an emissary's, perhaps.

". . . Well, I was born to a fine family, only slightly beneath the finest. Cambridge-born in Boston Township. I was taught the past and present. I read and write and configure the mathematics . . . within reason."

"Within what reason, Impatience?"

"Within the quadratics, but not fluxions."

"Do you *have* Newton's work? The mathematician, I mean, not the dead River King."

She smiled at me. "Why, NP, you just came to life!"

"Do you have it—and original, complete?"

"No. We, like all the world, are only copybook people, though there are rumors of a great library where the ancient campus was, by old Harvard Yard."

"Under the ice. . . ."

"Under a *mile* of ice." She toyed with her saber. "Someday . . . someday, since you will be my friend, perhaps you could come to Boston, help us excavate, search for it. Someday perhaps become librarian for those endless shelves of Warm-time books, waiting now in cold and darkness with all their secrets."

"Secrets. . . ."

"The secret of flying to the moon. The secret of the so-tiny bad things that make sickness happen—though Boston already knows some of that secret. The secrets of waves of radio, of black boom-powder . . ." She leaned closer. "NP, the pupils of your eyes just changed the littlest bit! Have you been naughty?"

"I don't—"

"Have *you* found . . . could you have found, in the Great Khan's fine library, the making-means of boom-powder?"

"No."

"No?" The predatory attention of a teasing child. "You didn't discover the method mentioned—perhaps unbind the book to take that page away and write another in its place? . . . Then burned that taken-away page?"

"No." This 'no' spoken, I believe, fairly convincingly.

"Well, I won't mention even the possibility to the Captain-General or his officers. I'm afraid of what they might do to such a little old man, to have that secret out of him."

"I know no such secret."

"Well, of course I believe you. I believe you, NP—though Boston suspects that several scholars, over the centuries, have found the making-means of boom-powder . . . then burned those pages, rather than accomplish even more mischief in a mischievous world, than sharp steel has done."

"I said, I know no such secret."

"Even if you did," she reached to pat my knee "even so, I would never betray you, NP—as you must never betray me. In any case, Boston prefers that secret remain secret, so the city not be overrun by any crowd of fools trained with tubes and flint-sparkers for its use. The present state of affairs suits superior talents very well."

"I do not know the method."

"As you say.—You see? We're friends, NP, and would have been friends as children, except you would have been too old."

"And you, too dangerous a child."

"I was. . . . You know, I killed a friend. I sliced her with Merriment, and sometimes I feel sorry for it. I miss Teresa. I'm glad I killed her—but I miss her."

"Yes. . . . Which of us isn't partly a child, who still wants everything?"

"She called me All-Irish. I wouldn't have killed her except for that."

"I understand. A serious matter."

"Well, you think it's funny, NP—but it isn't funny in Boston."

Someone spurred by my tent, close enough so the cloth billowed slightly as the rider passed. "And so, Impatience, you all live on the ice?"

"No. Only trash lives *on* the ice. We live *in* the ice. Boston is in the ice, and of the ice."

"But I'd heard there were great buildings . . ."

"Yes, and ice is what we make them of. We carve beneath buildings—and very big—all white white white, or clear as water. I thought you people *knew* how we lived in the ice."

"The city?"

"All frozen fine. We have an opera theater and a prison. We have our college, of course, our town-meeting hall, and places where other things are done, secret and not so secret. We are *civilized* people, NP. We have churches to these people's Mountain Jesus and Kingdom River's Rafting one, and to our Frozen Jesus, as well as chapels for every other Possible Great, so Lady Weather is sung to, also. There is nothing Boston doesn't have!"

"I see. Houses?"

"*Apart*ments. Gracious, don't you know what apartments are?" Apparently startled by such ignorance.

"From copybooks, I do, yes."

"Well, that's what we have! My mother's apartment is almost on the Common. My Uncle Niles—a true Lodge—lives *on* the Common. He has eleven rooms, not counting the un-mentionable."

"The unmentionable would be . . . the toilet?"

This strange girl nodded Yes, apparently embarrassed to speak it.

"But how . . . how does everyone keep warm?"

" 'Everyone' doesn't keep warm, NP. People of good birth, people with the right piece in their heads, keep *themselves* warm—warm enough that a cloth coat will always do. The Less Fortunate go around in fat fur boots, and wrapped in furs, and complaining. But they *have* furs; the Trash-up-top hunt furs for them. I had friends who had to wear furs."

"A city of ice . . ."

She tapped my knee gently with the tip of her sword's scab-bard. "Wouldn't you like to see it? I think you would. You'd *love* Boston—and we could hunt for the Harvard library to-gether!"

"Perhaps one day, Impatience."

She stuck her tongue out at me. A rude child. "But you're old. You may not have enough days to get to that 'one day.' "

"Time will tell."

"Oh, I know that saying. That's a Warm-time saying."

"Yes."

"Now . . ." She settled back on my cot, tucked my pillow under her armpit for support. "Now, I want to hear your story."

"But you haven't finished *yours*. How, for example, you came to be an ambassadress."

"Oh, my Uncle Niles likes me, so I was made diplomat to North Map-Mexico and here I am. . . . Do you want to hear the oldest song?"

"The oldest song?"

She slid to her feet—supple as a deep-southern snake—dropped her scimitar onto my cot, struck a sudden pose, and astonished me with a prancing, impudent little dance, back and forth, her arms crossed at her breasts. And she sang.

" 'Ohhh . . . I wish I was in Boston, or some other seaport town . . . !' " Quick little kicking steps back and forth along my tent's narrow aisle. " 'I've sailed out there and everywhere . . . I've been the whole world round . . . !' "

There were two more verses—their simple ringing melody sung out in a clear soprano, and danced to with no trace of self-consciousness at all. There was great charm in it . . . charm I found an uneasy decoration for what might lie beneath.

She came to the end suddenly as she'd started—and sat back on my cot, placid, breathing evenly as if there'd been no song, no vigorous dance.

"Now, NP, how did you come to be a slave of the Grass Lord Khan? Is he a pleasant young man—or cruel?"

I was still digesting the performance, her singing echoing in my ears. "His father's Border Roamers came into our forest. Too many to drive away."

"Then killed your people, surely."

"Yes, in the fighting . . . and after the fighting was over. But I was Librarian, and pushed one of them off the library's walk when he tore a copybook for pleasure, to watch the white leaves fall so far to the ground."

"A very *high* library, then?"

"Yes. We built in trees, and of trees, and they loved us."

"Well done to kill a fool! But NP, why didn't they throw you after him?"

"I think I amused them. I think his being killed by me amused them. Then one of the Khan's officers came and ordered the library sent west to Caravanserai—and me with it."

"I would never be a slave." The Boston girl made a face and shook her head. "I'm almost a Lodge—I *am* a Nearly-Lodge Riley." For emphasis, she slid a few inches of her sword's bright steel free of its sheath . . . then slid it shut.

"You have not met the young Khan."

"If I did, he would like me for my spirit and beauty. He would never harm someone so pretty and intelligent!" This strange little creature then swooned down along my cot's pillow like a romantic child. "He would fall in love . . . and I would be his queen."

I was startled, charmed afresh—then, as she lay there, her saber cuddled, I saw in those handsome black eyes (eyes dark as the Khan's, in fact) a gleaming amusement, beneath which seemed to lie dreadful energy, incapable of weariness. . . . Something struck me, then, and though I've never been certain, could never be certain, it occurred to me that the New Englanders might have made with their minds more subtle monsters than those that groaned and flapped great wings—might have made these more intricate others out of their own unborn and beloved children. . . .

There were sudden trumpets then, and stirring in the camp.

The Boston girl was instantly up and off the cot—smiled good-bye—and was gone. The tent-flap, swinging closed, stroked the vanishing curve of her sword's sheath. She left, as formidable people do, an emptiness behind her, as if the earth had nothing to offer in her place.

A sergeant was shouting. The ground shook slightly to the hooves of heavy horses.

I followed outside in time to wave an armored trooper to slow. He sat his sidling impatient charger, a roan already becoming shaggy with winter coat, and gave me a courteous moment.

"Are we breaking camp?"

"No, sir."

"Then what *are* we doing?"

"What we're told," he said, smiled, nodded, and spurred away.

. . . The camp's tumult finally done—an expedition apparently suddenly undertaken, and most of the soldiers gone with it—I wandered the hill-top, asked questions of those few left behind, was given no answers, and returned to my tent for a nap. It did occur to me that trouble might have come to the northern border while the army's commander was occupied here. . . . That trouble, of course, would be of my previous master's making, with the appearance of horse-tail banners, and horse archers with angled eyes.

I had, I suppose, convinced myself that my unimportant defection would be pardoned, if the Grass Lord ever met me again. But that conviction proved fragile as smoke when I tried to sleep in the quiet of an almost empty camp, and I realized that I would certainly be casually strangled by my student—Evgeny Toghrul being not a bad loser, but no loser at all. Not even of elderly librarians.

I slept at last, dreamed of perfect painless poisons milked from lovely vines—droplets certain to provide ease and freedom's easy end. I dreamed of dark doses through the afternoon, could taste them . . . then woke to early evening. I drew a cloak over my shoulders against the chill, and trudged over an encampment scored by horses' shod hooves, dappled with their manure, to a lamp-lit mess tent almost deserted.

The walking wounded, unfit to ride, had been left behind—left behind to cook supper, as well, a grim portent. A corporal I knew, called Leith, was limping among the pans and great kettles, blood spotting her bandages, while she spooned and stirred this and that, exchanging obscenities with two soldiers still staggering from injuries.

Portia-doctor, darkly handsome in a stained brown robe, and seeming weary, sat eating at a bench-table in the big tent's back left corner—and I was interested to see the Boston girl sitting across from her. The girl's tin platter was piled with the army's dreadful Brunswick slumgul, stew enough for two hungry men. This evening, apparently, boiled goat and halved turnips.

Patience saw me, nodded me over . . . and was well into her

supper when I came from the serving kettles to join them.

I bent to kiss the doctor's cheek, a privilege—and sensible precaution—of age, and sat beside her to watch Patience Nearly-Lodge Riley eat. It seemed important eating.

Portia-doctor smiled. "Fuel after flying, I believe." And I saw that of course she must be right.

Patience nodded, swallowed a large bite, and said, "Nothing comes of nothing.—Where have the soldiers gone? People won't tell me."

"South," Portia-doctor said, and poked at a piece of goat with a two-tine fork. "South through the mountains, to hunt down the cataphracts."

"Good God." Perhaps my favorite Warm-time phrase. "Can they catch them, three days gone?"

"Probably." The doctor ate her piece of goat. "The imperials will be leisurely, have no reason to hurry."

"Impatience, I thought you would have followed the soldiers south."

"I would have, NP. I wanted to see fighting, but they refused me permission—cited my safety and that sort of shit. The Big One-eye wouldn't lend me a horse to follow them." More spoonfuls of turnip eaten.

"Ah—Voss. Howell Voss."

"Yes, the Big One-eye. But I'm going to get a riding horse of my own—buy it out of my expense fund. Then, fuck him, I'll go where I want!"

"But you could have Walked-in-air."

Patience had very good table-manners; she finished chewing, and swallowed before she answered. "NP, I'm not a stupids' witch. I have just come over two thousand Warm-time miles. And I've stopped traveling, and said to myself, 'I'm here. I've *arrived.*' "

"And therefore?" Portia-doctor, interested in this phenomenon.

"Therefore, Doctor, if I air-walk again too soon, my head might ache, and I might fall."

"So, a rest."

"Yes, a few weeks, then I'll be able to say to myself, 'Now, I'm *going*. I'm going somewhere *else*. Then I'll do it, and my head won't ache, and I won't fall."

"I see."

"The piece in the brain doesn't like to be hurried, Doctor. One thing at a time is what it likes, with a long rest between." She demolished a last piece of goat meat, then attacked the rest of her turnips—which, frankly, were barely edible.

"And your beast?"

"The occa's risen and gone north. I had to kick her to get her up and going; they depend on you, then they want to stay. She'll wander awhile, but end with her mother." Salt sprinkled on turnips. "They're better than pigeons, for going back where they come from."

I tried the most promising piece of goat. "And how are the wounded, Doctor?"

Portia turned those sad brown eyes to me, eyes into which too much of others' suffering had reflected. "We've saved some—saved some of those for sitting, blind or legless, to beg in town squares."

"An army doctor is, I suppose, something of a contradiction."

"Yes, 'something of a contradiction,'" Portia said, and smiled—was almost beautiful when she smiled. Then she took up her platter, stood, and was gone.

"Is it true," Patience said, "that Big One-eye likes her?"

"Howell Voss? Where did you hear that?"

"I scented it from him while he was telling me I couldn't follow. He talked to me, but looked at her for a moment when she walked by. Then, he smelled of sad desiring—as *you* did, NP, when I mentioned the ancient Harvard library."

More Boston tinkering, apparently, and for sense of smell!

"Impatience, I believe we'll all be happier with you if you don't sniff around us like an eager hound."

"Well, then . . ." A slight pout. "Then I'll keep it to myself, what I discover that way."

"Please do."

"Why aren't you eating?"

"They have not peeled the turnips."

She smiled. "Do you know the Warm-time word 'eccentric'?"

"There is nothing eccentric about wanting turnips peeled."

"How are your teeth?" Patience showed me her small white teeth in illustration.

"I still have my teeth."

"Here." She reached over quickly, took my platter, and began to peel the halved turnips on it. She'd reached very quickly, and she peeled very quickly, so the blade of her knife flashed and flickered. "Now, eat them. They're good for you."

I ate them, and could only hope they were good for me, since they were good for nothing else. I do not imagine there is any more reliable sign of civilization than food that is a pleasure to eat, not simply grim forage. In Gardens, we had bird stews flavored with little forest friends. . . .

Having finished my slight platter as the Boston girl finished her weighty one—Corporal Leith had limped over and snatched the tin dishes up, muttering—I walked with Patience out into darkness and a cold wind come down from the mountains.

"Isn't this an *adventure*, NP?"

"If it ends well." Stepping carefully to avoid horse manure.

"Oh, adventures are ends in themselves."

"And what is it you want here, Impatience—besides adventure?"

"Want? Here, I want to watch warlords' grand clockwork tick, whir, and turn—have you ever seen wind-up clockwork?"

"No. Read of those time-pieces, of course."

"We have a large weight-wind-up clock at the entrance to

Ice-clear Justice, though it keeps uncertain time. . . . What *I* wish, is what Boston wishes, NP. I wish for perfection, as Boston wishes for perfection—and we will have it, or make it, so the sun is satisfied at last and comes to us as it did before, hot as fire."

"I see. . . ." But I didn't, then.

5

Colonel Rodriguez had come from Indian people—and wasn't ashamed of it. He'd never kissed a man's ass because that man was pale under sunshine, and could grow a fine mustache.

His mother had told him that good comes to those who wait for it, and Colonel Rodriguez—though not yet forty—had waited out several such officers, milky as girls, who spoke only the Beautiful Language, not *Nahua*, and knew women at court. The northern bandits had worn those men out, or killed them— and the Emperor, who knew truth when evil men permitted him to see it, saw the value in officers such as Michi Rodriguez, and gave him at last his regiment.

And see the result—with only three squadrons brought north! *Victory.* The troopers had celebrated every evening since the battle. Six slow marches riding south through the passes, the men dancing in camp every evening—and drinking *aguardiente* they were forbidden to have with them. Easier to find a cavalryman's soul than his hidden leather bottle.

Victory. A *first* victory. Now, the court ladies would coo and flutter . . . then moan, lie back and raise their lace skirts in dark, secret rooms smelling of the oils of flowers, so that a hero might do as he pleased, and so please them.

Perhaps . . . Though perhaps only smile and murmur behind their fans. 'See the little *Indio* . . . watch our brown hero try to manage both his chocolate cup and cake plate. See him spill crumbs on his uniform, perhaps a drop or two of chocolate as well. . . .'

But either way—a victory. The Indian colonel would come with his regiment to The City, and the Emperor would see he brought a battle won, as his banner.

"Something shone, high in the mountains." Tomas Reyes, a

milk-face but a decent fellow, had spurred up alongside on that showy gray—a trumpet-horse color.

"What something?"

"Colonel, I don't know. Two of the men saw it."

"Bandits. Curious shepherds."

"I don't know, sir. Should we arm a squadron?"

Rodriguez considered. It was the cataphract problem.—Well, there were two cataphract problems. One was the size of horse required to carry both the heavy chain-mail that guarded its own chest and flanks, *and* a man wearing that same chain-mail draped and belted from helmet to boot.

So, the proper horse was one problem; the full suit of mail was itself the other problem. No man, not even a very strong man, wished to wear it day and night.

Bandits, probably, high in the mountains above the pass. A spear-tip or sword-blade flashing an instant in the sun. Too far south, too many days south, now, for any interference by the northerners. They wouldn't have more than a few hundred Light Cavalry left at This'll Do. Would have been busy for a day or so just burying their dead. And wouldn't have had time to bring more than . . . say, a headquarters' detachment down through Please Pass to follow.

"Unlikely," Rodriguez said.

"Sir?"

"I said, 'Unlikely.' But just in case"—a favorite Warm-time phrase of his father's—"just in case, have Third Squadron fall out and arm."

"Sir." Captain Reyes saluted with a cadet-school flourish, showed off with a rearing turn, and galloped back along the files. Fair enough, the man was a fine horseman—unlike, say, a certain nearly-plump Indian, who nevertheless had won a victory.

Almost a sand-glass later by the sun's shadow across the narrow pass, and deep into an afternoon now truly warm, his guidon-bearer, Julio Gomez, saw steel glittering on the steep mountainside above them—and properly called it out.

There was, as Rodriguez had quickly discovered, a sadness nesting amid the pleasures of command. It was the sadness of knowing—knowing more than his officers and men. Knowing unpleasant things they did not yet know.

—Such as realizing immediately that this second conveniently revealed sparkle of steel was deliberate, meant to provoke him to action, and so, was no affair of bandits, but a military matter.

Which therefore meant that some of the northerners *had* followed him down. And since no local commander would have taken the remarkable risk, after a lost battle, of pursuing days deep into imperial country—certainly riding day and night to do so, certainly killing horses to do so—and with what must be a modest force of the few troops at hand, it meant as well that this northern commander was probably *the* commander, Monroe himself.

Rodriguez felt chilled and hot at once. Chilled, because such determination, such an extraordinary pursuit of several days south, was frankly a surprise, and disturbing. But hot as well, at the notion of doubling a triumph and bringing to Mexico City not one victory, but two. And the head of Sam Monroe.

He stood in his stirrups, turned, and called for Captain Reyes. It was going to be . . . it was going to be all right. This pass, *Boca Chica*, was narrow, its sides much too steep for cavalry to come down on his flanks. So, whether the northerners maneuvered in front of him as the pass widened, or tried to attack from the rear, the result would be the same. His people would hammer them, ride them down.

The colonel saw Captain Reyes cantering to him for orders . . . and felt the early autumn wind's caress as a promise of victory.

* * *

"He's armed a squadron—no, he's arming all his people down there." On the mountainside, Howell Voss sat slumped on a sweated horse, a remount. He'd left his wonderful Adelante wind-broken and dying two days back, as they'd left other horses his troopers had ridden to death on the fast chase south through these mountains. A brutal cost in fine animals. They had no fresh mounts left.

Beside him, Sam Monroe sat his horse, a weary sore-backed bay, looked down the mountainside's steep slope, and said, "Perfect."

In the narrow defile below, the cataphracts were lifting their heavy folds of chain-mail from the pack-horses' duffels, shaking them out, wrestling into them, fastening latches and buckles. Then, weighty, lumbering to their chargers to dress them in oiled jingling steel skirts.

" 'Perfect'? I don't see how this is going to get done at all." Voss leaned from his saddle to spit thirst's cotton. His empty eye-socket itched, as always when sweat ran into it under the patch. "We've got only Headquarters' Heavies, that's two hundred and fifty of my troopers—and what's left of Ned's Lights fit to fight, another two, three hundred."

"Yes."

"Sam, there are maybe seven hundred cataphracts down there."

"Seven hundred and fourteen."

"Our people are tired, and our horses—the ones we have left—are even tireder from chasing these imperials for almost a fucking Warm-time week."

"So?"

"Sir, go down there, I'd say we're asking for another cavalry disaster."

Sam smiled at him. "That's what I'd say, too, Howell, where

cavalry's concerned. But what we have down there, to quote old Elvin, is 'an infantry situation.' "

"We're not infantry."

Sam swung off his horse. "Ah—but we're going to be."

* * *

"Pass begins to widen up ahead," Rodriguez said, "past the next turn of rock." Captain Reyes stood in his stirrups to look.

"Scouts out, sir?"

"To report what, Captain? That the pass widens slightly past the turn, as we know it widens? That the enemy has come down and is waiting, as they surely are? . . . Now, I want our formations shaken out into ranks three deep across this *Boca*, wall to wall. Third Squadron to reverse order and hold in place farther back up the pass to cover the rear. If any of the northern cavalry—and it must be cavalry to have caught up with us—if any have followed down the pass, Davila is to immediately charge and strike them."

"Yes, sir."

"He is *not* to wait for my command."

"Understood."

"If most, or all their force, has come from the hills and is waiting before us—Mother Mary, please make it so—we will charge them in march order. First Squadron, then Second in support, if there's anyone left to ride over."

"Yes, sir."

"Pass those orders—and see they are understood, Tomas."

"I will!" A fine salute—and another sample of horsemanship as he turned and galloped away on the gray. . . . Man was a pleasant fellow, but really an ass.

Soon enough, another rider came up. Major Moro—practically elderly, and would never be more than a major. Very dark, too, well named *Moro*.

"Am I to suppose, Colonel, that this time Reyes got an order right? My squadron remains as marching, and first for the charge if the *cabróns* come down to meet us?"

"That is exactly right," Rodriguez said. "And be careful of your language, Major. The angels may be watching us, now."

Major Moro made a face. "It is those things from the north the angels need to watch, and carry their filthy souls away!"

"Absolutely." Rodriguez crossed himself to seal that truth. "The orders are as given. Now, get back to your men."

Moro saluted and was gone.

The pass was turning . . . opening. Two long bow-shots, now—no more.

Rodriguez held up his right hand. First Squadron's trumpeter immediately blew three short, rising notes—and the colonel heard, behind him, more than two troops of heavy-armored cavalry spur to the trot, horses' hooves beginning a rhythmic hammer, draped chain-mail making soft music as they came.

Proud of them, he said to himself, certain such pride was forgivable. The pass was turning. Turning. An edge, a sliver of open grassland was becoming visible past the mountain's slope. Steel sparkled against that hint of green.

Rodriguez reined Salsa far to the right—his guidon-bearer, Gomez, following—to clear Moro's men for the charge.

Called commands. . . . Then First Squadron began to wheel in stately turn to the left, ranks in good order as the pivot files slowed. It swung ponderously out into the pass's mouth; Salsa, champing his bit, was shouldered into the *Boca*'s rough wall as the right-flank ranks rode by.

No mounted troopers were waiting at the pass's narrow entrance. No horses.

Only big, bearded men—and what seemed to be a few women—in polished cuirasses, black-plumed steel helmets, brown wool, leather, and black thigh-boots. Two long rows of these people, all holding short, square shields grounded, and gripping twelve-foot lances like pikemen, heavy straight sabers sheathed at their sides.

There were two more ranks behind them. Those, Light Cavalry—men, and many more of their godless northern women—in hauberks, and armed with lighter lances, curved sabers.

And all on foot, drawn up as infantry.

Clever, if they're up to it . . . don't miss having horses under them. Rodriguez wanted a moment to think, to consider the situation, but Major Moro was not a thinker. First Squadron's trumpeter sounded two bright notes, then a long silver third—and more than two hundred huge horses sprang from the trot to the gallop, kicking stones, sending red dirt flying. They launched themselves and their riders as one, so chain-mail shook and rang like bells above the drumroll of hooves. As they passed, Rodriguez smelled coppery dust, horse sweat, oiled steel.

The first rank of cataphracts leaned to the right in their saddles, lifting their battle-axes free. And as if in a dance agreed upon, the northerners' long lances swung down in response into a glittering needled hedge, the men crouched low behind them, shields braced.

For a few moments that seemed more than moments, the space of air and light between the gallopers and those waiting ranks contracted, grew shadowy . . . then collapsed as the ground jarred and shook.

They came together in a great splintering crash that smothered trumpet calls. Bright steel shone through roiling red dust, and horses screamed—not men, not yet, though the cataphracts' own furious armored weight drove them to impalement, even through their draperies of chain-mail. Their battle-axes, flailing down right and left, struck with the solid sound of woodsmen's axes into ripe wood—or rang skidding off shields set slanting.

A black charger—all Moro's squadron rode blacks—exploded

out of confusion riderless, bucked and raced away, kicking at its dragging entrails as it went. Under red dust, horsemen spurred in, shouting as they hacked with heavy axes, while the northerners, fighting silent, caught these men and mounts on ranked lance points that rose and fell in rippling lines.

"Column!" Rodriguez shouted for that fool, Reyes. *"Second Squadron to form column!"*

"Yes, sir!" And there Reyes was. A fine horseman.

"Second Squadron into column—and advance!" There was an extraordinary amount of dust now . . . clouds of it, hard to shout through.

"Sir!" Reyes turned his horse—and seemed to meet an arrow come down out of nowhere, that rang off his chest's steel and whined away. "Look!" He pointed up.

Rodriguez looked up and saw infantry—no, more fucking dismounted cavalry, Light Cavalry by their mail shirts—high on the steep slopes of the *Boca.* Not many, perhaps thirty of them on each side, but they were using bows—those fucking longbows with the short lower limb. Barefoot, too—most of them he could see—to keep from stumbling and falling into the pass.

Using their bows—as I should have had each squadron's archers deploy to do. Too late now. Rodriguez waved Reyes away. "Into column! Column!"

"Sir!" Reyes spurred—and galloped into another arrow. This one took him in the belly by worst chance, just where the heavy fall of mail divided at his saddle-bow.

Dead. Rodriguez looked to see the captain fall, but he didn't. He rode bent over his saddle like an old woman—his fine seat gone in agony—but galloped out to Major Ticotin. Second Squadron was shouted slowly out of extended line . . . slowly into column of ten.

"Receive these!" Colonel Rodriguez called to the enemy as he rode, intending to go in with Ticotin. "Receive these, you fuckers!" He had no need to see what had happened to Moro's troopers. His ears told him. At the mouth of the pass, under the screams of dying horses, sounded the bright swift hammering of steel . . . the sobbing, grunting, barely caught breaths of men gutted on the pikes the northerners had made of their long lances.

"Well, you're very clever!" Rodriguez, galloping to Second Squadron's guidon, addressed Sam Monroe. "Now, let's see you stop cataphracts in column!"

"You are not going in with us. Absolutely *not!*" Major Ticotin looked furious, face pale above his beard. Dust was drifting around them like red fog. "You are staying *back*, Colonel!"

"I'm going in with you!"

There was a squealing sound—a damned pig somehow mixed up in this—and Rodriguez saw Captain Reyes off a way, saw him quite clearly leaning far back in his saddle, plucking at something.—The arrow shaft, of course, sticking out of his belly. He was making the sound.

"Your ass is staying back!" Major Ticotin reached over with the blade of his saber and sliced through Rodriguez's reins. Almost took his hand off.

"You're under arrest!" Rodriguez laughed at having said something so stupid. He tried to turn Salsa to follow with knees alone, then climbed down to catch the reins and knot them together.

Second Squadron poured past him like a river. Chestnut horses. Trumpets . . . trumpets.

He found the rein ends—goddamn horse circling around—knotted them, and swung up into the saddle, grunting with the jingling weight of his armor, just as Second Squadron, at full gallop, struck the center of the northerners' line.

Struck it, broke it, and thundered through.

I have him. I have him—thank you, Mother of God. "Reyes!" . . . *No Reyes. Reyes was gone.* Rodriguez spurred back up the pass. A long bow-shot down the defile, Third Squadron still waited, facing north, where now no enemy would come. "Orders! Gomez!" His guidon-bearer, not very intelligent, seemed startled to be transmitting orders in place of Captain Reyes.

"Go to Major Davila. Third Squadron to reverse front, and advance! *Now,* you idiot!"

Gomez hauled his horse's head around and kicked the animal into a gallop as Rodriguez watched him go—watched for a moment to be certain an arrow didn't come down to Gomez, cancel the order. *Worse rider than I am. Really a ridiculous figure . . . bouncing on the goddamn saddle as if he were fucking it.*

No arrow for Gomez. It seemed to Rodriguez that fewer arrows were coming down. Harder to mark targets, now, through the dust—and thank God's Mother for it. He turned Salsa back to the noise of fighting, cantered that way . . . and heard trumpet calls behind him. Third Squadron would be reversing files.

Rodriguez rode to the fighting—glanced back, and saw Gomez galloping down the pass to catch up . . . saw Third Squadron reforming. The noise of fighting ahead was extraordinary—crashes of metal, shrieks of injured horses echoing off the *Boca's* narrow walls as if the devil had sent a band from hell to serenade the dying.

Through a haze of dust, Rodriguez saw that the northerners' line was certainly broken. Ticotin's men had driven deep into their center, so the long ranks of dismounted lancers were swinging away to either side of the breach like *cantina* doors, their dead dotting the dirt and grass behind them.

Swinging away . . . so Second Squadron, galloping in, cheering, ax blades flashing through red dust, rode deeper between the northerners' ranks. The noise was terrific, the clangor, and thunderous sound of the chargers' hooves.

Then, louder, answering thunder sounded behind him, behind and high above. Rodriguez turned in his saddle, but there was only clear blue sky over the pass's rim, and Third Squadron now in motion, starting down the pass at a steady trot.

"Sir . . . *Sir!*" Gomez rode up, shouting, miming listening, his hand cupping his ear. Rodriguez thought he meant that odd sound of thunder—then heard a trumpet call out of the fighting, an imperial call. *The rally.*

Why?

Rodriguez spurred Salsa to a gallop, drew his saber, and rode into the hammered dust of fighting, his guidon-bearer still calling after him.

There was, he thought, as he leaned to strike one of their wounded cuirassiers staggering past—there was an odd satisfaction in seeing the difficulty.

The ranks of northerners, that had swung so wide apart at Second Squadron's charge, were now slowly swinging shut to enclose it. *Remarkable, such a maneuver, and accomplished by dismounted cavalry. Fine officers. . . .*

The rally sounded again, Ticotin trying to keep his horsemen together—to drive deeper yet, break the trap's jaws. . . . It would not work.

Rodriguez longed to charge into the fight. He felt that he could ride into the battle, gallop *over* the battle like an angel, and save his men. He spurred Salsa closer to the fighting, and rode against a file of men, bearded, covered with dust, clumsy in their high boots. One saw him, turned, and presented a lance-point. Rodriguez parried it aside, cut down at the man, struck something—perhaps only the lance shaft—and that man and all of them were gone, swallowed in clouds of dust, shouted commands, confusion.

Dust was in the colonel's mouth, but a breeze had come and bannered red haze aside to show clearly how Ticotin's troopers were dying, as if a great carnivorous plant—its petals treacherously open—now closed bright thorns upon them from either side.

More thunder behind him—odd sliding thunder. Gomez, that idiot, was shouting again. . . . Ticotin was stuck in shit and would not get out, but Third Squadron was coming. Rodriguez turned in his saddle to wave them on and into a gallop. They'd be in time . . . but barely.

He turned to see their bannered ranks now spurring into the gallop—and saw, a moment later, the mountainsides coming down into the pass.

The steep slopes to right and left were suddenly brown and gray rivers of bounding, rolling, skidding boulders. A torrent of stone was coming down in landslides, great granite monuments tilting, toppling to swell those catastrophic currents.

Of course. The Light Cavalry archers had stopped shooting only to climb to the ridges . . . begin those slides of stone.

The sound was beyond sound; it buffeted Rodriguez like blows. Salsa shied and reared away.

He controlled the horse—had time to see Davila and his trumpeter, at the head of Third Squadron, both staring up like astonished children as the mountainsides fell upon them. Avalanches of rock, a flood of stone, flowed and thundered down into the narrow pass and over the horsemen. Here and there bright steel wavered for an instant, ranks of men and horses screamed—and were gone, vanished beneath tons of rumbling granite that seemed to come down forever, while dust billowed, eddied in the air.

. . . Perhaps forty, perhaps fifty men and horses—saved by miracles—staggered here and there as the last showers of stone, the last great boulders skipped, crashed, rolled and settled. Several of these horses had broken legs dangling. Many of the men, dust-coated, swaying in their saddles, were shouting warnings— as if what had already happened was only about to happen.

Rodriguez heard a trumpet call—a call unknown to him— back at the entrance to the pass. He turned Salsa's head and rode that way. Gomez reined up beside him. "How?" he said. "*How?*"—as if their ranks were equal.

The destroyed men were still shouting behind them. There were also screams, but not many.

Rodriguez smiled at his guidon-bearer as if they were old friends, the best of friends riding together. "How? By my misjudgment, and the northerners' commendable initiative."

"Ah . . ." Gomez nodded, apparently satisfied.

At the mouth of the pass, now only those northerners stood—though there were slight disturbances within their ranks as the last of Ticotin's men were pierced with lances or dragged from their big horses to be hacked to death.

"Yes," Rodriguez said aloud, and meant he'd been right before, to wish to ride into the fighting. "Go with God," he said to his guidon-bearer—drove in his spurs, and galloped out of the pass toward the ranks of his enemies. He felt very well, really quite well . . . though he was saddened to hear Gomez following, riding behind him. Well, the man was a fool . . . always had been.

* * *

The fighting dust had settled, so the southern sun shone richly to warm the men and horses still alive. Now, near silence lay as if there'd been no noise in these mountains, no shouting, no trumpets, no hammering steel on steel in *Boca Chica* Pass.

It was a familiar quiet, the stillness after battle. Sam Monroe closed his eyes, eased his muscles to enjoy it. He was sitting on a dead horse, its skirts of chain-mail dark with blood and shit. Its rider lay with it; he'd been caught with a leg under the animal when it fell, and had been killed there.

Sam hadn't drawn his sword through most of the fighting.

He might have; he'd met several of their horsemen in the battle's dust and fury. It had been odd—perfect Warm-time word. Odd.

He'd ridden here and there, watching his men maneuver—and so well, obedient to their officers and sergeants as if they'd been veteran infantry, never cavalry at all. Wonderful, really, and all the more appreciated when a man simply rode—his worried trumpeter reining behind—as if terrible noise, dust, savage struggles, and the screams of hurt horses and dying men had nothing to do with him at all.

He'd met two cataphracts. They'd spurred at him, then passed, never striking—as if he were a person separate from the fighting. At the battle's end, one imperial, galloping blind out of clouds of dust, *had* come swinging his battle-ax.

Sam had swayed to the side and away from the ax's stroke—drawing sword as he did—then straightened in his saddle to slash the cataphract just under his helmet's nasal. And as the injured man reined past, spitting teeth and blood, Sam struck again, a back-stroke and much harder, to the nape. Though the chain-mail there caught the sword's edge, the blow's force broke the man's neck, and his charger trotted him away dying, his head rolling this way and that.

. . . Sam opened his eyes to hoofbeats as Howell Voss rode up, looking furious. An ax, that must have been swung very hard, had chopped his helmet's steel, snicked off the tip of his left ear. Voss, bareheaded now, was holding his bandanna to it.

"Howell. . . . Lucky for the helmet."

"I know it." Blood still ran down Voss's wrist. "You want their colonel's head to take back?"

"No, don't disturb their colonel. Leave him lying with his troopers." There was a spray of blood across Sam's hauberk.

"You hurt?"

"Not anymore," Sam said. Just the sort of vainglorious

phrase the army would like, with a defeat so thoroughly revenged. The sort of phrase that seemed to come to him more and more easily.

Small black shadows printed across the battlefield. The ravens had come to *Boca Chica.*

"We have two hundred and eighteen prisoners, Sam—we finished the worst wounded. Nine of the prisoners are officers."

"Behead those officers. And please tell them I regret the necessity."

". . . Yes, sir." A battle-made gentleman himself—his mother a tavern prostitute, his father a passing mystery—Voss had a soft spot for officers.

"Someone else can do it, Howell."

"*I'll* do it."

"Okay." That strange Warm-time word 'okay.' Yet everyone seemed to know what it meant, without explanation. "We'll let the troopers go. Leave them twenty of their horses for the wounded, and a few bows and battle-axes in case bandits come down on them."

"As you say." Voss saluted, and started to turn his mount away.

"And Howell . . ."

"Sir?"

"Sorry about the ear."

Voss smiled. And when he smiled—the handsome horse-face with its eye-patch suddenly creased and looking kind—Sam understood what women saw in him. "It's just a fucking ear, Sam. And I've still got most of it."

"True. And, Howell, it was very well done of your people—*very* well done for cavalry to maneuver so decisively on foot."

"Your idea, sir."

"Ideas are easy, Colonel. But shaping horsemen into infantry formations in the middle of a fight, is not easy."

"The people paid attention—and I was lucky."

"That, too." Sam held out his hand, and Howell leaned down to take it. "Thank you."

I weld them to me. Sam watched Howell ride away, holding the bandanna to his injured ear. *As I hammer, polish, and sharpen all my tools and instruments . . .*

Howell Voss would be the man to take the Rascob brothers' place.—Ned Flores had a sense for horses and distance and country. And both old Butler and Charmian were wonderful infantry commanders. . . . But here at the pass, Howell had turned from commanding Heavy Cavalry *and* Light, to commanding them as unaccustomed infantry. And he'd done it perfectly, as Sam had stood aside—needing only the hint that the imperials would likely come, the second time, in column.

"Good!" Howell had said. "I'll let 'em in—then re-form, and swing the doors shut." The important word in that, of course, had been 'Good!' That swift-reasoned eagerness.

So, a decision taken—and old Jaime and Elvin Rascob both now ghosts, though they didn't know it. It would also be useful—certainly sweet Second-mother Catania would have agreed—to manage Howell and Portia-doctor together at last, so Voss's loneliness didn't end by crippling him as a commander.

New instrument prepared; old instruments discarded. And instruments for what? The peace, and peace of mind, of two hundred thousand North Map-Mexico farmers, shepherds, tradesmen? Was that sufficient reason for the cataphracts dying here at *Boca Chica?*

How much difference would it make if the Emperor came back up to rule the north? If the Khan came down to rule it? Careless rule, or cruel—how much of a difference? Enough to be worth the deaths at This'll Do, then *Boca Chica* . . . and all the deaths in the years before?

No difference now to fourteen Light Cavalry, caught on the slopes by their own avalanche.

No difference to the one hundred and eighty-three troopers killed playing infantry against the cataphracts.

The soft sunny day was fading, laying long shadows across beaten grass, across dead men and dead horses. A fading day, but still warm so far south. . . . Sam took a drink of water from his canteen. He imagined it was vodka—imagined so well that he could taste the lime juice squeezed into it.

Flies had blanketed the dead horse he sat on, and veiled the pinned cataphract's ruined face. This crawling, speckled drapery rose clouding when Sam stood to walk away, and drifted humming along with his first few steps, as if he might be dead as well.

6

"Am I clever, Razumov?"

"Very, my lord."

"And you will have the courage to warn me when I'm not? . . . Should that ever happen."

"I will try to find the courage, lord."

"Good answer." The Lord of Grass was in his garden—a summer garden now past the end of its delicate temporary blossoming of sweet peas, pansies, and bluebonnets. The sweet peas were already gone, the bluebonnets and pansies withering in Lord Winter's earliest winds. . . . The garden and its paths were at the center of a small city of yurts, tents, buildings and pavilions set on gently rolling prairie, a few Warm-time miles north of the mound of Old Map-Lubbock.

There had been, not opposition, but complaints at moving Caravanserai from Los Angeles to the mid Map-Texas prairie, only eighteen horseback days south of the Wall of Ice. However, after one complaint too many on the subject had cost Colonel Sergei Pol his breath, there was an agreeable acceptance.

From his childhood, Toghrul had been fond of flowers. "Of course," he'd told his father, when that silent Khan had raised an eyebrow on finding his only son digging in the dirt with a serving fork, "of course, we cannot have the best Warm-time blossoms. None of their hollyhocks, lilacs, dahlias, roses."

His father had watched Toghrul at work for a while, then grunted and strolled away, seeming neither surprised nor disappointed.

Silence had been the Great Khan's weapon. Silence—slow, dark, deep as drowning water. In conference, from the time he was a child, Toghrul had watched his father's silence slowly fill with other men's talk—their arguments, defiances, explanations . . . and finally, their submissions. Their pleas.

The Khan, a short man, nearly wide as he was tall, would sit listening until at last the others came to silence also. Then, he spoke.

Toghrul's was a different way, from boyhood. He chatted with those who chatted with him, was quick in humor and appreciative of humor in others, so it came each time as the grimmest shock when pleasant conversation ended pleasantly . . . and the stranglers stepped, yawning, from behind their curtain.

The Lord of Grass bent to examine a dying bluebonnet. "How I wish for roses."

"We can get them, lord, from the south."

"Yes, Michael, we can get them from the south. They will arrive . . . then die as soon as our north winds touch them. I would rather not have them at all, than lose them."

"They might be kept in warm little houses, with windows of flat glass."

"Michael, I'm aware the coarse queen of Middle Kingdom keeps her vegetables and flowers alive in those sorts of houses, even after summer's over. But the notion of captive roses doesn't please me."

"No, my lord; I take your point. And if we find a painter to paint the most beautiful roses for you?"

"Razumov . . . Razumov. I would rather not *have* roses, than pretend to have them."

The chancellor bowed, and left the subject prettily. "The blossom of good judgment, however, *is* yours, Great Khan, since the Captain-General Monroe *has* followed his lesson of defeat with a triumph in revenge."

"Yes." The Khan swung his horse-whip to behead a windburned bluebonnet. "A mercy, it was too pale a shade of blue. . . . Yes, a thoughtful Captain-General. He was clever, and I was clever concerning him. Now, I believe we'd better send just enough bad weather to see what shelter he runs to."

Yuri Chimuk—an older man, large, flat-faced, and badly

scarred—had followed along on the flower tour, silent. Chimuk had been an officer under the old Khan, and had seen enough death on the ice from Vladivostok to Map-Anchorage—and in slightly warmer country farther and farther south as the years went by—to have lost any fear of it. The old general was one of the few men Toghrul knew, who weren't afraid of him.

"Your thoughts, Yuri?"

"Lord, our serious men are occupied commencing your campaign against Middle Kingdom. Since Manu Four-Horsetails is useless as tits on a bull, send him down to peck along the Map-Bravo. He's capable of that, at least."

Manu Ek-Tam was the old man's grandson, the apple, as Warm-times had had it, of his eye—and already a very formidable commander at twenty-four, having completed, it must be said, an exceptional campaign in Map-Nevada.

"Five thousand cavalry might be too heavy a peck, Yuri. I don't want North Mexico disturbed to war, just when we're striking east. The river people will be troublesome enough."

"Manu shouldn't *be* commanding five thousand; he's not capable. Give him a thousand, lord."

"So few? You don't want him killed, do you, old man?"

"It would be a relief to be rid of him."

". . . Umm. We'll say *two* thousand. Send some of Crusan's people down from Map–Fort Stockton to reinforce Manu. And remind your grandson, Yuri—pecks, harassment, *not* an invasion."

Yuri Chimuk got down on his hands and knees—something he'd been excused from doing years before, but persisted in as an odd independence. "What the Khan has ordered, I will perform."

When the old man stood and stomped away, Toghrul watched him go, absently switching the top of his right boot with the horse-whip. "Your thoughts, Michael Razumov."

"First, why wake a sleeping dog, my lord? And . . ."

" 'And'?"

"And, second, Yuri Chimuk loves his grandson even more than he loves you."

"Well ... first, the North-Mexican dog must be wakened *sometime*. And I need to know whether, when kicked, he will run yelping south to the Empire, or east, to Middle Kingdom. ... Second, as to Yuri's love for his grandson, it is only required that he blame *himself* for that brilliant and ambitious young officer's death, when—as it must—that occurs. We have room, after all, for only one genius of war."

"Is this in my hands, lord?"

"Not yet." The Khan leaned over a pansy. "Look, Michael, look at this brave little face. A tiny golden roaring lion, pictured in a Warm-time book."

"It is charming."

"Do *you* love *me*, Michael? You loved me when I was a boy, I know. I used to watch you, watching me."

"I did love you, my lord, and still do. Being aware that that remains entirely beside the point."

The Khan laughed, and bent to stroke the little pansy flower. "You are full of good answers, today."

"And, I regret to say, a question, lord."

"Yes?" The Khan stood.

"Map–Los Angeles and Map–San Diego—"

"The Blue Sky damn them both. What now?"

"Complaints, Great Khan. Ships do not arrive from the Empire with goods we've already paid for. Buk Szerzinski complains particularly, saying he has a Map-Pacific supply depot with *no* supplies of lumber, rope, grain, barrels of citrus juice, slaves, steel, or horses. All things to be needed by your generals as Lord Winter comes, and fighting increases in Map-Missouri."

"The problem being silver money?"

"Absolutely, lord. Money is the cause. The Empire accepts our silver, but discounts it against their gold. Szerzinski, and

Paul Klebb in Map–Los Angeles, both claim they pay the full price agreed upon, only to have the dirty lying bank of Mexico City discount its worth, so barely half of what was bought is delivered north."

The Khan ran his whip's slim lash through his fingers. "Those two are not lying, stealing from me?"

"They're not nearly brave enough for that, lord. And my men have examined the transactions."

"So, the Emperor comes to agreements; his orders are sent—but the dirty bank decides. A matter of civilization *versus*—wonderful Warm-time word, 'versus'—a crowd of savages galloping around in the chilly north."

"Precisely, Great Lord."

"Fucking clever currency exchanges and shifting values—gold up, silver down. How are we simple, honorable warriors to comprehend its principles?"

"Just so."

The Khan stooped to touch another surviving pansy, one black and gold. "Well, Michael, since we have the savage name, we might as well play the savage game. I will not be caught short at Middle Kingdom's river."

"Your command?"

"Arrest the . . . five most important members of the Imperial Order of Merchants and Factors in both Map–Los Angeles and Map–San Diego. Pour molten gold down their throats. Then ship the corpses to Mexico City, with the note, 'Herewith, lading payments in gold—as apparently preferred. Complete deliveries expected soonest.' "

"Perfect, lord."

"Sufficient, let us hope. . . . Anything else this evening?"

"Only a last question, if permitted."

"Yes?"

"As to your intention, lord, of going east to Map-Missouri to command personally."

"Oh, I'll wait until Murad Dur and Andrei Shapilov begin to make mistakes, which will likely be soon enough."

"Then I have nothing further worth your attention, Great Khan." Michael Razumov went to his hands and knees, then touched his forehead to the gravel of the Cat's-Eye Path. He was a fat man, and it was awkward for him.

. . . Toghrul had often considered relieving his chancellor of the necessity, but each time, a voice—his father's, perhaps—had murmured caution. He liked Michael Razumov, and almost trusted him. Reason enough to keep him on all fours.

When Toghrul was alone—but for twenty troopers of the Guard's Regiment pacing here and there—he said his farewell to the dying flowers . . . which had wanted nothing from him but sheep shit and water. Then he walked the Turquoise Path to his great yurt of oiled yellow silk, spangled with silver . . . set its entrance cloth aside, and stepped into the smell and smoke of cooking sausage.

His wife, and the slave named Eleanor, were preparing dinner at the yurt's center stove.—The caravanserai cooked and served for hundreds . . . thousands, if need be. But Toghrul had learned to avoid those kettles of boiled mutton with southern rice and peppers, though he would poke and fork at the food on occasions of state. The old Khan had loved that sort of cooking.

His wife looked up from cluttered pots and pans, through smoke rising to the ceiling's small Sky's eye. "What today, sweet lord?"

"Oh, Ladu, the tedious usual—causing fear and giving orders." He tossed his horse-whip onto a divan, then sat while Eleanor wrestled his boots off. Eleanor was a handsome woman with braided hair the color of autumn grass. Once, she had looked into Toghrul's eyes in the way a woman might gaze at a man while offering, while considering possibilities, advantages.

Toghrul had then had Chang-doctor remove her left eye—it

had been done under southern poppy syrup—with no explanation offered. But Eleanor had understood, and Toghrul's wife had understood. So now, the slave offered no more impudent glances of that sort, and seemed content.

"We have pig sausage and onions and shortbread cake. Will those help?" His wife smiled.

"They will certainly help."

Where the old Khan had mounted any pretty female oddment the armies found—enjoying the novelty, apparently—Toghrul, after some experiment, had decided on a traditional wife. Ladu, a Chukchi, somewhat squat and a little plump, had been chosen from the daughters of several senior officers—officers safely dead in battle, so dynastic entanglements were avoided.

Toghrul often considered that choice his best proof of good judgment, since Ladu had not found him frightening, then had come to care for him. One morning, waking beside her and watching that round, unremarkable face still soft in sleep, her short little ice-weather nose, the deep folds over slanted eyes closed in dreaming, he'd been startled to find that he loved her. This still surprised and amused him. It warmed him too, in a minor way, on winter rides, campaigning. . . . Only sons were missing—or had been. Ladu's little belly had been swelling for months, and properly, according to Chang-doctor.

So now, of course, there were expectations of a son. The staff had expectations . . . the chiefs and generals, also. Toghrul could disappoint them, and they would bear it. Ladu could not. She, and old Chimuk, were the only ones who never stood before him without anticipating a possible dreadful blow. That fear, its wary distancing, was certainly tedious, certainly made ruling more difficult, but Toghrul had found no way to remove it, since it was what the clans, the troops, expected and had always expected. In that sense only, he was the ruled and they the rulers. They were certain to be afraid of him; and what they required, he must perform.

. . . Ladu and Eleanor set hammered brass platters on the green carpet, a campaign spoil, and one of the last of its kind, with wonderful figures of racing blue-gray dogs woven into it. Toghrul slid off the divan and sat cross-legged to eat. The women stood by the stove, watching him, his appetite their reward.

"Delicious!" The sausage *was* wonderful. Bless the pig herd, though many of his men—those still worshiping Old Maybe—wouldn't go near the animals, certainly wouldn't eat their flesh.

Both women had nodded, smiling at his 'Delicious!' The Great Khan, He Who Is Feared and Lord of Grass, had paid for his supper.

* * *

"They're inside, came down yesterday." Margaret Mosten, by torchlight, motioned to Sam's tent.

"Charles *and* Eric?"

"Yes, sir."

"No quarters of their own?"

"They wanted to speak with you."

"Nailed Jesus. . . ." Sam swung down off his horse. Not *his* horse—Handsome was dead, left in the mountains, south. This was a nameless hard-mouthed brute, one of the imperials' big chargers. . . . They'd ridden back north by slow marches—more than a Warm-time week—the last returning days hungry, and all but the wounded taking turns on foot.

"Sir"—Margaret's eyes shone in the pine-knot's flaring—"what a wonderful thing." She'd been left behind to mind the camp.

"Killing their people, did not bring ours back to life." Sam walked sore and stiff-legged to the tent's entrance, put back the flap, and stepped into lamplight.

Charles Ketch, tall, gray, seeming weary of the weight of administration, sat hunched on Sam's locker. Eric Lauder, livelier, alert, perched cross-legged on the cot. A checker-board was propped between them. In age, they might almost have been father and son, but in no other way.

"Make yourselves at home."

"Ah"—Eric jumped a piece and took it off the board—"the conquering hero comes."

Sam swung his scabbarded sword's harness from his back, set the weapon by the head of the cot, and shrugged off his cloak. "Get off my bed, Eric. I'm tired."

"Are you hurt?"

"No. I avoided the fighting." Sam waited while Lauder stood and lifted the checker-board away. "Been injured in my pride, of course." He sat on the cot, then lay down and stretched out, boots and all. It felt wonderful to be out of the saddle.

"You seem to have made the best of a bad blunder." Eric emptied the checkers into their narrow wooden box.

"I was winning that game," Charles, annoyed. "You owe me five *pesos.*"

"*Would* have owed—*had* you won."

"I suppose the best of a bad blunder." Sam thought of sitting up to take his boots off. It seemed too great a task.

"Yes." Eric set the board against the tent wall. "But what sort of blunder was it?"

"A serious one—sending Ned Flores and a half-regiment to do a larger force's work." The tent's lamp smelled of New England's expensive whale oil, and seemed too bright. Sam closed his eyes for a moment.

"And what 'work' was that, Sam?"

"The work of winning a fight here, Eric."

"*Winning* a fight?" Eric sat on the locker beside Charles, nudged him to shift over. "You know, there is nothing more stupid than keeping a secret from your chief of intelligence."

"Except," Charles said, and winked at Sam, "telling him all of them."

"I made a mistake, Eric, doing something that was necessary. I was clumsy, and it cost us good people." Sam sat up to take off his boots. "What I could do to retrieve the situation has been done. Now change the subject."

"Fine," Eric said. "What subject shall we change to?" Smiling, his voice pleasant, softer than before, his dark eyes darker than his trimmed beard, he was very angry.

"Sleep."

"Before sleep, Sam"—Charles leaned forward—"there are questions in the army. Not complaints; more surprise than anything."

"Charles, the army is to be told this: We fought a battle, lost it—learned—then fought again and won. We will likely fight more battles, and may lose *another*, then fight again and win. Only children are allowed to win every time. That's what the army is to be told. Any officer with more questions, can come to me with them."

Charles sat on the locker, looking at him. ". . . Alright."

"A good answer," Eric said. "The fucking army thinks it's Mountain Jesus come down from his tree."

"Anything else?"

"Yes. Sam, there's serious fighting now, in the north. The Kipchak patrols are already in Map-Arkansas—and probably up into Map-Missouri as well; going to be trying for the river fairly soon. The major clans—Eagles, Foxes, Skies, and Spring Flowers—all gathered into *tumans*. It's to be winter war, no question. . . . Merchants we talk to, say Middle Kingdom is spending gold in preparation, particularly on their fleet. Frontier companies of their West-bank army are already skirmishing."

"No surprises there. Anything else?"

"Yes."

"Eric," Charles said, "it can wait."

"No, it *can't.*"

"Rumors, Sam."

"Not rumors, Charles," Eric said. "First informationals."

"Alright." Sam felt sick to his stomach—from being so tired, he supposed. "Let's hear it."

"Pigeon news from Texas, Twelve-mile," Eric said, almost whispering. "Our Secret-person there tells us a regiment, under Vladimir Crusan, rode out of Map–Fort Stockton yesterday. Riding south to Map-Alpine, then probably down to the Bravo. Also indications that another regiment is coming south to join him."

Sam sat up straighter, rubbed the back of his neck to stay alert. "That's interesting. You'd think they'd be too busy to trouble us. He has Seventh *Tuman?*"

"The Ninth," Eric said. "And I think the idea is to remind us to keep *out* of their business."

"What do we know of Crusan?"

"Only half-Kipchak," Charles said. "A good, steady commander, but not the independent type."

"Crusan is a good cavalryman." Eric frowned, considering. "But we don't think—my people don't think—he's up to commanding more than the Ninth."

"Coming down at full strength?"

"Apparently, Sam. One regiment . . . so, Warm-time's give-or-take, a thousand horse archers. And if, as seems likely, he joins with another detached regiment on the border, that would make about two thousand men."

"Maneuvers? Blooding recruits for the campaign against Middle Kingdom?"

"That's possible, Sam." Charles stood, stooping slightly under the tent's canvas. "But more likely just to keep us out of it, since we flank them to the south."

"Which"—Eric smiled—"makes them a little nervous. Pigeons have been coming in from my people, Map-California on east. The Kipchaks are being careful to stay well north of our border while they move their supplies through Map-Texas, mule and wagon-freight from the coast. . . . They're having some difficulty getting goods out of South Map-California—we don't know why—but they're still gathering remounts at Map–Fort Stockton, Map–Big Spring, Map-Abilene."

"Supplies for more than a year's campaigning, Eric?"

"No, Sam. Not for more than a year."

"So, the Khan expects to beat the Boxcars, take their whole river kingdom, in Lord Winter's season."

"That's right," Eric said. "And I'd say he can do it."

"Not easily." Charles shook his head. He looked tired as Sam felt. Looked his age, stooped, graying. "He'll have to whip their West-bank army, then campaign up and down the Map-Mississippi once it's frozen to easy going for cavalry. And even if he destroys their fleet, he still has to deal with the *East*-bank army."

"Alright, not easily," Eric said. "It's a big mouthful, but the Khan has a big appetite. And in any case, these regiments coming south are a different matter. They're just for us—a little reminder."

"*If* they're coming down, yes." Sam could smell himself in the tent's closeness. Horse sweat and his sweat. "But when— and if—the Kipchaks break the Kingdom, control the river, it will give the Khan all the West, give him the Gulf Entire. . . . Then we come next."

"He might not be able to do it at all." Charles pursed his lips, considering the Khan's difficulties. "Kingdom's West-bank army is what, now, fifteen thousand regulars? All heavy infantry. And they're only the first Boxcars he'll meet."

Sam saw Charles trying to talk things better, take some of the decision-weight from him. It didn't help. The conversation, repeating the heart of many conversations, seemed dream talk, difficult to stay awake for. "Charles, the Kipchaks can do it, if Lord Winter helps them and freezes the river fast. I think I could do it with the Khan's forces—and if I could do it, it's damn sure Toghrul can. . . . Now, Eric, this attack on our border. You believe those people are coming down—or you *know?*"

"I know they rode south. And I'd say they'll cross the Bravo above Map-Chihuahua."

"Coming down west of the Bend. Alright, I accept that—and on your head be it."

Lauder smiled. "Sam . . . what an unpleasant phrase."

"Two thousand wouldn't do to come against us seriously, and Crusan apparently not the commander to try it. Still, it makes sense, if only as an exercise, to act as if it were a serious threat." Sam thought a moment longer. "Charles, see to it all border towns and posts in the area are notified of possible trouble. They're to prepare their people to leave and march south up into the hills if the order comes, *or* considerable forces of Khanate cavalry are scouted. And by 'considerable,' I mean horsetails maneuvering in more than one area, in near-regimental strength. Then—and *only* then—they are to burn any standing crops, destroy any animals they can't take with them."

"*Good.*" Lauder struck a fist into his other palm.

"Sam, it's premature," Charles said, "even as a preliminary order. The Khan's people are not even near the border."

"Better too early than too late. And if Eric's wrong about this, we'll cut his pay."

"If I'm wrong, you can *keep* my pay." Lauder stood up. "Well, keep a month of it, anyway."

"—Also, Charles . . ." Sam lost the thought for a moment from weariness, then recalled it. "Also, all militia captains in Chihuahua are to be prepared to act against light-cavalry raiders. By harassing only, cutting off straggling small units, then retreating to broken or high ground. They are not to engage in *any* considerable battle—and if that order is disregarded, I will hang the captain responsible, win or lose."

"Alright, Sam." Charles sighed, resigned. His sighs, it seemed to Sam, more and more frequent. "But even this—if it proves to be for nothing—is going to cost us tax money we can't afford to lose. Crops burned, sheep and cattle killed or taken."

"If it proves to be for nothing, Charles, we've at least got Eric's pay. These orders are to be sent without delay. Riders tonight, birds in the morning."

"Yes, sir." Definitely displeased.

"And, Sam," Lauder said, "while you're still awake . . ."

"I'm not awake."

"Do we have an answer for the merchant Philip Golvin?"

"Oh, shit." Sam lay back down, felt sore muscles settle in relief.

"Unavoidable. I'm sorry."

"Eric, is there any question he speaks for the Queen?"

"None. Golvin factors goods for Island, for river traffic generally, *and* acts as an unofficial emissary. Queen Joan has used him before. Sent him all the way to Boston, once—apparently he didn't care for the journey. Went by ship across the Gulf, then up into the Map-Atlantic, sea-sick all the way."

"Sam," Charles said, "she definitely wants a visit from you."

"Wants more than that," Lauder said. "Queen Joan's getting old, has only a daughter—and ruling those barely-reformed cannibals can't be a pleasure. Two armies, for Weather's sake! West-bank and East-bank, and the men and officers of each kept absolutely separate!"

"Good reason for that," Sam said. What sort of hint did it need to be, when a man lay stretched on his cot, to leave him alone to sleep?

"But only a king's reason, Sam, to hold power balanced between them. And there's the Fleet."

"Still, Eric," Charles said, "the lady manages, keeps the throne. And with the King dead, now, for seven years."

"Charles, I don't say she isn't formidable—Middle Kingdom's formidable—I'm just saying she's looking for someone to hold the throne for her daughter, when she's gone. . . . Looking for someone, Sam, who *isn't* one of their river lords, *isn't* a general in either army. Queen Joan has a bookish daughter, and no sons. She needs a son-in-law who won't cut her throat—or force her to cut his."

"What a prospect. 'Bookish daughter' and a cut throat." Sam closed his eyes against the lamplight. "I doubt very much that the Queen is serious about my marrying her daughter. She's presenting the *possibility*, so I'll send troops to the Kingdom, help them against the Khan."

"More likely," Charles said.

Eric smiled. "Still, a possibility may become . . . probable."

"Worse," Sam said, eyes still closed. "Necessary. Now, I'm tired, and I would appreciate being left alone."

"Alright." Eric stood. "Alright . . . but this girl the Boston people have sent—"

"It'll wait. Now, if you two will put out that lamp and leave, you will make me very happy."

"In the morning"—Charles leaned to blow out the hanging lantern—"back to Better-Weather?"

Sam spoke into darkness. "Yes, we'll go, if the wounded can bear traveling. There's nothing useful at this camp but the dirt my dead are buried in."

. . . He lay, feeling too weary to sleep. Heard Charles and Eric murmuring, walking away. Lauder already, apparently, with a good notion what had been intended down here, what had gone wrong with Ned Flores and his people.

Eric was a razor with a slippery handle—bad temper and arrogance his weaknesses as chief of intelligence. . . . Charles, as administrator, hampered in a different way. His fault lay in fondness for Small-Sam Monroe, young enough to have been his son. And that, of course, the more serious weakness, leading to errors in judgment too subtle to be seen until suddenly damaging.

Fierceness and fondness . . . vulnerabilities balanced fairly enough between the two men most important to North Map-Mexico. Most important beside the young Captain-General, of course.

And now, it seemed the Khan was sending regiments south. A quick decision, probably, taken the last few days. It was interesting to study the Kipchak's Map-Nevada campaigns—see the pattern of them, far-ranging, swift, gather-and-strike, gather-and-strike. A herding pattern, a hunting pattern also, formed by generations lived in great empty spaces. A people, and an army, in motion. All cavalry.

They wouldn't care for close, tangled places. Wouldn't care for high, broken country, either.

Now, it seemed the Khan had decided, in the guise of two regiments, to greet and become acquainted with North Map-Mexico's Captain-General—as a wrestler might gently grip an opponent's arm, begin to try his strength and balance. . . . Toghrul perhaps grown weary of being locked into the western prairie, his way east blocked by Middle Kingdom and its great river. A river, according to the little librarian, Peter, much greater—with even short summers' meltings of a continent of ice and snow—than it had been as the Warm-time Mississippi.

The Khan might have difficulty campaigning against that kingdom while leaving his underbelly exposed the whole winding length of the Bravo border. So, he was sending—gently at first—to see how the metal of North Map-Mexico rang when struck. A touch, and a warning.

And why was that news so welcome? So good to hear? Why seemed so rich with opportunity?

The answer came like certain music as Sam began to drift to sleep . . . came as dreamed trumpet calls, sounding, *Duty, duty, duty.* What trumpet call did not?

. . . Had he taken his damn boots off? Couldn't remember.

7

Martha had washed herself, and her hair—drawn it up into a loose knot and pinned it, then combed and finger-curled a long ringlet in front of each ear. Charlotte Garfield had told her that her long hair, dark as planting ground, was her best feature. "*Only* feature," Charlotte's sister had said, and had neighed in fun at Martha's size.

Though clean, her hair done, Martha was scrubbing home-spun small-clothes—just discovered dirty beneath her father's bed—in the tub on the dog-trot, when she glimpsed metal shining through the trees. She took her hands off the rippled board, shook hot water and lye suds from her fingers, and watched that shining become soldiers marching up along the River Road.

There was a short double-file of men, East-bank soldiers armored throat to belly with green-enameled strips of steel across their chests . . . lighter steel strips down their thighs, sewn to the front of thick leather trousers. An officer was marching in front, and so must be a lieutenant. Lieutenants marched with their men, and never rode.

Martha watched them through the trees—her wet, reddened hands chilled by the early-winter air. Many soldiers traveled the River Road, now, because of fighting in Map-Missouri. . . . Though that was the West-bank army, fighting over there. She'd heard that army wore blue steel.

As Martha watched, the lieutenant and his men reached the cabin path—then turned neatly and marched up it. They were coming to her father's house, something soldiers had never done before. These were crossbowmen—heavy windlass bows and quarrel bundles strapped to their packs, short-swords and daggers at their belts. Long, green-dyed woolen cloaks, rolled tight, were carried over their left shoulders.

"Daddy!" She thought surely William Bovey had died after all, and they were coming to take her to hang.

Her father came to the door, said, "What is it?" Then saw what it was.

More than three Warm-time weeks before, Big William Bovey and two other large men had come out to the cabin, angry over a deal for a four-horse wagon team, and begun to beat Edward Jackson with sticks and their fists. It had seemed to Martha they were killing her father.

She'd run into the farry shed, taken up a medium hammer, and come out and brained William Bovey. Then she'd beaten his friends so bones were broken, and they'd run.

Bovey, a corner of his brain tucked back in, had been asleep ever since at his aunt's house up in Stoneville. It was the opinion of Randall-doctor that he would never wake up.

"No death done," the magistrate had said, "and some excuse for the fighting on both sides, since Edward Jackson is a horse-dealer and cheat. Yet his daughter, only seventeen, had reason to fear for his life." The magistrate, who chewed birch gum, had spit a wad of it into a brown clay jar on his table. "All parties are now ordered to both peace and quiet under the Queen's Law. Nothing will save any who break either."

And that had been that. Until now.

"Run!" her father said—too late, as the old man was usually too late.

Martha stood waiting, drying her hands on her apron, and wished for her mother.

. . . The lieutenant was young, but not handsome, a freckled carrot-top in green-steel strap armor. His face was shaved clean, like all soldiers'. He swung up the path to the door-yard, and his men marched behind him—twelve of them and all in step, their steel and leather creaking, till he put up his left hand to halt them.

"Well—" Though slender, the lieutenant had a deep voice. "Well, Honey-sweet, you're certainly big enough." His breath steamed slightly in the morning air. "You *are* Ordinary Mattie Jackson?"

"What do you want here?" Martha wished her father would say something.

The lieutenant smiled, and looked handsomer when he did. He had one dot tattooed on his left cheek, two on his right. "It's not what *I* want . . . not what the *captain* wants . . . not what the *major* wants . . . not even what the *colonel* wants."

A big man behind the lieutenant—a sergeant, he seemed to be—was smiling in a friendly way. The sergeant was bigger than Martha, as a man should be.

"No," the lieutenant said, "it appears to be a matter of what *Island* wants. And Island's wishes are our commands."

"You leave us alone."

The lieutenant shook his head, still smiling.

Martha's father said nothing. Edward Jackson was worse than having no father at all.

"Get what things you can carry," the lieutenant said, not in an unpleasant way. "You're coming with us."

"Is William Bovey dead?"

"I don't know any William Bovey, though I wish him well. I do know that you are ordered to come with us. So, get your whatevers; put your shoes on—if you have shoes—and do it fairly quickly."

"No," Martha said, and couldn't imagine why she'd said it. The big sergeant, standing behind his lieutenant, frowned at her and shook his head.

"Ralph, be still," the lieutenant said, though he couldn't have seen what his sergeant was doing. "Now, Mattie—it is Mattie?"

"Martha."

"*Martha.* Right. Now listen, even though it may cost my

men some injuries"—his soldiers smiled—"I will have you subdued, bound, and carried with us as baggage, if necessary. Don't
make it necessary."

"But . . . *why?*"

"Orders."

Her father still said nothing, just stood in the doorway silent
as a stick. Suddenly, Martha felt she *wished* to go with the
soldiers. It was a strange feeling, as if she'd eaten something
spoiled.

She turned to Edward Jackson and said, "You're not my father, anymore." Then she went into the cabin to get her best
linen dress, her sheepskin cloak, her private possibles (a bone
comb, clean underdrawers and stockings folded in a leather
sack), and her shoes—one patched at the toe, but good worked
leather that laced up over her ankles.

. . . They walked south—the soldiers marched, she walked—
through the rest of the day. Martha had started out beside the
lieutenant, possibles sack on her hip, her cloak, like theirs, rolled
and tied over her shoulder—but he'd gestured her behind him
with his thumb, so she'd stepped back to walk beside the sergeant, Ralph, the one who'd frowned and shook his head at her.
He was even taller than she was, and wider.

It had always seemed to Martha, when she'd seen them in
parade at Stoneville, that soldiers marched slowly. But now, going with them, she found they moved along in a surprising way.
It was a steady never-stopping going, nothing like a stroll or
amble, that ate up time and Warm-time miles until her legs
ached and she began to stumble.

Ralph-sergeant took her left arm, then, to steady her. He
smelled of sweat, and of leather and oiled steel.

They camped at dark, but lit no fire, though frost had filtered
down. The soldiers drank from tarred-wood canteens—the sergeant let her drink from his—and chewed dry strips of meat.

He gave her some of that as well. . . . Then the soldiers went into the woods to shit, came out, and lay down in dead grass in their long woolen cloaks as if they were under a roof and behind house walls—the lieutenant, too. Only one man was left standing under the trees, watching, with a quarrel in his crossbow as if this was enemy country.

The sergeant had stood guard, yards away and his back turned, while Martha did her necessary behind a tree. Then he'd cut evergreen branches for her to lie on. . . . She supposed her ringlets had straightened some from walking and sweating, so she had no good feature, now.

And that was the first day, traveling.

The second day, they rose before dawn, ate dried meat and drank water. Then the soldiers brought river water up in a little iron pot, made a small fire to heat it, and shaved their faces with their knives, the lieutenant first. After that, they went marching again. No one spoke to Martha—or spoke among themselves, either—except the lieutenant once said, "Pick up the pace," and they did, marching faster down the middle of the River Road, crunching through shallow, ice-skimmed puddles with everyone they met standing aside to let them pass. They went faster, but Martha kept up, her cloak flapping at her calves. It had became a pleasure to her to march with soldiers, to leave where she'd always been to go to someplace new, someplace that would be a surprise, with a surprising reason for coming to it.

Even so, sometimes a dread came rising that she might be being taken where an example would be made of girls who hammered men. But Martha swallowed those fears like little frozen lumps, managed to keep them down, and decided not to ask again where she was bound, or why, for fear of the answer.

Instead, she gave herself up to marching, and often could see the river on their right, flashing gray-white through stands of trees along the bank. Its icy current—still fed by Daughter

Summer's melt, far upstream at the Wall—was too wide to see across, and milky with stone dust washed from the great glacier in Map-Ohio.

Several times, she saw barges and oared boats far out from the shore, still summer-fit this far down the river, sailing with black-and-orange flags and banners fluttering in the river's wind.

Martha's legs were aching in the worst way by the time they came to Landing in the afternoon. Landing was the farthest from her home—the farthest south—she'd ever been. The Yazoo River came to Kingdom River there—though her father had said it was the other way round, and Kingdom had grown over to Yazoo as blessing and welcome. Her father had brought horses down for the fair, that time, and she'd come with him, riding Shirley. Some rough river-boys had made fun of her.

But now, though hard Ordinaries—wagoneers, sailors, warehousemen, and keel-boaters—stood drinking outside whorehouses and dens with their girls or pretty-boys all down the muddy road to Rivers-come-together, none had a word to call to hurt her feelings. They were quiet as the soldiers marched by—still in step through mud, horse-shit, and wagon ruts . . . then past a summer storage yard of huge racks of ships' skates and runners, long beams whose heavy bright blades gleamed greased and sharpened for winter-fitting.

They marched past loads of stacked lumber, sheep hides, sides of beef, pig, and goat . . . sacks of coal from Map–West Virgina, crates of warm-frame cabbages, onions, cucumbers, broccoli, cauliflower . . . barrels of pickles, brine kraut, smoked and salted river char.

The docks were even busier, noisier. Martha hadn't remembered everything being so large, loud, and confusing. The soldiers marched past starters shouting and flicking their slim blacksnakes at sweat-slaves trotting pokes of last potatoes up the ramps of two big pole-boats painted dark blue. Martha could spell out the letters on the company flags. *Jessup's Line.* . . . A herd of spotted cattle was being run down to a black barge, forty or fifty of the animals, driven by rust-colored dogs and three men with long sticks to prod them.

Martha had had a dog named Parker, when she was a little girl, a coon-hound with a blind left eye. Because of the eye, she'd been able to buy him with fifteen buckets of blueberries—no softs and no stems. Only two days' picking . . .

Those herding the spotted cattle, though, were different dogs, squat, barky, and quick. Interesting to watch work. Martha thought it had been worth such hard marching to come to Landing, with so much to see. And smell, too; the docks had the rich stink of the Rivers-come-together running beneath them, dirty float-ice, rotting mud, and fish guts. . . . Someone was playing a pluck-piano; she could hear the quick, twanging notes up the road behind them as a den door opened.

"Some moments for beer, sir?" The first thing Ralph-sergeant had said since morning.

"No," the lieutenant said, and led them to a dock at the far left, calling, "Clear the way!" to a work gang of skinny tribes-women, naked, with fox-mask tattoos covering their faces. They were smeared with pig-fat against the cold wind the river brought down. . . . The women stood aside as the soldiers marched out onto the planking, the wide boards booming beneath their boots. One—thin, and with teeth missing—stuck her tongue out at them. Two of the others called out to the soldiers together, in an up-river language that sounded like sticks rattling. It wasn't Book, wasn't even near book-English. Martha couldn't understand a single word.

A ruined barge was sunk along the left dockside, so only its rails and pole-walk showed above swirling water. Gray sea-birds—come all the way up from the Gulf Entire, Martha supposed—strutted and pecked along the railings. The birds had pale yellow eyes, crueler than crows'.

There was a wonder floating at the end of the dock—a galley beautiful as the circus boat that once came down from Cairo. But this one was painted all red as fresh blood, not striped green and yellow, and there was no music coming from it. A long red banner hung from the mast, stirring a little in the breeze.

The galley had one bank of oars, just above where the iron skate-beam fittings ran—and a red sail, though that was bundled tight to a second mast slanting low over the deck, reaching almost from the front of the boat to the back. A lateeno, Martha's father would have called it.

The lieutenant marched his men and Martha right up a ramp and onto the red galley. Everything there was the same bright red, or brass this-and-thats so bright in the sunshine they hurt her eyes. A line of men sat low on rowing benches along each side. They were naked as the tribeswomen had been, but with steel collars on their necks, and none of them looked up.

"You're late!" A soldier, standing on a high place at the back of the boat, had called that. This soldier wore a short-sword on a wide gold-worked belt. A long green-wool cloak, fastened in gold at his throat, billowed slightly in the river wind. His chest was armored in green-enameled steel, but with pieces of gold hanging from short green ribbons there.

"*Late,*" he called again, as they came along the deck. He was much older than the lieutenant, and had an unpleasant face, made more unpleasant because his lower lip had been hurt, part of it cut away so his teeth showed there. He had five blue dots tattooed on each cheek.

. . . Martha had never seen a Ten-dot man before. Never seen more than a Six-dot, and that was the Baron Elliot, and she'd seen him only once at the Ice-boat races.

"I'm at fault, milord," the lieutenant said, "and have no excuses."

"No excuse, is not excuse enough," the Bad-lip Lord said.

"So, three months pig-herding on Fayette Banks, for you and your slow men."

"Yes, sir."

"And this"—Bad-lip pointed at Martha—"this Ordinary is the object of the exercise?"

"Yes, sir."

"You, Big-girl—sit up here out of the way, and rest. We have cranberry juice; would you like some of that?"

"Yes, thank you." Martha came and sat on a little step below where he was standing. She wrapped her cloak around her and thought, too late, she should have said "milord."

The Bad-lip Lord leaned down and gripped her shoulder. "Some muscle there. Did the soldiers treat you with respect and kindness?"

"Yes, they did . . . milord." Martha thought of saying "especially Ralph-sergeant," but didn't.

The Bad-lip Lord nodded, then called, "Captain! South, to Island—at the courier beat!"

"At your orders, milord." A black man in a long brown cloak was standing back by a sailor at the wheel. "*Loose! Loose and haul!*"

Then, barefoot sailors Martha hadn't noticed were running here and there untying ropes. The whole boat swung out into the river, dipping, rolling slightly. And so suddenly that she jumped a little, a deep drum went *boom boom.* Then *boom boom* again, and the rowers' long oars came out, flashed first dry then wet as they struck the water all together, and the boat started away like a frightened horse. They were surging, hissing over the water, gray birds flying with them, circling the long crimson banner that unfurled, coiled, and weaved in the wind. Martha could hear it snapping, rumbling.

A boy in white pants and white jacket came running to her, knelt down, and held out a blown-glass cup—glass so clear she

could see the juice in it perfectly, juice the same blood-red as
the boat.

Martha thought of asking the boy why she was going where
she was going, then decided not.

She had heard that Kingdom's rowers were whipped—and
this was certainly a Queen's boat—but no soldier whipped the
red boat's rowers. Still, they worked their oars like farming
horses in summer furrows. She could feel the boat's *heave* . . .
and *heave* at each stoke they pulled together. The red sail was
still furled . . . the wind blowing cold upriver, into their faces.

It seemed odd to be sailing in a summer-fitted boat through
still-wet early-winter water. Martha had imagined one day traveling on a winter-fit's slanting deck as the ship skated hissing
over the river's ice on angled long steel runners . . . lifting, tilting as the wind caught its sails, so it almost flew, banners and
wind-ribbons curling and snapping through the air.

But this was still a summer-fit, with rowers. She wondered
what work the rowers would be put to, with Lord Winter already striding down to bathe in the river, and freeze it.

The juice—cranberry juice—in the beautiful glass, was sweet
and bitter at once. Martha'd never tasted it before, and didn't
know if she was supposed to finish it all, or only sip, and leave
the rest. She looked up to see if the Bad-lip Lord was watching,
and he was.

"It's for you, Ordinary. Drink it."

So she did. The juice grew sweeter with each swallow, and
she hoped it was a River-omen of sweeter things to come.

The west bank was too far away to be seen. She'd never seen
it, though her father had when he'd worked fishing. But they
were staying close enough to the east side of the river that
sometimes she could see a piling-dock there, its house or ware-
house high above the water, back under the trees. Then, a log
house . . . and a while later, another.

Martha saw little eel-skiffs as they passed. The men crewing them stood, balancing, and bowed as the red boat, the long red banner, went sweeping by. She sat holding the pretty glass in her lap, concerned it might tip over and break if she set it down on the deck. The deck was as clean as a worn washboard.

The lieutenant and his men were standing in the front of the boat. She could see them, see Ralph-sergeant past the great mast, its long, furled red sail. He turned his head, talking with another soldier . . . saw her looking, and smiled at her. Martha supposed the wind had completed the ruin of her ringlets.

They passed more log houses . . . then a lord's strong-hold. It rose above the river's bank, three gray stone towers within gray stone walls, all higher than a man could throw a rock—almost high as a crossbow quarrel might reach. Two ladies were standing on a little carved-wood porch, halfway up the middle tower, their hands tucked into fur muffs. Their hair was combed up off their necks and coiled; Martha saw gold combs glinting. They were wearing woolen gowns, paneled—perhaps in linen. One's dress was dyed soft blue and gold, the other's darker. The ladies, standing so high, seemed perfect little dolls, dolls made for children like their own.

Both together, they dipped behind the little porch's carved railing, curtsying as the blood-red boat went by.

Martha imagined their brothers, their husbands, in the hold. Tall, handsome men with clean hands and several-dot tattoos— and their father, scarred, bearded, brave as a bear. All the men very big, but kind, so that nothing more than a mouse in their wardrobe had ever frightened the doll-ladies, or ever could.

Martha waved up to them, but the blood-red boat had passed down the river, and the ladies didn't seem to see.

A while later, after a ferry had sailed past them, borne upstream on the wind—its passengers had stood, crowded, to bow to the Queen's boat—Martha grew restless, and shifted where she sat.

"Need relief?" The Bad-lip Lord hadn't moved from where he stood in all the traveling.

He'd looked down to ask the question, and when Martha didn't answer, made an impatient face. "Do you need to piss, girl?" His breath smoked slightly in the cold.

"... Yes, lord."

The Bad-lip Lord muttered, "*Rafting Jesus ...*" and lifted the forefinger of his right hand. The boy in the white jacket, who had been squatting by the rail, stood and came running.

"Bring this girl and a piss-pot together in the captain's cabin." The Bad-lip Lord looked back at the Brown-cloak Captain. "With your permission, of course."

"Does me honor," the Captain said, and he and the Bad-lip Lord both smiled.

... Relieved—a word that seemed so much nicer than 'pissed-out'—Martha had come to sit on her step again, her sheepskin cloak tucked tight around her against the wind. She watched the river run down with them, sometimes seeming to flow faster than the rowers could labor, though the drum kept beating like a heart, so steady that she forgot it from time to time.

Now, the river—great gray pieces of raft ice drifting by— was crowded with more and more ships and fisher-boats, rowed barges, and poled barges along the shore, so there were masts and long oars and banners and house flags of all colors wherever she looked.

Sometimes, as the wind blew this way or that, Martha could hear men singing on other ships as they passed—Gulf sailors and river-boatmen singing as they rowed or worked their lines. These men didn't interrupt their labor to bow to the Queen's boat, but only paused a moment to cup their right hands to their ears, to show they listened for any command.

The river had become alive with people and boats. Along the shore were more holds, more stone walls and towers, and wide two-storied timber docks on square stone pilings set marching out into the current. Slaves—still naked though Daughter Summer had died—were working on them, stowing and transferring the goods come in, the cargoes going out. Her father had called slaves 'the Ordinaries' bane' and said they took fish and honey from free men's mouths. . . . A band was playing on some pleasure boat, horns and flutes.

There seemed more to see than Jordan-Jesus could have noticed, though he was a river god, with all drops of water for his eyes.

The sun's egg had sunk west to almost touch the water when the Brown-cloak Captain said, "Passing Vicksburg bluff." Martha looked over and could just see a line of green and perhaps a fortress, east, high along the bank.

Soon after, the Captain said, "Island." And Martha saw, downstream, and far, *far* out into the current, what seemed a great walled town rising from the river, its stone gray and gold in early evening light.

Amazed, she clapped her hands—thought it might be magic—and looked up to see if the Bad-lip Lord was also astonished. She pointed it out to him.

He looked there, nodded, and said, "Island."

It was a place Martha'd heard of all her life, but had never thought to see. She swayed where she sat, then swayed again as the rowers' slow steady beat shifted, and the blood-red boat swung farther from the shore. They were going out and out where the great town grew from white water.

After a while, she saw fewer boats, fewer sailing ships. . . . And later, almost none, but huge tarred barrels floating, with signal masts on them flying flags of different colors. Martha noticed that what ships there were, steered by those flags and no other way.

Now, she could see the town was made of walls and towers, all built on hills of heaped boulders, each larger than a house.

Everything was heaved up and up out of the river, so the cold current foamed white and struck in waves against the stone.

"Two hundred years of granite rock brought down from the Wall's lap by ice-boat and wet-boat, with a good man lost to the savages for every Warm-time ton." The Bad-lip Lord was looking at the distant walls and towers. "And those tons dropped into the river there to make the kings' island."

"What a wonderful thing!"

"Do you think so, Ordinary? Clever, certainly. . . ."

A horn sounded, deep and distant as a pasture bull's crying out. Martha looked that way and saw, over the ship's red rail, another ship just as blood-scarlet but much larger, with two rows of oars on a side. It was coming toward them so fast that it carved white water with its black iron ram. Ranks of oars flashed, rose, beat, and fell, seeming only to touch the river's skin as it came, banners streaming from its masts, gulls wavering in the river wind above it.

The deep horn sounded again, calling to them.

It was the most wonderful thing. Martha stood and stepped to the low rail—though no one had said she could—to see it better. She could hear drumbeats, now, even the soft spanking as its oars struck the river. It was coming terribly fast, and it was very big. There were men . . . men in ranks standing along the two decks, one above the other. These were soldiers, and each man's armor was enameled in halves, helmet to hip, left side blue, right side green.

"Soldiers," she said.

"Marines," said the Brown-cloak Captain—and shouted, *"Still . . . oars . . . to heave to!"*

There were machine things on the great ship coming to them—things like giant hunting bows, but lying on their sides and fastened to timbers—and fire was burning in bronze braziers alongside them.

Martha clapped her hands and jumped a little up and down.

It was worth everything to have come to see such a ship. Beside it, all the other river boats were nothing.

Another horn sounded behind her. She turned and saw, much farther away, two more of the great ships, both blood-red and flying blood-red banners.

"Three of them!"

"Three of the Fleet's two hundred and more," the Bad-lip Lord said. "Now, sit down, girl, before you fall overboard."

Martha sat on her step again, but still could see as the great ship came to them, drums rolling and thundering so the gulls' cries sounded like music above it.

It came almost to smash into them, so Martha held up her arm to ward it—then swung suddenly sideways in spray and clashing currents. Spaced along its hull, the iron fittings for its winter runners were massive as great tree-stumps . . . and as it turned, rows of white oars rose dripping, folding up together so it loomed over, high as a riverside cliff, blood-red and ranked with two-color soldiers. The ship was named in dark metal at its bow. QS *Painful.*

At once a long, narrow wooden bridge fell from beside a mast, came swinging humming down through the air and crashed across the rail paces from Martha and the Bad-lip Lord.

Soldiers—marines—came running the steep planking with battle-axes in their hands, and two officers—their helmets striped blue, green, and gold—came running with them, short-swords drawn, and all jumping to the deck so it shook under Martha's feet.

One of the officers, the bigger one, stopped near her and called out, "*Who comes toward Island? And why?*"

His sword was shaped like a butcher's knife, but bigger.

"I come," the Bad-lip Lord said. "Sayre. And on the Queen's business."

"And come properly? With nothing and no one hidden on this ship?"

"Properly. Nothing hidden."

The officer unfastened a little latch at his throat, and took his helmet off. He had four blue dots on one cheek, three on the other, and a round pleasant face spoiled by eyes withno color. . . . It seemed to Martha the helmet must be uncomfortable. None of the soldiers who'd brought her to Landing had worn their helmets. They'd kept them strapped to their packs.

"Afternoon, milord." The officer bowed a little.

"Afternoon, Conway—how does your father do?"

"Dying."

"Sickness . . . a sad end for an admiral."

"Yes, sir. He would have chosen otherwise."

Martha saw the marines with axes going here and there about the boat. Some of them went downstairs, under the deck. The other officer was talking to three sailors; they stood barefoot before him, their heads down.

"We'll look through, and question—but quickly. Won't delay you, milord."

"Better not. I'm bringing Her Majesty a present . . . of a sort."

The officer looked down at Martha, and raised an eyebrow.

"Don't ask," said the Bad-lip Lord.

8

"This vessal to the Iron Gate," the big officer had said, speaking to the Brown-cloak Captain in a different voice than he'd used in conversation with the Bad-lip Lord. "—To the Iron Gate, directly and in order, otherwise at your peril."

"Understood," the Captain had said, "and will be conformed to."

And, after the officers marched the marines back up their ramp, the great two-decked ship had lunged away, its ranks of oars striking all together, its drums sounding slower beats, its trumpet a different call.

Soon, Martha saw much closer the cliffs of gray stone, the river's milky rapids foaming against them. Along those stone walls, another boat came in order behind them . . . then a second one, and a third, so there were four in line. Martha stood to see them better, and was told to sit down.

Then there was slow steady rowing into the river's wind, Island's gray wall, on their right, seeming endless as they passed—and high, so the gulls looked like snowflakes along the spaced stone teeth at its top.

"Big," she said.

"Very big." The second thing the boat's captain had said to her. "More'n a Warm-time mile long; near a mile wide. An' got more people on it than live on Isle Baton Rouge—well, damn near." He turned, talked with the sailor at the wheel, then turned back. "Milord, looks like a stuff-boat ahead of us for the gate."

"Pass them out of line," the Bad-lip Lord said. "Queen's business."

The Captain cupped his hands to his mouth and called, "Row up! *Row up!*" Martha heard their drum go *rum-a-dum, rum-a-dum, rum-a-dum.* The boat surged, surged . . . then swung left and slowly overtook a big barge that smelled of sheep and sheep shit.

A fat man in boots and a hooded raw-wool smock stood by the barge's steering oar, two rivermen behind him gripping its long loom. The boat's great cockpit was crowded with sheep's backs, sheep's puzzled black faces.—As they drew alongside, the fat man made a nasty fuck-finger at them and yelled, *"Get back, you bottom-holes!"*

"That's Peter Jaffrey," the Captain said. "I know him. Probably drunk."

The Bad-lip Lord frowned. "Drunk or not, he should know a Queen's red ship when he sees one." He went to stand at the rail, and gave the barge captain a hard look across the distance of river. Martha saw the fat man's mouth, which had been open, suddenly shut, and he made a bow, then cupped his right ear for any command.

"Not a bad guy," the Captain said, using a Warm-time word. "Lost his little boy to throat-pox years ago. Only son."

When the Bad-lip Lord smiled, it made his lip look worse. "All right, Crawford. But you might suggest the wisdom of courtesy to him when you meet again."

"I will, milord."

They swept on past the barge, then steered in again, closer to the wall. Martha, looking ahead through the boat's rigging, saw Ralph-sergeant near the bow, talking, laughing with another soldier—and beyond them, a great tower of gray stone standing out into the river.

The boat swung out to pass the tower's base where the river's flow curled against it like goat's cream. Chunk ice bobbed there, striking the granite.

Beyond, there was a great stone gateway, wide as a meadow and arched over high in the air with what seemed a spiderweb of iron . . . the span of a bridge where Martha saw tiny soldiers looking over. Harsh wind blew through the gateway, and a river current seethed into it. They turned with that tide—the red boat leaning, pitching—and ran on into the harbor, oars lifting, then falling to splash in foam . . . which became quieter water.

They were in a made pond-lake, oars now barely stroking, with walls rising high around them like the eastern mountains Martha had heard of, where Boston's creatures hunted. She saw a row of long gray wharves with boats and great ships tied to them, and sweat-slaves working, loading and unloading. . . . Even in this deep harbor, the current swirled, complaining. There were slow whirlpools, and the river's icy wind gusted here and there, trapped by stone.

A file of marines stood in order on a far dock as the red boat rowed slowly in. The Captain said something to his wheelman, and Martha felt the boat slowly turning toward those men. She had gotten used to that lifting, sliding motion, and thought she might become a barge-woman, being so at ease riding a wet-water ship.

They drifted in, the oars folding up and back like a bird's wings . . . and the red boat struck fat canvas cushions at the stone dockside with a squeak and three thumps. The sailors heaved out heavy lines; three wharfers caught them and cleated them in.

"Up." The Bad-lip Lord gestured Martha after him, as the gangplank was sliding out and down.

She had no time to smile good-bye to Ralph-sergeant— needed to nearly run down to the dock, her possibles-sack flapping at her hip, to keep up with the Bad-lip Lord. The file of marines, who had struck their two-color breastplates with armored fists to greet him, now followed, marching very fast. The harbor and docks were quickly left behind. Their bootsteps echoed off stone walls, stone steps, echoed down passages under overhangs masoned from great blocks of granite. Down those passages . . . then others, and turnings left and right and left again. In shadowed places, Martha sometimes saw, through narrow slits, a flash of steel in lantern light.

Other marines—more than a hundred in blue and green— came marching toward them down a way just wide enough, and passed so close as their officer called out, "Milord," and touched his breastplate, that Martha heard their armor's little clicks and slidings, smelled sweat and oil and sour birch-gum chew. Then they were gone, leaving only the fading sounds of their boots striking stone all together.

The Bad-lip Lord led on, striding so Martha had to trot to keep up, the file of marines trotting to keep up with her. They came to broad stone stairs, and went right up them past many people coming down, who smiled and nodded to the Bad-lip Lord. One of the men said, "Later," to him as they went by. All these men and women were rich beyond doubt—wore linen, velvet, and thick fur robes that blew against their fine boots in the wind. The men belted heavy short-swords; the women wore long, sheathed daggers in wide, jeweled sashes, and every one looked a lord or lady, except for several Ordinary women in brown wool, following their mistresses as tote-maids.

Martha stopped to do a stoop-curtsy to a group of no-question Extraordinaries, so as not to get into trouble, but the Bad-lip Lord took her arm and pulled her on up the steps. "Move!" he said.

Two of those women smiled at him and called, "Sayre . . . !" But he didn't answer. When one lady's fur robe blew a little open, Martha saw she wore a wide skirt embroidered with yellow thread and paneled in blue, perhaps silk from the south. . . .

They hurried on through four high-ceilinged rooms, one after the other. There were people in all of them, the same kind of people as on the stairs outside, any one of them looking richer than a mayor. . . . Then the Bad-lip Lord led down steep steps and into a long tunnel of curved stone courses—the first tunnel

Martha had ever been in, though she'd heard of them. The marines' boots, as they followed, sounded like the red ship's rowing-drum. The wind blew bitter after them along the stone, whining like a puppy.

They came out of that darkness into daylight, then through a wide iron-barred gate into a great sunny garden in a gray stone square. But the garden, the whole space of plantings, was an inside-outside! The ceiling, wider than any other ceiling Martha had seen, was made of pieces of clear glass set in frames of metal. It was all held up by iron posts three times the height of a man, and as many as trees in a crab-apple orchard. There seemed to be at least a Warm-time acre under it, with rows of broccoli and cabbage, and what looked like onions planted at the distant edge. "*Vegetables . . .*"

The Bad-lip Lord made a face, said, "Flooding Jesus . . ." and walked even faster, but she kept up.

They walked through that wonderful garden along a graveled path—the file of marines still coming behind them—went out another door, then turned and turned down a twisted staircase to a stone walkway, and into another glass-roofed garden. They were going so fast now, they were almost running. It seemed to Martha there was no end to Island, no end to gray stone and the cold smell of stone. No end to icy river wind, to soldiers—marines—and Extraordinaries in jewels and fine furs. No end to women who smiled at the Bad-lip Lord as if he was alone, with no up-river girl, big as a plow horse, trotting behind him in a wrinkled homespun dress, a greasy sheepskin, and muddy shoes.

Martha had begun excited by so much size and strangeness, so many new people—likely more than in Cairo, and she hadn't yet seen them all. She'd been excited, but now began to feel a little sick to her stomach with too much newness and hurrying. She missed her mother as if she was still a little girl, and her mother was alive and feeding the chicken-birds in the yard.

The Bad-lip Lord stopped at last, at the top of broad stairs where two guards—who must be soldiers, Martha supposed, and not marines, since one wore East-bank's all-green armor, the other West-bank's blue—stood to each side of iron double doors painted red as blood. Behind her, the marines stopped all together with a stamp *stamp.*

"Her Majesty in audience?"

"Yes, milord," the guard in green steel. "At the Little Chamber."

"Shit. . . ." The Bad-lip Lord spun on his heel and went back down the steps two at a time, with Martha and the marines hurrying after. He opened a door made of squares of glass, and hurried down a black-stone walk through a roofed garden of flowers. The garden light wavered like water across rows of marigold blossoms, roses, and another sort of flower with a cup of red and yellow on a slender stalk.

The Bad-lip Lord led them running up a narrow staircase to other iron doors painted blood-red and guarded by two soldiers as the first had been, one in blue armor, the other in green.

"Still in audience?"

"Yes, milord," the blue-steel soldier said. He reached to turn down a heavy latch, which looked to Martha to be made of gold, and swung the left-side door open to perfumed air, bright oil-lamps shining . . . and many people.

The Bad-lip Lord went in—then stepped out again, took Martha's arm, and pulled her inside with him.

It was a narrow room, its walls painted scarlet, with many old flags, banners, and lit chain-lamps hanging down from a ceiling shining with gold. At least it looked to Martha like gold—though there seemed too much of it for even a Queen's Island. The gold, or whatever bright metal it was, was hammered into shapes, possibly stories. Things flew among golden clouds up there—things like birds, but with stiff straight wings—and there were buildings appearing taller than buildings were made, taller even than fortress towers. . . .

A woman was laughing, down at the end of the room.

Behind all these people, who looked warmed by red paint and lamplight, Martha stood with the Bad-Lip Lord beside her. He was tall as she was, no more or less. A steel edge of his breast-plate's hinged shoulder-guard touched her arm. . . . There were so many men and women crowding, they made the narrow room seem smaller. The most surprising thing was there was no stink of old sweat or foot-wraps—none at all—as if everyone had come fresh from a summer washtub bath, their clothes just off a summer line.

A few of these people were talking with each other, but softly. Martha saw not one man who wasn't dressed richly, not a single lady who wouldn't have put any rich wife of Cairo to shame for her finery. Several had blue panels sewn into their long skirts. A few had green.

The woman at the end of the room laughed again—she was a loud laugher. Being taller than most, Martha could see it was a lady dressed in red velvet, sitting one step up on a big black-enameled chair, her head back, laughing careless as a man. She was holding a short spear in her left hand; its narrow steel head shone in lamplight. . . . Martha thought this must be the Queen, to be so loud amid grand people.

The woman stopped laughing, and said, "Fuck them and forget them is the rule for you, Gregory. You're not deep enough for love!" She had a strong alto voice, like a temple singer's; it rang down the room.

The person she was talking to was tall, mustached, and seemed to Martha beautiful as a story prince. His long, soft copper hair lay loose, and he was dressed all in velvets, coat and tight trousers made in autumn greens and golds. "—And that very shallowness, ma'am, I've confessed to Lady Constance, and asked her pardon. It's her brothers who concern me. They, apparently, *believe* in true love and marriage. In fact, they're insisting on it. Marriage, or my head."

People standing near Martha laughed—but not the Bad-lip Lord beside her.

"Well, you naughty *man*." The Queen was smiling. "You can tell the fierce Lords Cullin that I would be displeased to be deprived of your company."

"Thank you, Kindness," the tall lord said, and bowed graceful as a harvest dancer.

"Um-hmm. Now, go and get into more mischief." The Queen shooed him away, then looked down the length of the room and called out loud as a band horn, "You! Tall one! You must be the strong-girl. Ordinary . . . *Martha,* isn't it?"

Martha looked around as if another Martha must be there.

"Answer her!" a woman said.

Martha nodded and said, "Yes," but too softly to be heard.

"You come closer. Come closer to me!" Queen Joan's voice seemed younger than she was.

The Bad-lip Lord took Martha's possibles-sack and rolled cloak from her. A hand—she didn't know whose—shoved at her back, and she stumbled, then walked down the room as people stepped aside. She felt everyone looking; their looks seemed to touch her. A woman said something softly, and laughed. They'd be looking at her shoes, the poor leather, and the mud. Looking at her hair . . . her ugly, *ugly* dress. A big stupid up-river girl, in an ugly dress.

She stopped almost at the step and made a bow, then began to get down on her hands and knees, in case bowing wasn't enough.

"Stay standing, girl. We're not Grass Barbarians here; a bow or curtsy will always do." The Queen, though sitting, looked to be tall as a man if she stood, and had a man's hard blue eyes set in a long heavy-jawed face. Six dots were tattooed on her

left cheek, six on her right. There was a scar on her pale forehead, one on her chin, and another at the left corner of her
mouth.

Martha bowed again, very deeply, then straightened up. She
saw the Queen was smiling, and supposed she'd bowed wrong
after all. . . . Queen Joan's hair, its dark red threaded and
streaked with iron gray, had been braided, then the long braids
coiled like slender snakes crowning her head. There were many,
many jewels—little red stones, blue and green stones, and
strange bright stones clear as water—pinned to her braids here
and there, and fastened to her deep-red robe in intricate patterns, so she seemed to shine and glitter in the lamp-light as
she sat.

"No, no," the Queen said, still smiling, "you bowed very
well. . . . And the shining stones you see, ice-looking, are diamonds. They are old as the world, and change never."

Martha understood the Queen had read her mind by reading
her face, and supposed that was a skill all kings and queens must
have.

"Now." Queen Joan leaned down from her throne, and held
out her right hand. "Now, since you are so large, and supposed
to be strong and a bone-breaker, come take my hand in yours,
Martha-girl . . . and try your best to break *my* bones."

But Martha just stood and shook her head *no*. Her heart was
beating hard as the boat's drum had sounded. "No—I'd hurt
you."

But the Queen didn't seem to understand 'No.' She didn't
appear to have even heard it. She held out her hand.

Martha reached up and took it—hoping that gripping firmly
might be enough. The Queen's hand was white and long-
fingered, warm as if fresh from hot-water washing.

They held hands like friends, for a moment. Then, slowly . . .
slowly the Queen's grip tightened. The long fingers seemed to
slide around Martha's hand as if they were growing, and the

Queen's grip, terribly strong, tightened and tightened as though Martha's hand wasn't there at all.

It was uncomfortable. It hurt . . . then hurt worse—and Martha, frightened, began to squeeze back. Her hand was losing feeling; it seemed separate from her, and she had the dreadful imagining that the Queen was going to crush it, break its bones. Martha tried to keep that from happening—gripped against that happening with all her strength.

Suddenly, there was no pain, no terrible pressure—only the Queen's long white hand lying relaxed in hers.

"Strong enough, Large-Martha." The Queen took her hand away, and sat back on her enameled throne. "And no tears. You do please me."

Some people in the room said, softly and together, "And should be *always* pleased. . . ."

"You're seventeen years old?"

"Yes . . . Queen," Martha said, though 'Queen' didn't seem enough to call her.

"I'm told—by those I almost trust—that you beat three strong men down with a smith's hammer. Is that so?"

". . . I did. I did, Queen—but none of them died. I'm sure none of them has died!"

"Don't be frightened. I don't care if *all* of them have died."

People laughed at that.

"But you *did* it, Martha? And you did it alone?"

"Yes. They were hurting Pa."

"Mmm . . . And did you enjoy what you did with the hammer?"

Martha looked around her for a friend—but she had no friends here, as she'd had none at home. Her hands were shaking, and she put them behind her so the Queen wouldn't see.

"—I don't ask questions twice."

"I didn't want to . . . but I was angry."

"Alright. Good. And I understand your mother died of insect fever years ago?"

"Yes . . . Majestic Person."

Queen Joan laughed. It seemed to Martha she had good teeth for a woman her age, teeth strong as her grip. "Please, *please* don't ever repeat that 'Majestic Person.' I'm manured with enough titles."

A man in the room laughed.

"Michael, don't you dare!"

The man laughed again, and said, "The court won't use it, ma'am. We promise."

There was a murmur of promises.

"So, Large-Martha," the Queen said, then said nothing more for a while, but only sat looking into Martha's eyes as if there was a secret there she must find out. . . . Then, she nodded. "So, you have no mother. And, I'm told, not much of a daddy. But what if I promise to be *nearly* a mother to you, if you will come and live with me? If you will serve me, stay by me always, and guard me with your life until the evening I lie, a very old lady, dying in my bed?"

It was such a strange thing to hear, that Martha waited for someone to explain it to her. It seemed the Queen could not have meant 'guard,' since there were soldiers standing against the room's walls, and a soldier in blue-enameled armor standing on one side of the throne, a green-armored soldier on the other.

"Yes, I have guards, Large-Martha, but they are *men*. And there are occasions when even a queen must be with women only. I'm tired of having to guard myself at such times . . . lying in my bath, sitting on my toilet-pot with an assag across my lap." She tapped her short-spear's butt against the stone floor, and raised her head and her voice. "—And if it were not in the River Book that soldiers *must* be men, I'd have women soldiers, as The Monroe has in North Map-Mexico. . . . Proper in that, at least, though our currents might, were matters different, have flowed to drown that boy—as they *will* the fucking Kipchak Khan! I knew Small-Sam when he was a baby, carried him tucked in his blanket . . . wiped his ass."

Silence in the Red Room.

The Queen looked down at Martha. "Now, girl, you give me an answer—and make that answer *yes*."

Martha said, "Yes, ma'am."

The Queen smiled and sat back on her throne. "Oh, there's a sweetheart. My Newton would have said you'd make a Trapper-girl. A great compliment. . . . *Lord Sayre!*"

"Ma'am?"

"See that the Master teaches my constant companion, Martha, neater fighting than with a smith's hammer."

"You have in mind . . . the sword, ma'am?"

Martha knew the man's voice without turning to see him. It was the Bad-lip Lord.

"Mmm . . . no. I have in mind . . . a light, long-handled double-headed ax. Blade and spike-point, I think."

"Yes, ma'am."

"But not *too* light—something suitable to her size and strength. Rollins is to forge the ax-head from a cake of the Emperor's gift, hammer that steel to tears, as if for me."

"Yes, ma'am."

"No plate armor. Only best fine-mesh mail to rise from thigh to shoulder, then fasten turtle at her gown's neck—oh, I'll see you have such pretty dresses, child! . . . And a long knife, same steel and straight-bladed for strike or throw. A *knife*, no lady's frail whittler."

"I'll see to it."

The Queen raised her head and called out, *"Now, she is mine . . . and no longer an Ordinary!"* Then she spun the javelin she gripped in her left hand, and held the shaft down to Martha.

"Take this, Strong-girl—then come up and stand behind my throne, to give your life for mine."

Martha reached up to take the spear, and felt as she'd felt the motion of the river, when the red boat had heaved and pitched with its rowers' labor. Now, everything seemed to shift beneath her in just that way—and she would have been sure she was dreaming but for the rich colors of everything, the strange voices . . . and the Queen's eyes.

"—I said, 'Come up.' "

Martha climbed the step, her knees shaking, and the soldier in green armor turned aside to let her pass. She stood behind the throne, her breath coming so short she was afraid she might faint, and had to lean on the spear's smooth shaft. . . . Over the Queen's jeweled braids, Martha looked out on people in velvet, fine leathers, feathers and fur, wearing daggers, short-swords, and gold. Most of the men's and women's faces were tattooed in dots across their cheeks—some faces soft, some fierce, but none with pleasant eyes.

"Are you where you should be?" The Queen did not turn her head to look. She was wearing the perfume of a flower Martha didn't know.

". . . Yes," Martha said. "I am."

9

"I keep my pay!"

Eric Lauder had lathered a fine paint pony, and called as he rode down to the column in early evening, five Warm-time miles from Better-Weather.

Charmian Loomis rode just behind him—bone thin, taller than Lauder, and awkward in her saddle. Her long black hair, always loose as a child's, never tied or ribboned, bannered behind her. She rode in the army's brown wool and tanned leather, and wore Light Infantry's chain-mail hauberk with a colonel's gold C pinned at her right shoulder. A rapier hung to the left of her saddle-bow.

Howell Voss, then Carlo Petersen and his captain, Franklin, reined aside for them.

". . . I keep my pay, Sam." Eric was short of breath as if he'd been doing the galloping. "Two regiments. They crossed the Bravo together, day before yesterday, assembled in the brakes east of Ojinaga. Their outriders caught and killed two of my men, but not the third."

A cloud shadow, as if in memorial for the two, drifted over on chill wind. The sun, throughout the day, had been hiding in shame at the Daughter's death.

Charmian Loomis climbed off her horse, said nothing.

"Have those border people obeyed my orders, Eric?"

"Yes, sir, they have. I've pigeoned with Serrano—"

"Paul Serrano?"

"Yes, and Macklin. Our people are already out of Presidio, and we're clearing every village and hacienda from Ahumada past the Bend to Boquillas."

The pinto stretched his neck to nip Sam's big black, and Sam turned his horse—the imperial charger now named Difficult—

a little away to avoid a reprisal. "And John Macklin understands my orders about fighting?"

"He does. Cut throats, but no set battles."

"And the Old Men?"

"Sam . . . the brothers are not pleased."

Howell Voss slapped a fly on his horse's neck. "For Weather's sake . . ."

"Howell, let it go. The brigadiers are owed a part in this. Eric, where's Charles?"

"In town. None of my business, but people in Sonora aren't paying their taxes."

"They will." Sam swung off his horse, relieved to be out of the saddle. More than a year ago—almost two years ago—an imperial Light Cavalryman had sabered him across the small of the back in a stupid scrambling fight below Hidalgo del Parral. His mail had turned the cut, but still some soreness there came and went. "Now . . . all of you get down. We're going to talk a little campaigning."

The others dismounted, then stood or squatted, holding their horses' reins.

"Howell, Carlo, call your officers up here. All of them. Is there any dirt to draw on?"

Voss drew his saber, sliced frost-burned turf, then bent and tore it away to clear a patch of ground. Major Petersen, bulky as a bear and awkward out of the saddle, went to speak to his banner-bearer, and the man rode away down the column.

Sam sat on his heels, waiting for the others to come up the road. "Eric, we have the wounded with us. They stay in Better-Weather; Portia-doctor and her people stay there with them."

"How's Ned?"

"No rot in the stump. He'll do well enough . . . already up and walking a little. The wounded stay, and Jaime and Elvin stay as well."

"The Old Men won't like that."

"Eric, I know they won't like it. . . . I want *all* Butler's Heavy Infantry concentrated here, every unit, all reserves. Then, if they have to—if this Kipchak raid proves not to be harassment, but more serious—Phil can move either east or west to the mountains to hold any major force moving down. The old men can command that move, assemble any militia forces to join."

"Understood." Lauder was writing with a charcoal point on a fold of poor brown paper.

Sam waited as officers rode in from the column, waited until they'd gotten off their horses and gathered close. He stood so they could see him better.

"Orders. . . . Our cavalry's going north. All our cavalry—and reserves—will move up into Map-Texas *east* of the Bend, while the Khan's people move down across our border to the *west* of it. We strike up—as they strike down."

Someone said, "Lady Weather, be kind."

More officers rode up. The last, the rear guard's lieutenant, swung off his horse and knelt behind Captain Wykeman, reins draped over his shoulder.

"Going up into Texas," Captain Franklin said to them. "All the cavalry."

An officer said, "Jumping Jesus!"—a Warm-time phrase that would have gotten his great-grandfather burned by his neighbors.

"Now. . . ." Drawing his belt knife, Sam went to a knee and sketched with the blade's point the great southern angle of the Bravo's Bend. "The Bend."

Eric and the officers nodded.

"The Kipchaks, about two thousand of them, have come down a long ride, many from Map–Fort Stockton, and seem to intend raiding into Chihuahua, west of the Bend."

Someone was arguing with a woman down the road.

"Nailed Jesus," Major Petersen said, "it's that fucking Boston girl."

Sam stuck his knife in the dirt, stood, and turned in time to see the girl—very small on one of the captured imperial chargers—reach out and hit his trumpeter, Kenneth, with her sheathed saber. Kenneth took the blow on a raised arm as his horse shied away. The girl was yelling, "I go where I wish to go!" and seemed prepared to hit him again.

Sam walked through the officers and down the road, the troopers in his way reining their horses aside. The girl saw him coming, her small face white under the wide-brimmed blue hat.

"Get down," Sam said.

"What?"

"Get down, or I'll pull you down."

"Not so . . ." Patience slid a little steel out of her sword's scabbard.

"If you draw, I'll take you off that horse and whip you here in the road, before everyone." He slid his quirt's loop off his wrist. . . . It was one of those odd moments, coming more and more frequently for him, when anger and laughter seemed to coil around each other to become one thing. Sam was careful not to smile.

A pale mask stared down, wrinkled in fury, the girl's small teeth showing like an angry grain-store cat's.

"—And you'd deserve it, Ambassadress, for such improper and unladylike behavior."

Slowly, slowly the small face relaxed to its usual smooth perfection. "And beating a True Emissary of Boston Town is a gentlemanly thing to do?"

"Only to recall her to her duty."

Patience sighed, swung a leg over the saddle, and slid down to the ground. "That man tried to stop me going where I wished to go. I wanted to come listen to your conference."

"No." Sam turned and walked back up the column. Grinning troopers watched him pass.

The girl called after him. *"Unkind . . . !"*

"What did you say to her?" Howell was smiling.

"I said, 'No.' " Sam knelt, picked up his knife. "Now, these troops the Khan is sending south . . ." He drew their route with the point of the blade. "Sending about two thousand men west of the Bend to test us, so we'll *let* them test our militia bands, our deserted border villages, our empty pastures and fields. And while they're doing it, we're going to take all four thousand of our cavalry—plus militia horsemen and volunteers—*east* of the Bend"—he drew the curving line of march—"and north into Texas, to take and burn Map–Fort Stockton."

Silence. Then someone whistled two notes.

"That's at least three days, Sam, riding up into Texas." Carlo Petersen, an older man and sturdy as a tree trunk, had Ned Flores' command.

"That's right, Carlo."

"Leaving just local militia to hold them in the west?"

"Leaving local militia to *trouble* them in the west, with our Light Infantry reserved in the hills. . . . Charmian, your people are not to engage unless absolutely necessary. The whole point is to keep them busy, give them work and wear, but *not* a battle. Should be good practice for our people, thanks to Toghrul Khan."

"Hard practice," Captain Wykeman said.

"—Jaime and Elvin will stay here with the Heavy Infantry, so the brothers will be in charge strategically. But Phil Butler will be in tactical command."

"Uh-oh." The previous whistler, a lieutenant named Carol Dunfey.

"—I'll inform Jaime and Elvin that the infantry only moves on Phil's orders."

"Sam," Petersen said, "are you saying the Old Men are out?"

"No. They're *up*. In overall command—but not battlefield."

Nods. Those close enough, were looking at the outline of the Bend cut into the ground.

"Howell," Sam said, "will command the cavalry campaigning into Texas—as their general."

The officers stared at Voss.

"And not you, Sam?" Petersen, bulky, rosy and round-faced, looked like a startled baby. An aggressive baby, saber-scarred.

"No.—Howell."

Voss stood at ease. Not surprised. Sam saw he'd expected the command might come to him.

"Well, in that case," Eric said, "I should go north with him."

"No, Eric. You'll be more useful here."

"Sam, I'll need to be up there."

"You need to do as you're told."

There was a moment of silence . . . silence enough that the wind could be heard, and the nickering of restless horses down the column.

" . . . As you order, sir. I stay in Better-Weather."

"Phil and the Brothers will have to know what's happening in Texas, Eric. Your people will pigeon down to you, and you will keep the Old Men and Colonel Butler informed. It shouldn't be necessary for you personally to go out in the kitchen to taste the soup."

"You're right, sir. I apologize."

Charmian Loomis leaned over to look at the drawing again, nodded, then straightened and walked to her horse . . . mounted, and rode away.

"It's clever, Sam." Howell stood staring down at the dirt drawing as if it might change. "But the Kipchak's clever, too, and we'll be raiding deep into his country. If he realizes, and sends more people across and south of us . . ."

"Then, Howell, you'll learn to like mare's milk."

Smiles at that. They seemed willing enough, even after

This'll Do. Sam supposed there might come a time, after other losses, when they would no longer be willing.

Eric stood. "Good plan." His pinto backed a little, tugged at its rein.

Sam got to his feet with a small grunt of effort. "Good as long as it's only ours. I want you to ensure that, Eric. If there are any people you're uncertain of—bought agents, particularly east of the Bend—I don't want them sending pigeons to Caravanserai as Howell rides past."

"We know of five. I've left them *because* we know them."

"Don't leave them any longer."

"Yes, sir."

The others were up, gathering their horses' reins.

"And all you officers," Sam said, "keep in mind that your lives and your troopers' lives depend on these plans being held in silence." He bent, scored his diagram to nonsense with his dagger's point.

Murmurs of agreement.

"In *silence*, gentlemen and ladies. I'll hang the officer who makes this known by word or note or indication. Drunk or sober."

A perfect silence then, as if they were practicing.

What did it mean? Sam climbed into the saddle for the last stretch to Better-Weather. *What did it mean that a man was most at ease, felt truly comfortable, only when planning battles?* He spurred his horse—well-named Difficult—out in front of the column. Kenneth came trotting after him, the trumpeter seeming untroubled by having been struck by an angry ambassadress. *And what did it mean that others were also more at ease, were also only truly comfortable with a man when he was planning battles? The younger officers' faces had only been pleased at the notion of war. Was the Captain-General becoming* only *a Captain-General, with nothing else left of him at all?*

"More than likely," Sam said.

The trumpeter said, "Sir?"

An early-winter rain had followed the column for the last few Warm-time miles. Now, it caught them, dark, cold, and driving, seething in swift puddles under the black's hooves. What plans he'd made in dirt with his dagger, then erased, were gone now under mud and water.

* * *

Better-Weather's fortress, built of granite blocks four years before, squatted gray in dawn's cloudy light amid the town's scattered wood and adobe houses, liveries, small manufactories, and inns. Three-storied, deep-moated by Liana Creek, and shaped a square, it enclosed a large, grassed siege-yard for sheep, a roofed swinery for boar, and runs for chicken-birds.

Charles Ketch's office was off the courtyard, at the northwest corner of the third floor. Its four tall windows were barred with thick, greased steel, and armored men and women of Butler's Heavy Infantry mounted hall guard in six-hour shifts. These sentries, recruited deaf and dumb, had calmed their watch-mastiffs—and grinning, apparently pleased with news of *Boca Chica*, saluted Sam past.

". . . Sam, Sonora doesn't *pay*. Tax payments denied by three separate pigeon-notes. Two, day before yesterday. One, yesterday afternoon."

"Late, you mean, Charles." Sitting on a three-legged stool with his scabbarded bastard-sword across his lap, Sam straightened to ease his back, and wished he'd had a hot bath in the laundry before coming upstairs and down the hall to duty. Wished he'd had a second cup of chocolate at breakfast.

"No, sir. *Withheld.* Stewart claims they need their money for their roads, this year—says an elected governor should have that decision." Charles—looking, it seemed to Sam, older each time he saw him—sat with his desktop and the floor around him piled with papers, paper scraps, twine-knotted bundles of papers, and wooden boxes of the tiny rolled notes of pigeon-carries. His copy of *The Book of Jew Jesus*—a very old and precious copy concerning the first Jesus known—rested like a thick battlement of sewn binding and time-browned paper in front of him.

Eric Lauder had once said to Sam, "Charles thinks the truth hides in that Warm-time Bible like a bird in a bush. He puts his ear to it for little chirps and twitters of sweetness . . . kindness."

"Charles, you're sure he's serious about withholding the province's taxes? He's picked a very bad time for it."

"Yes, I know."

Ketch's office, gloomy in a cold and clouding morning, was packed to its rafters with narrow crates of bound volumes containing the records of what each year had brought to the provinces of North Map-Mexico. Reports of gold or silver earned or spent, of diseases—animal and human—of good crops or bad, of crimes and hangings. Bitter complaints and boasts of success. Everything carefully entered on paper from Crucero Mill.

All news came to Better-Weather, and came fairly swiftly—by messenger, by pigeon—or several were made sorry for slowness. Rumors came as well, and were always stacked in seven boxes at the end of the highest shelf—hard to get to, and so the more carefully considered before setting in place.

"Our memories are all in my paper-work," Charles Ketch had once said to Sam. And each short summer, when Lady Weather's daughter had wed the sun, he cleaned out his office, transferred all the crates to storage down the hall, and ordered new boxes built for the memories of the new year.

"Oh," Sam had said to him, "I still keep a few memories in my head."

Charles had smiled and reached out, as he often did, to grip Sam's arm, as if to be certain he was still present, young, and strong.

"Very worst time for refusal." Sam leaned forward to pour a clay cup of water from the fat little pitcher on Ketch's desk. "What makes Stewart think he can get away with it?"

"A habit of making important decisions. It's the risk with governors: the tendency to independence. They are elected."

"Elected with my permission, Charles."

"Easy for them to forget that, after two or three years in office." Charles took a pinch of snuff, but didn't sneeze.

No one smoked the Empire's tobacco in Ketch's office—there were never flames there that might cause fire, not even lamps at dark, so all reading and copy-work was done by daylight.

No flame, so no heat through the nine months of hard winter. There were leaded panes of clear glass in the windows, so the wind, at least, could not come in.

"And this is your worst news for me, Charles?"

"Yes—except for the Kipchaks coming down, of course."

"You're mistaken." Sam stretched his legs out. His right spur scraped the stone flooring. "This tax thing is much more serious than two thousand horse archers."

Charles smiled. Approval . . . fondness. "Yes. That's right, of course. Stewart's is just the first of an endless succession of conflicts between Better-Weather and the governors elected locally. Each province will challenge you, sooner or later. Roads, mutton prices, wool prices, cabbage prices. You'll need certain taxes, and they'll wish to make them uncertain, to use the money locally, if only to insure their reelections. Stewart, and Sonora, are only the beginning."

"And you've done . . . what?"

"Nothing, Sam. It's too important for a decision of mine."

"Then you advise . . . what?"

Charles sighed, seemed embattled behind his stacks of paper, his massive copy of *The Book*. "Sam, you can have any recalcitrant governer removed from office, or killed. But that would mean *always* having them removed or killed at any serious disagreement. Taxes being the most serious—"

"Aside from recruitment."

"All right, aside from recruitment."

"Which would be the next refusal, Charles."

"Yes, which might very well be the next refusal."

"And your advice?"

"What I think we need to do, is limit their time in office. Make it law that a person can be elected only once as governer in each province. Then there'd be no building of little lordships to break us apart—or at least it would become less likely." Charles's voice from gathering shade, as rain came down outside.

"Yes. My fault for not thinking of this before."

"*Our* fault."

Sam considered Patricio Stewart. Big, bulky man with direct blue eyes and a bad temper. Broken nose, possibly *because* of his bad temper. For some reason, wore his long black hair in pigtails, held with silver clips.

"Alright." The stool had been doing Sam's back no good. He stood up, leaned on his scabbarded sword. An aching back at twenty-seven; he'd be a bent old man, no doubt about it. "Alright. We'll issue that order of a single term only, for governer of any province."

"Still five years?"

"Yes. Still a five-year term, once elected against all comers. But one term only."

"And if the other governers object? Follow Stewart?"

"Charles, I won't kill them; they were elected by their people. And I won't kill Stewart, for the same reason." The rain swept like a slow broom down the windows, dimming the daylight so Ketch, behind his desk, seemed to fade with it. "Instead, when this happens, I'll kill the person most important in supporting their independence."

"... I see."

"Might be Eric talking?"

Charles shrugged. "Eric has his uses."

"Who is Stewart's most important friend in this tax thing? Who stands behind him in Sonora?"

"... His wife's father, I believe. A formidable man, Johnson Neal. I know him, raises spotted cattle."

"Have Neal arrested, Charles. See that he's tried for treason in the tax matter. For plotting to destroy our unity ... possibly in the Khan's pay, or the Emperor's. Then hang him."

In deepening shadows, Charles had become a ghost. "And if the magistrate makes some difficulty, Sam?"

"Choose a magistrate who won't. This is to be done at once. And the same magistrate is to issue a judgment referring to payment of provincial taxes as duty inescapable."

"That's ... that should be effective."

"*Also*, find a discontented priest of Mountain Jesus, a man who may have had problems with Stewart's people over shares of altar gifts, distributions ... whatever. Bound to be one. Advise the man to preach, publicly and often, proper obedience to Better-Weather. Three gold spikes will be sent, later, to be driven into any temple tree he wishes."

The ghost sat silent.

"—And all a legal and administrative matter, Charles, and your responsibility. Neither Eric nor the army are to have anything to do with it. ... Understood?"

"Meaning, I suppose, that I tend to avoid unpleasant necessities?"

"Meaning that, Charles—*and* that it should be seen as a matter of law, not of my will and my soldiers."

"I'll see to it."

"Quickly, in the next few days, so send fast pigeons. We're

going to need that money. . . . Oh, and once the taxes are received—and all in coin, not kind—spare what we can for road-
work in Sonora. Build a bridge, and name it after Stewart. A
modest bridge."

"Yes. . . ." The spectral Charles Ketch seemed to smile. "Really very sensible, I suppose."

"But sad for Johnson Neal's daughter?"

"Yes."

"Only if she's stupid, Charles." Sam slung his sword on his
back. "If she's clever, she'll know her father hanged in her husband's place."

"Then, let's hope she's clever. . . . And the matter of remounts for this . . . excursion up into Texas?"

Sam paused at the office door. "Every damn horse in Nuevo
Leon, if necessary. Have your people pay their price and bring
them in. If it has four legs and can carry a man, Howell is to
have it."

"May have to pay with script."

"Get them in, Charles."

"Yes, sir."

"I want the first draft corralled in Ocampo in four days. The
second, three days later in La Babia."

"Sam—I'll need more time, just a few days more."

"Charles, I don't have the time to give you. First and Second
Regiments of Heavies and Second Regiment of Lights, reinforced, will be there; Howell is picking them up as he goes."

"The reserves?"

"Every trooper."

"Nailed *Jesus*. How are we going to pay them? We have no
plans for calling up the reserves, Sam, except for war. For war,
they'd wait for their money. This will be thousands of gold
pesos every day!"

"This, Charles, is war's beginning."

"Dear Weather . . ."

"And what money we don't have later, I'll borrow from the Emperor."

"Oh, of course! Would you tell me why Rosario e Vega would agree to pay our army?"

"Oh, I think he'd prefer to, Charles, rather than see it coming down through *Zacatecas* to pay him a visit."

Ketch laughed, laughter from darkness, over the sound of rain. "Might work, at that. . . . Alright. The remounts will be there, Sam. At Ocampo and La Babia. But it will cost us a fortune, and make enemies in Nuevo Leon."

"Any rancher who objects to parting with his horses, Charles, is welcome to go with them up to Map—Fort Stockton."

"Understood."

* * *

. . . In the corridor, two big soldiers with curved body-shields at rest, short-swords drawn, stood spaced down the passage a few yards apart. In greased boots and horse-hide trousers, with straps of oiled steel body-armor from shoulder to hip, they stood still as if frozen, their faces obscure behind helmet nasals.

A watch-mastiff's rising—and Sam's shadow, thrown by sconced lamplight along the walls—alerted both deaf-mutes as he came, and their helmets turned toward him smoothly as Warm-time machinery must have done.

The first guard was a woman—taller than Sam was, and wider. She made a comic face, wiggled her eyebrows at him as he passed her great grumbling dog, so he went smiling past the second soldier to the stairs.

10

Martha was lost. Almost two weeks in the Queen's chambers had taught her nothing of Island's directions, passages, and endless ups and downs.

The Queen's chambers were the whole top of North Tower, three great whitewashed drum-round rooms, one above the other. The lowest was guarded on narrow left-winding stone steps by six soldiers, three in green-enameled steel, and three in blue. Very polite soldiers, who'd nodded and smiled at Martha every time she went up or down.

They'd smiled and nodded, but never spoke to her, and all six unsheathed their swords each time the iron doors opened at the top or bottom of the stairs. They drew their swords . . . watched her coming to them, up or down, then sheathed their swords, smiled and nodded.

In those few days, Martha'd learned that tower. Queen's chambers above, guardroom below, kitchen and pantry below that . . . then down more winding steps to the scrub-laundry, with its water barrels, kettles, stone tubs, and ever-hot iron stove. The laundress was Mary Po, a big silent scrubber with hands ruined by lye and hot water; there were no nails on her fingers. The girl Walda helped her, and ironed the Queen's robes and woven linen with flat polished stones hot from the Franklin, so the room smelled of cloth heated to nearly scorching.

There were all those levels of the Queen's tower, and places deeper still, down steeper steps through little iron doors. Darker places, where Martha was not permitted. The green-steel Guard captain, Noel Purse, had ordered her not, her first day.

"Guests, down there," he'd said. "Her Majesty's important guests, resting in chambers beneath. And that will never be your business."

"Yes, sir," Martha'd answered as if she were a soldier, since she felt like a soldier, though a girl, and was armed with her spear as a guard herself.

Down there, someone must have heard the captain talking to her, because the faintest howling began, so she supposed one of the guests had brought his dog-pet with him.—But later, when she mentioned the dog-pet to Maid Ulla, Ulla had made a child's warning face and told her it was people, and the Queen would visit them, but never let them out.

So, there was no dog-pet under the tower.

At first—perhaps because she was tired—Martha had thought she might be dreaming of the Queen's chambers, dreaming and drifting through them as she sometimes drifted in dreams. The huge round rooms, their stone walls lime-washed snowy white, were draped in great soft sheets of orange cloth and gray cloth, purple, rose, sky-blue and pinewood green, so there was color everywhere. Some cloths hung against the walls, and others fell across from round alder rafters to divide one place from another—so each great room was like a house with smaller rooms within it.

There were those richly colored cloth curtains, and woven tapestries of war, of hunting, of handsome Extraordinaries playing banjars, flutes, and drums among flowers in glass-ceilinged gardens. Then others of the same people kissing and fucking, and also summer wet-ships and winter ice-ships sailing the river through the three seasons. . . . The tower chambers always bright with many hanging lamps, and sometimes sunlight shining through stone-slit windows sealed with glass very close to clear.

There was also see-through southern gauze—which Martha'd heard of but never seen—that hung here and there like smoke, and stroked her as she walked through it behind Queen Joan. All almost a dream, and seeming more so since the women—Ulla, fat Orrie, and the great ladies who waited on the Queen—

stepping quietly on the carpets, appeared as if by magic when a curtain was suddenly pulled aside.

So the Queen's daughter, Princess Rachel, once appeared for breakfast with her mother—a princess seeming to Martha more serious than the story ones. Tall, dark-eyed, dark-haired, face too strong-boned for beauty, she'd stalked through drapery unsmiling. But introduced, had taken both Martha's hands with gentle courtesy, and said, "Welcome to our household."

Though later, buttering muffins with her mother at table by the solar's iron stove, she'd glanced at Martha—standing nearby with her spear—raised an eyebrow, and murmured, "Mother . . ."

"What? . . . *What?*"

The Princess had sighed, and said, "Never mind."

Ulla told Martha that Princess Rachel lived in a different tower, came to breakfast rarely, and the black stains on her fingers were writing-ink.

. . . As the Princess had come to breakfast, so other great ladies came to visit through the days. Some brought their children, others little dog-pets to play with—but none stayed long. The Queen preferred privacy. In these wonderful, cushioned, quiet rooms, only she was harsh and noisy, striding here and there, making rough jokes and criticizing her women's sewing as they sat at the long table in the gauze-curtain room, doing fine stitchery in linen kerchiefs, and on the Empire's white cotton underthings.

Martha had touched and dirtied a kerchief her second afternoon, and been sent down to the laundry for a bath. "With lye soap!" the Queen had called.— "I'll have no pig to guard me!" So, in a stone tub, with Mary Po pouring buckets of hot water, and the ironing girl, Walda, scrubbing with a bristle brush, Martha was made clean enough to touch Jordan Jesus' altar cloth. Then she was dressed in heavy sandals and fresh linen, in underclothes and overdress, with long sleeves like almost a lady—though one who would soon wear padded fine-mesh mail under her gown. That had been fitted-for, but not yet finished.

When done, her hair dried at the laundry hearth and pinned up, a finger ringlet before each ear, Martha took her spear, went up the many stone steps—smiled at the six soldiers as they smiled at her—and climbed past them to the Queen.

"Better," Queen Joan said, looking her up and down. "You'll never be a pretty girl, but 'handsome' may be possible in time, though a fairly large 'handsome.' The ringlets, the ringlets have their charm." And Martha, now so clean, was invited to sit beside the Queen at a mother-of-pearl table, to sort old earrings for keepers and pairs.

"Trumpery crap, most of these." The Queen's long fingers sorted and shifted, flicking silver and gold, bright stones and stones softly-rich this way and that. "Those I had from my sweet Newton, I know and keep—what are you doing?"

"Separating the plain hoops."

"Well . . . the silver; put those aside."

"Yes, ma'am."

The Queen began to hum as she worked, then said, "What do you think of these?"

"They're very pretty."

"Yes. I thought so too, many years ago. Now, of course, I know better—and so they are spoiled for me." She began to hum again, fingers deft among the jewels. "I do not remember the names of half the men who gave me these . . . made flowery fucking speeches, bowing, asking Newton's permission to gift me this or that. Once, my sweetheart smiled at Liam Murphy—Lord Murphy's gone, of course. Whole family's gone, and a daughter eaten. Newton smiled at him and said, 'You may give my lady what you please. As it pleases her, it pleases me . . . though doesn't turn me from my way.' "

The Queen set green studs aside. "Poor Liam should have

listened more closely. . . . Do you think of men, Martha?"

". . . No."

The Queen stopped sorting. "Martha, you're going to be with me for many years. You've just told me a lie. Never, ever, lie to me again about anything."

"I'm sorry. I do think of men, sometimes."

"And in particular? The truth, now."

"Well, I liked Ralph-sergeant."

The Queen found a little gold lump, with no pin or clasp. "Trash. . . . You liked Ralph-sergeant. And who is he?"

"A soldier. He came to get me at my father's house."

"And why did you like this soldier?"

"He was big—bigger than me. And he was kind."

"Ah . . . 'kind.' I have many large sergeants in my armies, East-bank and West, but I hope not too many that are kind. . . . Do you have a match for the turquoise?"

"No, ma'am."

"Of course not; that would be too fucking lucky. How am I to get a turquoise to match with that Kipchak squatting on Map-Arizona? This is a useless earring."

"You could give it to Lord Pretty."

"Yes, Gregory'd wear it. Damn fool. . . ."

Through the following days, Martha had learned the attendant ladies' names and titles, learned the servants' names: Ulla, Francis, Orrie, and Sojink—a tiny Missouri tribeswoman with filed teeth and a bluebird tattoo across her face. . . . Martha'd learned the cloth-draped spaces of Upper Solar and Lower, and where Queen Joan slept by a window in the high chamber, curtained in cloudy gray. She'd learned also to stay very near the Queen, just to her right and a little back, the spear always in her hand.

Still, Martha could go up and down the tower, and visit as she wished—but never for very long. That was decided when the Queen was choosing a robe for Wintering the Gardens, and didn't care for the velvet that fat Orrie showed her. She said, "Everything from that clothes-press smells of river mold! Orrie, take them all down to the laundry to be cleaned and pressed again. Martha, help her, and stay there to see it properly done."

"No, ma'am."

The Queen stood very still, then said, "What did you say?" Seeming startled, as if there'd been a birdsong she'd never heard before. Fat Orrie was panting like a puppy.

Martha said, "No, ma'am. I won't go down with the laundry, and stay there."

Then, though the Queen's face didn't change, she put her hand on her dagger's pommel. That knife was a soldier's weapon, long-bladed and heavy enough to weight her jeweled sash.

"I'm here to guard you, ma'am," Martha said, though she was frightened. "I can't guard you if I'm sitting waiting in the laundry."

The Queen turned her head as if she were listening to voices . . . then took her hand off her dagger. "Yes, that was a *proper* 'No, ma'am' from you. You'll help Orrie take the laundry down— then come right up again to be near me."

"Yes, ma'am."

"But, Martha," the Queen said, "don't become too free with *noes.*"

. . . And Martha had been careful not to. She'd shut her mouth and opened her eyes and ears through her first days, and learned the solar chambers, the tower and its people, very well, except for the deep places below. But now, with another place to be at mid-day by the glass exactly, she was lost and wandering Island like a pony loose.

After she'd asked directions of two people—people who seemed Ordinaries, and not too great to answer—then asked a third in a granite passage along her way, Martha climbed, at last and late, two flights of stairs in the South Tower . . . tapped on a narrow oak door, received no reply, then slowly opened it onto a wide sunny room. It was very bright with windows. The floor, polished white marble streaked with brown, was puddled here and there by something spilled. Smelled like a lamp's Boston oil.

A man was standing by a long oak rack of weapons. He was short and seemed massively fat, big around as a cabbage barrel. He wore low boots, loose tan trousers, and a yellow shirt, and though he appeared to be only in his middle years, his hair—cut evenly in a circle just above his ears—was dappled gray. A bowl-cut, they'd called that in Stoneville.

"You're the Queen's Martha, I suppose. I'm Master Butter-boy." He set a slender sword into the rack. "Don't come late to my class again." Master Butter-boy had a pleasant deep voice, sounded to Martha like a good glee singer. His eyes were dull green, and small.

She closed the door behind her, and set her spear leaning against the wall. The streaks and spills of oil made the marble floor slippery. "I couldn't find the way, Master."

"You *have* no master now, only the Queen for mistress. 'Sir' will do." Butter-boy strolled a few steps nearer, moving like a pole-boater, with an easy rolling gait. He stood looking at her—and Martha saw he wasn't fat, only very wide, and thick with muscle. Scars were carved into his round face, and three blue dots were tattooed on each cheek. Thinner white scars laced his heavy forearms. "—You are the Queen's, and no other's. You might keep that in mind when some try you for this or that favor, or attempt to command you."

"Yes, sir."

"And you say you couldn't find your way here?"

"Yes. I went to West Tower."

Master Butter-boy gave her a hard look. "Then *learn* your way. Learn Island well enough to run its passages blind. Because on some dark night of trouble, you may have to. We *are* at war, though many here don't yet seem to realize it."

"Yes, sir."

"Mmm . . . Well, you've got size, if it doesn't slow you. None easier to butcher than Large-an'-slows. And thank the River you don't carry big teats—very much in the way, fighting hand to hand. No big teats, and no balls to guard, either. . . . Your age?"

"Seventeen, sir."

"Better and better. Youth makes the third fighting gift. No comment? We stand silent?—though I hope, not stupid." Butter-boy smiled, drew a small knife from his belt, and threw it at her spinning.

Martha thought of ducking away, but there was no time. Thought of catching the knife by its handle, but that seemed unlikely. She swung her hand as the knife came whirling, and slapped it to the side to clatter across the floor. Her palm was cut a little.

"Did you think of catching it?"

"Yes, sir."

"Then why didn't you try?"

"I think I thought . . . better a cut, than chance the point coming in."

Master Butter-boy smiled. "You and I, Martha Queen's-Companion—may I call you Martha?"

"Yes, sir."

"Well, Martha, you and I are going to settle in very well when it comes to murder." He walked over to pick up his knife. "You do know that all killing is murder, though often for worthwhile reasons?"

". . . I suppose so."

"She 'supposes so.' " Butter-boy began to sheathe his knife, then spun and threw it at Martha again, but underhanded, with a swift shoveling motion.

Since it wasn't spinning this time, Martha thought she might catch the knife's handle as it came—stepped a little to the right, reached out, and just barely managed to. Then, for no particular reason, it seemed reasonable to immediately throw it back.

". . . I can't tell you, Martha," Master Butter-boy said, "how pleased I am with you already." They were at the weapons racks, putting yellow ointment on their cuts. "You are the season's surprise!"

"Thank you, sir."

"Now—not to waste instruction time . . ." Butter-boy put the ointment pot back on a shelf, considered a moment along the racks, then chose a plain, long-bladed, double-edged dagger. "Ah, is there any creation as honest as an honest weapon? No, there is not."

Master Butter-boy stepped out onto slippery marble. "Difficult to be sure of your footing on this. Deliberately difficult. Did you think I'd spilled oil come all the way from Map–New England—rendered out of whatever sea beasts—in carelessness?"

"I wasn't sure, sir."

"Well, I didn't. Learn to fight on treacherous footing, and firm footing comes as a gift." In illustration, Butter-boy began to stride, the long dagger's needle point balanced on his thumbnail. Suddenly he slipped, slid, and tripped stumbling across the floor. But the weapon went with him perfectly, didn't sway as he mis-stepped and staggered, didn't threaten to tumble and fall. It seemed to have grown, become rooted, where it stood on his thumb.

"The knife . . . the knife . . . the knife." Master Butter-boy jumped suddenly forward, then sideways, then high-stepped back and back on the oiled marble—very light on his feet, it seemed to Martha, for so wide a man. The dagger stayed with him as if they were partners in a dance.

"Listen," he said, always moving—turning in circles now. "Every steel weapon, sword to ax, flowers from the knife and

its discipline of timing, force, and distance to strike. The swinging ax, the parrying sword, are only children of the knife. Never
despise it—though there are fools who do, until its blade slides
between their ribs." He flipped the dagger off his thumbnail,
caught it casually by the grip, and stood easy.

"Some courtiers—you know that word? It's a Warm-time
word, and means those who linger in a king or queen's court.
Some of those will stare at your ax, which I understand is being
fettled for you, and consider it your first weapon in protection
of the Queen. They will think of the ax—perhaps one or two
plan for the ax—and forget the long knife entirely. See to it
you do not."

"Yes, sir."

"And always remember this: Your weapons, if across a room
and out of reach, are no weapons at all, but only a source of
amusement for those butchering you, then your Queen."

"I understand."

"Never, never, *never* go unarmed."

"I won't."

"*And* never unarmored. Always at least fine chain-mail over
a padded shift to protect your breast, your belly—and your
back, above all."

"Yes, sir. They're making it."

"Now, Martha, choose a knife from our weapons stand, and
come see if you can cut off some portion of me—keeping in
mind there are no dulled instruments here, bleeding being the
best teacher."

* * *

"The Queen is among her pickles." The East-bank soldier, steel
armor-straps enameled to gleaming jade, stepped aside to let
Master Butter pass into storage—household storage, not the

great, dark, echoing chambers beneath Island's inner keep, stacked with barrels of crab-apple, barley, pickle-beets and onions, salt beef, salt mutton, salt pork, and salt cabbage.

Here, in Household, were small rooms of special cooked and jarred far-south fruits, condiments, compotes, and particular meats—boiled and poured into clamp-lid crocks, then sealed with wax, so they almost always lasted more than a year. Though sometimes not, and burst with hard sounds and messes.

Butter walked down the narrow stone corridor, his shoulders wide enough to often brush the walls. He heard the Queen muttering, ahead and off to the left, in the pickling room. . . . One of her dear things, pickles. Apparently they hadn't had them in the savage mountain world she'd been born to, so she ordered foods pickled that most had never thought to. Broccoli, carrots, cauliflower.

The court had taken to these, so every gathering and ball saw bowls of pickles along the sideboards, with the smoked meat, honey candy, hard-cooked eggs and hot barley rolls. The salting prompting thirst, of course . . . Butter stepped to the left.

"So, Master Butter . . . ?" Queen Joan, in ropes of freshwater pearls over a gown of soft imperial cloth—dark blue, with dark-blue lambskin boots to match—was shaking a great blown-glass jar of the tiniest gherkins, finding treacherous sediment. "Look at this sad shit," she said—the Warm-time phrase so apt—and held the jar up to a deep arrow-slit through the tower's stone, so daylight might aid lamplight.

Master Butter straightened from a bow. "Susan-preserver is getting old."

"We're all getting old, Butter. But not all of us careless."

"She's *very* old."

"Then let her get her trembling ass off my island. Let her hobble back where she came from." The Queen shook the gherkin jar again. Peered into it. ". . . So? What of my Large-Martha; is there prowess there?"

"Your Large-Martha will do, Majesty—when she learns Island, and always to be a little early rather than late. Should do better than some who call themselves fighting men. She has size and strength, but more important, quickness. A big man, stronger and just as fast, could likely beat her down, but not easily. She doesn't mind bleeding."

"But can she learn to *fight*, Master Butter?—fight serious men and sudden, not just bumpkin Ordinaries brawling in her father's yard."

"I'm sure so."

"And you're 'sure so' . . . why?"

"Most men and women, Queen, if steel or any trouble comes suddenly, throw their heads back in startlement—and so, of course, lose a moment to defend themselves. This Martha does not. She lowers *her* head to look closer, to watch what comes and how it comes."

"Hmm . . . And once she's trained, could you kill her in a fight?"

"Oh, yes, Majesty, though not easily. But I can kill anyone."

"Well, Master Butter, I've known two men you couldn't have killed."

". . . Ah, the King, of course. Very strong. Was *very* strong."

"My Newton, yes. And another . . . I don't think you'd find me easy, either, though I'm not what I was."

"I would cut my throat before *that* contest, My Dearest Majesty."

The Queen set the gherkin jar down on its shelf with a *clack* that almost broke it. "Then you're an ass, and impertinent in your affection!"

"My apologies, Queen. But of course, I'm mad."

"Yes, so Paul-doctor says. He says you hear unpleasant voices, but so far manage to disagree with them. And you are useful as master of arms."

Master Butter bowed.

"Now, get out of my sight. Hone my guardian-girl to a fine edge, but do not come private into my presence again for a year."

"A year, Majesty," Master Butter said, "—a year is not so long a time." And bowed himself out of the Chamber of Pickles.

Webster was furious from long imprisonment. Patience had kept him basketed by day, allowed only the shortest night flights for exercise. He bit her thumb to the bone when she reached in with a piece of lunch's mess-kettle mutton, then huddled stoic as she shook his basket—cursing while little drops of her blood flew—then threw it onto the tent's canvas floor and kicked it under the cot.

Sleety early-evening rain came in a gust, as if Lady Weather were angry also.

"Very well," Webster said from under there, speaking in a thin, weedy little croak that someone unfamiliar might not have recognized as speech. "*Very . . . well.*"

It sounded like a threat, but was surrender.

Patience held her thumb down a moment to bleed it, then insisted that bleeding stop. Even so, it took a while. Webster's teeth, though few and small—a baby's milk teeth in fact—were capable, as he'd proved on a robin once.

When the thumb stopped dripping, Patience wasn't angry anymore, and went to hands and knees. Under the cot, through the basket's woven willow strips, pale blue eyes—the right, wandering—looked out at her. "*Very well.*" Almost a whisper.

"Are you hurt?" She meant his wings.

"No."

"Oh, thank Who Comes," Patience said, reached in, and rolled the basket out while the Mailman scrambled to stay upright. No bitten thumb was worth damaging its wings. More expensive than any two or three occas, this was an embryo halted and kept halted at four months in the womb, while what were becoming arms, wrists, and fingers were encouraged to shape wing-struts instead, and anchorages of muscle were enlarged in the breastbone. All mind-managed, observed through slender glass tubes stuck inside a tribeswoman's belly.

Delicate work, not to be compared to the easier earlier interventions that almost always produced an occa—delicate work, and often unsuccessful. No apartment on the Common cost as much as one of these wonders. And this—she'd named him Webster, since he spoke so well, had forty-three words—this was Township property, not hers.

She set his basket on the cot, and unlatched the lid; Webster tried that constantly, but the method was beyond him, his fingertips too tiny. She took the lid off, and reached in to stroke and lift him out. He was withered, very small—a double handful—and brown as an old leaf, his round bald head the heaviest thing about him. He smelled of milky shit, and had left little slender yellow turds in his folded bedding.

"You bad boy . . . making messes." And he was a boy, or would have been; there was the tiniest pinch of spoiled cock and balls nested at his bottom.

Webster was still angry, said none of his words while Patience unfolded one of his comfort cloths and wiped him. She reached up to set him against the tent-pole, where he clung with skin wings and little nearly-legs wrapped around the wood, while she took the messed cloths from his basket and folded two fresh ones in.

"Want cheese?" Patience smacked her lips to demonstrate how wonderful the cheese would be.

Webster stared down from the tent-pole—little left blue eye looking straight at her, the other drifting away.

"Cheese?" Patience dug for the crock in her duffel. Table scraps were often fed Mailmen—little meat pieces they could munch and gum to slurry—but farmer's white cheese was recommended, mashed with goat's milk if possible. Both things produced south of the ice, and very expensive.

"Oooh, look at this . . . look at *this!*" She held a caked forefinger up to him. "If you bite, I'll make you sorry."

'Make you sorry' was a phrase all Mailmen were taught in training—when occasionally they *were* made sorry for flapping off the glacier flyway from Cambridge to New Haven and back again. Webster apparently recalled it. He closed his eyes, opened his mouth . . . and Patience felt eager wetness and heat, the rhythmic tickle of his little tongue as he licked and sucked the clots from her finger.

Five loaded fingertips later, Webster burped and said, "Fly?"—his first courteous word since their fight.

"Yes." Patience lifted him down and set him on her shoulder, which he clutched with fanned translucent amber wings. "—To Map-McAllen."

Webster understood 'McAllen' at least, and nodded. He had— as all completed Mailmen had—a perfect map stuck in his understanding by weeks and weeks of careful feeding of treats for remembering, weeks and weeks of careful scorching with candle flames for forgetting, say, where Map-Charleston, or Map–St. Louis, or Map-Philadelphia, or Map-Amarillo were, and their direction either way and any way. Scorching, as well, for forgetting the how-to-get-theres of much smaller places. All to fashion a messenger so superior to silly pigeons, who could only return where they came from.

"Not sunshine." Webster was a coward, and frightened of hawks.

"No," Patience said. "Moonlight." And turned her head to him for a puppy kiss. He didn't kiss very well . . . really only licked little licks.

The near-frozen rain peppered the tent's canvas as Patience sat on her cot, and using her small silvered-glass mirror for backing, while Webster watched from her shoulder, wrote a tiny note in tiny printing on a tiny strip of best-milled white paper.

fm better-weather. dear cousin louis, voss and 4000 cav going probably north to be bad in probably texas. now send webster back. yrs, p.

She reread it as Webster crawled down to the blanket beside her and thrust out a fragile little leg. It barely had a knee, had toes too small to count.

It seems probable, Patience thought. She'd heard the word 'north' spoken by a trooper in horse-lines. And a farrier cursing over the lack of replacement shoes for Voss until Boquillas del Carmen. *So . . . probable.*

She gently wrapped the strip of paper around Webster's leg— there were tiny soft bones in it—then looked in the covers for the piece of string she'd had ready to fasten the message on. She found the string on her pillow . . . and found also that she'd changed her mind.

"Why," she said to the Mailman, "should we make my so-old Cousin Louis look wise in Map-McAllen? Why let him interfere with my camp's campaigning? Though it would serve a certain rude ruler right, who threatened to pull me off my horse and hit me with a whip. . . . Still, what could be more foolish than helping foolish Louis rise to Faculty, when he'll deny us credit?"

Webster watched her from the blanket.

" 'Oh,' he'll say, 'I knew it before, that cavalry coming up.' His so-old wife will agree. And you know, Webster, if Monroe's people lose severely in Texas, there will soon be no North Map-Mexico. And with no North Map-Mexico, no need for an ambassadress *to* it."

Patience unwrapped the note from the Mailman's leg, tucked the paper into her mouth, chewed thoroughly, and swallowed. "Instead, let's adopt the Warm-time attitude of wait-and-see."

" 'Wait and see,' " Webster said, his voice thin as the piece of string, though he had no idea what those words meant. He had suckled his white cheese too greedily, and proved it by burping a mouthful up.

* * *

Howell Voss, having restrung the banjar with true cat-gut—
two silver *pesos* a coil, shipped from Imperial Trading & Market
in Cabo—leaned back on his cot and played a tuning chord,
Warm-time G. Or so it was assumed. He'd long had the sus-
picion that ancient tuning was slightly different from the
present's—different enough so the music said to have been
theirs, notated as theirs in surviving copy-works, now probably
sounded somewhat off.

He twisted his pegs, plucked . . . twisted his pegs again, and
was in modern tune at least.

He'd just taken a singing-breath, when someone scratched at
his tent-flap.

"I heard you tuning," Ned Flores said, stooping to come in
out of gathering darkness. He wore an ice-spangled army blanket as poncho, and was pale as a weary girl. "—Thought I'd
better interrupt before the camp suffered."

"You might remember that wasn't your sword hand you
lost."

"No." Flores dropped the blanket, gently kicked open a folding camp chair, and sat. "But you wouldn't duel an officer for
an act of mercy."

Voss sighed and set the banjar down. "Truly refined taste is
so rare. . . . And how *is* that wound? Should you be up and
walking?"

"Well, after five days in a mercy wagon with a fresh-sewn
stump, I'm glad to be up. As for this," holding out a thickly
bandaged left wrist, "—not, by the way, as comic as your fresh-
trimmed ear—I'm told I can have something made, and strapped
on."

"What something?"

"Your Portia says, a hook."

"The doctor's not 'my Portia.' But I think a hook would do."
The sleet was rattling, coming down harder.

"I've been considering tempered steel, Howell, forged from
knife stock a flat inch and a quarter wide by a quarter inch
thick—in-curving to a wicked fish-hook point. And, *and* its
outer edge filed and sharpened."

"The whole outside curve of the hook?"

"Hollow ground to a razor edge. Hook in, slash out."

"Mountain Jesus. You'll have to be careful with that thing,
Ned."

"Others . . . will have to be careful of it. I don't suppose you
intend to share any tobacco. You're getting damned rude,
Howell—or should I say 'General'?"

"A curtsy will do." Howell dug in a trouser pocket, tossed a
half-plug over. "Don't take it all. That's Finest."

Ned bit off a chew. "Oh, of course it is; it only *smells* like
dog shit. Who sells you this stuff?" He tossed the remainder
back.

"Maurice."

"Maurice, the Thief of Reynosa?"

"He was acquitted. And that was about mules; the store was
not involved."

Ned tucked the chew into his cheek. "Remind me, How-
ell . . ." he leaned far back in the camp chair, paged the tent-flap
aside with his bandaged stump, and spit over his shoulder out
into the rain. "Remind me to play pickup sticks with you again.
For money."

"Yes, I will—and what the fuck happened at This'll Do?"

"What's the Warm-time for it? Got . . . 'too big for my
britches.' "

"Elvin always gets that wrong." Howell bent to pick up the
banjar.

"Please don't. I'm an invalid."

"Healing music." Howell commenced soft strumming. "So, what happened at This'll Do?"

Ned shifted his chew. "Absolute dog shit. . . . Well, nothing as wonderful as the *Boca Chica* thing, from what I hear. Our Sam standing aside to watch you make an ass of yourself—which, by some miracle, you did not."

"Which—by some miracle, Ned—I did not." Howell struck a chord, then lightly muffled it with his fingers. Struck . . . muffled. Struck . . . muffled.

"At This'll Do, I thought . . . Howell, I thought there was a very good chance to beat those people."

"You did?"

"And I would have, if they'd had the usual old fart commanding them."

"But they didn't; I know. He gave us a hard time. Rodriguez, one of the new ones."

"So"—Ned leaned back to spit again—"a lot of our people killed. All my fault."

"Ned . . ." Howell plucked out a soft *fandang* rhythm. "What in the world were you doing down there at all? And with only half a regiment of Lights? Why would Sam send you? We could have waited for those people to come up, get into real trouble."

"Oh, both of us thought it seemed a good idea."

"At the time."

"Yes. Seemed a good idea at the time."

"Mmm . . ."

"Change of subject from my command blunders, Howell. . . . I'm interested in going up into Texas with you. Map–Fort Stockton."

"No."

"No?"

"If you were four weeks better healed, Ned, you wouldn't have to ask. I'd have asked for you."

"I can sit a horse."

"Not for a three-day ride north, and then a fight. You're not going."

"I'm not going. . . ."

"No, you're not."

"And if Sam says I am?"

"You're not going."

"Well . . . play me a tune on that fucking thing, if you're going to sit there with it."

Howell bent his head to the instrument, watched his large hands as if they were another's, and picked out a swift, soft, twanging melody.

"That's not . . . not terribly offensive." Ned, grown paler, leaned back to spit the chewing tobacco out.

" 'Camp Ground Racers,' supposedly," Howell said. "But I doubt it."

Ned sat back with his eyes closed, listening.

"Ned?"

"I'm not dead. Though I'm sure I look it."

Howell stopped playing, set his instrument aside. "Come use my cot. Lie down for a while."

"Tell you something funny, Howell . . ."

"Come on, lie down."

"Tell you something funny." Eyes still closed. "I have—had—always assumed I'd be next in line. Take command under Sam. Take command if anything happened to him. Always assumed it would be me."

"Ned—"

"And of course, that very assumption demonstrated I would never be any such thing. But I didn't *see* it."

"Stop the horseshit, and lie down."

"I don't know how it happened." Ned sat up, looked across the tent as if there were distance there. "When Sam and I were kids, *I* led, more often than not. Then, when we got older—

when the fighting started—I don't know how it happened. Just . . .
after a while, people were coming to Sam and saying, 'What
now?' "

"Ned—"

"They asked *him*. They didn't ask *me*. And that fucking
This'll Do thing is beside the point. I've made damn few mistakes in seven, eight years fighting. I've been a hell of a commander. Better than you, Howell, Light Cavalry ranging."

"That's true."

"It wasn't that I made mistakes. It was just that people didn't
come to me and say, 'What now?' "

"Come on." Howell got up, took Ned's good arm. "Come on.
Lie down and get some rest."

Ned stood, and staggered. "Lie down, or fall down. Not ready
for Map–Fort Stockton, after all. . . ."

* * *

Coming back from john-trench in gusting sleet—and regretting
he hadn't moved into his rooms at the fort, after all—Sam heard
music, banjar playing from Howell Voss's tent on officers' row.
Bright music; surprising how lightly those big fingers
strummed. . . . It was a temptation to walk over, sit laughing,
listening to sleety rain and music, while talking army. Three
years ago, even two years ago, he would have done it. But the
distance of governing had grown between them, or seemed to
have, which made the same difference.

Voices over there. Ned; certainly off his cot too soon after
wagoning in.—Interesting that loneliness was never mentioned
in the old tales of kings, presidents, generals and heroes. Those
men and women somehow told as sufficient of themselves, and
never, after crapping, walking alone under freezing rain.

Going down tent lines to the third set-up, his boots scuffing through ice-skimmed puddles, Sam heard another conversation—one-sided conversation, it sounded. He scratched at the canvas flap. "May I enter?"

"Oh, Weather . . ." Unbuttoning canvas. Then the Boston girl's sleek head, white face. "It's the leader of all!" It was difficult to find her pupils in eyes so dark. The wind spattered her face with tiny flecks of ice.

"A freezing 'leader of all.' "

"A moment." More unbuttoning, then the flap drawn aside. *"Ice-rain!"*

For a moment, Sam saw no one who could have said it. Then the girl's little creature moved down the tent-pole, opened its mouth, and said again, *"Ice-rain!"*

It was the first time Sam had seen the thing—known to all the camp, of course, despite some effort to conceal it—as more than shadowy motion in its basket. More, proved unpleasant.

"Webster loves ice-rain," Patience said, closing the entrance flap behind them. "He loves what hawks hate."

"But you haven't sent him flying." Sam brushed meltwater off his cloak.

"Not yet." She stood, observing him. "Are you going to fight the Kipchaks now, or wait? Fight seriously, I mean, not these little scootings back and forth across the border."

"Well . . . I would prefer the little scootings back and forth."

"Please sit; my tent is your tent. . . . So, you are going to fight him *seriously*—and would have to be allied with Middle Kingdom."

Sam lifted his sword's harness from his back, then shrugged his cloak off and laid it along the tent's canvas floor. He sat on the girl's cot, the sword upright before him, resting his folded hands on its pommel. "We're discussing the possibility, Ambassadress."

The girl clapped her hands together. "It's going to be a *war!*" Couldn't have seemed more pleased.

"I would appreciate it—the army would appreciate it—if you could delay a report of that possibility. Delay it . . . three weeks? Four?"

"And why should I do that, Captain-General?"

"Well, you've already delayed sending your . . . ?"

"Mailman. Webster is a Mailman."

"Ah . . . well, you haven't yet sent him to report our cavalry's preparations to go north. And there was no disguising that from someone already in camp."

Patience stared at him, head slightly turned. Perfect pale little face. Perfect teeth. "I haven't sent him—for my own reasons."

"Then might you also . . . pause, before reporting the possibility of a *larger* movement to the Boston people in Map-McAllen? Again, for your own reasons."

The Boston girl smiled. It seemed to Sam to be a smile in layers, like a bridal cake—but one baked in sweet and bitter layers. "You believe that pride is my fault? Wishing to be ambassadress to greater and greater?"

"I hope so."

"But, milord, New England doesn't want you winning—you and that fierce Queen—against the so-brilliant and, I believe, very handsome young Khan." No smile now.

"I know. But New England—Boston—is going to be disappointed, and will have to await a later occasion. If I live, and the Kingdom fights with us, Toghrul will probably lose."

"And you say that—why?"

"Because he's certain of victory . . . and victory's never certain." Sam stood with his sword in his hand, bent to pick up his cloak, and swung it to his shoulders. "Also, the Khan enjoys war. I don't. His enjoyment is a weakness."

"I see."

"And, in exchange for three or four weeks of silence—your little friend *not* flying to Map-McAllen—you can come with our army to the River war, and see everything. You can come and hover above the dying, like Lady Weather."

"Mmmm . . ." Patience thrust out her lower lip like a child. "You are a bad man, to tempt me."

Her little monster toed the tent-pole where he clung, and called, "*Weather.*"

. . . Outside, in darkness, Sam trudged a long diagonal of freezing mud behind the Boston girl's tent, over to the next set-up's small, canvased toilet trench. A Light Infantry corporal, one of Margaret's Headquarters people, sat behind the screen, balanced on the poop-pole and peering through a little gap in the rigged canvas. A great horned owl, huge golden eyes furious under soaked feathers, shifted on his right wrist with a soft jingle of jess-bells.

The corporal stood up. "Sir."

"Sorry to stick you with this duty, Barney. She probably won't be sending her creature tonight. Probably won't be sending him at all."

"If she does, sir, Elliot'll hear it fly, and go kill it."

The owl, Elliot, hissed softly at its name, and fluffed its feathers.

"Who has the daytime, now?"

"Elmer Page, sir. Civilian. He's got a hunting red-tail."

"Okay. In the morning, tell Citizen Page that his help is much appreciated.—And Corporal, remind him politely to keep silent about it."

"Sir."

Sam walked down to the tent. Finding the entrance flap unbuttoned, he set it aside, said, "May I?" and ducked in.

"Milord." Neckless Peter, in a hooded brown robe too big for him, stood up from behind a small camp desk.

"Sit," Sam said, set his sword against the tent's wall, and let his cloak fold to the floor. "What are you reading?"

"Please . . ." The old man gestured to his cot. "I was writing, sir. A record . . . a memoir of our doings."

"Well . . ." Sam sat on Peter's cot, and stretched to ease his back. "Well, if you're troubling to do that, you may as well write the truth. No use wasting the work on inaccuracies."

"The truth, sir. Yes."

"Sit, Peter. *Sit.* And let me thank you for the use of your toilet trench. An inconvenience, but necessary."

"I understand. And the watchers have courteously stood aside for *my* necessities."

"Still, my thanks. . . . We're going to have a dinner, Peter, at the fort. In . . . oh, about a glass. I'd like you to come over. Any guard will direct you to officers' mess—one of those all too appropriate Warm-time names."

"Yes, sir."

"Peter, smile for me. You're not on the menu."

The little man smiled. "But perhaps your officers would prefer I not come."

"My officers' preferences, I think, we can set aside in favor of good advice from you. And, by the way, I won't permit questions about Toghrul Khan that might offend your honor as his teacher."

The little man sat looking at Sam—a librarian's regard, as if Sam were a copybook that might prove interesting. "There are . . . there *are* two things that may prove useful, and that Toghrul would not mind my telling you."

"Yes . . . ?"

"First, I've seen that you and your people—officers and soldiers—are friends."

"Not always, Peter. But usually, yes."

"Toghrul Khan has no friends."

"Mmm . . . A disadvantage, when friends might be needed. An advantage, when friends might be lost."

"That's so, of course, sir. And second, I believe you are sometimes afraid. The Khan, however, is afraid of nothing and no one."

"Now that's *very* useful. Very much worth knowing."

"Yes, so it seemed to me."

"Then . . ." Sam bent to pick up his cloak, stood to fasten its catch at his throat. "We'll see you at dinner?"

The old man got up from behind his desk. "Yes, milord."

" 'Sir.' Or 'Sam,' if you prefer."

"Sir."

"And bring an appetite, Peter. It'll be army food, but plenty."

"I will."

"By the way"—Sam paused at the tent's entrance—"since you're now in our councils. I'm sending Howell Voss north, with all our cavalry assembled. North into Texas. First, as a counterblow to the Khan's harassment across the Bravo to the west. . . . And second, for a more important reason."

"Heavens," Neckless Peter said—a perfect use of that wonderful old word. "A 'counterblow.' Toghrul will find that . . . interesting."

"So I hope," Sam said, set the tent-flap aside with his scabbarded sword, and ducked out into sleet become snow.

* * *

An Entry—which, I suppose, must be only a footnote to my history of North Map-Mexico and its Captain-General. In his person, the young man represents his land and people so well that that alone may be his guarantee of command. Young, strong—certainly ferocious, but never, I think, wantonly, carelessly. A fierce shepherd of the mountain shepherds' country.

He sat on the edge of my cot, and the light of my lamp went to him so he seemed outlined, vibrating with energy to be released as, supposedly, did the internal engines of wheel-cars on Warm-times' hard black roads.

A sturdy, broad-shouldered young man, sandy hair cropped

short and shaved at his neck—looking very much like a countryman come to a fair to wrestle for prizes. A prosperous young
countryman though marked by harsh weather, dressed in good
cloth, soft leathers, fine boots. His forearms thick as posts, his
large hands as fat with muscle as most men's fists.

He sat, elbows on his knees, and spoke to me—welcomed me,
really, into his close company. A closeness likely to cause me
difficulties with Eric Lauder. . . .

What marked him commander? The light that seemed to go
to him was surely only my attention. So, his calm . . . yes. A
readiness to act—certainly that; when he wears his long sword,
its grip hovers over his right shoulder like an odd impatient
demon, close enough to whisper in his ear.

It seems to me, considering, that the marker of his command
lies in the great division, a canyon's space, between the young
man as plainly seen—intelligent, forthright, absolutely capable—
and the infinitely subtle expression in his eyes. Eyes the color
of those semiprecious stones comprised of mixtures of light
brown, light green, and light yellow, seen sometimes in streams
run down from the mountains of Map-California.

In his eyes was nothing forthright or simple, but rather com-
plication, inquiry, examination . . . and an odd affection—perhaps
for me, perhaps for everyone.

When he left, I sat as one sits after reading an important
copybook, of which only a portion has been understood.

12

"Get that damn rat off the meat!"

Elvin, quick for a dying old man, picked up a roll and threw it down the table. It missed Butler's dog—a yapping single-handful—and hit Sam as he was carving. The mutton seemed tenderer than usual, and had little bits of pepper stuck in it here and there. Oswald-cook grown enamored of southern spices, after cooking a thousand dull kettles of Brunswick slumgul.

"Don't hurt my Poppy!" Phillip Butler wore ground-glass imperial spectacles held to his eyes on thin, twisted wires that curled behind his ears. He looked over the spectacles more often than through them. Short, gray-bearded, he seemed more a children's tutor than a colonel of Heavy Infantry.

Poppy scurried down the table with a mutton scrap in tiny jaws, jumped a platter, and leaped down into Butler's lap. "There, Candy-lamb," the colonel said, looking still wearied by the five-day ride from Hermosillo Camp to Better-Weather.

"What's this about Howell going up into Texas," he'd said to Sam that afternoon, "and what nonsense are *you* up to, sir?"

"Serious nonsense, Phil."

Sam stooped, found the roll on the floor, then threw it back, sidearm. The brothers leaned apart so the roll flew between them, and Sam went back to carving mutton—cutting Ned's portion into small pieces, for one-handed eating. Oswald-cook had put *many* little peppers in the meat. . . . Sam handed the loaded pewter plates to Margaret to pass down the long, narrow table. They were eating in a room of stone walls; ground floor in the fort, therefore no windows.

Around the table were all those close to him—except Portia-doctor, still with the wounded at Clinic, and Charmian, already gone west to annoy the Khan's people come over the border.

Margaret sat to his left, looking somewhat harried, preoccupied. Below her, Howell, looming eye-patched over his plate. Then Phil Butler, then Ned, eating one-handed and looking grim. The Rascob brothers at the end of the table, backs to the iron stove—called a Franklin, after some Warm-time person. And up the other side, Eric, who seemed annoyed, then Charles, then the little librarian, shy and silent, on Sam's right.

His friends, and only family . . . though there'd been others through the years. From the Sierra, and later. Paul Ortiz . . . Lucy . . . John Ott. All dead. Paul killed at Tonichi. Lucy caught by imperials, raped, then burned to death tied to the Jesus tree in the temple at Malpais. And John Ott lost for nothing, wasted for what had seemed a useful notion.

"I'm glad I'm dying," Elvin said through his bandanna, as if he'd mind-read Sam's thoughts. "Better death, than these fucking dinners with those dogs!"

Jaime elbowed him. "Be quiet."

"Don't tell me to be quiet." Elvin, his plate arrived, settled to mutton and potatoes, tucking forkfuls under a flap of bandanna to prove his good appetite.

The plates went round. Sam sliced and served, Margaret passed . . . and with thanks to Lady Weather or Mountain Jesus by those who cared to give it, they ate spiced mutton, broken potatoes with mutton gravy, and broccoli steamed with garlic. They ate this main course quickly and in silence, from campaign habit . . . then took second helpings for the same reason.

Margaret got up from the table-bench twice to go round, pour barley beer for them. She bent beside Elvin to whisper in his ear. "You don't have to eat what you don't want, Old Sweetheart."

"Mind your own business," Elvin said, then put down his knife and two-tine fork—like all their mess silver, a spoil from God-Help-Us. "I've had enough. Those little rats of Phil's have spoiled my appetite, running around the damn table."

"You can have some custard, El," Jaime said.

"*You* have some fucking custard."

. . . When—after the last of mutton, almost the last of potatoes and broccoli—the custard bowl was passed with a cruet of honey, conversation came round with it.

"Anything at the races, Howell?" Charles and Howell both placed long-running wagers on the races at El Sauz—though betting only with civilians.

"I won on Barbershears, Charles. I'm sorry, pigeon said Snowflake didn't show."

"Surprise me," Charles said. "*Amaze* me. A horse with three first finishes—and for me, no show."

Ned was eating a dish of chicken-egg custard with his left wrist's bandaged stump held carefully away from the table's edge. "Lesson, Charles—don't bet on white horses. Does anybody here know of any white horse winning consistently? There's something wrong with their bones . . . more white a horse has on his hide, the more easily broken down."

"Silver," the little librarian said, the first thing he'd said at dinner.

"What?"

"The Warm-time horse," Neckless Peter said. "Hi-yo Silver was extraordinary."

"Oh . . . Well, Warm-times." Ned poured honey on his dish. "Different breeding."

Sam listened to horse talk for a while, then set his beer-jack down, pushed his custard dish aside. "I'm sorry," he said, "to break the rule of no war conversation at mess."

There were several small sounds of metal on oak, as knives and forks were put down. The duller taps of horn spoons. . . . Margaret stood and went to the dining-room door, by the weapons rack.

"Empty corridor," she said, "except for two of Charles' silent people on guard. One dog. Louis."

"Louis?"

"The dog, Sam. Name's Louis."

"Okay.... What's said here, is not repeated." Sam waited for nods. "You all know that Howell's going north into Map-Texas."

"With all the cavalry we've got."

"That's right, Ned. Picking up the divisions on his way. Every mount, every man and woman."

"And if he loses those people?—Excuse me, Howell. But what if all those people are lost?"

"Then, Ned," Sam said, "we go for a swim in Sewer Creek. So Howell is ordered *not* to lose those people."

"Takes care of that," Howell said, and cut a small chew of tobacco.

"—Also Howell, when you reach Map–Fort Stockton, kill what fighting men you can, of course, and any women who fight beside them, but otherwise, harm no women or children."

"That's tender, Sam." Howell tucked the tobacco into his lower lip. "Tender . . . But why?"

"Because, in the future, I want the Khan's troopers fighting only for him, not for their families' lives."

"Good policy," the little librarian said, then closed his mouth when the others looked at him.

"But bad policy"—Eric drummed his fingers on the table—"bad policy to have one here who was the Khan's . . . and still may be."

"My Second-mother, Catania," Sam said, "found Neckless Peter to be a good friend, and honest. Is there anyone now in North Map-Mexico with better judgment in these matters?"

Sam waited through what Warm-time copybooks called 'a pregnant pause.' A small gray moth, alive past its season, fluttered at a hanging lamp.

". . . None I know of," Eric said. "Librarian, I apologize."

"Unnecessary," Neckless Peter said. "A chief of intelligence should act the part."

"Okay. Charles, any problem with the staging of remounts—any problem with payments, with moving the herds up the line?"

"Lots of problems, Sam. Lots of angry ranchers. But your horses will be there, Howell."

"Eric?"

"Sam, fodder's already wagoned and waiting. Hay and grain at Ocampo and La Babia. Rations, horseshoes, spare tack, sheepskin blankets for the horses. Sheepskin mitts, cloaks, overboots, and sleep-sacks for the troopers. Ten of Portia's people mounted to accompany with medical kits and horse stretchers."

"All costing an absolute fortune," Charles said.

"And only the first expense, Charles."

"Meaning what, Sam?"

"Meaning that Howell and the cavalry are not coming back south. . . . Meaning that during the next two to three Warmtime weeks—presuming the Kipchaks intend nothing serious west of the Bend—during the next two to three weeks, *all* the army, all reserves, *and* selected militia companies, will gather to march north over the border, up the Gulf coast into Map West-Louisiana, then north again into Map-Arkansas and the Hills-Ozark."

Sam finished speaking into a silence that seemed deep as dark water.

"*. . . My God Almighty.*" An oath from Jaime Rascob that would have called for burning, a few decades before.

Another silence, then, until Phil Butler broke it. "About time." Butler had a rusty voice. "If the Khan takes the Kingdom, we're next. There's no doubt about that." One of his tiny dogs—not Poppy—climbed up onto his left shoulder like a cat.

"Yes," Eric said. "I suppose . . . about time. But surely after the winter would be better."

"*After* the winter," Elvin Rascob said, "with the Kipchaks already campaigned down that frozen river, Middle Kingdom would be dead as me."

"Right," Howell said. "He'll go up into Map-Missouri now, take a river port—and as the Mississippi freezes, send his *tumans* down the ice. Split the Kingdom, East-bank from West . . . and the whole thing will be in his hands."

"And then," Jaime said, "he'd come for us."

Lamplight seemed to waver slightly in Sam's sight, move to the rhythm of his heartbeat. Relief . . . relief and a deep breath no one must see him draw. These men, and Margaret, might have said, "No. No war. We won't have it unless we're invaded. The army won't have it. The people won't have it!" . . . They might have said so, knowing he would never stand, take his sword from the rack, and walk out to gather loyal soldiers, order the hangman to stretch and grease his ropes.

"Once in the Hills-Ozark," Sam said, "we'll threaten the Khan's lines of supply and communication with Caravanserai, and with his ports on the Ocean Pacific. Very *long* lines of supply. Everything for his army will have to come through broken country just north of us." Sam picked up the carving knife, stroked its edge across mutton bones on the serving platter. "He will not be able to let that stand. He'll have to turn from the Kingdom's river to strike us."

Howell nodded. "And when he turns . . ."

"We fight him, and hope Middle Kingdom strikes the rest of his army, in the north, at the same time."

"Their armies are supposed to be good enough," Ned said, "and if, as we hear from Eric, those warships are truly capable, skating around on the ice . . ."

"My people have reported on those ships, Ned. And what they report is so."

"No offense meant, Eric. But we would be *depending* on those people. What's the guarantee of their fighting hard enough in the north to tie down half the Khan's army?"

"As yet—none." Sam tapped the carving knife's point on his plate. A soft ringing sound. "But it makes good sense for them to do it. Together, we'd have the Kipchaks in a toothed spring-trap, with jaws even Toghrul might not be able to break."

"If you can persuade the Boxcars—and then, as Ned says, *depend* on them." Eric smiled. "And they've always been slow at war. Strong, but slow. Two armies, Left- and Right-bank— always kept separate—*and* the Fleet, *and* the river lords, don't make for quick response."

"Ah..." Butler stroked a dog. "But *if* Middle Kingdom will move, we can play kickball with him. Toghrul campaigns north to the river, is heavily engaged—then has to turn south to us, while hoping the rest of his army still holds in the north. We've given him two chances to lose."

"Yes," Sam said. "The Kingdom to his front, and us coming up his ass right across his lines of supply. We'll see how Kipchak *tumans* enjoy campaigning with enemies north *and* south of them. We'll see how they enjoy fighting us in hills and forest, our kind of country. And they'll have to fight us, or winter-starve." Sam examined lamplight gleaming down the carving knife's blade. "Which reminds me; our dear Catania said there were likely still the old Trappers, though only a few, in North Map-Texas. Perhaps, Eric, if you sent a person riding far north now, to ask in her name and mine, they might sled down to interfere with those supply lines here and there. Teach the Kipchaks lessons in deep-snow fighting."

"That can be done."

"All very nice," Ned said, "if Lord Winter and Lady Weather cooperate. Nice, if everything goes perfectly."

"*Almost* perfectly will do, Ned." Sam put the carving knife down. "I know no other way to beat him."

"He could withdraw early," Howell said. "Take his losses ... plan to deal with us next year. And after that, go back to the Kingdom."

"He could," Sam said, "if his pride can bear a thousand-mile retreat, his tribesmen swallow it. And after that, he'd find us and Middle Kingdom firmly allied, and the more ready to deal with him. . . . Truth is, the Khan has made a mistake. He's sent a small force against us, thinking we'll be concerned about our border, and will only deal with that—for instance, by return-raiding up to Map–Fort Stockton—while he passes us by in his campaign against the Kingdom. I don't think it will occur to Toghrul that Map–Fort Stockton might be only *cover* for positioning Howell's cavalry to screen our army as it moves north past the Gulf and up through Map-Louisiana and Map-Arkansas."

"That *is* nice." Ned blew gently on his bandaged stump, as if to cool it."

"So I hope," Sam said. "The Khan's made a serious mistake, but I doubt he'll make another. Our time against him is now . . . or never."

Consideration to that was given in silence around the table. It seemed to Sam to have become an evening of silences.

"I agree," Jaime said, and Elvin grunted behind his bandanna.

"Yes," Ned said. "We go for the son of a bitch."

"Keeping in mind," Howell said, "that if the Boxcars aren't with us, don't fight in the north—then we are fucked, and the Kipchaks will chase us all the way to Map–Mexico City."

"Phil?"

Butler sighed, and bent to set a dog on the floor. "Seems an opportunity to me, Sam. Man spreads his legs—your pardon, Margaret—why not kick him in the nuts?"

"Still"—Charles shook his head—"still . . . organizing this in a matter of days. And paying for winter campaigning, Sam. The whole *army*, for Nailed Jesus' sake!"

"I know, Charles. I know. But we couldn't prepare properly for war without the Khan knowing it. It's important he feels free to move east to invade the Kingdom, commit most of his forces to it."

"And will our soldiers appreciate this short notice, Sam, when they're freezing, starving in winter hills?"

"What they will appreciate, Charles, will be those supplies that you and Eric see come up to them, at whatever cost."

"And if—even supplied, even aided by the Boxcars—the army loses this war?"

". . . Then, Charles, I suppose some young officer will gather new cavalry—draft-horse cavalry, wind-broken cavalry—and skirmish over the foothills while new infantry gathers in the Sierra." Sam smiled. "Old-man infantry, young-boy infantry, girl infantry, thief-and-bandit infantry. And our people will raid out of those mountains, and suffer the Kipchaks' raids, while the Khan Toghrul grows old and dies. And while his son lives, and his son's son, until finally a weakling rules at Caravanserai, and the Khanate breaks apart. Then, our people will come down from the mountains, and make North Map-Mexico again."

The evening's fourth silence.

"Well . . ." Charles stared down at his plate, as if the future might be read in mutton bones and remnant potato. "It will mean no relief of taxes. Not for years."

"And, speaking of taxes," Sam said, "any pigeon from Sonora?"

"The tax thing?" Lauder made a note with charcoal pencil on a fold of paper.

"What tax thing?" Howell said.

"None of the army's business," Charles said.

"Well, that's rude." Howell shifted his tobacco chew, leaned to spit into his saucer.

"He's right," Sam said. "A civil matter. The governor had been encouraged, by his friends, to withhold payment of taxes to Better-Weather."

"An *un*civil matter, as it happens," Charles said. "There was . . . some opposition."

"How bad?"

"Four of Klaus Munk's reeve men were killed at Neal's home, day before yesterday. His vaqueros fought for him."

"And?"

"Munk arrested Neal, is bringing him to court with three of his men."

"And?"

"He'll be found guilty by Magistrate Caminillo, and sentenced to death."

"The vaqueros?" Ned said.

"Will also be sentenced to death, Ned." Charles glanced at Sam. "We can't have cow-herds killing law officers."

"Just," Sam said, "as we can't have people not paying their taxes. You did well, Charles. Sorry I had to give you the job."

Eric reached over, patted Charles's arm—an unusual gesture for a man who didn't care to touch or be touched. "My sort of work."

"No, Eric," Sam said. "It had to be a civil matter, and straightforward.—Make certain the matter's finished, Charles. See that Magistrate Caminillo understands, no mercy."

"Who the hell is Caminillo?" Howell said. "I don't even know the name."

"He was a hide dealer," Charles said. "Elected judgment-man in Nogales, then Ciudad Juárez. The old governer, Cohen, suggested him for magistrate. Called him honest, and no coward."

"Duels before he robed?" Howell smiled. "Probably fewer than Cohen's."

"None, actually," Charles said. "I believe Caminillo was challenged twice for his judgments, but refused to duel. Sought those men out, and beat them with a ball-stick. He's quite highly regarded out there."

"Well and good," Sam said—a very old copybook phrase. "But see he does what has to be done."

"I said I'll do it."

Disapproval, and anger. Sam let it be. *Losing an old friend to these necessities. But it's only fair—been losing myself to them for some time.*

"One thing's sure, Sam," Eric said. "You've made an enemy of the governer."

"There's something surer than that. Governer Stewart has made an enemy of me." For a few moments, there was no sound but the stove's fire dying. *No fear. Please don't let me find fear in my friends' faces. . . .*

". . . Jaime," Elvin said, "pass me some of that custard. What in the world did Oswald-cook put in the mutton? Tasted like fucking pepper soup!"

"Sam,"—Howell spit tobacco juice onto his saucer—"Map-Louisiana and Map-Arkansas are both Boxcar states."

"Howell," Margaret said, beside him, "where's your spit-cup?"

"I've put civilization behind me, Trade-honey. . . . Sam, we'll be crossing the Kingdom's territory most of the way north."

"Yes—but with the Kipchaks already striking to their river up in Map-Missouri, I don't think the Boxcars will mind. I think they'll be pleased to see our army coming."

"And *if* they mind, Sam?"

Sam smiled. "Tough titty." It was one of Warm-time's oldest military sayings.

"More beer, anyone?" Margaret lifted the clay pitcher.

"There's not *enough* beer for this," Ned said, and the others smiled. Sam felt the tautness in the room slacken. There was a turn at the table, a turn from worry to work to be done. There was also—he'd felt it many times before—an odd feeling of relief from the others. They'd been commanded, commanded to a grave but reasonable risk, and there seemed to be subtle enjoyment in that for them. . . . For them, not for their commander.

"So, Sam," Phil Butler said, "who does what?"

"Howell leaves day after tomorrow, picks up the cavalry as he goes. Elvin and Jaime order the army assembled—*with* the regular militia companies of Coahuila and Nuevo Leon. You two are in charge until the forces are brought together here at Better-Weather. . . . Phil, once that's done, you command the army's movement north, taking Portia-doctor and the medical people. Charmian and the western militias will still be busy playing games with those Kipchak units come down west of the Bend. She and her light infantry will be the last to join you."

"Join you," Ned said, "if she isn't enjoying herself too much."

"Ned, you'll be well enough by then to scrape together what few mounts Howell hasn't taken. You'll command rear-guard cavalry scout as the army moves north."

"Alright, Sam. And once we're in Map-Arkansas?"

"Howell should already have come east from Map–Fort Stockton, brought the main body of cavalry there to join you." Sam paused a moment. ". . . And in the Hills-Ozark, Howell commands the army. You, Ned—and Phil and Charmian—serve under him."

"*Howell*, Sam?" Phil Butler said. "Not you?"

"I . . . will be visiting the Kingdom."

The fifth silence. Sam supposed Charles would be first to break it.

"No! Absolutely not!" Charles hit the table with his fist. "Sam . . . they'll cut your throat for you, no matter the Queen knew dear Catania, no matter she knew you when you were a baby. *I'm* the one who should go."

"Queen Joan won't cut my throat."

"If she doesn't," Ned said, "the generals and river lords will."

"And cook and eat you, besides." Jaime shook his head.

"It's the Queen," Eric said, "who wants this meeting. Asked for it."

"Don't do it, Sam." Ned cradled the stump of his wrist. "You're not fucking immortal, no matter what you think. They'll kill you—or keep you under stone until you rot."

"They might want to, Ned, but they won't. They need us."

"They may *not* need us, Sam. They can fight the Khan and maybe beat him without us. And New England will help them."

"A point," Eric said. "Sam, our Light Cavalryman has a point. I doubt if the West-bank generals or East-bank generals—let alone two or three hundred river lords—consider us ideal allies."

"Perhaps not ideal, Eric. Still, it can't be comfortable for the Kingdom with the Khan to the west, savages and tribesmen north, and New England breeding Mountain-Jesus-knows-what to the east."

"True . . . and, of course, we also need them."

"Yes, we do, unless we want to face the Kipchaks alone once Middle Kingdom goes down—and then have to conduct a fighting retreat south through the mountains, where the Empire's army will certainly be waiting for us."

Neckless Peter cleared his throat. "I believe New England will *not* help the Boxcar Kingdom. I felt so when they sent the girl, Patience. New England wants them to lose. Wants us to lose."

"*Us?*" Eric smiled.

"Eric," Sam said, "that's enough."

"Boston wants the Kipchaks winning?" Ned looked better with impatient color in his face. "Horseshit, old man. That would leave the Khan ruling all the civilized river-country!"

"Yes, Colonel. But the Khan *isn't* civilized, and his people aren't civilized. He orders, and they obey. They have no Warm-time law. No law but his word."

"You might ask the governor of Sonora about laws and words

and obedience, Librarian." Charles took a sip of beer.

"Charles," Sam said. *Certainly a friend beginning to be lost.* "That's almost the same, but only almost. If the state reeve had refused to arrest, if the magistrate now refuses to convict, I'll have to come to some accommodation."

No answer from Charles Ketch.

"To hell with Stewart and Sonora," Ned said. "Eric—this visit to Middle Kingdom. This was your idea?"

"The Queen's idea, Ned," Sam said. "And she wouldn't want the visit just to toss me in the river. She's looking for what help we can give them."

"Looking for more than that," Charles said.

"More?" Howell spit into his saucer.

"There's a bride-groom question." Eric smiled. "Her daughter."

"*Wedding* bells with the Princess Rachel?" Ned grinned and thumped his wrist-stump on the table. "*Ow!* Weather damn this thing!"

"An engagement, perhaps," Sam said. "I doubt the Queen really intends a wedding."

"Look, Sam," Howell said, "your plan makes good sense. But that will make no difference if Middle Kingdom doesn't agree, doesn't care to listen to you. The Boxcars don't like our holding the Gulf's west coast. They don't like us freeing serfs that run south. They don't like North Map-Mexico having an army, and especially not a *good* army. And they don't like you ruling down here with no dots on your face."

"Still, the Queen needs us."

"And afterward, Sam, if she no longer needs us?"

"By that time, the Princess Rachel and I may be engaged—if a serious engagement was ever intended. It's likely a notion of the Queen's to keep the river lords unbalanced."

"Right," Eric said.

Neckless Peter said, "Probably."

"And it's possible"—Sam smiled—"that the Queen will grow fond of me."

"Oh, how *not*, boy?" Elvin said through his bandanna. "And you such a charmer!" He found a strip of mutton fat on his brother's plate, and threw it down the table. Missed Sam, and hit Margaret on her shirt's shoulder.

"That's my fucking red southern-cotton!" She kicked her bench back and jumped up. "If you weren't dying, Elvin, I'd kill you. I've got to get warm water on this." She went out into the hall. "*Louis, get down.*"

"But Sam," Charles said, "engaged? Is it necessary?"

"I think it's going to be."

"Nailed Jesus." Jaime picked up a fork, toyed with it. "Nailed *Jesus*, Sam. Engaged . . . then married into those people?"

"Cannibals." Ned rested his wrist stump on the table.

"*Used* to be cannibals, Ned."

"Sam," Howell said, "you talk of the Princess and the Queen. But the river lords, the generals, the admirals of the Fleet—will they 'grow fond' of you?"

"Perhaps they'll learn to seem so. . . . And, another matter. Phil, forgive me, but the Boston girl goes north with the army."

"You're joking."

"No, Phil, I'm not. A price of her silence, her not at least trying to inform Map-McAllen that you're coming over the border."

"Sam," Eric being patient, "her silence could have been assured otherwise. And her little flying-thing gone the same way."

"Eric, I think we have enough on our plate without murdering Boston's ambassador, and her pet."

"As I understand it," Neckless Peter said, "New England would likely regret the Mailman as much as the lady. The creatures are very expensive."

"There you are, Eric—both too expensive to murder."

"I hope, Sam, they won't prove too expensive kept alive."

"A concern for another day. So, Phil, arrange a small guard detachment for her, see to her comfort and supplies. And apparently she's a killing lady; watch that that scimitar doesn't get her into more trouble than she can get out of."

Butler took off his imperial spectacles, polished them with a linen napkin, "This must be punishment for sin."

"Punishment for bringing those damn dogs to dinner," Elvin said. "Have we more business here? I have to pee."

"*Louis, get down. . . .*" Margaret came in from the hall. "And let me tell another old dog that he's very lucky that stain seemed to come out. I hope it came out." She settled onto her bench.

"I wasn't throwing at you."

"Elvin," Jaime said, "just be quiet."

"Don't tell me to be quiet.—*Baja.*"

"What?"

"Jaime, Baja militia should be ready to move east with Sonora's, if Charmian has trouble with those Kipchaks come down."

"I think Charmian and Chihuahua can handle them. But alright; we'll pigeon Oso. Tell him to stop fucking his sheep and get his people assembled."

"What *about* New England?" Howell spit into his saucer again, winked at Margaret.

"As I said"—Neckless Peter no longer so shy—"Boston wishes the Kingdom defeated."

"And why would New England want the Khan to win, Librarian?" Ned took a swallow of beer. "How does that help them?"

"They want it, Colonel, because the Kipchaks are a fragile force—"

"Right. Only thirty, forty thousand cavalry."

"Still fragile, Ned," Sam said, "in time. The Khan will die

someday, and his son, or his successor, is unlikely to be as formidable. But their Khan is all the Kipchaks have. Without Toghrul, or another like him, they're only separate tribes of shepherds and raiders."

"That's true enough." Howell bent to spit in his saucer again, but Margaret reached over and snatched it away. "Well, for Weather's sake! Women in trousers . . . never a good thing—oof!"

"Now, *children,*" Phil said.

"She has an elbow like an ax!—Give me the damn dish."

"Spit in your fucking pocket," Margaret said.

"A brute with tits."

"You two finished?" Sam said. ". . . I think Peter's right, and New England takes the long view. Middle Kingdom, if it survives, will certainly grow to threaten Boston in time. The Kingdom is a book-civilization; formidable even under weak rule. New England would certainly prefer, in the future, to deal with the Kipchaks."

Eric nodded. "It does make sense that Boston would like to see us *and* Middle-Kingdom go down. Also, considering the future, most of Map–East America is wooded, close country. Some mountains also, apparently. Kipchak horsemen wouldn't be as comfortable campaigning there."

"And," Charles said, "whatever womb-things the New Englanders are mind-making are likely to enjoy dark woods."

"Can we leave the future alone?" Elvin said. "Sam is going off to the Kingdom—likely get his throat cut—and we're to kick the Khan in the ass. Now, if there's nothing else, I need to get out of here, or piss under the table!"

Sam smiled. "Only this: Charles holds here as administrator—with Eric, in case one or two governers see a chance for independence with the army gone north. . . . Eric, failure to produce supplies, *or* nonpayment of taxes, is to be regarded as treason. Charles knows how I want such cases handled."

"Understood."

"Also, Neckless Peter is to act as adviser to both of you. And is to be consulted on *all* important matters."

". . . Very well."

"Okay. Then there is no more business at mess.—I leave in two days, and I'll want a written plan of action from each of you before I go. We'll work on supply and reinforcement matters tonight . . . troop movements, dispositions, and objectives tomorrow and tomorrow night."

"Not enough time."

"Howell, it will have to be enough time. I leave day after tomorrow." Sam shoved his bench-seat back and stood. "Good dinner. Margaret, please thank Oswald-cook. The little peppers in the meat were . . . interesting. I'll be leaving for the coast; you'll be coming with me—and a *small* escort."

"How small, sir?"

"Four or five presentable men."

"Not enough, Sam."

"Ned, four or five *are* enough. I don't want the Boxcars to think I'm afraid of them."

"Still," Eric said, "not enough."

"Sir, you're a head of state!"

"Yes, Peter, I am. The head of a *minor* state, coming to make great demands on Middle Kingdom for cooperation in war. I think going modestly will better serve the purpose.—Margaret, only four or five presentable men come with us. Men only, the Kingdom doesn't approve of women soldiers."

"Margaret's a woman soldier," Howell said—and was elbowed again.

"Margaret," Sam said, "will be an exception, *and* a useful lesson to them."

"You don't want us going up with the army?" Jaime said.

"Stupid question," Elvin muttered through his bandanna.

"No, Jaime. You two don't go up. If this ends badly, take the people into the Sierra and find a wiser Captain-General." Sam took his sword from the weapons rack, and walked out. They heard him say, "*Louis,*" then murmured talk to the mastiff about behavior.

" 'Into the Sierra.' " Howell made a face. "I can see myself, an old man eating goat hooves and setting ambushes."

"He will not come back," Jaime said.

"Shut your mouth." Elvin, looking tired, sat with his eyes closed.

"Perhaps he'll come back," the little librarian said, "but not the same. A Captain-General is one thing. A future king, is another."

* * *

Neckless Peter, carrying a lamp, was skirting frozen puddles to the tent lines when Eric Lauder caught up with him. They walked side by side though gusts of bitter wind, so Lauder had to lean close, raise his voice a little.

"Your opinion, Librarian?"

"If one thing goes wrong, all goes wrong."

"Yes—but if all goes right?"

"Ah . . . Then, it seems to me, Toghrul will be destroyed, and Middle Kingdom will have our Captain-General for husband to their princess—and likely, heir to their throne."

"Then to be our king, as well."

"Yes."

"And should the Khan *be* destroyed—regrets?"

"I will have regrets. He was a wonderful boy. And his mind . . . you know the Empire's fine-cut gems?"

"Yes."

"So, Toghrul's mind."

Peter slipped a little on ice, and Lauder took his arm. "But this fine mind seems interested only in war, conquests."

"Of course, to battle boredom—the cancer of all conquerors."

"Not our reluctant Sam." They'd come to Peter's tent.

"No. His sickness is sadness at what must be done."

"Well . . ." Eric patted the frosted shoulder of Peter's cloak. "Well, welcome to us, Wisdom."

Peter called after as Lauder walked away. "And am I now trusted?"

Eric turned and smiled. "By all but me," he said, and went into the dark.

13

Sam, his farewells said in camp at Better-Weather—farewells only by-the-way in the hustle and hurry of the army's business—rode along the frozen path to meet Margaret and the others, come from south stables. They and the baggage waiting on the road leading to Saltillo, then Montemorelos . . . and finally the port of Carboneras on the Gulf Entire.

Howell already gone to La Babia to join the First Division of Cavalry, then move north. Ned gone, too—west to gather what spavins were left, gather Charmian and the Light Infantry as well—allowing any surviving squadrons of Kipchaks there free rein to plunder and burn vacant farms and fields.

Phil Butler, circumferenced by little dogs—was that a correct use of the Warm-time word, 'circumference'? Phil would be muttering in his tent, peering over copy-maps many centuries old, showing ways to go to many places nowhere now. His captains would be scratching at the tent-flap to ask questions, only to be told he'd answer when he damn well pleased, and meanwhile, get out!

The brothers still the irascible center of it all; the gathering army's every problem coming to them. And almost every problem solved. . . .

Sam was tired—sleepy, really. Last evening, he'd gone down for a hot-water bath in the laundry at the fort, and found Ned there, submerged in the deep stone tank, all but his bandaged stump. He'd held that up out of the steaming water. . . . They hadn't spoken of war or the campaign at all. Hadn't even mentioned it, splashing, scrubbing with lye soap. They'd spoken of old sheep stealings, recalled boyhood friends. Remembered, laughing, Catania coming up one morning to north pasture, where they'd folded two fine stolen rams—Catania walking up the mountain with a slender peeled pine branch in her hand.

When she'd seen them, higher, poised to run away, she'd called, "*Stand still.*"

And they had. She'd walked up the slope to them, loosed their belts as they stood, then yanked their sheepskin trousers down. And as they still stood, not moving, not avoiding, she'd whipped them until their legs and asses were striped, and bleeding here and there.

"Steal," Catania'd said, tossing the pine branch aside, "steal— and pay the thieving bill." Then she'd said, "In these times, those who are men find better things to do."

That night, sore and stiff-legged, they'd taken the rams back down the mountain to Macleary's place—and the next day, went west to serve under Gary Jeunesse, fighting the Empire's soldiers.

Sam and Ned had recalled and laughed . . . claimed scars still from the whipping. Ned's mother had been long dead then, and it had seemed to Sam at the time that while he might have run after the first few blows, Ned never would, so hungry for a mother's attention, even though punishment.

They'd laughed, splashed, and not spoken of the war at all.

Sam—for some reason never at ease in fortress chambers— had dried, dressed, went out the postern gate, and trudged over frozen mud to his tent, finding Margaret there amid possibles, garments, and a large cedar chest.

"What's this?"

"A clothes chest."

"We'll leave it. Duffels will do."

"Sir—Sam, you're going to a kingdom, a queen's court! They'll expect you to *look* like a Captain-General. It will hurt us if you look otherwise."

"No."

"Why? We have gold and silver, jewels and jeweled weapons. We're not savages."

"Why? Because, Margaret, they will have more gold, more

silver, more and finer jewelry, furs, and velvets. If we try to meet them on that field, we *will* seem savages."

"Alright. . . . Alright. What do you want me to pack? Just tell me and I'll do it."

"Don't be angry."

"Sam, I'm not angry. What do you want me to pack? I don't give a damn how I look before those ladies."

"We pack as if for campaigning. New woolens, warm and clean. Good cloaks, ponchos. Best-quality leathers and good boots. Plain fine-steel weapons, plain fine-steel armor—showing signs of use."

"Going too far the other way. . . ."

"Yes, it would be, so I'll take one set of rich cloak-and-clothes for ceremony, and each of us will also wear a ring from the treasury—one of the imperials' we took at God-Help-Us. Gold, with a considerable stone."

"So, at least *something*."

"And a matching bracelet for you."

Margaret gave Sam a wife-look. "And that's to bribe me to silence about appearing in Middle Kingdom looking like a file of lost troopers?"

"That's right. Margaret, it's our army standing behind us that they'll see. We dress to remind them of that army."

"Well, I'm not going to argue with you. I'm tired of arguing." She dropped the chest's lid closed with a thump.

"Good. Finish packing, then go to Charles' people and wrestle that treasury jewelry from their grip. They'll want a signed receipt."

"They'll want several receipts."

Margaret gone unsatisfied, Sam had lain on his cot, holding a vodka flask for company—and found, oddly, that even holding it helped.

He'd tried to sleep, but only planned dispositions in Map-Arkansas. On the border, really, between North Map-Arkansas and Map-Missouri. He'd seen, as he lay there, how quickly the Khan was certain to act when he realized what they'd done. Toghrul wouldn't hesitate, wouldn't consider—he'd turn back from Kingdom's river and attack. There would be no delay.

By then, Howell *must* have brought the army up into place. In proper country—steep, but not too steep, and wooded. There'd be barely time to prepare for the blow. . . .

Sam had lain awake long glass-hours, the war's possible futures folding and unfolding like one of the decorated screens the Empire's ladies were said to love, colorful with signs, secrets, and portraits of their families and lovers intertwined with painted flowers.

He'd risen before dawn in cold and darkness, set his flask aside, draped his cloak, and strapped his sword on his back. Then walked icy ground to north stables and the brute imperial charger from *Boca Chica*—Difficult. The stableman, Corporal Brice, had tacked the big animal up—kneeing the horse's belly to burp air out of him for the cinch—stood aside while Sam mounted, then reached up to touch his knee. "Good luck, General."

"Jake—you people, the army, *are* my luck."

. . . Sam saw the camino from the ridge. Six people mounted, with four packhorses on lead, were waiting at the roadside, their cloaks blowing in a cold wind. The rising sun threw their shadows sideways.—As he'd seen the riders, they'd seen him, and watched as he spurred down the slope.

When he trotted up, Margaret heeled her horse to meet him . . . seemed troubled.

"Sir—"

"What is it?" Sam said, then looked past her at the others. A lieutenant of Light Cavalry, and three sergeants—one each, apparently, from Heavy Infantry, Light Infantry, Heavy Cavalry. The army's four divisions represented. . . . There was also a grinning civilian, very fat in a stained red-wool cloak, holding the packhorses' lead. Undoubtedly one of Eric's dubious people, acting as cook, hostler, strangler on occasion. . . .

Sam knew the lieutenant. And two of the sergeants.

"Margaret, what in the *fuck* did you think you were doing? I said, *'presentable'!"*

"Sir, the brothers, and Eric, *and* Phil Butler—they all insisted."

"They ordered these men here?"

"Yes, sir, ordered them with you as escort."

"I gave you a different order, Margaret. And I want it obeyed."

". . . Sam, I agree with them."

He reined Difficult past her. "You men get back to camp."

The young lieutenant of Light Cavalry saluted him. "Sir, wish we could, but we've been promised hanging if we don't travel with you." The lieutenant, Pedro Darry, was wearing a marten cloak as costly as a farm. Son of one of the richest merchants in North Map-Mexico, handsome and spoiled, he'd ornamented the Emperor's court in Mexico City while serving as a factor for his father, before destroying two marriages and running one of the husbands through in a duel.

"I see, promised hanging. . . . Then go back and *be* hanged, Lieutenant. And take these other men with you."

"Please, sir—if we *swear* to be presentable?" Red-haired, green-eyed, and slender, with a pale and elegant face, Darry smiled winningly while managing a restless gray racer.

"No," Sam said. The lieutenant, sent back north in disgrace, had managed to fight three more duels in the last four years—while on leave, so permitted though not approved of—and had killed all three men, Pedro being not only a spoiled son of a bitch, but an accomplished swordsman. . . . And, to do him justice, one of Ned Flores' favorite troop commanders.

"Sir, if we swear word-of-*honor?* Otherwise, well . . . I'll have to resign my commission, and these men desert, so we can follow after you."

"Might be useful, sir." Margaret, behind Sam—and meaning, of course, Darry's skills at court as well as with the sword. His looks . . . his manner. Not the sort of young man to be considered a back-country barbarian—as another young North Mexican surely would be, ruler or not.

And it was possible that the three sergeants—professionally expressionless, and sitting their saddles at attention—though *not* presentable, and obviously chosen for ferocity, might also prove useful as visible reminders of the army they represented. . . . Sam knew David Mays, a silent, squatly massive Heavy Infantryman with a face like a fighting dog's, a man avoided even by those considered dangerous themselves. Sam knew him, *and* Sergeant Henry Burke, a tall, lank, hunch-shouldered Heavy Cavalryman. Burke was known for his savage temper—and the ability, on a sufficient bet, to bend his knees, reach both arms under a horse's belly, and lift the animal slightly off the ground . . . holding it there for a count of five.

Sam didn't recognize the third sergeant—a Light Infantryman, lean and boyish, so pale a blond his hair looked white, his eyes a very light gray. He carried a longbow on his back, a short-sword on his belt.

"Name?"

"Wilkey, sir. Company of Scouts."

He smiled at Sam, seemed perfectly relaxed and at ease, containing none of the fury the other two sergeants carried locked within them—and for that reason, was perhaps the most dangerous of the three.

Sam looked past him. "—And you?"

The fat man saluted badly, with a flourish. "Ansel Carey, milord. Cook, hostler, rough-medic, and . . . what you will."

'What you will' Sam supposed, included any necessary murders, though the man wore no weapons. . . . Phil, Eric, and the others must have enjoyed choosing these guards and companions. A dandy and duelist, three dangerous sergeants, and a servant with certain skills. And, of course, Margaret Mosten. On consideration, a useful party . . . though *not* perfectly presentable.

"Darry . . ."

"Sir?"

"If you cause any trouble in the Kingdom—any problems with women, any embarrassment at all—you will wish to Lady Weather you hadn't."

"Understood, sir."

"And the same for you men! If trouble comes, it had better come *to* you, not *from* you."

"Sir."

"Sir."

"Sir."

"Master Carey?"

"Hear an' obey, milord."

" 'Sir' will do." Sam hauled Difficult's head around, and spurred the charger down the road and into its customary punishing trot. Four days, at least, to the Gulf Entire, with a boat pigeoned to wait for them. Then, a two-day crossing to the mouth of Kingdom River . . . and what welcome the Kingdom chose.

* * *

It was odd to ride where no mountains rose in the distance . . . oddly calming, dreamlike, as if riding might continue forever.

Howell turned in his saddle, as he'd done before, to confirm that more than four thousand cavalry rode behind him, raising no dust on the prairie's frozen grass and ground. Carlo Petersen at the front of First Brigade, with his trumpeter and the banner-bearer—the great flag restless in the breeze, its black scorpion threatening on a field of gold . . . though scorpions were deep-south creatures. The only scorpion Howell'd seen had been in a glass bottle, looking furious.

Petersen, then the banner, then three brigades coming after, side by side in long, long columns of ten—regiments broken into squadrons, then troops, then companies. Light horse, Heavies, and militia troops as well. The horse-archer companies deployed Warm-time miles east and west. And deployed the same distance behind them.

But ahead, only two scouts rode, nearly out of sight in high, frost-killed grass, and out of sight completely when they rode down the other sides of long soft swells of land.

Howell would have preferred no scouts before him, nothing but distance with no stopping place, no purpose but going.

After almost four days over the border, guided by an iron-needle compass and two ancient Warm-time copy-maps—an Exxon (mysterious word) and half a BP (mysterious initials)—they were fifteen, perhaps twenty miles south of Fort Stockton. He could, of course, choose to ride wide around it, lead on north and north to the Wall. Perhaps ride up onto the ice itself—there must be canyons, melt-slopes that horses could manage. Then all four thousand and more might ride over endless ice to the turning tip of the world, until they slowed . . . and slowed . . . and the horses froze, the riders were frozen fast in their saddles. An army of steel and ice—shining in sunlight or coated in blizzard white—that could not harm or be harmed, could not lose or win.

In nearly four days riding north in absolute command, a command that might end with the destruction of all the army's cavalry, Howell had begun to learn the lessons he'd seen traced on Sam Monroe's face. Sadness, and necessity. All these people following behind the banner, behind Howell Voss—sole commander, and responsible.

It took much of the pleasure out of war. Not, of course, all the pleasure.

He heard grass-muffled hoofbeats coming up behind him. A cuirassier drew up on his right, hard-reining a big bay. "From Colonel Petersen, sir."

Howell recognized the man, but couldn't remember his name—then did. "You're one of the Jays—Terrence."

"Yes, sir." The corporal pleased as a child to be recognized. How was it possible not to take advantage of the innocence of soldiers?

Jay wrestled his bay to keep it close. "Sir, the colonel suggests holding the column here. Cold camp."

"Cold camp, yes, Corporal—but not here. Tell Colonel Petersen"—as new a colonel as Howell was a general—"tell him I've changed my mind, decided to move closer. Tell him I want to be able to take the Kipchaks in darkness, a glass before dawn. They're horse archers; no need to give them good shooting-light."

Corporal Jay hesitated, digesting his message. "In the dark before dawn. Yes, sir."

As he started to rein away, Howell said, "And be easy with your mount, Trooper. Later, you'll want all the go he's got."

"Yes, sir." The corporal, carefully slack-reined, cantered away back to the Heavy's column, and Howell noticed some chaff rising where the big horse went. *I want a light snow—very light, but enough to weight this dead grass.* A prayer, he supposed, but asked of what Great? Lord Jesus?—still, the shepherds thought, hanging spiked to a piñon pine somewhere in North Map-Mexico's mountains. The shepherds, and the bandits there, thought he might be found someday and rescued, taken down and brought to Portia-doctor for healing. . . . In the

Sierra, they used to think Catania-doctor could certainly heal Mountain Jesus when he was found—and the man or woman who found him made Ice-melter in reward, and ruler of a new-warmed world.

No use now, though, for a new-made general—come north into enemy country—to pray to Lord Jesus, fastened in early Warm-times to his piñon and left there asking why, and saying, 'Please not.'

Portia . . . Portia. If we were together now, and some savage stuck a blade point in my only eye—or a piece of this dry chaff was blown into it—you would have a blind oaf stumbling after you, mumbling love, and asking where his cup might be, since there was still some chocolate in it. A burden added to a thousand others wearing you away.

Sam might have earned you, might be sufficient. No one else.

. . . What Great, then, to send us a very light snow? Lady Weather? The Kipchaks' Blue Sky brought snow or clearing, but undependably. Some savages worshiped one of the old All-makers, a Great too busy doing—and often doing badly—to listen to any prayer. And the white-skin tribesmen up by the ice-wall, their red-skin shamans and chiefs, called to the Rain-bird for weather they wanted, which seemed to make as much sense as any.

Howell closed his eye as he rode, picturing the Rain-bird in his mind. He saw it flying. Not big as a mountain—only large as a small lake, green and blue as that same lake in Daughter Summer. Its wings rising and falling, all wind and breezes blown from those wings. . . .

They camped at sunset. Cold camp. But though there'd been no snow, neither had Kipchak horsemen—though four had been met—escaped to warn Map–Fort Stockton.

Howell walked the high-grass swales in failing light, his boots crunching, breaking dead stems. He chewed mutton jerky and talked with the troopers—all of them cheery, all apparently pleased to be in the Khan's country, and readying for battle. . . . Howell joked with them, especially with the women—the lean Lights in their fine mail and leather, smiling, girlish, some sharpening their curved sabers with spit-stones, and the fewer bulky older women serving in the Heavies, ponderous in cuirass, with long, scabbarded straight sabers, and helmets hinged with neck and face guards. The perfect images of war, but for cooing altos as they groomed their big horses.

Howell chewed the last of the jerky as he walked the lines. He found Carlo Petersen sitting in deep grass, playing checkers with his captain, Feldman.

"Not for money, sir," Petersen said, as he and the captain stood. In the army, only equal ranks could play for money, horses, or land. All could play for sheep.

"Who do you have out, Carlo?"

"Same as the march screen, sir. But rested."

"Send riders to them. Remind them they're to avoid the enemy tonight, as before, but kill any they can't avoid or take prisoner. *No* Kipchak is to ride out from Fort Stockton, then back to it."

"Still retire before force, though?"

"Yes, still retire before company strength or more. Send a galloper, and fall back on us."

"Yes, sir. Billy, see to it."

"Yes, sir," the captain said, saluted, and trotted away, acorn helmet under his arm, mail hauberk jingling.

"We hit them in the morning, dark, and no trumpets?"

"Yes. I know, Carlo, that there'll be some confusion, even going in brigades-in-line. But the Kipchaks will be even more confused. I don't want whatever garrison is there, to have the chance to hold fortifications or buildings against us. I want them surprised and scattered. . . . I'll be with Second Brigade. Make certain, *certain* that your officers know to keep contact with our people to their right and left—no gaps, darkness or not."

"Not easy."

Howell said nothing, and Petersen grinned. "Okay, I'll re-mind 'em.—Do we take prisoners? Major Clay supposed not."

"We'll take no fighters prisoner, Carlo, but if your troopers catch a coward—or wise man—running, then that's a Kipchak I'd like to speak with. And remember, by Sam's order, women and children are *not* to be harmed in any way."

"Yes, sir. And you'll be with the Second."

"Right. First Brigade's yours, Carlo. I'll be trying to hold Reese back."

Petersen laughed. Willard Reese was more than forty years old—a moody man, cautious as an infantryman before he was engaged, then almost insanely aggressive. Fighting, the man foamed at the mouth.

Howell returned Petersen's salute—Sam was right, the sa-luting had certainly set in—and walked on in the last of sunset light. The western horizon was colored rich as a deep-south orange, though the air was weighty with Lord Winter's early cold.

He kicked through dead grass, wishing Ned were command-ing at least the First Brigade's Light Cavalry. Not that Carlo Petersen wasn't a fine officer, and a driver. Only he lacked that instinct (wonderful Warm-time word) that told an officer—not that something had gone wrong—but that something was *about* to go wrong.

Ned had that—or used to, before This'll Do. And Sheba Tate, Third Brigade, had it. No need, this evening, to find Major Tate on the right flank, advise her. . . .

A group of horse archers called to Howell as he walked past. "There he is—a general!" they called, and laughed, delighted as he gave them the so-ancient finger. A tribal sign, but one all people seemed to know.

Valuable men . . . and only men, those troopers. No women could draw longbows on horseback, the six-foot bows looking so odd and awkward with their long upper arms and short, deep-curved lowers. Valuable men, who could outshoot even the Khan's cavalry—once they'd spent a young lifetime learning to work their longbows at a gallop—shooting fast to either side or to the back, over the horses' cruppers. If he had more of them, if they didn't take years to train . . . If Ned had had more than two files of archers with him in the south, they might at least have covered his retreat.

Howell found a place as night came down, thick frost-killed grass in a fold between slight rises, with no tethered horses, no murmuring soldiers.

It was cold and growing colder, Lord Winter strolling down from the Wall. . . . It was supposed to be hot in summer, deep south in the Empire—hot enough in those weeks to burn and kill a man lost under the sun. Probably true, considering the Warm-time vegetables they grew with no warming beds, no flat-glass frames . . . but still difficult to imagine.

Howell decided to sleep for only three sand-glass hours. He'd wake then, though no one tapped his shoulder. The little librarian, Neckless Peter, claimed these hours were not quite the old Warm-time hours. Perhaps . . . perhaps not, though twelve of them still made a day, though a dark day in winter. What did the poem say? *Winter, that turns in snow like a tiger.*

Howell spread his wool cloak on brittle grass. . . . Phil had seen one of those snow tigers. 'Big as a pony,' he'd said, 'all yellow and black so he looked on fire.' A tiger in the reed brakes along the Bravo, likely come down hunting wild spotted cattle. Something to see.

Howell unbuckled his scabbarded long-sword, drew it, then lay down with the blade beside him and gathered the cloak around them both. A one-eyed soldier, and his cold, slender, sharp-tongued wife.

* * *

Sam had seen the Gulf many times before—had seen the wide Pacific Sea as well—but never lost his wonder at such lovely water, that seemed to beg traveling over. Lovely even now, gray, rough, hummed across by an icy wind. . . . As a boy, he'd dreamed of sailing in a fishing schooner across the Pacific, sailing to islands with sweet Warm-time names . . . sailing on and on, living his life over water. Coming to his death there, finally.

His Second-mother, Catania, had told him of the great wind-sailors of Warm-times, that she'd read of in *Or the White Whale*. And the great machine-engine sailors, later. The *Queen Elizabeth* . . . the *Harry Truman*.

Perhaps from those stories, from that imagining, great water had always been a pleasure to him, though he'd never been out for more than a few sand-glasses in small boats. . . . It had occurred to him, the last few years, that small coastal navies—east on the Gulf and west on the ocean—might be a means to secure North Map-Mexico's water rights. Might be a means to transport troops north and south as well.

Not a subject to bring up at Queen Joan's court. But a temptation. The Kipchaks had conquered a long western coast—a coast vulnerable to attacks by sea. Horsemen who'd come by riding across from Map-Siberia to the Alaskan ice, the Kipchaks used curses and charms to protect themselves from open water, running water. Thought them full of devils.

No question that navies, even small navies, were a temptation. . . . What if he mentioned to merchants, to fishermen at Carboneras—and across the country at La Paz—that some ship-won plunder might become legal plunder? That flags of Warm-time piracy might become flags of profit if taken from the Kipchaks' coast of Map-California in the west . . . if taken from the Empire's coast, south, along the Gulf. With, of course, government paid its share and fee for licensing such ventures, shares that might lesson reliance on taxes raised by reluctant governers.

It was a notion. . . .

"Dust," Margaret said.

Young Sergeant Wilkey called, *"Dust."*

A troop of welcome was riding out of Carboneras. Fifteen, twenty people, their mounts raising dry-sand dust, even in the cold. Sam knew who, without seeing them. The mayor. Town councillors. District militia commander—that would be Ed Pell, very competent, a harsh disciplinarian who had, perhaps, too many close relatives serving in the militia companies. The local garrison commander would be Major Allen Chavez, an older man who didn't care much for Ed Pell.

Pigeons, of course, had had to come so a boat would be held for them. But pigeons would have flown in any case. It had proven a great annoyance that pigeons flew to warn of his coming on every occasion, no matter what he ordered to the contrary. An annoyance to set beside many others.

"It'll be the mayor," Margaret said. "Mark Danilo. And local city people, couple of their wives. Ed Pell will be with them; his cousins, too. And Major Allen Chavez and his officers. Trooper escort."

"Right," Sam said. "Let's ride to meet them and get this over with, then down to the docks. I want to be on the water well before evening."

"Boat's the *Cormorant*," Margaret said.

. . . It took a while to reach the *Cormorant*, though Sam—by refusing to rein in—forced his welcome to be one of conversation moving at the trot. They rode past people lining narrow streets of low adobe houses . . . past occasional taller mansions of red and yellow brick, where men, women, and little children stood by wrought-iron gates, calling out, applauding in the old style. Pigeons had certainly flown—and as certainly flown to New Orleans as well, then up Kingdom River to its ruler's island.

A crowd, and more applause, at El Centro. A priest of Edgewater Jesus stood off to the side, watching with two of the Weather's ladies.

Sam reined Difficult slowly through the people to them, swung down from the saddle, bowed, then took their hands in turn and bowed again. Great applause, and a smile on the oldest Weatherlady's pale, crumpled face, framed in her purple hood. . . . Purple, Sam supposed, for storm clouds. It hadn't occurred to him before.

Remounted, he moved steadily along. Flowers sailed through the air, little red summer flowers from some magnate's glass-windowed garden. The expense that must be. . . .

What was that wonderful line from a poem or acted-play?— translated from the Beautiful Language in one of the Empire's copybooks, though it had seemed perfectly at home in book-English: *'Is it not passing brave to be a king, and ride in triumph through Persepolis?'*

Passing brave—as long as there were flowers thrown, not stones, not crossbow quarrels. And those, important flowers in this province, little messengers that no hard feelings remained over the dead at This'll Do.

Once out of the market square, Ed Pell wished to speak privately. Margaret, not Sam, regretted there wasn't time—reducing Pell slightly, as intended, and pleasing Major Chavez and his officers, also as intended.

. . . The caravan of welcome turned away at last by the dock gates, Sam and the others rode out on echoing tarred planking over shallow gray Gulf-water flecked with small shards of floating ice. A beamy fishing schooner lay waiting one dock-finger over, and they dismounted and led their horses to it.

A large two-masted boat, painted a near-midnight color, the

Cormorant's name was painted along its bow, the last letter becoming a black eye over a black beak. As they led their horses to the ramp, a gull, silver-white with dark wing tips, sailed by and shit neatly as it went.

An elderly man with a large nose and red woolen cap appeared above them at the rail, turned his head, and called hoarsely, "Cap—it's the big cheese!"

"You watch your fucking mouth!" Margaret called up to him, and the old sailor smiled down, toothless, and blew her a kiss.

14

The Lily Chamber of Large Audience was a single great room—
a room and a wooden building, all of itself. The chamber, quite
lovely, was painted in lily colors of white and gold, and had a
wide hearth on each of its four sides. The huge logs that burned
beneath those brick chimneys had been wheeled and dragged
five hundred Warm-time miles from the mountains of Map-
Arizona. And still, it seemed to Toghrul Khan, gave less heat
in commencing winter than the fat little metal stove in any
yurt.

The room was cold enough to keep cut meat sound . . . but
the four fires did give warmth to the chamber's painted ivories
and golds, and so an impression of comfort.

The odors of much of the audience—sweat, smeared sheep
fat, and mare's-milk fartings—made an unpleasant counter-
point.

The audience subject for today—traditionally a Please-and-
Thank-You, with wishes that Blue Sky turn trouble away—was
not, however, lightning, grazing land, floodwater, or sheep scra-
pie, the tribesmen's traditional concerns. The subject today was
salary . . . payment . . . wages.

There had been, over the past few years, more and more
interest by the fighting men in money—as opposed to gifts of
flocks, horse herds, honors. Razumov had noticed it early, and
warned it would increase. "A penalty of civilization, lord, and
reward of conquest. The old ways now being *seen* as 'old
ways.' "

Sadly true—and having to be dealt with by such audiences
as this, in which little bags of silver coin, minted in Map-
Oakland, were handed out to officers whose only interest should
be in service to their lord. There was no question how the old

Khan, his father, would have dealt with these more and more frequent requests for currency. He would have picked an officer past his prime, and ordered silver spikes driven into his skull, as a lesson on the perils of greed.

It was in the midst of distribution—a rank of rewarded men bowing over their clutched little bags of metal before him, while he smiled and smiled (the watching crowd hissing in approval)— that Toghrul became aware of a disturbance at the doors.

Two men had pushed in past the guards, then immediately had fallen to their hands and knees and begun the long crawl down the center aisle toward his cushioned dais. An excess of debasement, and a very bad sign.

The rank of officers glanced behind them at the crawlers, bowed once more, and got out of the way.

No more hissing approvals. Only silence.

Toghrul waited while the two fools came toward him, baby fashion, crawling more slowly the closer they came. Watching them, copybook Achilles-and-the-Tortoise occurred to him.

He waited, then beckoned them on to finally rest before him, still on hands and knees. They'd come dirty from long riding. He knew one—a minor officer of supply, with Ikbal Crusan's tuman. The other was just a soldier.

"Great, *Great* Lord—" The officer of supply.

Serious trouble, if it required two 'greats' as introduction. Toghrul sat silent. His father would have approved.

"Map–Fort Stockton . . . O Khan, live forever." The sweating officer was Kipchak, the steppe still in his face.

Toghrul waited.

"The . . . the North Map-Mexicans have come up and destroyed it, lord!"

Ah, a fact at last, though likely faulty. Murmurs in the Lily Chamber.

"And with what forces did they accomplish this?"

More groveling. Both men had their faces on the carpet. "It seemed . . . three or four thousand riders, lord. Heavy and Light. They came from southeast, in the dark before morning."

Listening, a flush—an absolute flush of pleasure, of amusement—rose in Toghrul so he couldn't help smiling, then chuckling at such a surprise, a blow struck as clever as one of his own! An interesting event, and at *last* an interesting enemy. The joys of complications arising . . .

"So, I'm to understand that this Captain-General, this Small-Sam Monroe, seeing us striking to the south—west of the border Bend—has taken the opportunity to strike north at *us* from east of it!"

Silence from the grovelers . . . well, a little nod from the officer. A nod into the carpet.

"And the place is destroyed?"

"Yes, lord." The Nodder. "Burned and destroyed and all the men killed."

"Only the men?"

"I believe only the men, lord—the seven or eight hundred left behind as guards, herdsmen, and storekeepers." A pause. "I believe the women and children were spared."

"You believe, or you saw?"

"I saw . . . a little."

"And you—soldier—what did you see?"

But the soldier seemed to have seen nothing, and only burrowed into the carpet, his ass in the air.

"The horses?"

The Nodder murmured, "Gone, lord."

"Almost two thousand—four herds of fine horses *gone*, taken? Driven away?"

A nod. There were strands of drool on the carpet.

"But you weren't killed . . . and you were mounted?"

A nod, but a reluctant nod.

"Why then didn't you send . . . this one . . . with the report? Why not, yourself, have followed those clever thieves, made certain of their route of retreat? Then you might have become a wind ghost, cut throats in the night to unsettle them, and so secured at least a little of my honor."

"I . . . lord, I didn't think."

"You didn't? Your head was at fault for not thinking?"

Barely a nod.

"Well then, your head's proved of little use to you. You'll do much better without it." Toghrul lifted his right hand, made a little spilling motion—and four guardsmen, two from each side of the dais, jumped down on the Nodder like swineherds on a shoat, and bound his hands behind him. They lifted him up, and trotted away with him down the chamber's aisle while the officers, chiefs, and important men of audience fell aside as if the pops were carried there in rot and puss and buboes. The Nodder made no sound, going, seemed almost asleep with terror.

The soldier remained silent on the carpet.

"*Soldier . . .*" Toghrul waited patiently until a grimy, teary face rose from warp-and-weft. "Soldier, your Khan would never punish a man for obeying his officer's orders, even if the officer has proved a fool and coward. Go then, and report to the commander of the camp for rest, rations, and honorable assignment."

The teary face, astonished, then turned to a lover's, looked up rich with affection and gratitude. There was a subdued murmur of approval at such generous and lordly justice.

The soldier, turning, began to crawl aside, but Toghrul smiled, gestured him up onto his feet, and waved him away into the rest of his life.

There was an odor of urine; the carpet would have to be cleaned.

* * *

There was no denying blood.

Thought on a throne was well enough; thought in a summer garden well enough. Thought on a cushion couch with a dear wife by one's side, also well enough.—But none the equal, for a Kipchak, of horseback consideration. Consideration, this sunny, clear, and cold afternoon, of the morning's information: the surprising counterstroke from North Map-Mexico. A counterstroke absolutely Monroe's in conception, though Razumov's people—and an after-the-fact pigeon from the Boston creatures in Map-McAllen—suggested the immediate commander was Colonel (now General) Voss, apparently a very competent officer. Banjar player, also, according to Old Peter's farewell report. Monroe, it seemed, had gone to Middle Kingdom.

Toghrul whipped his stallion's withers, lifting Lively to a lope out into Texas prairie endless as an ocean. A frozen ocean now, brown and yellow with frost-burned grass. He rode as if he flew as New Englanders sometimes flew, and smiled again at what Monroe had managed. Very much—oh, *very* much what he might have done himself. An enemy, a thief, puts his head into a yurt's entrance, intending mischief. What better response, what more humorous response, than to wriggle under the yurt's fabric at the back, circle round, and kick the fellow in the ass?

So, the Captain-General apparently possessed imagination, and certainly a sense of humor. He also now possessed two thousand fine horses, which would remount his cavalry handsomely, *and* likely help pay the expenses of the expedition.

Well done, and more than worth killing him for. Worth killing Voss and many of his people, too, for laughing, as they must be, at a Khan's discomfiture. But how sad that the only interesting person in the West must be done away with. . . .

Toghrul reined Lively to the left to avoid a deep runoff ditch half-hidden in the grass. A trace of short summer's melt.

. . . And of course, the North Mexicans would not go into Blue Sky alone. There were others, a troublesome few of a ruler's own, that in time must join them. Manu Ek-Tam, that so-brilliant young officer. And two or three of his dear friends. All brilliant young officers, perfect at everything but keeping silent. Was there any spy or agent so effective as kumiss in revealing disloyalty, arrogant ambition? Disrespect?

So, the treacherous cut their throats with their own tongues. And the Uighur tuman, of course. Foolish, grumbling tribesmen, needing to be worn away by enemy lances—as, in the past, the Cuman and Kirghiz had been. So, an army of many differences, many purposes, was shaped and whittled into an army with one purpose only. Obedience.

But was any great man ever brought down except by those closest to him? The generals, the ministers, the great of Caravanserai with their velvet tents, musicians, women, and fuck boys—it had been many months since one of these was peeled and stuck on a stake.—Now see the result of forbearance. Murmurs, judgments made, requirements of the *Khan's wife* that she produce a boy.

Expectations impudent in themselves.

The sheriff of the camps was just such an impertinent man. Who, after all, would miss him? Who miss the lesson he presented, perched screeching on a stake?

All so tedious. Was it impossible men could be ruled by reason? Old copybooks claimed, improbably, it had been done—by which they certainly meant not by reason at all, but greed, and its parceled fulfillments. . . .

Sul Niluk, a Guardsman galloping a hundred Warm-time yards away, whistled and pointed. Toghrul saw movement ahead at the side of a slight rise, a stirring through the grasses' tall ruined stems.

Jack the rabbit. And up and away he bounded, already mottling snowy into his winter coat. Toghrul, spurring from a canter to the gallop, lifted his left arm so his hawk's jesses jingled.

Reaching over, he tugged the bird's yellow velvet hood away and launched him into the air.

The prairie hawk spiraled high, saw the rabbit going, and slid after it as if the air were ice. Toghrul pulled Lively in to watch.

Jack the rabbit jinked swiftly here and there, going away. Not even wings could carve those sudden angles after him, and the hawk didn't attempt it. It flew, it sailed straight to a place just past the runner—suddenly stooped, and struck as Jack came fleeing to it, sure as if there'd been an appointment.

The rabbit screamed—Toghrul had heard two children screaming just so at Map-Sacramento, when his father took it. He'd been no older than the children, but much safer, sitting on his pony in the midst of the Guard. The children had been put into fires, held there with spears while they blistered and shrieked, burning. The old Khan hadn't been cruel, only very practical, and people frightened by frightful things were easier to manage. A *sort* of applied reason, after all.

Sul Niluk rode on to bend from the saddle and lift the hawk hissing from its prey, a tuft of fur already bleeding in its beak. Sul bent down again, picked up the rabbit as well, tucked it in his saddle-bag, then rode back to bring Toghrul his hawk.

. . . And by winter's end, with the campaign against Middle Kingdom completed, then, in just such a way as the hawk's— as Monroe defended his border with quick and clever little strokes and dodges—in just such a way the tumans would sail over the grasslands to meet him where, sooner or later, he was certain to go.

When that was accomplished, of course, the world would become a little less interesting.

* * *

Well-balanced, her laced, low boots as firmly planted as flooring brushed with oil allowed, Martha grunted with the apparent effort of an ax-swing that was not. Master Butter accepted it for fact, raised a swift sword-parry against it—and was, by surprise, backstroked across the face with her ax's heavy handle.

He staggered away, calling, "Wonderful!" in a goose's honk, since she'd broken his nose.

Martha came after him fast, mimed a finishing stroke across his belly, then set her ax aside, said, "Oh, poor Sir," and went to him with her yellow handkerchief to stop the bleeding.

Master Butter set his sword into the rack, pinched and tugged at the bridge of his snub nose to painfully straighten it, and said, "Owww!" Then he took her handkerchief and held it to his nostrils. "No one has had as much blood out of me in months—and that was a West-bank captain quick as a cat."

"I'm sorry."

"You *would* be sorry, if you hadn't so correctly followed to kill me. Never, never let an opponent recover, whether in duel or war. If someone is worth fighting with fist and foot, they're worth kicking unconscious. If they're worth fighting with sharp steel, they're worth killing. *Always* fight to finish."

"Yes, sir."

"I think now 'Butter-boy' will do. It was a hurtful nickname—you know those Warm-time words, 'nick-name'?"

"Yes."

"Sit down . . . sit on the bench; I'll get some vodka. Practice is over today; I'm bleeding like a pig." The handkerchief to his nose, he went to the table, picked up a blue-glazed bottle, pulled its stopper, took several long swallows, then brought it back and sat beside her. "I have no cups; I apologize. . . . Well, I took the nick-name they'd used to hurt me, and made it my True-name. *Master Butter-boy*. One deals with insults as one deals with any opponent who possesses a long and punishing reach. You close as soon as possible, grapple him to you—then use the knife." He took another long drink from his blue bottle, then offered it to her.

"No, thank you. Is your nose alright?"

"It'll be alright, Martha. A good lesson, though, for both of us. Should only the mildest corrective injury be required, the nose is as good a thing to strike as any other. In a more serious case, involving weapons, you will keep in mind that a person struck hard on the nose is blinded for an instant"

" 'Blinded for an instant . . .' "

"Yes." Master Butter took another swallow. "After which, of course, more will have to be done. *Never* strike a first blow without having prepared a second. Each stroke, each slash, is an introduction for the next . . . and I am ruining your handkerchief."

"It will wash."

"I hope it will." Master Butter sighed, then took the cloth away and examined it. "And how do you go on in court, Martha?"

"Oh . . . I mind my own business."

"Well, that may do for a year or so, but not forever. You're with the Queen day and night; that's too close for some lords' comfort . . . some generals' comfort, too. And what makes great men—and women—uncomfortable, is sooner or later set aside."

"The Queen will keep me safe," Martha said, "as I will keep her safe, for certain."

" 'For certain.' " Master Butter threw his head back and laughed. "You *are* young." Then he said, "By the way, a very good time to reach over and cut someone's throat—while they're laughing."

"Yes, sir."

"For certain . . ." Master Butter sighed, and took a deep drink from his blue bottle. "Still, properly said. Our Queen is a wonder, but wonders may grow careless. You may not. *Particularly* not with this war to the west, since it has certainly occurred to the horse savages that our Queen presents an obstacle."

"I won't be careless."

"See to it. . . . So, you two deal well enough together—must, for good guarding. And the Queen's daughter?" He handed over the vodka bottle.

"I like Princess Rachel. I don't know if she likes me or not, but she's kind." Martha held the vodka bottle, but didn't drink. Her father had given her tastes of potato vodka, but she hadn't liked it.

"Sons and daughters, daughters and sons." Master Butter took his bottle back, displayed it. "Map-Louisiana work. Enamelware." He sipped, set it down on the floor beside him, then sat silent for a long while, looking at Martha, blinking slowly like a wood owl.

Martha sat, her fine new ax resting across her lap, its head's blade bright as silvered glass and sharp enough to shave down from her forearm. The head's spike, on the reverse, was a slightly curved claw, coming to a needle's point. The Queen's own Weapon-smith had made it, and engraved an ancient Warm-time saying on the side of the ax's steel. *Deadlier than the male.*

". . . My father," Master Butter said after a while, "was Lawrence, Baron Memphis, which does make me a 'sir,' by courtesy. Sir Edward. He was Memphis, but not a brute . . . would eat no talking meat." Master Butter was silent for a time, seemed distracted in liquor.

Then he said, "My brother, Terry, the present baron, loved our father and still honors his memory. My brother was *not* squatly fat, heard *no* voices, had *no* falling fits—and has no great talent for killing, either. He sends me an allowance, and, of course, as one of Island's household, I have my servant, my rooms, my place in the hall at meals. No one treats me with disrespect. Those who aren't afraid, are sorry for me. . . . I mention this, as I'm considering you for a friend."

"I see. . . ."

"—Not, I hasten to add, a lover. I have whores for the one thing, and have given my Forever-love to another." He took the handkerchief away, examined blood spots on it, then pressed it against his nostrils again. "My love, comic as it must seem to those few who know of it, is for Her Majesty alone. So it has been from the moment I stood beside my father on the pier of Silver Gate, and saw her first come ashore to Island beside Newton Second-Son—the River rest His Majesty."

He blew his nose gently. "She was tall, looked like a beautiful bitch wolf, and though frightened by the noise and crowds and newness, was too brave to show it. . . . And a foolish fat boy, despised for his falling fits, saw her, lost his heart, and never got it back."

Martha sat silent beside him.

"This . . . quiet of yours, is the reason I consider you for friendship, Martha. Knowing that a friend would never repeat what I've just told you for commons' casual amusement. Very few at court would dare laugh to my face—but many when my back is turned."

"I won't tell anyone."

"Thank you. . . . And that was very nice work with the ax. Most forget an ax has a heavy handle, and see only the blade and spike—as I did, to my shame. That stroke was *very* nice, and followed quite properly by the belly cut."

"But your poor nose . . ."

"Yes. You've made a friend of me—but an enemy of my nose." Master Butter laughed a goose's honk. "My dear, I think the Queen chose better than she knew."

15

Sam had occasionally seen Kingdom warships at a distance, rigged for the Gulf's summer wet and ponderously tacking off-shore, great white seashells of sail taut with wind—or their ranks of oars out, flashing yellow in sunlight. Banners streaming from their masts.

And in winter, once, riding high along the coast with a file of troopers, he had heard a great hissing, like some monstrous southern snake's—and seen one of the Kingdom's great ships, driven before the wind, skating the Gulf's ice on huge, bright steel runners.

But to have seen at a distance was not the same as seeing close when the *Cormorant*, intercepted under a storm-darkened sky by a Kingdom cutter at the river's mouth, was held rocking in the tide while a warship came drum-thundering, oar-thrashing down upon them.

"Nailed *Jesus*," Margaret said, as it came.

After a shouted interchange over gusting breezes, they were invited to board by clambering up the great ship's side on a dripping rope ladder, as it heaved and rolled in the delta's swell. The ship's name was worked in bronze at its bow: QS *Naughty*.

Their packs and baggage followed them, knotted to slender ropes—'whips,' by the orders given—and drawn up to the ship's deck by silent sailors, working barefoot in the bitter wind. Heavier tackle was rigged, cable and belly bands, to haul the kicking horses up one by one to the warship's deck, then to be chivied into a large shelter of heavy canvas and taut-stretched cord, made in moments.

"Your people, sir, to remain on this section of deck—and wander nowhere else." A pleasant officer in Middle Kingdom's naval-gray cloak, jacket, and trousers—and young, a boy no more than fourteen or so, his dark hair cropped short. A blue dot tattooed on each cheek, a heavy curved knife at his belt, he swayed to the ship's motion as Sam and his North Mexicans staggered.

"My men," Sam said, "and Master Carey, will stay where you put them, with our packs and gear. They're to receive refreshment. My officers come with me."

"Sir, the captain's orders—"

"Belay those orders, Fitz." A very small man strolled down the deck, stepping without looking over fixtures, lashings, and coiled lines. This man—with hard black eyes, a weather-creased face tattooed with three dots on one cheek, four on the other— wore frosted silver moons on his gray cloak's shoulder straps.

"Captain." The boy officer saluted himself away.

"Milord." The small captain bowed to Sam, raised his voice against the wind. "Ralph Owen. I have the honor to command this Queen's ship. You are welcome aboard—and your officers, of course, stay with you."

Sam saw the man's surprise, noticing Margaret Mosten. "A lady . . ."

"It's our custom." Sam smiled. "Captain Mosten has commanded light infantry in several battles. Presently, she acts as my aide and executive."

"Ah . . ."

"And I'll introduce Lieutenant Pedro Darry."

Pedro stepped forward, snapped to attention. "Captain Owen. A pleasure, sir."

"Darry . . . *Darry*," the captain said, ushering Sam and the others down the deck. "I believe I know the name."

"My father, Elmer, has been to Island twice, I think, sir. On business."

"Oh, *yes*," the captain said. "Heard him spoken of."

"Admiral Reynolds had become a friend, I believe, sir. And an associate in developing larger milling saws."

"Planks." Captain Owen nodded, moving them along.

"Planks and sawn members; that's it. The admiral mentioned that to my brother some time ago."

Margaret, stepping around a large metal obstruction left on the deck for some naval reason, raised an eyebrow at Sam as they went, at Pedro's already proving useful.

The captain's cabin, arrived at through odors of sawn wood, paint, damp canvas, and old sweat, was reached by a dim, narrow passage, then up a steep and even narrower stair. Its door was guarded by a large soldier—a marine, Sam supposed—in hoop armor enameled half-green, half-blue, from helmet to hip. The marine struck the butt of a pole-ax on the deck, then stepped aside.

Ushered in by the captain—out of shadow into light—Sam saw a room painted all white, fine as those described in Warm-time copybooks of sea travel, sea fighting. Spacious enough, though low overhead under massive beams, with crossed short-bladed sabers and two painted pictures on its side walls—one of a fleet of ships on winter ice, the other a yellow boat in stormy waters. The room was furnished with a woven blue carpet, a wide wood cabinet on the wall across, and round-back chairs at a polished fir-wood table bolted to the deck.

There were six large, wonderfully clear pane-glass windows across the cabin's back wall. Against two of them, big wooden machines, fitted with heavy windlasses and long steel bows set horizontal, were drawn up and fastened to thick ring-bolts with heavy rope and tackle.

Past these, Sam saw the river through the window glass; its current, surface roughened by the wind, streaked dark and silver in cloud-shadowed light.

The cabin was a chamber fine enough—as the warship was massive and complex—to put a provincial in his place. Sam had a moment's admiration for the Khan, for the perfect confidence necessary to assault this Kingdom.

The small captain waited while an elderly sailor in gray shirt and gray trousers—come silent through some trap or door—took the visitors' unbuckled long-swords, sabers, and rapiers, and then the cloaks to hang beside them on pegs along the near wall. "Please . . ." Owen gestured to his beautiful table, and when they were seated, took a chair across from them.

Seated, Sam thought, just in time, as the ship suddenly rolled steeply to the right . . . then seemed to swing half-around, timbers groaning as they took the strain.

"I can offer you berry juice," the captain said, "imperial coffee, or imperial chocolate. No vodka or barley whisk, I'm sorry to say. Queen's ships carry no liquors."

"Juice would be appreciated," Sam said. "And my men?"

"Are being attended to, milord."

" 'Sir' will do, Captain. I don't require 'milord'ing."

"As you wish . . . sir." Captain Owen smiled, and sat silent while the old sailor padded in through what seemed a pantry door with four silver mugs on a fine brass tray. He set the tray on the table, and handed the mugs round. To Sam first, then—with only momentary hesitation—to Margaret, then Darry, and his captain last.

Sam had heard that sailors toasted sitting, so he stayed put and only raised his mug. "To the Queen."

"To the Queen."

"The Queen."

The juice was blackberry. Sam had tasted it before, but never served hot as coffee. ". . . Wonderfully good."

"You'll be my guests at supper, of course. We'll have a two-day run up to Island, milord—"

" 'Sir.' " Sam smiled.

"Sir. Two days up to Island. The Fleet had been noticed, some time ago, of the *possibility* of your coming, though not how or when."

"Events determined," Sam said, "as they must in your Service."

"Truer words never," the small captain said, and looked as pleasant as a narrow and ferocious face allowed. He reminded Sam of the champion Sonora jockey, Monte Williams, a bane of Charlie Ketch's betting-luck. "The ship's honored to receive you, sir, and you'll honor me by using my cabin."

"No, Captain Owen; I won't displace you on your own ship. But if other officers will be kind enough to make room for us, it would be appreciated."

". . . Of course, sir, if you prefer."

The old sailor came back from the pantry with a silver platter of what seemed to be large honey cookies.

"Do try these," the captain said. "Peter *claims* to be a baker, though some doubt it."

"An' haven't I baked goods for you since ever?" the old sailor said to him. "*An'* taught you stem from stern when your nose was still runnin'?" He set the platter firmly down, and padded out.

"There you have years of shipping together," Captain Owen said, "from when I was a boy. And in battles and Gulf hurricanes. After such a time, you see friendship has overcome discipline."

"And should in that case," Sam said, "or an officer's no officer."

They sat silent for a while, sipping steaming berry juice. . . . Sleet came lancing across the great stern windows, and as if discomfited by it, the ship seemed to swing and swing away. Sam was glad to be sitting; he had a vision of himself stumbling across the uncertain deck, perhaps vomiting, to sailors' amusement.

And having imagined that, he saw himself, Margaret, and Darry, as this veteran little captain must see them. . . . Three young people, Margaret the oldest, but still three *young* people. Soldiers—scarred, though not by passing years—and all wearing tanned-sheepskin tunics, brown woolen trousers, riding boots, and hauberks of light chain-mail.

Pedro Darry, of course, also sporting his own gold hair-clips, gold broach, and jeweled rings, leaving Sam and Margaret comparatively unadorned, though she'd insisted on a wide silver and sapphire bracelet for Sam's sword arm—an imperial piece, acquired from the duke's baggage at God-Help-Us—and a massive signet ring as well, onyx scorpion on an oval of gold.

Which decorations, of course, might only add a certain barbarous air. . . . So, three provincial soldiers sitting at the captain's table, young enough to be his children—and ignorant as children, both of sea war and the complications of Middle Kingdom. But still representing a land, a people, and a veteran army.

The captain would be making judgments, and likely others in Middle Kingdom would tend to judge the same as he. So, if a certain simplicity was bound to seem obvious to such people, then why not *be* simple—and certain. Let them grasp directness, feel its edge.

Sam set the silver mug down; it slid a little on the tabletop with the ship's motion. "I won't pretend not to be impressed, Captain. Impressed by this ship, and the Kingdom it represents. You seem a formidable Service, the more so since we have no experience of navies whatsoever. My people are mountain people—though we've learned to fight where we have to."

Captain Owen put his own drink down. "Good of you to say, sir. And from what we hear, your army fights very well on any field. . . . We also do well enough, and are going to do better, patrol the Ocean Atlantic in force—as we now patrol the Gulf and Carib Islands."

"My father," Lieutenant Darry said, "spoke of the great expense of the Fleet, Captain."

Owen nodded. "And he was right. We are expensive. Good timber, imperial cotton and manila for sails and rigging. Longleaf tempered steel for the catapults and mules."

"And of course, your people," Sam said.

"Yes, sir. The largest expense. Our rowers are serfs, but serfs must be fed, and well fed, to row a warship. Our sailors have River Freedom of course, and must be paid, as the marines are paid."

"Furs and hide," Margaret said.

"Why yes, lady—excuse me, *Captain.* Exactly; we can't winter-dress our people only in woven wool. It soaks in spray and freezes. We use sealskin cloaks when we can get them, other leathers when not, Those, usually oiled."

"So," Sam said, "without supplies from Mexico City on the one hand, and Boston on the other, your Fleet might find itself in difficulty."

Owen smiled. "That's absolutely right, sir. Of course, in that case, the Empire's coastwise traffic in the Gulf, *and* New England's coastwise traffic down Ocean Atlantic, might also find themselves in . . . difficulty."

"Still, you'd always need a year or two of supplies laid up."

"We would indeed," Captain Owen said, still smiling. "Try the cookies."

"I already have, sir," Darry said, chewing. "Damn good."

"*Smart soldier.*" A voice from behind the pantry door.

Darry hesitated a moment, thrown off stride. "Very good cookies . . . It occurs to me, Captain, that my father might be interested in providing your fleet with sheepskins. We wear them in the army—warm, light, and well greased with the animal's own fat."

"Hmm . . . But a sufficient number of those skins?"

"Captain," Sam said, "we have many more sheep than people. Your supply vessels could pick up the shipments from our Gulf coast. And, of course, that source would lessen your fleet's dependence on New England's sealskin."

Owen nodded. "That's of interest, milord—sir. I'll mention

it to my admiral. We do lose a number of sailors to frostbite, and a sailor with fingers and toes gone is no longer a sailor."

The ship suddenly heaved forward, then heaved again, so they swayed in their seats.

"What's that?" Margaret gripped the arms of her chair.

"They're rowing, Captain?"

"Yes, sir," Owen said, as the ship seemed to rise slightly and heave forward again. "We've turned upriver and upwind. This is to the beat of Lose-no-time. For the rowers' stroke speeds, there's Loiter, Keep-station, Lose-no-time, Pursuit, and Battle-and-board."

The ship surged . . . surged . . . surged. Sam seemed to feel the great effort through his bones—the rowers' strength straining at the long oars to drive forward this monument of oak and fir, of supplies, gear, and tackle, of men and steel.

"Captain, how long can they do this work?"

"Oh . . . at this beat, sir, a glass-hour and a half, before relief. At Battle-and-board, of course, a much shorter time."

"And years of service?"

"Ten years would be the usual, though there are men rowing who've been with her for . . . fifteen, sixteen years. Of course, those started young."

"Changes with Lord Winter?"

"Oh, when we rig to skate, sir, rowers are transferred to the Carib, and coasts south. No ice there."

"And if," Darry said, "or when, they break down in service, sir?"

"Well, Lieutenant . . . that depends on the original reason for assignment." The captain took a cookie. "If they're indentured serfs, they're put to lighter duty, longshore labor and so forth. That's routine for many of them in any case, when the ice comes down. But if assignment was for a criminal or treasonous matter, then, with the sentence no longer in abeyance, it's carried out."

"So," Margaret said, "a man may row your ships for fifteen years, and when he can row no longer—"

"Hanged. Burned. Whatever his original sentence. It's hard, ma'am—sorry, *Captain*—but the Fleet is a hard mistress, even for those who aren't serfs, and who don't row. And the custom does insure that those who are criminals, lean into their looms."

"And," Sam said, "in the Ocean Atlantic?"

"Ah . . . in those waters, sir, we've found oars of little use. Water's too rough, waves too high. Out there, a man must *sail* his ship." The captain finished his cookie as Sam reached to try one.

The cookie was soft, crumbling, rich with honey . . . and something else. "Spotted-cow butter, and what flower spice?"

Margaret took one and tasted. "Rosemary . . . ?"

"*Southern sunflower seed!*" From behind the pantry door. "*Ground fine!*"

Sam raised his voice. "Delicious!" And received a possibly pleased grunt in response.

"Old Peter," the captain said, "used to bake certain savages taken in fights off Island Cuba. It was the beginning of his cookery."

"Better the cookies, sir," Margaret, chewing hers.

"Yes. . . . That's becoming the general opinion. Though there are old captains who still hold to celebration roasts on long voyages. I served under one, Jerry Newland. 'Old school,' as the copybooks say. Newland's father had filed teeth. Codger came aboard once to visit . . . had a smile one remembered. Map-Louisiana family."

"It seems," Sam said, "that the ships become villages to your people, with village memories."

"Oh, that's exactly so, sir. They do become our worlds, so much that after months on the water, particularly if there's been fighting—pirates always, of course, and imperial ships from time to time, though those not *officially*—"

"We meet them much the same, Captain. Fighting, some-times very serious fighting, but not war declared. Mexico City is . . . cautious."

"Right, sir. Absolutely. And after such cruises, it does often seem the land is less *actual* than the river, gulf, or ocean, and home a poor substitute for a ship of war."

"Promotion?" Margaret said.

Owen smiled. "Ah, Captain, the fundamental military ques-tion. Promotion is as always, everywhere. Merit, to a point. Influence, to a point. And luck, above all." He took another cookie, and called out, "This *is* a good batch, Pete."

"Not speakin' to you." Muffled, from the pantry.

The captain grinned and ate his cookie.

It occurred to Sam that just this sort of man would be re-quired to found coastal fleets for North Map-Mexico. Now, having met Ralph Owen, he saw that fishermen wouldn't do. *Would* do for corsairs, certainly, but not for naval officers. That would require men like this one, persuaded somehow from the Kingdom's service or the Emperor's. . . . It was something to consider.

Captain Owen leaned back in his chair. "I doubt if Admiral Reuven would garrote me, sir, if I mentioned some news pi-geoned in to New Orleans yesterday. Not Kingdom news, after all."

"Yes?"

"I understand you sent a force up into Texas, or so the Boston people at Map-McAllen claim."

"Yes."

"You may not have heard what has been reported."

"We haven't."

"Ah. Two days ago—this only by McAllen's pigeon, of course—your people are said to have taken and burned Map–Fort Stockton."

"*Weather!*" Margaret said, and hit the tabletop with her fist.

"Took, burned . . . killed many hundreds in the garrison, and, according to the McAllen people—who, I suppose, can be trusted in this—came away driving well over a thousand of the savages' remounts."

"By the Nailed Jesus!" Darry stood up, then sat down.

"On Kingdom River, Lieutenant," Owen said, "we thank Jesus Floating. He rules here, as much as any Great can."

"Sorry, sir."

"Oh, no offense taken."

"Losses, Captain?" Sam saw Howell for a moment, trotting through the dust at *Boca Chica*, holding a bandanna to his ear.

"Apparently too few, sir, to burden a pigeon with."

"I'm in your debt, Captain, for the pleasure of that news." *Now, Howell—ride east. And ride fast.*

"Courtesy to a guest, sir."

"And news that *is* your Kingdom's news? If I may ask, how goes the fighting in Map-Missouri?"

"Oh, the little I know would only bore you, sir." Captain Owen held out the cookie platter. "Another?"

* * *

Sam woke to a change. The ship was moving differently . . . the rowers' rhythm slightly slower, as if even effort must drowse so near the morning. There was slower surging, a lower pitch to the groaning music of the ship's hull and fittings—and less of that wallowing side to side that had almost sickened him at supper.

He'd gone to bed in the first-officer's cubby—more closet than room—and somewhat stifled, had regretted the captain's cabin. Now, with the ship rolling only a little, he could still reach out from the narrow, swinging cot to touch each side wall, alternately. As he swayed one way, then the other, a hanging tin lantern sent shadows after him—its little wick burning as his night-light privilege, in a ship where any fire but the galley's was usually forbidden.

Sam lay awake for a while, then tossing aside his canvas cover—blankets apparently considered softening influences in Kingdom's Fleet—swung his legs out, managed a get-down rather than a fall-down, and staggered about the cubby, dressing. Finally, bracing himself to buckle his sword's scabbard down his back, he considered the unhandiness of long-swords in ships' close quarters.

The lamp blown out, the cubby's curtain—pulled open—brushed a heavy shoulder. Sergeant Mays, standing at ease in full armor, dagger, and *short*-sword as the ship shifted, turned his helmeted mastiff head and said, "Mornin', sir."

"Morning, Sergeant." Comforted by such formidable night-watch, Sam jostled down the swaying corridor and climbed a dark ladder-stair to the next, the big infantryman behind him. They managed down a slowly pitching passage to a hatchway—and out into near dawn, and a gentle freezing wind over a deck sheeted with ice.

"Footin', sir." Mays stepped close behind, hobnails crunching.

Sam, passing two sailors at the ship's great steering wheel, reached the right-side—*starboard*—rail, got a grip, and the sergeant stood away. There were serried small waves on the river—what North Mexico fishermen called 'chop'—and swirls of dark current here and there. Leaning over the rail's thick oak banister, Sam saw the two ranks of long yellow oar-looms rise all together . . . pause . . . then dip like birds' beaks into wind-roughened water. Dip . . . bow slightly with the strain of the stroke, then splash up and out together. Pause . . . then dip again.

He could hear what sounded like wooden blocks struck together to keep the rowers' time. A hollow, almost musical note.

"*Morning, sir!*"

Sam turned, looked up to the high stern deck—apparently, and rather comically, called the 'poop'—and saw Captain Owen, in a tarred canvas cloak too big for him. The captain stood with one of his officers behind a low railing that ran across that higher deck, with entries only for two narrow accommodation ladders.

"Morning, Captain . . . !" Sam's breath drifted in frost for a moment, then was whisked away on the wind.

He turned to the river again, and saw no shore, even with dawn streaking the eastern horizon pollen-yellow. No shore, no margin, only the odor of fresh water and ice coming on the wind. Only that, its smaller waves, and what seemed a tidal race, marked it different to a landsman from the Gulf Entire. Sam could see two distant lights—ship's lanterns, each far enough away to seem only glimmers, like dying sparks risen from a campfire.

Somewhere to the east, likely already passed in the night, the old New Orleans—of so many copybook tales—lay, as most ancient river cities, long drowned. Owen's first officer had claimed at supper that a church bell tolled in its sunken tower there, and could be heard as deep currents swung the bronze. . . . The town now called New Orleans, seemed to be one of the Fleet's headquarters and harbors, so was barely spoken of.

"Sam. . . ." Margaret came and stood by him, yawning, her cloak's hood drawn up against the cold, its dark wool pearled with mist-droplets.

"Others up?"

"Roused or rousing, sir. Short sleeping seems the rule on these ships."

"Hmm. Look at this river, Margaret. Big with summer melt off the ice. According to Neckless Peter, at least three times, maybe four times, what it was before the cold came down. So the cities on it now, all named for flooded Warm-time towns that had been near, aren't really the old Map-places. According to a ship's officer, aren't called 'Map' at all."

"Why not 'New' this or that?"

"I don't know. Perhaps concerned their Floating Jesus might object."

"It's a perfect prairie for the Khan's *tumans*, sir, once it freezes."

"A prairie for them from the north, *as* it freezes."

"Sam . . ." Margaret put her gloved hand over his bare hand on the rail, as if to warm it. An unusual touching, for her. "Sam, I know . . . we know what you intend to do. And you can do it, no matter how big the fucking river is."

Sam smiled. "Without my vodka?"

"With *or* without it, Sam." She took her hand away. "These Boxcars seem to be a formidable people, but they're like the Kipchaks, full of pride and horseshit. Both are ripe for a kick in the ass."

"And I'm the boot?"

"You're the boot, Sam. You, and the rest of us sheep-stealers." Margaret glanced behind them, saw only Sergeant Mays, standing weighty on the deck. ". . . We have interesting news. Master Carey shared beer with the cooks in the galley last night, and helped with pots and pans. Ship's gossip is that Jefferson City, Map-Missouri, has been taken by the Khan's general, Andrei Shapilov. And every man in the garrison there killed. Three . . . four thousand of the West-bank army."

"*Weather.* . . . But I knew, knew there was something. There was more on the captain's mind than cookies."

"Jefferson City might wake them."

"Wake some, Margaret. And send others deeper to sleep." Sam lifted his hands from the rail, blew on them to warm his fingers. "—But I'd guess, not the Queen."

16

"My *regiments . . . !*"

Queen Joan had cried this out several times through three days and nights, but not as if requiring comfort. And even men and women who ordinarily weren't wary of her, hadn't dared offer it.

It seemed to Martha that the Queen's rage, like a lightning stroke near a bee tree, had set the hive of Island humming.

Officers of both bank armies—very senior and important men, usually seen allied at court—were suddenly absent. And very different officers, lower-ranked, harsh-faced, and grim, suddenly appeared to take up posts, positions, responsibilities . . . work they never seemed to rest from.

So, in only three days and three nights, Martha saw what queens were for.

"A poor time," the Queen said, holding a green velvet gown out at arm's length to see what window light did to it. "A poor time for that puppy Captain-General to decide to come calling."

"But you invited him. . . ."

"Martha, don't use my past actions against me. I might have invited him—and I might not."

Distant trumpets and drums, preparing welcome at the Silver Gate, sang softly through the tower's stone.

"The young jackass." The green velvet was dropped to the floor. "I'd look like some pricey whore, rowing up to Celebration. Well"—she smiled at Martha—"perhaps more like the whore's mother, along for bargaining."

"No, ma'am. The whore herself, and beautiful."

The Queen, at the wardrobe, turned with a look. "So, I'm flattered and put in my place at once. I've come to suspect, girl, you've a brain along with your muscles." She rummaged, disturbing pressed gowns. "Probably should have you whipped. . . .

What about this?" A long dress striped black and silver.

"Seems . . . gaudy, ma'am."

" 'Seems gaudy, ma'am'! Well, *what* then?"

"The dark blood-red."

"Hmm. Worn several times before."

"And worn well, Majesty."

The Queen found the gown and hauled it out. "Pressed, at least. I'm amazed it's cleaned and pressed. Lazy bitches. . . ." She held it up to the light, then held the dress to her and went to stand before her long mirror's almost perfect silvered glass.

"That fucking stupid Merwin dog," she said, examining her reflection. Martha had heard her say it before, referring to General Eli Merwin, dead with his men at Map–Jefferson City. The Queen had written and sent a letter to the Khan's general, Shapilov, thanking him for ridding her of a fool.

Queen Joan turned a little to the left, a little to the right. "I suppose it might do."

"Do nicely, ma'am," Martha said, and with Fat Orrie, began to dress her.

"Well, this Small-Sam Monroe deserves no better. Get it on me. The black shoes—I'll freeze—and only jet for jewelry, as mourning for my poor dead soldiers." Cascades of band music now drifted into the tower. "Who in Lady Weather's name do those people think they're *greeting*? Jesus come rafting by?"

"We need to hurry, ma'am."

"Don't rush me." With both hands, the Queen lifted the Helmet of Joy from its silver stand and settled its weight carefully on her head. "Terrible for my hair . . ."

Then the Queen *was* rushed, though apologetically, by Martha, her waiting women, and finally the chamberlain, Brady, come panting up the tower stairs in as much temper as he dared to show.

"For the—! Ma'am, we have a head of state now landing!"

"Calm yourself, old man." The Queen made a last pass before

her mirror. Then, satisfied with red and black, led out and down the flights of stairs, her soldiers saluting as she passed.

Princess Rachel, wearing a simple, long, white-wool gown, with a thick goat's-hair shawl paneled in blue and green—and with only one lady in company—was waiting for them at the tower door. Her dark-brown hair was ribboned down her back in thick braids.

"Dressing to be plain?" the Queen said. "Fear rape, do you?"

The Princess didn't seem to hear, took her mother's hand and kissed it, then stepped back beside Martha as they walked down the long north staircase, past the glass Flower House. The Princess's lady—a blue-stocking named Erica DeVane—waved good fortune as they went.

Martha had seen Island's Silver Gate—had become familiar with almost all of Island, as Master Butter had advised her—but never with nine or ten thousand people, Ordinary and Extraordinary, packing its cut-stone landings and docks. Men, women, and children, all dressed for holiday, and so many that she saw stirs here and there where someone, shoved by crowding, had fallen into the harbor and had to be fished out before the icy water killed them.

The Queen's throne had been perched on the wide first-flight landing of the Gate's middle staircase. She settled into it, warmed by an ermine cape and lap robe, and crowned with the Helmet of Joy, its thirteen human hearts—shiveled knots bound in fine gold netting—dangling, swinging in the bitter wind.

Deep drums rumbled as a warship—Martha thought she saw the name *Haughty* as it turned—swung in to tie at Central Finger.

"Well-handled," the Queen said. "But certainly with more important duties . . . better things to do." Martha could hardly hear her over the band music. One dull-voiced instrument in there sounded very like a plow-horse farting.

As she watched past the Queen's heavy helmet of hearts, gold, and yellow diamonds, Martha saw the warship put out a broad bow-gangway, as if a great sea beast had stuck out its tongue.

A little group of six appeared there, and the crowd cheered all together, a tremendous almost solid weight of sound, so even the bands seemed silenced. Martha thought the Queen said, "My, such enthusiasm." And she must have said something, because Martha saw Princess Rachel, now standing beside her mother, smile.

The little group came down the gangway, cloaks blowing in the river wind. They marched up the dock to the harbor steps with one man walking slightly ahead, then climbed the stairs between lines of soldiers, to shouts and tossed women's favors of bright kerchiefs and painted paper flowers.

In an almost-hush of cheering between one blared march and another, Martha heard the chamberlain say, "Seem pleased to see the man."

"Jefferson City," the Queen said, "has frightened them. So they look to even improbable friends." She said something more, but the bands had struck up Warm-time's 'Semper Fidelis'—or its fair copy—and Martha couldn't hear her.

But the bands and crowd quieted as the group climbed closer to the Queen.

"For God's sake, Brady . . . he's a *boy*."

"Twenty-seven years old, ma'am. And experienced."

"Experienced, my ass." The Queen ruffled her ermine cape and loops of jet beads. "Experienced at hanging sheep thieves— which he was himself, once."

"But is no longer, ma'am." Martha noticed the chamberlain had kept his voice low, apparently to encourage the Queen to do the same.

"Is to me; I changed his shit rags. Very noisy baby . . ." The

Queen was drowned out by a last blare of music with cymbals and rumbling drums, as North Map-Mexico came up the last steps.

Monroe—bare-headed, well dressed in dun velvet, with silver on his arm and a fine ring on his finger—seemed handsome to Martha, in a way. Broad-shouldered, a little shorter than she was, he looked tough and tired, like any young officer who'd seen fighting. He was wearing only a fine cloth cloak—dark brown as imperial chocolate—against the cold, and was armed with a long-sword down his back, even coming to greet the Queen. He looked strong to Martha. Long arms and big hands. *I'd have to close with him. Short-grip the ax, stay inside the swing of his sword. And quickly, quickly.*

He stood at the foot of the throne. His people had stopped well back. To Martha, almost all of them—the soldiers, the woman, too—looked Ordinary, but dire fighters. Only one, a tall young man in black velvet, and very handsome as the court judged handsomeness, seemed well-born though not dotted.

The music having crashed to a stop, the Queen raised her voice over crowd noise. "How *very* welcome you are, Captain-General, to Middle Kingdom—and in time for our Lord Winter's Festival!"

"I look forward to it, Majesty." A young man's light baritone, raised to be clearly heard. He sounded a little hoarse, to Martha. Perhaps from shouting battle orders. "Look forward to it . . . and with heartfelt thanks for your kind invitation to visit your great and beautiful river country."

"Your pleasure, Lord Monroe, is our pleasure!"

Martha supposed the Queen was smiling, to show how pleased she was.

"—And we hope your visit with us will be the longest possible, so we may come to know one another . . . as our people and yours may come to know one another."

Monroe bowed to the Queen, then turned a little to bow to

Princess Rachel. Not, it seemed to Martha, really graceful bows. They were too . . . casual. She supposed he wasn't used to it. "Your Majesty's welcome reflects your own graciousness, kindness."

Martha thought Queen Joan must still be smiling, but heard her mutter, "Is this shit-pup making fun of me?"

"No, no." A murmur from Chamberlain Brady. "All in form."

The Queen stood up. "Then come, welcome guest, and those you've brought with you, to rest in comfort from your journey!"

"Should say more, ma'am." Brady's murmur.

"Fuck that," said the Queen, stepped down from her throne, and offered Monroe her arm. He was smiling—Martha supposed he'd heard the 'Fuck that'—took her arm, and swung a slow half-circle with her as the crowd began a rhythmic clapping, loud, and with shouts.

Following the Queen close as they climbed the steps—the Princess had dropped back to walk beside the chamberlain—Martha glanced over her shoulder to be sure Monroe's five fighters were coming well behind. Then she set herself to watching those bowing as they went by, those clapping and cheering in the crowd, watching for anyone a little too tense for the occasion.

They passed Master Butter as they climbed to the second Grand-flight's landing. He was standing with Lord Vitelli's man, Packard—blew an almost-hidden kiss to the Queen, then winked at Martha as she went by.

"In the old days," the Queen said to Monroe, raising her voice through the crowd's noise, "Chamberlain Brady would have welcomed you naked, or nearly naked, with the 'My Sunshine' dance."

"Really?" Their guest looked over his shoulder. "Chamberlain, I'm sorry to have missed it."

"Just as well, milord. Not what I used to be, prancing."

"Oh," Monroe said, "I imagine you still step lightly enough."

Martha heard the Queen's little grunt of humor through the cheers and shouts around them, and there came a shower of perfumed paper flowers, tiny twisted petition-papers, and candies wrapped in beaten silver foil.

Ordinaries in the crowd were shouting, *"Mother! River-mother!"* and grinning at the Queen like—as she always said—the great fools they were.

* * *

"Thank Mountain Jesus *that's* over."

"The Jesus here floats, sir," Margaret said. "But Weather, this place is big!"

"Oh, I'd say these rooms are proper," Darry said, "a suite commensurate with rank."

"I think Margaret meant Island, Lieutenant, though these rooms aren't nothing."

Chamberlain Brady had led them a long way, commenting to Sam on the warmth of the people's greeting, and mentioning the banquet of welcome at sunset. They'd come a great distance through granite passageways and up granite stairways, to this 'suite.'

First, a high-ceilinged entrance chamber with a long, beautifully-carved table set in it—and woven tapestries along the walls, with scenes of men and women hunting animals Sam had never seen or heard of, dream animals from copybooks. . . . There was this great room, warmed by two corner Franklins with fires rumbling in them, and lit by lanterns hanging from its ceiling on silver chains. Then, on both sides of a wide hallway—its walls decorated with painted pictures of river people at common tasks—were six more rooms. The first was a small laundry room with both bath and wash-tubs. On the stove were kettles of hot water, already steaming. The other five were sleeping chambers, each very fine, with polished wood furniture, beds with duck-feather mattresses and pillows, and flower drawings on fine paper on every wall.

These rooms, also, each held a stove burning. And the last chamber, largest and most beautiful—with two glassed arrow-slit windows cut through yard-thick stone—was warmed by two stoves.

"This is all to impress us," Margaret said, and making a face of not being impressed, joined Sam and Darry sitting at the entrance room's big table. The three sergeants stood at ease along the near wall. Behind and above them, a woven hunting party of people wearing feathered cloaks rode after a six-legged elk.

"Well, it impresses *me*," Sam said, "to afford such warmth and comfort in this huge heap of stone in winter. Island does impress me, as that warship did. Great wealth, and great power—and they make it plain."

Master Carey came in with two liveried servants carrying the last of the baggage . . . and saw it stowed. His and the sergeants' gear in the two bed-rooms nearest the entrance. The lieutenant's in the next. Then Margaret Mosten's. Then Sam's.

"We should have brought finer things to wear," Margaret said.

"No, we shouldn't," Sam said. "Decoration won't win us anything, here." He waited for the last of Island's servants to leave and close the door behind him. "Now, first, remember that what we say in these rooms may be overheard, stone walls or not."

"Right," Margaret said.

"This is what I want done. . . ." He paused to pick an apple from a silver bowl.

"Apple should be tasted, sir." Carey, come to stand with the sergeants.

"Oh, I don't think I'll be poisoned today. That would be a little abrupt." Sam took a bite and chewed. "It's sweet. Wonderful, a *sweet* apple. . . . Now, Sergeants Burke, Mays, and Wilkey, you'll take Lieutenant Darry's orders as to guard-mount. But there is always to be a man on duty at the entrance, here. And, I suppose, I should have someone with me."

"No 'suppose' about it, sir," Margaret said. "You will damn *well* have one of the sergeants, or me, with you at all times."

"Alright—one of the men. Margaret, you headquarter here, but wander often enough to keep an eye on all of us, and on any change in our position with these people."

"Yes, sir."

"Lieutenant . . ."

"Sir?" Darry sitting handsomely alert, left hand resting on his saber's hilt. A hilt, Sam noticed, sporting gold wire on the grip.

"Since, Lieutenant, you're a very social fellow, you will *be* a very social fellow here. Get out and around in the court. Cultivate companions-in-mischief. I want to know who's important, and who's not. I want to know what they think of the war—and of us."

"I understand, sir."

"And, Pedro, limit your amusements to those that do *not* require duels."

"Goes without saying, sir."

"Um-mm. And, Master Carey, you're to do whatever it was Eric Lauder instructed you to do—once you've told me exactly what those instructions were."

"Yes, milord—sir. Really, only to guard you, particularly against long-acting poisons, and to . . . deal with any river people who might threaten you or our mission here."

"Carey, you will 'deal' with no one without my direct order. Is that clear?"

"Very well, sir. Ask you, first."

"Yes. . . . Now, all of you,"—the sergeants came to attention to indicate attention—"all of you, remember why we're here. We are *not* here to make friends; I think that's unlikely in any case. We're here to offer the Boxcars help that they already need, and will need more of when the Khan joins his army." Sam finished the apple, found no place to put the core.

Carey came around the table and took it away.

"Thank you. . . . As to official matters, I think Her Majesty will let me wait at least a day or two, and possibly more, before we meet in any private way. To put me in my place."

"She seems damn rude."

"Margaret, watch your tongue."

"Sorry, Sam. . . . But she does."

"The Queen is exactly as my Second-mother described her. Older, but the same. A fierce lady—and one, now, with great burdens, which probably include the people of her court."

"Those, my business, sir?"

"Your business, Pedro. . . . All of us need to remember that as this Kingdom manages against Toghrul Khan, so North Map-Mexico will have to manage. We need these people as much as they need us. Keep it in mind."

Nods and "Yes, sir's."

"Master Carey," Margaret said, "the horses brought ashore and cared for?"

"Yes, Captain. Stabled and fed."

"And how are we to be fed?"

"Banquet tonight for milord and officers, and otherwise, according to the kitchens, as we please. Meals brought up to us, or served in Island's Middle-hall, still called 'The King's.' Milord and officers have places held at south high table there, servants and men-at-arms, places at south low."

"Hours?"

"All hours, Captain."

It seemed to Sam that Better-Weather's imposition of Ansel Carey—and Darry and the sergeants—was proving to have been good sense. "Most times," he said, "we'll eat publicly. Roosting up here would not be helpful. We need to see, and be seen."

"As to tonight's banquet, and attending what they call Extraordinaries, sir," Carey said, "I'm told that presently there is still no Boston ambassador at Island. The Queen ordered him out last year, as we knew—quite a scene, I understand. She threw a cabbage at him in one of their glass growing-houses."

"I'll try to avoid cabbages," Sam said.

"As for the rest, sir, no ambassador from the Khan, of course. Left weeks ago. The others will be court officials, river lords, generals, commanders, courtiers and so forth. And their wives."

" 'And their wives,' " Margaret said, still apparently regretting finery.

* * *

"Thank Lady Weather, that's over." The Queen, weary from the Welcome-banquet, and half-submerged in scanty lye-soap suds in the great silver tub, rested with her eyes closed. Steam scented with imperial perfume rose around her. It had taken Orrie, Ulla, and a nameless tower servant, two trips up from the laundry with pails of boiling water to fill the tub.

Martha, ringlets ruined by wet heat, knelt to scrub the Queen's long back—a back softened here and there by age, but still showing ropes of muscle down her spine. And there were scars, though not the many that showed on her front—puckered white beside her mouth, across her left breast, her belly, her left shoulder . . . and a bad one pitted into her right thigh. Her wrists and forearms, like Master Butter's, seemed decorated with scars' pale threads and ribbons.

"It seemed to go well, ma'am. And the dancing." Though Martha had been struck, above all, by the Welcome-banquet's food, as if the Kingdom offered endless spotted-cattle roasts, baked pigs, geese, and goats, fried chicken-birds, pigeons, and candied partridges to overawe the North Mexican lord. All those foods, and many tables of others.

The evening's bright occasion, and its music, had pleased Martha very much—though after, something pleased her more. Climbing the solar tower's entrance steps behind the Queen, she'd noticed by torchlight a large soldier in green-enameled armor, who'd winked and smiled at her while standing sergeant of the guard.

"*Dancing,*" the Queen said, talkative after considerable imperial wine. "The usual strutting and sweating. Not a man of them could leap over a high fire."

"Lord Patterson paid attention to you."

"Lord Pretty would pay attention to anything with a hole between its legs—and crowned, all the better. Still, at least Gregory can dance, there's some sense of rhythm there."

"Yes," Martha said, distracted—and to her own surprise, bent and kissed the Queen on her temple.

"What are you *doing?* Don't be impertinent."

"It . . . it is a thank-you."

"A thanks for what, Country-girl?" The Queen surfaced a long leg, looked at her toes.

"A thanks for sending for Ralph-sergeant."

"Oh. . . . Well, 'kind' soldiers aren't good for anything *but* standing at my stairs. Another useless mouth to feed at Island. The expense of this manure pile is outrageous—thieves, every damned one of them. Sutlers, fucking cooks and clothiers . . . Do you know, I don't dare look at the stable bills? You would suppose the Kingdom would receive gift-privilege from these merchant hogs—oh, no. Overprice and thievery!"

"I could visit them, with Master Butter."

The Queen laughed, half-turned in the tub to hit Martha on the shoulder with a soapy fist. "No, no. My people and I play many games, Trade-honey, and your ax would break the rules."

"Then we won't," Martha said, and used a soft cloth to rinse. The Queen's torso had a fierce history, but her nape, revealed under pinned-up hair, was tender as a child's.

Standing with care, then stepping out into wide southern-cotton toweling, the Queen left wet footprints on the carpet, so a woven snow-tiger grew a damp mustache. Martha hugged and gathered her in cloth—felt a sweetness of care and attending as she stroked the Queen dry over softness here, hard muscle there.

Swaddled, the Queen turned and turned as Orrie took wet cloth from Martha, replaced it with dry.

. . . Burnished, smelling of flowers from the bath, the Queen sat on an ivory stool—the ivory once the teeth of a Boston sea-beast called the walrut, or perhaps sea walnut. She sat slumped while Martha unpinned and brushed out her hair, long, with weaves of gray running through the red.

Martha brushed with slow easy strokes of boar bristle so as not to tug or tangle.

"Now listen," the Queen said, her head moving slightly under the brush. "This sergeant of yours—Orrie, leave us."

"Yes, Majesty." Orrie, very fat and usually a stately walker, always seemed to scuttle away relieved when dismissed.

"Ma'am, he isn't really my sergeant."

"And may never be, Martha, and then never more than a lover. Don't talk to me about *men*. But this sergeant of yours, if it should come to love, it still cannot come to marriage and children as long as I'm alive—*ouch*."

"Sorry, ma'am."

"I must and will be first. My life *always* above his and yours.

Not because I'm such an Extraordinary, but because my life is the peoples', and they have no one else. . . . Though it's also true that I enjoy being queen. I don't deny it."

"I understand."

"Perhaps you understand, girl, and perhaps you don't—how many strokes is that?"

"Forty-three, I think."

" 'You think.' Alright, forty more. . . . What I was saying to you about coming first, about the necessity of it? I have one child, a resentful daughter only two years older than you, who misses her father still, and believes me a brute bitch who hasn't even wept to lose him."

"I know better, ma'am."

"Yes, you heard me wake crying for my Newton on End-of-Summer Night, after our Jordan Jesus rafted down. You heard that, and you've heard my dream groaning. And likely heard my grunts playing stink-finger under the covers, rather than have some tall man come up to give me shaking joys—then take advantage for it. . . . You've heard, Martha, and so are closer to me than my daughter ever has been, or ever will be. And who are you? Only a strong child, really, and otherwise no one at all. Rachel will never believe how I love her . . . wouldn't credit it."

"I know you love her."

"She's all I have of Newton. And more, Rachel was a charming child—*easy with that fucking brush*—and she was so intelligent that people made the River-sign, hearing her conversation."

"I believe it. And she's pretty."

"How many is that?"

"Seventy . . . I think."

"Oh, for Weather's sake, Martha, learn how to fucking *count*." The Queen stood, shook her hair out, put her hands back for the sleeves of her night-robe, then shrugged it comfortable as Martha wrapped the fine green cloth around her, then tied its soft belt bow. "Pretty? Well, if not truly pretty, then Rachel's handsome enough, I suppose." Queen Joan raised her arms high and stretched like a man, joints cracking. Then she stepped a little jigging dance, shook her arms out as wrestlers did to ease their muscles, before she strolled relaxed to the little silver bucket, rucked up the hem of her night-robe, and squatted.

"But. *But*. This Kingdom is crueler than my mountains ever were, Martha. Crueler than the tribesmen who came down. Well named the River Kingdom, uncaring, cold, and made of killing currents as the river is." There was faint musical drumming as she peed. "And full of men and women who once ate talking meat. Still do, sometimes. . . . This is what my daughter will someday rule, and I don't believe that she can do it."

"She has your blood."

The Queen tucked a tuft of cotton wool to her crotch, wiped herself. "But has not had my *life*. Hasn't seen what I've seen, hasn't fought as I've fought, hasn't learned what I've had to learn. Let me tell you, when my Newton was killed in Map-Kentucky coming to a fair agreement, I came this close,"—the Queen held up her thumb and forefinger, almost touching—"this close to being weighted with iron and thrown into the river. . . . Where's my nail-knife?"

Martha found it in the toilet cabinet's second sliding drawer. "Here, ma'am."

The Queen, quite limber, crossed a leg over a knee and commenced trimming her toenails. "Came very close, then, to going into the river. So, I fucked one man as if I'd secretly loved him always—then had his throat cut. *And* murdered two more before I felt free of that weight of iron chain." She bent closer, peering to examine a neatened nail. "A woman, a sister to one of those men, was thrown from her window in South Tower as a reassurance to me. Her uncle did it, Martha, for fear I would destroy their family, even the babies."

Those toes finished, the Queen crossed her other leg and began trimming. The little knife-blade twinkled in lamplight as she worked.

"I'm sorry," Martha said.

"Sorry? Sorry for what, girl? For necessity?"

"For you."

"Well, you're a fond fool." Paring with quick turns of her strong wrist, the Queen ended with her little toe . . . then stood up off the silver bucket and shook down her robe's skirt. "Those who think we're more than beasts, should study their toenails." She handed Martha the little knife. "It goes in the *top* sliding drawer. Now . . . what else?"

"Brushing your teeth, ma'am."

"The hell with it. . . . Did you know the Warm-time hell was hot?"

"Yes, ma'am."

"I always thought that was strange. . . . Where are my slippers?"

"By the bed."

"Not the woolen slippers—the sheepskins."

"I'll look for them."

"Oh, never mind." The Queen seemed to swim away through gray gauze curtains to her bed-nook. "Between Ulla and that fat Orrie, nothing is ever where it should be. I should have them whipped. . . ." Martha, following, had to brush a drift of fine cloth from the ax handle behind her shoulder.

Queen Joan sat on the edge of her bed and began rearranging her pillows—which she did every night. The maids had found no way to place them to please her.

She plumped a goose-feather one, tossed it to the head of the bed. "You see, Martha, Rachel would not be capable of what I did. She pretends to fierceness, but break a bird's neck before her and she goes pale as cheese." Another pillow tossed after the first; a cushion picked up and tested with a punch. "And I cannot live forever."

"Then she needs a fierce husband, ma'am."

"Oh, yes. Memphis, or Sayre, or Johnson—who's a monster—or Lord Allen, or Eddie Cline. My Newton despised Cline and so do I. *Or* Giamatti, *or* one of the Coopers, who have hated me and mine forever."

Pillows and cushions arranged, the Queen crawled into bed on all fours, like a child, then tucked herself under the covers and drew them up to her throat. "And all of these people, Martha—chieftains, lords-barons, lords-earls, generals, admirals and so forth and so forth—every one of them keeping at least five or six hundred sworn-men on their hold lands, all trained and armed and excused service in my armies."

She sat half up, elbowed an unsatisfactory pillow into place. ". . . Their 'River Rights.' River Rights, my ass! And not *one* of them—well, possibly Sayre, possibly Michael Cooper—but otherwise not one of them could hold this kingdom, keep its people from under the hooves of those fucking Kipchaks." The Queen lay down again, tugged the covers to her chin. "Those savages are breaking my West-bank *army!*"

Martha saw there were tears in the Queen's eyes. It was frightening to see, and ran goose-bumps up her arms.

"I cannot imagine," the Queen said, staring up into the bed's umbrella of pearly gauze, "I cannot *imagine* what possessed those Texas jackasses. And I saw them in the grassland just before. I saw them! What possessed those idiots to campaign in open prairie against the Kipchaks, and with all their forces? Was there no Map-Lubbock, no Map-Amarillo to fortify? No notion of fucking reserves?" She wiped her eyes with the hem of the sheet. "Are my slippers by the bed?"

"The wool slippers?"

"*Any* damn slippers."

"Yes, ma'am. Beside the bed."

"—They rode out singing hymns, were quilled with arrows like porcupines, and have left my kingdom naked!" The Queen thrashed under her covers. "I need a husband for my girl! Hopefully, one who won't kill me for the crown."

"A Boston person?"

"Oh, certainly, and introduce one of those half-mad oddities to the lords, the armies, the merchants and Guilds of Ordinaries as my son-in-law and heir? He would live as long as I would, then . . . perhaps a week, unless he flew away like some fucking bat."

"Then, if no one else will do, why *not* the North Map-Mexico lord?"

The Queen sighed and closed her eyes. "Martha, you're a young fool; it's a waste of time talking to you. You've seen him. Monroe is a *boy*—sturdy enough, clever enough—but what has he done? Beaten those southerners, those imperial idiots? That's as difficult as beating a carpet to clean it. That, and only the raid north by his man, Voss. . . . The river lords would cook and eat Monroe, and the Blue generals and Green generals would gnaw the bones."

"He seems fiercer than that."

"And if so, then fierce enough to take the throne from me!" The Queen opened her eyes, looked at Martha in an unpleasant way. "I won't be forced to have him!"

"But Princess Rachel—"

"Rachel doesn't know. She is a *child*. This is the Throne's business, and she will marry and fuck and bear children for the one *I* accept! . . . The woolen ones?"

"Yes. I can get the sheepskins—"

"Oh, never mind." The Queen seemed older lying down, her long, graying hair spread on her pillow. Older, and weary. ". . . Still, perhaps a long engagement. Long enough for his soldiers to be useful against the Khan. If that suits Boy Monroe, I suppose it may suit me. Time enough, afterward; engagements are often broken. . . . But the same baby who peed down my furs? Floating *Jesus.* "

The Queen lay quiet then, and Martha smoothed her covers . . . tucked them at her throat. "Sleep sweet, Majestic Person."

The Queen smiled at that, then sighed. "Oh, Martha. You know, I still have trouble forgiving my Newton—going off to Map-Kentucky to win a battle, and die doing it. He left these lords and generals to me, and they press and press against my power, and watch for me to stumble as I grow older. They all wait to see if I forget a name, a river law, or some common word. They bribed my maids so their doctors could examine my shit, see if I have bleeding in the turds—can you believe that?"

"Your shit is stronger than most men's muscle, ma'am."

The Queen threw her head back on her pillows and laughed. "Oh, that's very good—and true. But for how many more years, Martha? How many more years . . . ?"

"I'll deal with the chamber-maids."

"Hmm? Oh, those. Those two have been under the river's skin for more than a year, dear. Without their tongues." The Queen turned on her side, and lay looking through Martha into memory. "Michael Cooper came to me at the time, muttering something about summary executions without notice given to the Queen's Council, and I said, 'Lord Cooper, I had to silence them before they damaged the reputations of great men, even placing some in jeopardy of treason.' That shut his catfish mouth."

Martha reached up to the hanging lamp . . . lowered its wick till the flame went out. "Then there's nothing for you now to dream of, ma'am, but pretty birds and pretty places."

After a moment, the Queen's voice sounded out of darkness. "The only things I wish to dream of, Martha, are the Trapper mountains, and the Trapper days. . . ."

* * *

Sam woke to a savage wind—Lord Winter's serious wind—whining past stone walls like a great dog begging to be let in. There was a sandy shush and rattle in it as well. Hard-driven sleet and snow.

Strange he'd been dreaming of summer. Summer in the fourth week, when it was perfect in the fields of August, leaf-green everywhere, so winter seemed only a story that might not be repeated.

He reached under thick wool blankets to touch his long dagger's hilt. Sergeant Wilkey would be sleeping at the room's door. Carey'd wanted the man *in* the room, had gone round the walls under the tapestries, looking for any secret entrance.

The fat man's ways were Eric's. Secret, sly, often useful . . . often ineffective.

The Queen wouldn't send a killer to his room, certainly not before she'd heard him out, and likely not after. His death would be no advantage to her now, though it might be later, once—if—the Kipchaks were beaten. Now, she'd make him wait a few days, then be dismissive, just short of insult. It would be interesting to see how Queen Joan ruled and decided. Interesting to see how she managed a court that might kill her on a notion . . . how she managed a people who still occasionally ate people.

The duck-feather bed was too soft; it was hurting his back.

Sam got up with his dagger, tugged the blankets with him, and padded through the dark to a carpet near a stove's dimming coals. He rolled himself in wool, felt the support of cut stone stacked deep beneath him, and went to sleep . . . hoping for more dreams of summer.

17

After days of wandering, walking through glassed gardens, examining walls, fortifications, the great stone-built entrance harbors—the Silver, the Gold, the Bronze, the Iron—his inspections never seeming to disturb the officers and men guarding those places, Sam had seen enough of Island.

It lay, a mountain of snowy, wind-struck stone in an ice-flowed river, and seemed to him about as useful as any natural mountain might have been. A great redoubt, no question, and would be very expensive to reduce—but by that time, with an enemy having won to its walls, the war would already be lost. It seemed a poor substitute for a veteran field army, well led, an army not divided into East-bank and West, with a fleet uncomfortable with both of them.

After those inspections, Sam saw what Toghrul had seen, even though far away at Caravanserai in Map–West Texas. The Khan had seen—had sensed—the Kingdom as a giant, but bound in chains of long habit and regulation, often slow, awkward, and shambling. . . . All a hunting call to the Kipchaks, so numerous, so neatly swift, so wonderfully well-commanded.

And, of course, that very instinct, that eagerness, had exposed them. Toghrul had paid no heed—after his one warning attack south—to an enemy left behind him. As a wolf pack, chasing elk, might run by a bowman waiting in a snowy wood, with nothing but glances and a snarl as they passed.

But then, the bowman might follow, so that on a final field, the pack in battle with a furious great bull elk, arrows came whistling from behind.

These notions were confirmed for Sam as he walked the grand stone corridors of Island, whose high ceilings stirred and eddied with lantern smoke and the smoke of torches, which flowed to any outlet of air like a gray ghost of the great river sliding past them.

. . . During meals in an echoing dining-hall of granite and oak beams, huge as a roofed landscape, the Boxcars—Extraordinaries, of course, at the high tables—were courteous enough. They asked polite and apparently interested questions about North Mexico—its longer summers, its sources of labor, what beasts there were to hunt. Then chatted of hunting, of old campaigns against the tribes. Nothing was said about the Kipchaks.

Pleasant conversations, as by hosts to somewhat dubious guests, and all accompanied by very good food—cow roasts, stuffed geese, cabbage boiled or chopped cold—all meats spiced, carefully cooked, and sauced with gravies a little rich for Sam's stomach. And at every meal, even with breakfast's chicken eggs, fish, or pig-slices, various sorts of pickles and candied imperial fruits were served, with jellied berries from the river's thickets.

In that hall, only breakfast was eaten without music to listen to. Banjar men, a shaman-drummer from some backwoods tribe, and a blind woman with a harp were the orchestra—or more properly, a Warm-time 'band' that strummed and drummed and plucked to ease the later dining down.

Courteous and perhaps a little careful dealing with Sam and Margaret Mosten, the Boxcars seemed more than courteous to Pedro Darry, the lieutenant having become a favorite with the younger men—and possibly some older wives—so he laughed and joked with the Kingdom people as if born on the river.

Sam had been glanced at by a number of the Boxcar women, and found himself, a night or two, dreaming of jeweled and furred beauties . . . particularly one, smoothly plump, with fiery red hair. She was apparently of some notable tribal family allied to the Kingdom, since her small white teeth were filed to neat points.

Sam dreamed of her, but would have sought no introduction,

even if there'd been the time, and this the occasion for it. None of the high-table ladies came to dine without cold-eyed husbands, brothers, or a hot-eyed lover, as escort.

At ease with Pedro, these richly dressed men and women—their cheeks dotted with blue tattooing—remained more guarded with Sam, though friendly enough, smiling as they suggested second helpings of this or that. They appeared to wait for their Queen's decision on him, not caring to be caught wrong-footed.

The great tables, so piled with food being busily served by Red-liveries, seemed to Sam a hint of the Queen's contempt for the courtiers' greed. He grew used to their soft, slurred speech—and sudden eruptions of temper down a table's polished hardwood when enough vodka or barley-whisk was drunk. They all, men and women, came to meals armed—their children also armed with ornate little daggers—but never drew in argument.

"Carey says the tables here are all the Queen's," Margaret had said when Sam mentioned it, "with everyone her guests. No one draws steel on her or hers."

Queen Joan had joined the diners only twice, for mid-meals, while Sam and his officers were eating there. She'd seemed to enjoy herself at the north table, and ate very well—particularly a pudding of preserved fruits—but paid no attention to the North Mexicans.

On one of those occasions, the more than three hundred Ordinaries lining the low tables had raised their beer jacks to her, swayed in place, and sung a song, 'Mammy, How I Love You.'

The high tables hadn't joined in the singing, and the Queen had stood to shout the Ordinaries to silence—"*Stop that damned noise!*"—which had seemed to please the singers very much. Sam saw they loved her, and were her strength against the generals, admirals, and lords of the river.

On the fifth morning, at a breakfast of imperial coffee, slice-cut barley bread, cheese, eggs, and a sort of sausage, a servant in the Queen's blood-red livery came easing along the wall, past the high tables' seated diners.

Margaret Mosten slid her bench-chair back a little as the man came, and hooked her little finger in her rapier's guard to loosen the blade in its scabbard.

"Oh, I'd say no trouble there." Darry, on Sam's other side, reached for another slice-cut of bread. "Some errand. . . ."

The errand ended at Sam's place.

"Milord." The servant had a murmuring, messenger's voice. "Her Majesty is pleased to give you audience. . . . If you'll follow me."

"About time," Margaret said, and stood.

"Only the Captain-General," the servant said.

Even so, when Sam walked after the man down the hall's long center aisle—watched, it seemed, by every eye—and Sergeant Wilkey left his place at a low table to come with him, the servant said nothing.

It was, as usual on Island, a long walk. . . . The servant finally stood aside at a narrow door, opened it, and bowed Sam and the sergeant into a large, bare stone room. There were dark double-doors at its other side, and a single heavy, carved chair as furniture. The high ceiling, vaulted gray granite, echoed their bootsteps. There was no stove.

Sergeant Wilkey stayed standing by the narrow door, his longbow now strung. He'd taken three battle-arrows from his quiver and held them alongside the bow's grip with a curled finger, to be handy. . . . Sam walked to the middle of the room and sat in the carved chair, stretching his legs. He breathed out a faint cloud of frost, and wished for another mug of coffee. What was expensive and rare at Better-Weather—though so much closer to the Empire—seemed lightly come-by on Kingdom's river. Goods and gold by water shipping, he supposed.

How fine would made-roads have to be, to equal that ease . . . ?

After a while, footsteps, a latch's turning, and the double doors swung open across the room. The Queen's armswoman, Martha, stepped through first. She was wearing a heavy, green-paneled woolen gown, the dress's hem reaching just to her low boots, not long enough to trip her. Sam saw the handle of her ax just over her right shoulder, and a gray glint of fine mail beneath a wrist's cuff. He'd seen bigger young women, but not many.

Queen Joan came behind her, almost as tall as her fighting girl, though slender. She was dressed like a copybook queen, with an ermine wrap over sky-blue velvet laced and looped with pearls. She wore blue-dyed deerskin slippers, and a narrow crown of leaves of gold.

Princess Rachel, behind her, was nearly as tall, but plainly dressed in a gown the color of stone. Her long dark hair was down, bound only once by a slender silver chain.

Sam stood, bowed to the Queen and her daughter, though not deeply, then stepped back.

Queen Joan sat, her armswoman standing behind her—and watching Sergeant Wilkey. Princess Rachel stood beside.

"It occurs to me . . ." The Queen had a voice that seemed younger than she was, a voice unlined, with no age in it. "It occurs to me . . . do you know the tale of the Gordian knot? It's a Warm-time tale."

"I know it," Sam said.

"Then tell me, Captain-General—who was Small-Sam and peed down my front on occasion—tell me why I shouldn't cut one of my Kingdom's possible knots, by cutting your throat? Pigeons informed me this morning that you're no longer a guest, but an invader, with your foot soldiers marching up through West Map-Louisiana . . . your cavalry come, or coming, east into Map-Arkansas to join them there."

Silence and stillness by the narrow door, where Sergeant Wilkey stood with his longbow.

"If I'd asked your permission,"—Sam smiled—"you would have denied it. My army *is* crossing Kingdom territory, and intends to fight on it in North Map-Arkansas, South Map-Missouri—but fight the Khan Toghrul, not Boxcars."

"So you say. But with your throat cut, you'd say no more, issue no commands, invade no one."

Sam took a moment before answering. ". . . I think you won't kill me, Queen, for two reasons: Your war with the Khan has already begun badly, and I doubt you want war with North Map-Mexico as well. Kill me, and you'll certainly have it. And also . . ."

"Also?"

"My Second-mother, Catania."

Queen Joan sat and stared at Sam, her face bleached pale as bone. "Well . . . Well, you have a ruler's guts at least, to use her name to me, to assume I honor her memory so much."

"I don't know what memories you honor, Queen—I only know she honored yours."

"You young dog . . . to use my own heart against me."

"What weapon more worthy than *your* heart, Queen?"

Queen Joan stared at him; she didn't seem to need to blink. "I have courtiers—ass kissers—who speak to me in just that way."

"No, you don't. Those people fear you, and they lie. I'm as likely to bite your ass as kiss it."

The Queen glanced over at her daughter. "Rachel, what do you think of him?"

"He is . . . a change, I suppose."

The Queen looked back at Sam. "Let me tell you something, clever young Captain-General of minor importance—let me tell you that if I were even five years younger, and had a different sort of daughter, I'd put you under the river. . . . Yes, and *then* weep for sweet Catania's memory."

Sam nodded. "But you're not younger, Queen. You need help against the Khan. And you don't have a daughter fierce enough to follow you in this kingdom."

"I'm here," Princess Rachel said. "Don't speak as if I were not."

"I apologize, Princess."

"But you are *not* here, Rachel." The Queen spoke without looking at her daughter. "You're only present. To be here, you would have had to do more than read and write in your book tower. Do more than tame song-birds. More than conversations and philosophies and letters and studies of this and that. You have not *earned* being here."

"Then I will not be missed." Princess Rachel left her mother's side and walked out through the double doors. The doors remained open, so her footsteps could be heard down the hall as she went.

"I'm sorry," Sam said, "that the Princess was upset."

"Too fucking easily upset. My Newton wanted a boy. I gave him a girl—and am punished for it."

"A princess may become a queen."

"Some may. . . . Listen, Small-Sam Monroe, you care for your North Mexico, and hope to save it by joining us against the savages. All this perfectly understood, and sensible. Be assured, if I hadn't thought you might be useful to us in just that way, I would never have asked your visit, never offered the possibility of engagement to my daughter."

"Always more improbable than probable."

"Yet here you are, *Small*-Sam. And apparently intend to make the 'improbable' a fact!"

"Yes, I do."

"We're not in *that* much trouble. We're a civilized kingdom—well, coming to be civilized—while you lead only border tag-ends, roosting on land stolen from the Emperor. Land that any more formidable emperor will soon take back."

"Queen, if you didn't need me, if you didn't need my army . . . if you had any man to keep your daughter safe, we wouldn't be talking. I'd be dead, or gone."

"Still a possibility."

"Not since Map–Jefferson City."

Queen Joan sat watching Sam for almost a full glass-minute, then said, "You're fortunate that so many of my ghosts stand beside you."

"I know it."

Queen Joan rose, her armswoman looming behind her. The Queen was tall; she looked slightly down at Sam, her eyes the flat blue of sky reflected in polished metal. "You have my permission to try to persuade Rachel. And also my permission to . . . advise our commanders in all campaigns where your people will also be engaged." She considered him for a moment. "And I do hope that some foolish treachery of yours, some starving ambition, won't make it necessary to kill you."

"Poison," Sam said, "would be the only way with a chance to keep my army from your river, then your island. An absolutely convincing illness. And even then . . ."

"Oh,"—the Queen smiled—"you know the old copybook phrase 'Where there's a will, there's a way'?"

"I know it. And I depend on it."

The Queen walked away, laughing, her armswoman striding to cover her back.

Sam heard bootsteps behind him, the faint music of oiled mail. "Well, Sergeant?"

"Seems thin ice, sir."

"Yes. Thin ice . . . over deep water."

* * *

The Queen—with Martha nearly beside her, only a half-step back—strolled down the Corridor of Battles. Banners along the walls, some only woven memories, moth-eaten and frail as insect-gauze, billowed slightly in the faint breeze of their passing. The Queen, as always in this corridor, paused beneath the flag of battle Bowling Green—this great cloth, its years recent, still gleamed in white silk and gold thread, its only crimson a tear of loss, sewn at its center.

The Queen whispered to herself, as she always did under that banner. Whispered to herself, or perhaps the killed King . . . then walked on.

"So, Martha, *now* what do you think of our sturdy young Captain-General?"

"I think you should be careful, ma'am."

"Mmm. You think he might—if, for example, he and Rachel *become* engaged to marry—perhaps take advantage afterward, set me aside? Kill me?"

"He might, if he thought it best. Set you aside, I mean. But—"

" 'But?' "

"He wouldn't kill you, ma'am."

"And why not, girl?"

"Same reason you won't kill him."

"Clever Martha. . . . The past weighs on both of us like a fallen tree. And I see Catania, smiling at me."

18

There were two guards at the door to the West Tower solar. A chamber, as Sam had found—Sergeant Burke clanking up behind him—reached after a steep seventy-two-step climb from the tower gate. As usual at Island, one of the guards was armored in blue-enameled steel-hoop, the other, in green. Also as usual, both were armed with shield and short-sword for handiness in close quarters. . . . They were keeping an eye on Sergeant Burke.

"No entrance here, milord." Green-armor.

"Announce me," Sam said.

"Cannot do it, sir." Green again.

"Announce me," Sam said, "or stand aside."

There were few moments more interesting to a commander, than those spent waiting to see if a questionable order would be obeyed.

After those interesting few moments, Blue-armor turned and knocked gently on the iron-bound oak door. Sam had found no flimsy entranceway on Island, except on the glass greenhouses. Any enemy army reaching Kingdom's capital would find difficult barricades at every turn, on every landing, and before every room.

The door latch turned, thick oak and iron swung open, and Princess Rachel stood impatient in her slate-gray gown. She held a small copybook in one hand, a steel-nib pen in the other.

"I'm occupied, milord." Looking down at him a little, since she was slightly taller. "And I believe our conversation was just completed at my mother's audience."

"I've come to apologize again for that . . . clumsiness, Princess."

"You spoke your mind."

"Carelessly." Sam tried a smile past a guard's steel shoulder.

"As I said, milord, I'm occupied."

"And since I am not, Princess, I've taken a guest's liberty to visit."

Impatience *and* annoyance. "Very well." She stepped aside as he came in, then swung the door closed behind him. Sam saw, as if he still stood outside on the landing, the look exchanged by the three soldiers.

This solar was no lady's retirement, with cushions, harps, embroidery frames, little dogs, game-boards and so forth. It was a library and copying room, circled with shelves and copybook stacks, copy stands, and a flat-topped work-desk beneath the north window. . . . Only thick carpets—spiraled tribal work, Roamer patterns woven in greens, golds, and rust reds, with dreamed creatures chasing down the edges—relieved the room's simplicity. The light was good, a bright, cool reading light from four great windows spaced around the chamber—the only windows Sam had noticed at Island that were not narrow and iron-barred.

There was no scent of perfume—the Princess apparently didn't use it. The only odors were of fine laid paper and best black sea-squid ink.

Princess Rachel stood silent, watching him, pen and copybook in hand. She had her mother's lean height and length of bone, but what must have been her father's features, blunt, brown-eyed, with wide cheekbones. A handsome face, in its way.

"Forgive me, Princess, for intruding, but it's proved necessary." Sam walked over to a shelf, read copybook titles on fine sewn top-bindings. "Otherwise, you'll continue avoiding me all over Island, and I'm sorry to say we don't have the time for it. . . . *Martian Chronicles.* I've heard of Dreaming Bradbury, but not read him. I have read one copybook supposedly by G. Wolfe. Some argument whether it's really a dream of his. Might have been written of our time, in some ways."

Sam glanced over at her, saw no welcome in her face. *"The View from Pompey's Head . . ."*

"We have two of Basso's." Grudging, but a response. Sam supposed this princess could not *not* speak of books.

"Haven't read him."

"We have that—and the *Light Infantry Ball.*"

"Really? Well, light infantry, at least, is a subject I know something about." Sam looked for an empty chair; there seemed to be copybooks or copy paper stacked on everything. It was a room Neckless Peter would have loved.

"Not that sort of light infantry."

"Oh? What sort is it?"

A little color in those pale cheeks. "It . . . it is about social relationships before and during the very ancient Civil War."

"The Map-America civil war?"

"Yes," the Princess said, and certainly wished him gone.

"Not much use of light infantry there. Skirmishers, scouts, that sort of thing. Of course, the bang-powder bullets must have influenced all their tactics. . . . Have you read the *Right Badge of Courage?*"

" 'Red.' " Definitely blushing—and of course, very shy. What else could she have grown to be with such a mother?

" 'Red'?"

" '*Red' Badge of Courage.*"

"Really? You're sure?" Sam set a stack of paper on the floor and sat on an uncomfortable little stool set against the wall by the bookshelf. "I've seen the copybook. Book-English, though traded from Mexico City."

The Princess opened her mouth to say she was sure, then must have noticed something in his face. ". . . But you knew it. You *knew* that was wrong."

Sam smiled at her. "Yes, I did. There *is* no 'Right' Badge of *Courage.*" He leaned back, stretched his legs out, and crossed his boots at the ankle. His sword-hilt tapped the wall behind him. Shouldn't have worn his sword. It was a mistake to have come up to her chamber armed, a long bastard blade slanted down his back. *Think first*, was the rule at Island.

"I apologize, Rachel." The Princess blinked at the familiarity. A formal court, they held. "I shouldn't have come to your chamber armed."

A little smile. "I didn't consider your sword rudeness, milord." She went behind her work desk, and sat looking out at him over a low barrier of copybooks—as Charles Ketch so often did. Gentle people finding refuge behind written walls. "—Everyone goes armed at Island."

"You don't, I've noticed. Not even a lady's dagger."

"I have guards."

"You have guards, yes—each man from armies kept deliberately separate. West-bank and East. Guards commanded by ambitious generals. West-bank generals . . . East-bank generals."

"It has worked for us very well."

"And will, until the day a really formidable general joins the River armies together. Perhaps is forced to join them to meet the sort of threat that, for instance, the Kipchak Khan is posing now. That general will be king—and all the more easily if those who ruled are dead."

"I don't think . . . I don't think you need concern yourself with that, milord."

"Oh, but I do. You see, Princess, the government of Middle Kingdom depends not only on the strict separation of your two armies, not only on the Fleet as a third force. It depends on a ruler being strong enough to maintain them in balance."

"*You* being such a ruler, of course."

"Your *mother* being such a ruler."

"Then you had better discuss your ambitions with my mother." An angry face over the stack of copybooks. Now, Sam could see her father in her.

"I wish . . . Rachel, I wish we'd had the time to know one another better. If there'd been a year or more for visits, so we didn't meet now as strangers, and all this so . . . awkward."

No answer from the Princess. Her pale face, dark eyes, seemed to float above stacked white paper.

"—But, lacking that time, shall we have plain speaking?"

"Very well, milord. Plain speaking." She touched the papers before her. "My interests are my books and those people also interested in books and learning. Ours is an ignorant age—and forgive me, but you're an *example* of it. A provincial war-lord, who seems to wish to be a king! And assumes . . . assumes that everyone will fall in with those wishes!"

There was quiet, then, almost restful. Sam saw one of the river gulls, come up from the Gulf Entire, sail close past the room's south window. Its shadow marked a white wall for an instant as it passed.

"You're mistaken about my wishes, Rachel. Only an ass wishes to rule anyone. As only a coward . . . avoids necessity.—You know, I drink too much." He saw her a little disconcerted. "I have to be careful, at dinner and so forth here. I have to be careful not to drink too much—but not drink so little that it's *noticed* I have to be careful. I drink . . . to rest for a while from what I'm becoming." Sam waited to see if the gull would fly back, leave another quick shadow of its passing. "I'm becoming . . . an instrument, a tool for the work my people set me. And I saw the same in your mother, when I first met her, then again this morning. I saw that burden in her eyes."

The Princess listened, her head cocked slightly to one side, as if to hear him better.

"Of course, I knew the Queen, in a way, before I came to Island. My Second-mother mentioned Joan Richardson often, admiring her courage, and always spoke of her with love. As she spoke of your father.—You would have liked my Second-mother, Catania. I was told my First-mother was beautiful, but Catania was brave. She was the sort of person we all would wish to be."

The Princess looked down, cleared her throat. "You suggested we speak plainly. I didn't mean to be rude to you, milord."

"Rachel, my name is Sam Monroe. I am not your 'lord,' and never will be. But I hope, in time, to become your friend."

Still looking down at her desk-top, as if solutions had been inscribed there. "My mother is Queen. I have no interest in being one—in being like her."

"Thank every Jesus for that! As to your becoming queen, it's surprising how little choice we have in these matters. I won two, three battles after older commanders had been killed. Before that, I'd been a shepherd—and occasionally, a sheep thief and near bandit. I was very young, and very foolish. . . . Then, *because* better men were dead, I was looked to when unpleasant decisions had to be made. I made just enough decisions rightly, to trap myself into becoming Captain-General of North Map-Mexico—a slightly ridiculous title."

"Not ridiculous."

"You're too kind. But that's really all I am, a very good military commander, and a fairly good ruler otherwise. Though I probably use force, sometimes, when force is not quite necessary. . . . I also used to read a good deal; my Second-mother saw to that. She was afraid I'd pick up poor book-English, or the mountain tribes' signs and chatter. So, I've read, though now I have little time for reading—and by the way, you must meet Neckless Peter, our librarian and informational. The old man was the Khan's tutor, and he'd love this room."

"I'm to understand, then, that you are a *decent* provincial war-lord, and fairly well read."

"Exactly." Sam's back was hurting. He got up from the stool and walked over to the north window. The window's glass was very fine, some of the clearest he'd seen, each square pane bright as a mirror. The Kingdom people did wonders with glass. . . .

"Well, milord—Sir Monroe—you are trying to persuade the

wrong person. I am not the Queen. Put it another way: I can say *no*. I'm not interested in marriage; certainly not with you."

Sam saw gulls spiraling down past the tower. It was the view the Boston girl would have had, Walking-in-air. He was struck by what a strange people those New Englanders must be, to have—at least a few of them—such a gift, and treat it only as utility. . . . Beneath the gulls, the river Mississippi lay many miles wide, its current, beaten silver, reflecting the mid-day's winter sun like the oval yolk of the Rain-bird's egg.

"You misunderstand me." Sam turned back from wonderful airiness to the chamber's circling stone space. "I wasn't trying to persuade you, Princess. I was explaining the necessity. You cannot *say* no."

"I think I can." Princess Rachel stood up behind her desk— was certainly a little taller—and started to the door. "And you are leaving."

"*Don't* . . . do that." Sam stayed where he was, saw her hesitate. "If you call your guards in, my sergeant and I might have to kill them. It would be a bad beginning."

The Princess stood still.

"—A lesson, Princess. Power lies along the edge of the nearest blade, and the best. If it were not for the Queen's rule, my sergeant and I could kill your two guards. Then I might beat you—bend you over that desk, rape you, *force* you to marriage. I've known men who would do it. I've seen men at this court who would do it." Sam reached over his right shoulder, slid the long sword's blade a few inches up out of its scabbard . . . then slid it back. "You see, Rachel, this solar is no sanctuary at all, and never has been. Your safety has rested—since your father's death—in the hands of a tired lady, now growing old. A lady who goes to bed with fear and deep decisions every night of her life, so that you, and others like you, do not have to."

"My mother—"

"Rachel, the Queen has said I might try to persuade you. And when a Queen says 'try'—as when I say 'try'—what is meant is, *get it done.*"

"You lie! She wouldn't do that."

"I'm sure she wouldn't, ordinarily. She'd wish you married into one of the great River families, I suppose, since you seem not up to ruling more than book-shelves. But you might say Toghrul Khan has been our marriage-broker, Rachel. The arranger of our engagement at least, from the time your mother received pigeons confirming that Seventh and Eighth *tumans* had taken your West-bank army's garrison at Map–Jefferson City, and killed them all.—How many was it? Three thousand . . . four thousand men? And, of course, the women and children."

A silent Princess then, standing still as if savage dogs surrounded her, the blue dots on her cheekbones like spattered ink.

"—Which also was the reason she wasn't as angry as she might have been, hearing that my army had come up into Map-Louisiana."

"My mother doesn't confide her reasons to me."

"No. Why should she, Rachel?" Sam walked to the west window. That view was of Island's stone keeps, then the river. The coast of Map-Louisiana too far away to be seen. "Why should she? You're no part of her ruling." He turned back to the room. "She's a woman bearing responsibility for many hundreds of thousands of lives, in a kingdom still occasionally cannibal. And now, the Khan, a very great and merciless commander, is coming to your river."

"She never asks me for help!"

"Should she have to?"

"You heard her. I wasn't 'here'—only 'present.' "

"And was she right, or wrong? You allowed yourself to be only 'present,' walked away and came up here to your tower, where—it seems to me—you use books as walls, instead of ladders."

Definitely her father's daughter. Anger took her like a man, made her silent and still, except for her eyes. "You do not know me. And you do not know my mother."

"As women? No. But as present and future rulers, Rachel, I know you both very well, being one of those odd creatures myself. A creature whose army the Kingdom needs, a creature who might make a son-in-law who will *not* murder the Queen for the throne,"—Sam smiled—"even with what is bound to be great provocation. A son-in-law also capable of dealing with the river lords, the Kingdom's East and West-bank armies, *and* the Fleet."

"And you—of course—are capable of all that."

"No, not without you. Without you, without an engagement to marry you, Rachel, I remain only the provincial war-lord you named me, and unable to unite the Kingdom's armies with mine. Unable to command them."

"*I will not do it.*" The Princess walked back to her desk, and sat, seeming less secure behind her paperwork walls. "Now, you've said what you have to say. Please leave me."

"Rachel, your people and mine *need* my sword." Sam smiled at her, hoped she saw kindness in it. "And, sadly, where my sword goes . . . so do I."

"I would be no help in any of that." Perhaps there were tears in her eyes. "I'm happiest with copybooks. I enjoy . . . quiet." She tried a small smile. "I am not like my mother."

Sam glanced out the south window for the gull, and saw several a bow-shot away, riding cold wind. "I understand. You would be happy in some peaceful house. Perhaps with a peaceful man, but certainly with as many copybooks as could be gathered or lent from here or there . . . and visitors whose interests reached beyond present wars, present politics. You'd wish to correspond with others of like mind from Boston to the Pacific Coast—not all Kipchaks, I understand, gallop and shoot arrows—and from Mexico City, as well. Perhaps learn the Beautiful Language. . . ."

"Yes. That's very much what I'd like."

"Then let me tell you, Rachel, what *I'd* like. . . . There's a farm in the hills past Villa Ocampo. It's a place—we measure in Warm-time acres—a farm of about six hundred acres. A sheep farm, with more summer grazing higher in the hills. And there's hunting. Partridge and deer, of course. Brown bear . . . wolves. There's a fieldstone house on the place, with a little wall around it, and a garden and orchard. We have just enough summer, most years, for crab apples."

The Princess listened and watched him, as a wary young mare might watch from spring pasture. Ready to wheel and run.

"—A man named Patterson owns the farm I'm speaking of. Important sheep-runner, Albert Patterson. And I believe he'd sell the place to me. There's no guarantee, of course—we hold a citizen's property as part of lawful liberty—but I believe he might sell, if I met his price." Sam smiled at her. "That is what *I'd* like, and like to do."

"Milord—"

"So now, Rachel, we know what we'd wish our lives to be. But, since neither of us is a fool, I think we also know the lives we will *have*."

"Your obligations are yours only."

"Yes—as yours will be to continue the decency of your mother's rule here! Decent, at least, compared to what it had been, with men eating men for dinner, and the river lords seizing anything they *couldn't* eat."

"My . . . my mother rules and wishes to rule. I don't."

"Your mother will soon be old, Rachel. She won't be able to shelter your people much longer from the river lords and the generals of East-bank and West. She won't be able to shelter you from men who would take you, or simply cut your throat, in consideration of the throne."

"And you have no consideration of the throne?"

"I don't *want* the fucking thing." Sam saw her wince at the word. Gently brought up . . . too gently brought up. "I don't have a choice! You and I *have* no choices. The thousands of men and women on your river, *and* down in my North Mexico—many of them better people than we are, Princess—depend on us to do what we're *supposed* to do. Their children depend on it."

"*I* will decide my duty." She stood; her white fists struck the top of the desk before her, hitting the wood hard. Three long sheets of paper sifted to the floor. "I will decide—not *you.*"

Sam went to the door, so angry he felt his hands trembling. Angry at this stubborn girl, striking against a trap already closed upon her. Angry at himself . . . at this great pile of rocks filled with fools.

He turned at the door. "There *is* no 'I will' for you, Rachel—and none for me. The Queen sees to that. The Kipchak Khan sees to that. Boston, and the Emperor in Mexico City see to that. And the actions of some of our own people, fallen so far from Warm-times, also leave us no 'I will.' "

She stood staring at him as if he were some grim wizard, flown from New England on a storm. Sam saw tears in those dark eyes, saw the knowledge of her lost freedom in them—perhaps the same freedom her father was said to have regretted—and felt great pity for her.

"So, my dear,"—and why not? Perhaps, in time, she might even become his 'dear'—"like it or not, you will have to replace that pen with a dagger. And as for me, my farm will be the camps . . . my flock, soldiers." He swung the oak door open, smiled at her, and hoped she saw affection in it. "Welcome, Princess, to our engagement—and almost certainly, endless troubles." He stepped out and closed the door behind him.

Sergeant Burke, lounging by the guards, spit tobacco juice out into the stairwell and came to a fine attention with a clank of his saber's scabbard. "Congratulations, sir!"

"Fuck off, Sergeant," Sam said, pleasing Burke—and, he supposed, the two Island men as well—since soldiers liked nothing better than fond curses.

19

"I believe you're to be congratulated, Monroe." Lord Sayre stepped across West Keep's ground corridor, smiling at Sam like an old friend. "I say it, since you've come from the lady's solar without cat scratches." The wound at Sayre's mouth left lower teeth showing unpleasantly when he smiled, an effect apparently useful to the man.

Sam took the offered hand—a strong hand. "Since you're so . . . well informed and first with congratulations, except for my sergeant—I suppose I'd better be wary of you."

Lord Sayre laughed. "Always a good idea." He glanced over Sam's shoulder, where Sergeant Burke stood watching. "—And your sergeant, there, also a good idea."

Sam turned to Burke. "Henry, this is Lord William Sayre. Pass the word to the others. Lord Sayre can come to me at any time, his reasons his own."

"Sir."

"This . . . hasty engagement, with marriage *possibly* to follow, is going to be so interesting." Sayre walked beside Sam down the corridor, their boots silent on deep carpets, ringing on stretches of stone. "Too bad the war's confusing issues. You know, I'd thought I might have the throne myself, in time."

"You wouldn't have been suited to it, milord. Slightly too honorable, from what I've heard."

" 'Slightly.' Mmm, that's possible. . . . Do you play chess, Monroe?"

"No. My friend, Ned Flores, plays a strong game, but I've never really advanced past checkers."

"And I understand Colonel Flores will be playing one-handed, now?"

"Island seems always well-informed." They were walking through a huge room paneled with wood streaked rust and red.

Its ceiling, worked in hammered copper and gold, was two stories high—so high that Sam could make out few details in an
elaborately carved narrative, apparently of love and loss. . . . By
a polished granite fireplace, one of the few he'd seen without
an iron Franklin fronting it, a group of men and women dressed
in furs, and velvets in every color, were laughing at some notion
or remark. The jewels down their weapon scabbards sparkled in
the fire's light.

"Island well-informed? Informed about such as your Colonel
Flores, you bet, since our strength is not in cavalry."

"Wonderful Warm-time phrase, 'You bet.' "

"Yes . . . and your checkers game, Monroe." Sayre opened
the left of double doors, and ushered Sam through into a long
hall he'd seen before. It was decorated with musical instruments
of every different kind, hanging on the walls, or, if very large,
resting on polished stands. "—A game fairly successful, it
seems. You jump a few pieces, and are crowned." Sayre struck
a light chord on an ivory banjar as they passed.

"A move isn't the game," Sam said.

Near the hallway's end, rested what seemed a fair copy of
the ancient Warm-time piano, massive as a spotted bull, but
gleaming black. "Meanwhile . . ." Sayre, who seemed musical,
stepped over to strike a chord on the instrument's narrow keys
with both his hands together—a loud crashing sound, but beautiful. "Meanwhile, the Queen still rules."

"A very *long* meanwhile, I hope. I've had enough of ruling
to know the stink of its necessities. And, speaking of necessities,
Sayre, I've noticed Island doesn't seem much alarmed at having
lost Map–Jefferson City. Not much alarmed at the Khan's certain taking of all Map-Missouri soon—and the river, I'm told,
already freezing north of Cairo."

"Ah, well . . . *war.*" Sayre left the perhaps-piano, which, as
they walked away, still sounded softly down the corridor as if
reminding of times lost. "Monroe, we're always fighting wars.

We have over thirty thousand veteran regulars, taking both bank armies together. Pikemen, crossbowmen. They've never been terribly impressed by horsemen. You know the Warmtime phrase, 'Whoever saw a dead cavalryman?' "

Behind them, Sergeant Burke cleared his throat, his bootsteps, spurs jingling, even more definite.

"I've seen them," Sam said. "And horseback raiders are one thing, the Khan's *tumans* are another. Thousands of light and heavy horse, under perfect discipline, with fast supply trains and bridging-and-siege engineers behind them."

"Mmm . . . Jefferson City making your point, I suppose."

"I hope so, for the Kingdom's sake. Once the Map-Texans were beaten at Cut'n Shoot? The old Khan had their bones collected and ground-up to enrich horse feed."

"Yes. . . . A word of advice?"

"Of course." Ahead, polished dark wood, gleaming uncarpeted, ran to the West Keep steps.

"It occurs to me, Monroe, it might be useful for you to speak with Peter Bailey."

"Retired from East-bank army, isn't he?"

"Ah—done your informational! Yes, retired, but still our grand old man. Still the best general in either army, in my opinion. If the King had had him up in Map-Kentucky, the King would still be alive. . . . Bailey's here at Island now, over in East Tower, come for a law-case on some leased estate land."

A small marble statue of a crouching cat was set on a green-stone stand along the corridor wall. Sayre paused and ran a forefinger along the carving before walking on. "Jemima Patch's work. . . . As to General Bailey, the old man doesn't care for me, which you may consider a recommendation; he's not a man for the court. But if I were you—a provincial commander of note, and *possibly* soon to be a prince—I'd speak with him." Sayre hesitated, seemed to have more to say.

"Yes . . . ?"

"Well, with no intent to offend . . . most of Middle Kingdom, Monroe, will *not* find you an impressive heir to the throne. You're pretty much a savage as far as the River's concerned, a no-dot nobody. But Bailey was a great fighting man—both armies loved him, though the Fleet did not. His support would be worth more than regiments to you."

"Sounds like good advice," Sam said. They'd come to the Keep's stairs. "And if the old man bites me, I'll let him know it was your idea of amusement, and I only an innocent and honorable young soldier."

"Ah . . . checkers." Sayre smiled, bowed, then strolled away.

"Your impressions, Sergeant."

"Good man at your side, sir. Risky, at your back."

"Fair enough," Sam said. . . . And why not to East Tower, now, to see the old man? A long walk, then likely steep stairs. There was no place at Island reached without climbing many steps.

*   *   *

With Henry Burke slouching behind him like some great carnivorous stork in armor—and after two inquiries of the way—Sam climbed a last flight of stone stairs, went down an icy corridor, and found the door to Bailey's rooms.

He knocked . . . knocked harder, and wasn't answered.

Sergeant Burke eased past, and hit the door hard enough to shake it in the jamb.

Muffled curses from inside. A bolt slid back, and an old man with shaving soap on his face, looked out at them. He was barefoot, and wearing a deep-green belted robe, spotted here and there with grease.

"Oh . . . it's you." He stood back from the door.

"You expected me, sir?" Sam walked into the room, gestured for Burke to wait outside.

The general, bulky, but bent with age, went back to shaving at a enameled basin of hot water on a stand also holding a small, polished-metal mirror. There were suds and splashes on the stone floor by his meaty, white, bare feet.

The old man gripped a long razor in a knob-knuckled hand, peered into the small reflecter, and began to scrape his cheek. "Expected to be annoyed by some fool," he said, "since the Khan took Jeff City." He paused for delicate work along his upper lip. The razor's blade flashed in firelight. "Damn woman remarked my stubble this morning. Carping old bitch. . . ."

A small iron stove didn't seem to warm the room. Perhaps couldn't; the stone ceiling looked to be three men high.

"*This* fool, sir, is Sam Monroe."

The old man held his razor away, and smiled. "I know which fool you are, milord." Bailey's eyes, sunk in wrinkles as some far-south lizard's, were an almost topaz yellow. He recommenced shaving. "I used to have a servant for this chore—you know Warm-time 'chore'?"

"Yes. Very apt, sir."

"Mmm. . . . I *used* to have a servant, before spending every fucking piece of silver I have to settle with a land thief named Edgar Crosby!"

"I've heard of some court case." Sam noticed a faint odor of urine from the old man's chamber-pot.

"Not a 'case.' A *crime*. I'd intended Highbank for my granddaughter. Now, little Agnes will be a fucking pauper!"

"And if I promise to see to it, sir, that in the future, little Agnes *doesn't* become a pauper, can we talk about this war?" Sam swung his scabbarded sword off his back, and sat, without invitation, in the nearest of two fat, velveted armchairs facing the futile stove.

Bailey rinsed his razor. "And Crosby's head?"

"Your Master Crosby's head—and all our heads—may be used as *buzkash* balls by the Khan's horsemen, if this kingdom doesn't come fully awake."

General Bailey grunted, then concentrated on finishing shaving, flicking suds from his razor onto the floor's stone. He had four tattooed dots on one cheek, five on the other. "And from me—retired, aged, forgetful—you wish?"

"Some sensible advice."

"Oh, *that*. Do you intend to try to command this war for us?"

"The Queen, so far, allows only that I 'advise' Kingdom's forces."

"Ah. . . . And you intend to press that small authority as far as it will go?"

"Yes, I do, sir, since my people also stand under threat. The Queen is a great lady, and a fighter, but not a war *planner*."

Bailey rinsed his razor, folded it, and set it on the basin's edge. He mopped his face with a white woven-cloth towel. "I found your campaigns very interesting. The Boston people at Map-McAllen, for reasons of their own, reported them to us in detail. I suspect that demonstrated competence is why you are not at the bottom of the river. Apparently it's thought you might prove useful." The old man sat in the other armchair, lifted his bare feet onto a worn ottoman, and settled with a grunt, staring into the Franklin's small fire. "Who suggested you come see me?"

"Sayre."

"Ah . . . that oh, so clever man. Too fucking clever."

"A soldier, though."

"Yes, a soldier, if you keep an eye on him." The old man shifted slightly in his chair. "Your campaigns. The night thing at—God-Help-Us'

"Yes."

"Really not bad. Better than not bad."

"I was lucky."

"Of course. And lucky in the men—and women, by Lady Weather!—that fought for you. Did seem to me . . . and of course I wasn't there. But hearing of it, it did seem to me you spent your people a little too freely. Might have substituted maneuver for slaughter—certainly in the initial assault. It can be more useful to *confuse* an enemy, than kill a few more of them."

". . . Yes, you're right, sir. I thought of strong left-flanking, get them half-turned from me, but I was afraid the cavalry might just charge away into the night . . . turn up weeks later in Map-Guadalajara."

The old man's laugh ended with a liquid cough. "And by Jesus they might have, at that. I've found cavalry . . . not quite trustworthy."

"I've learned to trust them. And since I'm presently *looking* at a pair of flat, obviously-infantry feet, I'll dismiss an ignorant observation."

Bailey smiled and wiggled his toes. "Oh, no insult intended. All your people seem to know their business."

"Yes, they do."

The old man stroked his cheeks, evaluating his shave. "Stupid woman . . ." He turned from watching the fire to look at Sam, an examination as coolly interested as an elderly cat's. "And just what do you, as a young commander of rather limited ex-perience—no experience on the river at all—just what do *you* think needs to be done?"

"Sir, I think what's left of the West-bank army should be behind fortifications—dug-ditch and palisade, if that's the best they can do—until the river freezes, and they join East-bank army. Your General Pomeroy needs to stop sticking his neck out for the Kipchaks to chop. No more half-assed marching and countermarching."

"Hmm. Miles Pomeroy has had the fever-malaria for years.

It makes him short-tempered, restless. I doubt he'll take that 'advice' to heart. Though I also doubt that fortification will win the war."

"It will stop *losing* it, while East-bank army gets its thumb out of its ass and moves west across the ice. The Fleet should be sailing north right now, ready to rig its runners to join them. The river's already freezing at St. Louis—"

"It's freezing below Lemay.—And this combination of forces will, of course, terrify Toghrul."

"It will keep his generals and half his army busy in the north, sir."

"While . . . ?"

"While my army marches up through Map-Arkansas, threatening his lines of supply . . . then waits in good defensive country."

Bailey pursed his lips and made soft kissing sounds. "Well, young man, my information is—and I still receive *some* information, some useful pigeons—my information is that the Khan has already reached his people in the north, taken command from Shapilov. Which means your army had better move fast, or they'll be too late."

"They'll move fast. They should be well into Map-Louisiana now, with the cavalry coming east from Map–Fort Stockton to join them."

"Better be. A great deal seems to depend on your General Voss."

"He's a *dependable* man, sir."

"So, with your army coming up West-bank from the south . . . which the Khan probably knows already—"

"I think not. The cavalry, coming east, should screen the army's march for at least a week or so."

"Very well, Monroe, let's say that's true—"

"We'll have my army coming up the west bank, and your East-bank army crossing the ice in the north, supported by the Fleet. The Khan will find himself between two immediately threatening forces—and will have no choice but to divide his army to deal with them. He won't have time to attack one with all he has, then turn to face the other."

"He may try to make the time."

"Not with his supply-lines threatened north of the Map-Ozarks, sir. No fodder; no remounts; no replacements. Time will be against him."

The old man sighed. "From your lips, to the ears of Floating Jesus."

"And Mountain Jesus as well, General."

"Well . . . it's a very *young* strategy, Monroe. With many *ifs*."

"It's the only one, sir, I think has any chance at all."

"Mmm. . . . So, the Khan, once he realizes he's blundered by campaigning with an enemy left behind to cut his lines of supply, must send troops south to at least dislodge that enemy. But he must also leave forces in the *north*, to hold the river ice against the Fleet, and East-bank army."

"Yes."

"So he will send, or go south himself, to meet . . . you? I assume you intend to command that battle."

"Yes, sir."

Bailey put his head back and closed his eyes as if beginning a nap. "And what chance do you give this strategy, young man?"

"The only chance we've got, sir."

"Well, that's fair enough. A soldier's answer, at any rate." Still with his eyes closed. "—Of course, if he beats you, destroys your army without taking heavy losses, he'll use your own plan in reverse."

"Yes, if he won with light losses, he'd hook to the riverbank there, let his northern forces keep *our* northern forces busy until the river freezes down to him. Then he'd send his *tumans* out onto the ice to take Island."

"And the Kingdom."

"Yes. And the Kingdom.—But he won't *have* light losses, General. Win or lose, I promise we will ruin him in the fight. So Kingdom will still have a better than even chance against the rest of his army, in the north."

Bailey opened his eyes. "A fair-enough promise. Well, you have a notion, milord. And I like it—there's a nice, nasty unfairness to it. But it will depend, of course, on *our* people and *your* people fighting as one, though so many Warm-time miles apart."

"Yes."

"To deal with which difficulty, I suppose, I'm being recruited, though so old, and now impoverished."

"There would be pay."

"Um-hmm. Same nasty odor of taking advantage—always a sign of solid strategy."

"Horseshit," Sam said. "You'd have been very angry if you hadn't been asked to help by *someone*."

A sideways yellow glance. "And speaking of 'someone,' what does Her Majesty think of your 'advising' Kingdom's men?"

"She dislikes it extremely, and wouldn't have allowed even that if she had a better choice—and didn't need my army."

Bailey smiled. He had two teeth missing. "She is a remarkable woman. A better queen, in some ways, than Newton was a king. His heart was never really in it; he found us . . . a sad lot. And that Kentucky business, an absolute mess. General Ryan, and his so-faithful tribal allies!" The old man seemed to dream for a few moments, then roused. "So, you 'advise.' I doubt such grudging approval by Her Majesty will be enough."

"The Queen has allowed my engagement to Princess Rachel."

The general sat up. "*Has* she? Well . . . that might make a difference. And the girl will have you?"

"I believe she will, though reluctantly."

"Ah. 'Reluctantly.' 'Advise' and 'reluctantly.' Son, you're going to be very lucky to keep your head—even forgetting Togh-rul and his Kipchaks."

"I know it."

Bailey hauled himself out of his chair, padded to the Franklin, and struck the hot stove-pipe with his fist. A small belch of ash and smoke came from the fire. "Fucking thing. . . . If the Kip-chaks had *not* taken Map–Jefferson City—"

"I know. In that way, Toghrul works for me."

"He'll work against you, when he finds he has to take half his army down to Map-Arkansas." The general's robe was dusted with ash. "Think you can beat him?"

"If he fights my fight—yes."

"And your fight will be?"

"Wait for him in broken, wooded country, hills with some height to them. On perhaps a seven-to-eight-hundred-acre front, cut by narrow hollows. And all under Lord Winter's snow."

"Map-Ozarks."

"Yes."

Bailey tapped the stove-pipe again, absently. "So, you leave him no room for sweeping cavalry maneuvers. . . . He'll break his command into smaller units, try to work them along the ridges into your formations."

"I would, in his place."

"And, of course, he'll dismount most of his people—have them come against you on foot."

"So I hope, sir."

"He'll still have numbers on you, even with only half his army with him."

"Yes."

Thinking, Bailey touched the stove-pipe again, left his fingers on it too long. "Ow! Damn thing. It seem cold in here to you?"

"It is cold." Sam demonstrated by blowing a faint cloud of breath. "You need a bigger stove."

"What I need," the old man said, "are twenty fewer years and two thousand pieces of silver. You'll meet him on the ridges?"

"Cavalry waits *along* the ridges, in reserve. His dismounted men will have to attack up snowy hillsides; the Light Infantry will fight them as they climb the slopes. The Heavy Infantry will be waiting when—if—they reach the crests."

"Umm. Of course, the Khan will soon know of your army, and approximately where it will stand. There'll be no surprises for him, then."

"Yes, but it seems to me, no choices either. He'll have to come to us."

"Alright." Bailey dusted ash off his hands. "I'll do what I can, milord. As you 'advise.' But everything depends on your people marching north from West Map-Louisiana. If that army *doesn't* move north, *doesn't* threaten the Kipchaks' line of supply, there'll be very little either you *or* I can do."

"Understood. And Howell Voss should join them with the cavalry at any time; possibly already has."

"Let's hope so. What I can do, now, is pigeon to suggest strictly defensive formations to West-bank army in the south. Pomeroy will listen; he's not an idiot. It seems to me that Cotton is already doing the best he can in the north, at St. Louis."

"I think so. I'd be very grateful for that pigeon, sir. And East-bank army?"

"Ah . . . my old command. Mark Aiken will do as he's ordered, and there's the rub. Know that phrase?"

"I believe I've heard it, sir. Very apt."

"Well, there *is* the rub. Aiken will require orders, since moving even *toward* West bank is contrary to founding regulations. 'Advice' won't do—not even from me. He will move only at the Queen's command, or by the Queen's warrant. Won't do more, won't do less. . . . I'd say that up till now, no one has ordered him to do anything, other than local defense situations.

Still, once he's *told* what to do, Aiken will move, and quickly, and be glad to." The old man began to pace back and forth in front of the stove. It was slow pacing, with a limp. "We're . . . you must understand, Monroe, that we're an aggressive military. Defense is a poor doctrine for us. You know the Warmtime 'doctrine'?"

"I do, yes. Sir, the Kipchaks *want* to be attacked. They hope for it, as a knife fighter wishes for a clumsy thrust to counter for his kill. What they *don't* want, is delay, and a mobile and determined defense."

"Oh, I understand very well." Pacing away, the old man spoke that to a wall and glassed arrow-slit. "But what you must understand, young man,"—limping back, now—"is that by *being* aggressive, the Kingdom's forces have been very effective at controlling the river and six Map-states. Dealing for the most part, of course, with savages, tribesmen and so forth. Now, they're being asked to meet a military at least as formidable as ours—and commanded, I regret to say, by a genius of war."

"And the division of the army into East and West-bank commands?"

The old man stopped pacing. "Oh, that began as a sensible precaution on the part of our kings. Did you know it used to be a death-penalty offense for an officer of one bank army *ever* to cross the river . . . ever to have a close relationship with an officer from the opposite bank?"

"I'd heard that."

"And heard correctly. It was all a matter of careful balances— and now, of course, has become a weakness. It had occurred to no one, myself included, that it might be wise for both bank armies to *cooperate* against the Kipchaks, moving back and forth across the river to threaten his forces' flanks."

"Must be done now, sir." Sam stood, buckled his sword harness . . . reached over his shoulder to touch the weapon's hilt.

"Yes. Now it must be done, milord. And the Fleet won't like

it. They've always been pleased to deal with a *divided* army. But East-bank was my old command, and I believe Mark Aiken will at least prepare to move, if I convince him that a direct order will be coming. Then he'll be able to get his regiments out onto the ice with no delay."

"That is . . . better than I'd hoped for, sir. I owe you a great debt."

"You keep that in mind, young man. I believe you mentioned . . . pay?" Bailey stooped for a small piece of firewood at the stove's rack, tossed it into the flames.

"I'll see to it, General. . . . And I think I've taken enough of your time."

"Oh, nothing but time, now. Time, and a little widow—quite old, of course—but enough of a bitch to be interesting."

"The suggester of shaving?"

"The very one." He walked Sam to the door. "Remember, milord, your people have to be in place—and soon."

"I know it."

"And the other matter—"

"—Is Kingdom's fleet."

"That's right. If our fleet doesn't get north, and onto the ice to slice through those *tumans'* formations . . ."

"Any influence with the admirals, sir?"

The old man smiled. "Why, yes. The admirals are very much like sea-whales—they snort and wallow, roll and blow. And they hate my guts. That's always influence of a sort, if properly applied."

Sam paused at the door. "My thanks again, sir, for your help."

"You haven't got anything to thank me *for*, yet." The old man put a hand on Sam's shoulder. "When you can do a little better than 'advise,' you might take it upon yourself to see Lenihan. He's *supposed* to be coordinating command, here."

"I will. And I wish you could be fighting with me."

Bailey shook his head. "You *are* young. I can't tell you how grateful I am that I *won't* be fighting beside you. What's the copybook phrase? 'Scared to death'? I was scared to death, every battle I fought."

"I doubt it," Sam said, and swung the door open. Sergeant Burke came to attention.

"What's your name, Sergeant?" Bailey bent a yellow eye on him.

A more rigid attention. "Burke, sir!"

"Well, Sergeant Burke, watch this boy's back."

"Sir!" Followed by a very snappy salute—now, it seemed to Sam, as much a part of his soldiers as their belly-buttons.

. . . There was no temptation as great as inaction. Sam stood weary in the corridor's cold, drafty gray stone, Sergeant Burke standing silent behind him, and wished for rest, solitude, an end to persuading strangers. An end to maneuvers of words, as wearing as a battle in this great smoky warren of wind and rock.

The sergeant cleared his throat. And as if that had been a signal to march, Sam marched.

It would be the chamberlain's office, next—undoubtedly a mile away through freezing granite halls and stairways—to attempt to persuade that clever fat man to, in turn, try to persuade the Queen to loosen her grip, only slightly, on power.

It seemed unlikely—as everything on the river seemed unlikely, dreams flowing down in the current's ice with their Floating Jesus, so Sam felt he might wander Island forever.

* * *

Rodney Sewell had come down-river from Cooper Estate just two days before. Sent for to come quickly, he'd landed still wearing the family's livery, but changed in the dock shed to brown smock and sack trousers.

A preparation under-cook had been willing enough, for a bare handful of copper, to provide a place for a tall, shabby, ginger-haired stranger to sleep, deep in the kitchen cellars. Willing enough, if chicken-birds were properly gutted, potatoes peeled, and onions sliced by the basketful.

The people called him Ginger, since Sewell never offered his name, and were impressed by his gutting chicken-birds like a wonder. But though he always washed that mess off at the pump before the scullions' meals were served, and was quiet and decently mannered, the pot girls avoided him. Perhaps he washed too well, as if his hands—large, and long-fingered—had more important things to do.

Also, his first day working, he'd responded in an unpleasant way to the teasing any new kitchener was bound to expect. He'd stared at them, and was so oddly silent—while the gutting knife worked on, worked faster, its greasy blade flashing through flesh—that the teasing stopped.

Lunchtime on his third day, Sewell had strolled past the serving trays for a suite of Tower rooms. Strolled so near that the meat cook, Mr. Harris—in conversation with a fat servant belonging to those rooms—had cursed him and waved him back to his work.

Hours later, after filleting a deep basketfull of fishes to rest in ice as dinner preparation, Sewell ambled by the trays again. One held sliced carrots, turnip crisps, and pickled mussels. Sewell hesitated there, saw the idiot scrubber watching him, and walked away. He went through the second kitchen and down the cellar corridor to the turning for barrel preserves, and the jakes.

The storage there, shadowy and damp, extended from the corridor on either side down long, narrow aisles, walled by high stacks of barrels with more barrels packed behind them. All smelling sour with tons of brined cabbage—Warm-times' 'sour kraut'—some of it five, six years old. Sewell had never had a taste for it.

Down each dark aisle, hacked cabbages and huge open barrels—some half-filled, some crusted with salt shipped up from the Gulf Entire—stood beside long, knife-scored work tables.

Sewell had come to the end of storage, had the door to the jakes in sight, when something very heavy draped itself across his back and shoulders. It staggered him, with surprise as much as anything, but Sewell was quick, had always been very quick and strong. He would have had his gutting knife out, except that two fat legs had wrapped themselves around him, so his arms were pinned to his sides.

The knotted cord that whipped around his neck was inevitable, though Sewell did everything that could and should be done. He tried to scream—just too late—so made only a soft croaking sound. He bent, and bucked into a somersault to smash the strangler to the stone floor. Then he got to his feet—a difficult thing to do—and drove backward with great strength into a side aisle and a work table's heavy, seasoned edge.

With luck, the oak might have broken the strangler's spine, but hadn't. Whoever, he was a sturdy man, and he'd shifted a little just in time. Even so, given only one good breath—only one—Sewell felt anything might be possible.

But no breath was given, and Sewell thrashed and staggered this way and that down the narrow aisle, kicked and arched his back, writhed to work his arms, his hands, free of those fat legs locked around him. It was difficult to do with no breathing. . . . Soon it became impossible, and he knelt on the stone—that great weight still clinging, bearing on him. The cord buried deep in Sewell's neck seemed now made of diamonds, it sparkled so in his mind. He felt little things breaking in the back of his eyes from brightness.

He was lying down, face pressed to cool stone, and had no

idea how that had happened, where the time had gone. He could feel a thing in his chest trembling. He was warm in the seat of his pants. . . .

Ansel Carey, whistling a song his father had taught him, went up the aisle to the corridor, looked left and right, then came back to haul the corpse onto the work table, and go through its pockets. He found a gutting knife, another little blade hiding strapped to the right ankle, twenty-seven coins—copper, silver, and gold—and a tiny blown-glass bottle with a string-wound stopper. There was a thimbleful of ashy powder in it, that smelled like toasted almonds.

He tossed everything but the money into a brine barrel at the end of the work table, then slid the corpse that way. With grunts of effort, he doubled it over, lifted it . . . and stuffed it down into the big barrel butt first, so the feet and black, swollen face came together at the top, awash in pickling.

"Unappetizing," Master Carey said, fitted the oak lid down tight, then used a mallet to set the top hoop. . . . While he labored—rolling the barrel to the back of the narrow aisle, then, with the aid of a plank as lever, hoisting it level by level, deep into the storage stacks—he decided the matter had been, after all, too slight to have mentioned beforehand, orders or not. And too squalid to report now, to a young Captain-General with more important matters on his mind.

20

"Sir, what is the *matter* with these fools? As you suggested, whenever I'm out of these damned rooms, I've been having 'casual' conversations with a number of civilians and middle-rank officials—and those older officers who'll speak to a woman soldier without smirking—and none seem very interested in the Kipchaks."

Sam saw a tired Margaret Mosten sitting across from him at their suite's great table—as she undoubtedly saw a weary Sam Monroe. "The matter, Margaret, is they simply don't believe the threat is great. This afternoon, Chamberlain Brady dismissed the Khan with a wave of his hand. These people are not convinced this war requires that they let some war-lord from nowhere—"

"A *no-dot* war-lord, sir." Lieutenant Darry, still eating at supper's end, paused in forking up a baked apple.

"That's right, Pedro. A no-dot war-lord."

The long table supported the remains of food brought up under covered silver salvers by four servants in the Queen's blood-red livery. Servants accompanied from the kitchens by an untrusting Master Carey . . . who'd then uncovered platters of salt ham, broccoli and fresh onions, a roasted duck, potatoes creamed to pudding in spotted-cattle milk, and spiced baked apples—tasting them at random while the food cooled, the meats congealed.

Now, supper over, Carey—who remained mysteriously fat, since he never sat to eat—was collecting Island's silverware. The Chief of Kitchens, a tyrant laired deep in Island's cellar warren, counted all returned silverware, even from the Queen's table.

". . . But, do they think Toghrul Khan is just going to go *away?*"

"Margaret, except for some of the officers the Queen has just brought to Island, the Boxcars think he's basically only a more formidable tribesman. And they've dealt with tribesmen and tooth-filers many times."

"But they lost Map–Jefferson City!"

" 'A fluke,' is how the chamberlain described that. I got the impression he thought the Queen was making too much of it."

"The court tends to agree, sir." Darry poured himself more berry brandy. The lieutenant, though slender, seemed to have an extraordinary capacity—was always hungry, and never seemed drunk. "People I speak to, some of them officers of the better regiments, regard this war as . . . well, a career opportunity. Except for those like Stilwell or Brainard, who have estates to inherit."

"Fucking overdecorated roosters." Margaret made a face. It seemed to Sam she hadn't yet forgiven him for her boots, leathers, and mail, in a court where the women—and men—dressed like furred and velveted song-birds.

"Well, Captain, they're frivolous . . . and they aren't." Pedro twirled his silver goblet; those were counted in the kitchens, too. "Most of them have fought tribesmen. And if not, fought each other in duels. I feel . . . really, I feel quite at home. Though, of course, they are a little rough."

"A little rough?" Sam considered some brandy, then decided not.

"Well, sir, Jerry Brainard has killed a man who questioned his family recipe. A question of palms."

"Palms?" Margaret said.

"Yes, Captain. Palms. Girl's palms—of course hardly done at all, now. But the question was whether to cattle-butter them before broiling, or after."

"Lady *Weather* . . ."

"And which," Sam said, "did the Brainards favor?"

"Oh, Jerry said, 'Before.' Before, absolutely. Keeps 'em plump; keeps 'em from drying out on the grill."

"These people," Margaret said, "deserve the Kipchaks."

"But our people don't," Sam said, "and Toghrul will see to it that as the Kingdom goes, so will they."

"True."

"And speaking of deserving, I've seen no Jesus priests, no ladies of Lady Weather at Island."

"No, sir," Darry said. "I understand the Queen doesn't allow it, doesn't allow them to stay. She sends them back where they came from with silver pieces. Says to do good—and stay gone."

"Making enemies, Pedro?" Margaret said.

"Don't think so, Captain. I'm told she gives a *lot* of silver. And the winter festivals, very elaborate, supposed to be wonderful to see. Canceled this year, of course."

"Master Carey," Sam said, "do we have a healthy pigeon?"

"Two, sir. Only two since Hector died on the *Naughty*. Couldn' stand the motion." Ansel Carey kept the birds in his room, and expressed to them the only tenderness Sam had seen from him.

"Leave the silverware; let the Queen's people count it when they come for the platters."

"What message, Sam?"

"To Howell and Ned, Margaret, through Better-Weather. Howell's probably joined by now, and Eric can relay dispatch-riders up to them. I want them moving north fast as possible. Forward elements should already be out of West Louisiana."

"Sam, they *know* that." Margaret had carved the supper meat, and was cleaning ham juice from her long dagger's blade with a red woven-cloth napkin. "They don't need to be reminded . . . if a galloper could even catch up to them."

"Well, they may not need a reminder if they get it—but they might have needed it, if they don't."

"Sam, that doesn't make any sense at all."

"Does to me," Darry said, and pushed his dessert plate away. The lieutenant tilted his heavy chair back and sat at ease, gleaming boots crossed at the ankles. "Precious Miss Murphy's Law. What may be fucked up—your pardon, Captain Mosten—will be fucked up. So, better a pigeon, to be sure."

"My thinking," Sam said. "And it's possible that Howell . . . even that both of them have been killed."

"Nothing," Margret said, and got up from the table. "Nothing could kill both of those men. I don't think Ned is killable."

"Did lose his hand," Darry said.

Master Carey's room was down the corridor. Sam could hear him murmuring to the pigeons, apparently making his selection.

"Speaking of hands, Pedro; you've had more than a week dealing them out at the card-tables at court. And, I understand, have been successful. What news?"

"Master Carey exaggerates, sir. Just fun cards, small stakes; never enough to make anyone angry. Also, no involvement with any lady having serious connections."

"That's a comfort. Go on."

"Well, sir . . ." Darry brought his chair forward, sat at attention. "Well, sir—this *is* no court, in the sense of the Emperor's court at Map—Mexico City. It's . . . really more like chieftains gathering at a tribal longhouse in the mountains, or north, along the ice-wall. Though the longhouse in this case is stone, and miles each way." Darry paused, considering. "It isn't that there aren't *manners* here, sir, and decent precedence—there are. But it's all damn shallow."

"Meaning," Margaret Mosten said, "keep a sergeant with you, Sam."

"Yes," Darry said. "Absolutely. Not that murdering you would be undertaken lightly, sir."

"Glad to hear it."

"But it wouldn't be, well, regarded as . . . memorable."

"And no fucking consideration as to what might happen then?" Margaret leaned over the table like a storm. "With the Kingdom at war, and our army marching into Map-Arkansas?"

"Ah, but you see, Captain, the people who are the considering sort, wouldn't be the ones who killed our Captain-General." He smiled at Sam in encouragement.

"One or more of the sergeants," Margaret said, "*and* either Pedro or me in any public gathering."

Darry nodded. "We have no dots on our faces, sir, is what it comes down to. We aren't Boxcars."

"Neither was the Queen." Sam reconsidered the berry brandy, poured the barest taste into his glass and drank it . . . breathed its stinging sweetness in and out.

"No, but she is *now*, sir. She was married to their king—and, I understand, murdered to hold her own once he was gone."

"Watch your tongue, Pedro. Even stone walls can grow ears."

"Oh—oh, nothing out of the way in that sort of killing, of course, sir!" Darry said. "Admirable, really. An admirable lady . . . who having been a tribeswoman herself, knew what needed to be done."

"I'd leave the subject, Pedro. . . . Margaret, will you go and persuade Ansel to part with a fucking pigeon. I'd like to get that message sent. And Pedro, you might keep in mind that those · people at Island who do 'consider' before they act, might consider it useful to put one of my people into the river, as an indication we're not wanted here, long-term."

"I suppose that's true!" Darry seemed startled at the notion.

"So, if you find even *your* charm suddenly overvalued by new friends, a new lady, you might be careful what dark corner you're invited to."

"I keep an eye on him, milord." Master Carey carried in a bird basket, with Margaret marching behind him. "I've been Sancho to his Panzo, or whatever . . . keep close to any fun, or lady."

"Tediously so," said Lieutenant Darry.

"It was a question, sir, but I chose our Louella." Carey set the basket on the table. "She's small, but swift. And spirited— flies so hawks can kiss her ass."

Louella set a bright black eye to the basket weaving, examined them.

"Sir," Margaret said, "it would be a mistake. They'll think you have no confidence in them. They'll start looking over their shoulders for *more* messages."

"Good point, sir," Darry said. "Still, there's Miss Murphy's Law. . . ."

"Pedro," Margaret said, "be quiet."

Sam closed his eyes for a moment . . . saw Howell in camp, unrolling the bird's tiny message-paper and reading it. Then saying, "Well, for Weather's sake. What the fuck's the matter with Sam?"

"Alright. . . . Take the bird back, Ansel."

There were two very hard knocks on the suite's heavy door. It opened partway, and Sergeant Mays leaned in. "Her Majesty an' the ax-girl to see you, sir."

Master Carey snatched up Louella's basket, and waddled swiftly back to his room as the Queen, in a long wolf-fur cloak, came in past Sergeant Mays, her armswoman behind her.

"Where's that fat man off to?"

Sam stood with Margaret and Darry, and bowed. "Honored to welcome you, ma'am. . . . Carey's our schemer, spy, and supply person. Secrecy's a custom with him, so he snatched our pigeon away."

"One of your Master Lauder's people, I suppose?"

"I'm sure of it."

"This habit,"—the Queen stood in the middle of the room—"this habit you have of being so directly honest as to insult those you speak to, I find very unpleasant."

"I apologize, Queen. I do it to unsettle those older and cleverer than I am."

"And that's exactly what I mean—that sort of thing you just said."

"Perhaps I should try a *little* lying. Will you sit, ma'am? Have wine . . . berry brandy?"

Queen Joan shook her head, then was silent, as if she'd forgotten why she'd come. Her ax-girl watched Sergeant Mays, since he stood closest to them.

"What is it, ma'am?" Sam said. "What's happened?"

". . . Nothing. Nothing's 'happened,' Monroe. I visit where I choose, when I choose." Sam saw, by the hanging lanterns' warm light, that the Queen was pale as cotton sheeting.

"They're on the river?"

"Our difficulties," the Queen said, "our . . . difficulties are still *our* concern."

"They've taken St. Louis."

The Queen made a sound in her throat, and clawed her fingers as if she were about to fight. Then, spreading her arms wide, her long wolf cloak swinging open, she began a slow-stepping dance of fury. Her ropes of pearls swaying with her furs, she turned in drifts of flower scent, eyes rolled back, teeth bared to bite. She danced in paces her ax-girl mirrored to stay within reach. "*I'll kill . . . that fucking Kipchak. Every person, everything he loves, I'll kill. I'll skin his wife, his child*—I hear there's to be a child. *I'll skin that baby slowly, for him to see— and his horses, skin his horses alive before I skin* him, *roll him screaming in salt, and serve him roasted!*"

It was a promise frightening to see danced and almost sung. Sam noticed Sergeant Mays stand back a step, and saw that Margaret had closed her eyes, as if the Queen were a fire burning too close.

When Queen Joan stood still and silent, Sam went to her and took her hands while the armswoman watched. "Give me your warrant, dear."

". . . I am not your 'dear.' " But she let him hold her hands.

"Give me your warrant to assist you in this war, to command, so our armies can fight together."

"So you can prepare to take my throne—*boy?*" She pulled her hands away.

"I swear to *uphold* you on your throne, Queen—uphold your rule against any and all. I swear it on the memory of my Second-mother. . . . And will hold to it,"—he smiled—"no matter how inconvenient."

"Never," the Queen said. "—*Never.*" She turned and walked out. Her ax-girl, following, glanced back to be certain of no surprise, then closed the door behind them.

"What do we do?" Margaret said into silence. "Sam, what do we do, now?"

"What do we do . . . ?" Sam took a deep breath. "What *I* do is keep trying to persuade the generals and admirals here to cooperate with our army."

"Won't do it, sir, without her." Carey, out of his room like a mountain marmot, appearing in the hall. "Boxcars think we're shit, sir."

"Sad," Pedro Darry said, "but true." An ancient phrase.

"Then fuck 'em," said Sergeant Mays.

"No. We *need* these people." Sam reached for the brandy, noticed Margaret Mosten's glance, and set the crystal jug aside. "I'll go to the river lords, tomorrow—"

The chamber's door swung open again, and Queen Joan's ax-girl stepped in. "Her Majesty," she said.

The Queen stood in the doorway. "I've . . . changed my mind." She stared at them a few moments, then said, "Dear God." One of Warm-times' shortest sayings.

* * *

After an early breakfast delivered to their rooms—the roast pork, boiled eggs, oat pudding, and honey rolls all first nibbled for safety's sake by Master Carey—Sam, with Sergeant Wilkey pacing behind him, longbow down his back, coursed through Island's passages to East Tower's stairs, cubbies, and chambers, until a serving man nodded to "General Lenihan" and pointed them to offices at the end of a lamp-lit hall.

No guard was posted there.

Wilkey opened the oak door and stood aside as Sam walked in. Three soldiers, clerks, stood writing at stands beneath hanging five-flame oil lamps. They were wearing West-bank army's blue wool, but no weapons, no armor. They set their pens down as Sam and Wilkey came in.

"Brigadier Lenihan," Sam said. "I understand he's executive for plans and coordination—dealing with both bank armies?"

"And you are?" The tallest clerk, a sergeant.

"He's 'Milord Monroe' to you," Wilkey said pleasantly. "Now, see him in to your general."

The clerk said, "Sorry, sir—milord," trotted to an inner office door, knocked, opened it, and said, "Lord Monroe to see you, sir."

There was a grumble from inside. Sam walked past the clerk into a smaller space that reminded him of Charles' cramped office at Better-Weather, though more brightly lit. A stocky man with cold gray eyes and several days' growth of beard, wearing West-bank army's blue, stood from behind a desk piled with maps and message sheets. He had three tattooed dots on his left cheek, four on the other.

"General Lenihan, I believe we have some business."

"Sir—milord—I hardly think so." Lenihan's voice was hoarse with fatigue. "And, while I wouldn't wish to be rude, I must say I don't have the time for it." The brigadier looked down at his desk-top. "There are orders to be copied, orders to be sent. In short, sir, I have a war on my hands—at least portions of it."

"I see you do. And how does your war go, General?"

"That, sir, with all respect, is something I couldn't discuss with you. Perhaps the chamberlain's office . . ." Lenihan, impatient, glanced down and shifted some papers.

Sam shoved a stack of documents aside, then sat on the edge of the desk, one booted foot on the floor. "The Queen has allowed me to be what help I can in this war, Lenihan. So it's by her warrant and authority, as well as mine, that I suggest you drop this pose of 'responsible officer weary of interfering idiots'—and prepare to take my orders."

The general's face flushed. "I would need a *written* order, signed by the Queen, to do any such—"

Sam lunged across the desk, took Lenihan's throat in his right hand, and drove the man back against the wall. The brigadier was strong, struggled, and reached for his belted dagger. Sam covered that hand with his left to keep the blade sheathed—and heard Wilkey, behind him, draw his sword.

"Put up, Sergeant!" The sword whispered back into its scabbard.

Lenihan, who couldn't breathe, fought hard. His chair went over with a clatter; a fat folder slid from the desk. He struck with a heavy fist at Sam's head and belly, tried for his balls. Then plucked and tore at the strangling hand, to wrench it free.

The office door opened.

"Mind your own business," Wilkey said behind Sam, and kicked the door shut.

The general, though a tough man, was beginning to soften with lack of air. The punches and kicks slowly became random. Sam saw in the man's eyes the astounded realization this might be death—come so oddly, so suddenly, in an *office* of all things, and at the hand of a titled stranger young enough to be his son.

Sam let him go, and the general slid down the wall to one knee, took long, gasping breaths—then staggered up with his dagger drawn.

Sam, arms crossed, sat back on the desk edge, watching him . . . taking no notice of the knife.

"You . . . young *dog!*" A furious brigadier, and even hoarser now. There were tentative knocks on the office door.

"Get away from there!" Sergeant Wilkey said. There were no more knocks.

Sam was careful not to smile. "I apologize, Lenihan. I was hasty—but I needed to get your attention. We simply don't have time to waste with nonsense." He picked a paper off the desk-top, then another, and glanced over them. "Floating *Jesus!*" Pleased to have remembered the River's Great. "You people are moving units of East-bank army to cover these fucking towns!"

"That's right!" The general was still gripping his dagger. "The Kipchaks are raiding across the ice, up-river. They're burning East-bank towns. Killing everyone in them. Children . . . everyone!"

"Of course they are, General." Sam set the papers down. "Haven't you wondered why?—The Kipchaks *like* children. They have children of their own. So they must have a reason to be crossing the river up there, attacking those towns, and killing your people—including the little children."

"You . . . put your hands on me." Lenihan sheathed his dagger.

"Yes, I did. And if you don't begin to *think*, instead of sitting passing papers like turds, I'll put my hands on you again. Is that plain enough for you, General?"

Scowling silence.

"The Kipchaks *want* you people to break up your East-bank army. Shapilov, and now the Khan, want that army dissolved into little garrisons guarding civilians who *should* be moving back off the river into the forests. What the Khan *doesn't* want, is that army united into a single force that might cross the river ice against him!" Sam shook his head. "Lenihan, you and your people at Island have been doing the Kipchaks' work for them."

"We have not."

"Yes, you have. And it must stop. We don't have *time* for mistakes this serious. So far, you've been dealing with the Khan's generals. But now, Toghrul has taken command. Another blunder like this, he'll tear your throats out." Sam stood up off the desk. "You people are not dealing with tribesmen and savages any longer, warriors who don't know discipline. You're facing a great mechanical of war—do you understand? A veteran horse-army that can move fifty Warm-time miles a day, and fight a battle that evening. All commanded by a man more intelligent than both of us together."

Sam stood off the desk, and went to the door. "So, we do things right, General, and do them quickly and in cooperation— my people coming up into Map-Arkansas, and yours north, on the river ice. We do things *right* . . . or your head and my head and the Queen's head will end piled with thousands of others, here in your great courtyard."

"I . . . don't know."

"Yes, you *do* know, Lenihan. . . . Now, by right of the Queen's warrant to me, you will inform General DeVane of East-bank army, General Parker of West-bank army, the two senior admirals at Island—Pearce and Hopkins—and the River Lords Sayre and Cooper, that their presence is commanded this afternoon in the Queen's council chamber at . . . two glasses. Each may bring one aide. And General Bailey may choose to attend, or not."

Lenihan looked even wearier than before. "I will . . . inform them, milord."

" 'Sir,' will do; we don't have time for 'milord's. But you will do more than inform them, Lenihan. You will see to it that those officers and lords are *present*—if necessary, escorted and under arrest."

". . . Yes, sir."

"What's your first name?"

"Patrick."

"Two more matters, Patrick. You're to post a guard at your corridor door. Also, put your clerks up on charges, for not supporting their officer with more than timid tapping while he was being assaulted."

A grudging first smile from the general. "Sir."

"See you at two, Pat," Sam said, and left the office, Wilkey following.

* * *

Ned Flores, weary, stood by a hasty nighttime fire, his steel hook reflecting the flames' red. "Howell, we're not moving fast enough."

"We're moving as fast as won't exhaust the men and break down the horses." Howell spit tobacco-juice hissing into the fire. "Won't do us any good, Ned, to ruin the army moving it."

"Speaking of which, we should be nearing the Kipchaks' supply lines soon."

"Yes."

"What do you want done when we hit them?"

"Take what we can use, give the rest to the local tribesmen."

"And the escort?"

"Kill them all."

"Okay. . . . My men have had no trouble with the savages—called Bluebirds, apparently. And they'll like any plunder we can give them. No trouble with the Bluebirds—but we got some cold looks from those West-bank scouts, couple of days ago."

"We're just passing through, Ned. We won't give them any trouble, and there aren't enough of them down here to give *us* any trouble. If the drum calls coming down the river are true, the Kipchaks pretty much wrecked West-bank army up at St. Louis." Howell kicked a brand back into the flames. "Also, I intend to look to those river people for food and fodder as we go north to the Map-Missouri line, in case Charles can't get supplies up to us fast enough. So, let's not kill any of the soldiers they have left."

"Right. . . . It's really upsetting."

"What?"

"That you're actually *thinking*, Howell. It's difficult to get used to."

"You insubordinate asshole. You're lucky you're wearing that nasty thing."

Flores raised his hook and kissed it. "Don't insult my Alice."

"*Alice?*"

"Why not? Remember Alice Rodriguez? Cold, curved, and dangerous?"

". . . Oh, Mountain Jesus. Hadn't thought of her for years. Well, take 'Alice'—and your regiment—and move off north. Smartly, Ned. We'll night-march six glass-hours."

"General,"—Flores saluted with the middle finger of his good hand—"consider it done."

With Ned mounted and spurred off through falling snow, calling for his trumpeter, Howell stood warming his hands at the failing fire, watching down the hillside to the defile where Phil Butler's Heavy Infantry battalions were marching north in moonlight. Marching in good spirits, apparently, since they were singing "Gringo the Russians, Oh" as they swung along. Odd, how falling snow muffled sound.

"General?" Roberto Collins reining in his horse—and looking too young to be a captain on the staff. "Last units, sir, except for Colonel Loomis's rear guard."

"Al right. Orders."

"Sir."

"Colonel Loomis to deploy three companies of Lights as tail-end charlies. Double-time the others up to flank us, deploying lightly to the east, heavily to the west. We'll be approaching the Kipchaks' lines of supply, coming from Map-Texas to north on the river. Tell her I want *no* surprises."

"Sir."

"And Roberto, make sure Charmian understands that her people are to stand no engagement. If there's a problem, they're to skirmish, then fall back on the main body."

"Yes, sir." And Collins was off at a gallop through deepening snow. Young, it seemed to Howell, young for a staff officer. And where had "tail-end charlies" come from? Some copybook . . .

"Big One-eye!" Blue-coated scimitar at her belt, Patience Nearly-Lodge Riley came to the fire's coals—small boots stomping through the snow—and tilted her hat's brim back from a face perfectly white, hair black as blindness. "I could send Webster to our Captain-General at their island. He would find him, if you have a message, or need his advice."

"I don't have a message, don't need Sam's advice, and would appreciate your staying with the baggage train where you belong. Colonel Butler put you there, Lady, and you're to stay."

"*Only* until fighting. I was promised to hover over a battle like Lady Weather, picking out this one or that one for best luck or bad."

"Right. . . . Well, until that battle, please get your Boston butt back to baggage. We are *responsible* for you."

"And I so appreciate your protection." The girl smiled up at him, her small, white right hand resting on her sword's pommel. "The Captain-General—he'll be coming soon to fight the battle?"

"Can't be soon enough. Now, if you'll just get back where you belong. We have a night march—"

"You haven't visited dear Portia-doctor at all, One-eye, not a single time in this hasty travel north. Don't you think she would like a visit from you?" Another smile with that.

"Likely as much as I'm enjoying this one," Howell said. "Go back where you belong—or be tied and taken."

Patience made a comic grimace of terror . . . paused . . . seemed to drift a little up into the air, then swept away, long coat flapping softly as she sailed over hillside drifts of moonlit snow, and left the snow unblemished.

The Queen's Room of Conference, a high-ceilinged stone box, had been arranged for discomfort. This to encourage short conferences, and little in the way of comment or advice to her from anyone. No attempt had been made to cushion that fact, or the straight-back wooden chairs ranged around a circular too-wide table, so everyone had to call their conversation. No refreshments were provided.

There was a small stove in a distant corner, with a small fire in it, and the thick, blurred glass of four arrow-slits down the room had been opened just enough for a steady, bitter little breeze to enter, and fans of powder snow.

Introductions had been made. Sam had noticed few friendly glances.

His chair had diagnosed his bad back at once, and was making it worse.

Only the Queen, bundled in lynx and wolverine, with her ax-girl standing behind her, sat in comfort on a minor throne plumped with pillows. Her daughter sat to her right, then Brady, the chamberlain. Then Generals Parker, DeVane, Lenihan—and Bailey, just arrived, his greenwool uniform as food-stained as his chamber-robe had been. . . . Then Sam, at the foot, and on around to two admirals, Hopkins and Pearce, wearing storm-gray—both exactly the ocean whales Bailey had described, so Sam had had to be careful not to grin when introduced. Then, sitting side by side, though with careful space kept between them, Lords Sayre and Cooper. Cooper, almost elderly, and just returned to Island from up-river, sat tall, thin, and slightly bent in gray velvet and gray fur—looking, Sam thought, like a friendly grandfather, though perhaps a grandfather very close with money.

The last person around the table, sitting to the Queen's left, *was* a moneyman, Harvey Sloan, treasurer, looking more of a tavern tough than a book-keeper.

Each of these men had brought an officer or aide, and those—holding folios of fine paper, ink bottles, and steel-nib pens in narrow boxes—sat in more of the uncomfortable chairs, behind their principals and well back from the table. Margaret Mosten sat behind Sam, and Pedro Darry tended the cloakroom by the chamber entrance—though, since the room was near freezing, no coats or cloaks had been handed over.

Harvey Sloan had just spoken for peace—for discussions toward it, at least, with payments of silver promised for the Khan's withdrawal.

"Harvey," the Queen said, "the Khan Toghrul is not some nose-ringed savage down off the ice at Map-Illinois. We won't buy him with beads or banjars *or* silver pieces."

"How does it harm us, Majesty, to try? He can only say *no.* And if he should say *yes,* we have bought a year or more to become stronger."

"Harvey, for Jesus' sake use your head for more than a fucking abacus! He would say *no,* because he doesn't *want* us to have a year to grow stronger!"

"Sloan," General DeVane. "Sloan, this is not a money matter."

"Well, it will swiftly become so, General! Wars are fought with money as well as soldiers, and the financial affairs of the Kingdom remain uncertain, since I'm not allowed a central bank—which we sorely need to regulate the currency. Warmtimes had one, I understand, and so should we! And also, land taxes have been in arrears four years running. So, how is this war to be paid for?"

The chamberlain, Brady, called across the table, softly as he could and be heard, "We also still have a treasury surplus—or am I mistaken?"

"If there's a time to spend," Sam said, speaking up, "it's when a knife is at your throat."

"Oh, understood, milord." The treasurer smiled. "But perhaps in your ... realm, barter still holds a place. In Middle Kingdom, it's cold cash, silver or gold."

"And mostly in mine, as well." Sam smiled back. "Though sheep and stock are occasionally traded. ... When our Charles Ketch posed the same question to me that you bring to the table, Treasurer, I told him what I now tell you: Spend the fucking *money*. And if more is needed later, the Emperor will provide it."

"The Emperor?" General DeVane again. The general, slightly fat, was an amiable-looking man, except for his eyes. They were dead black as dug coal-rock. "Now why should Rosario e Vega send any treasure to your people, or ours?"

"Because, General, once we win this war he will either send us gold and silver, if we need it, or we will go down to South Map-Mexico and ask again."

Both admirals said, "Piracy!" speaking almost together, and seemed pleased with the notion.

DeVane said nothing, only stared at Sam a moment, then nodded. Pedro had mentioned that the DeVanes of Baton Rouge still ate talking meat at festivals. ...

"Well," Sloan said, "that may be, *then.* This is now."

"Harvey," the Queen said, "shut up."

As if a voice in his head had said, "Keep Harvey Sloan," Sam determined to do it, whenever that choice was his. A Charles Ketch, but tougher, slower to back off where income and outgo were concerned.

"Monroe ..." General Parker, uniformed in blue wool, was a strikingly handsome man, tall, with clear blue eyes and perfectly graying hair perfectly trimmed. "Monroe, I confess to some puzzlement why you, rather than Her Majesty, called this meeting, for which senior officers were threatened with arrest for nonattendance. I'm curious where you found the authority for *that*—and why now you're in council on matters concerning Middle Kingdom, particularly since no announcement has been made appointing you to command of anything."

"I'll make that announcement, General." Princess Rachel spoke quietly, and did not look at Sam. "Lord Monroe and I have agreed on an engagement to marriage. Also, he has my mother's warrant to pursue this war as commander, whenever his own forces are involved."

"Which," the Queen said, "will be in *every* important decision. If I thought, Parker, this occasionally annoying young man was a fool, he would already be on his way down-river with my foot up his ass."

Sam saw Rachel begin to smile, then stop. She said, "Are matters now clear to you, General?"

"Absolutely clear, Highness." He turned to Sam with a slight bow. "Milord."

"Generals," Sam said, "Admirals and Lords, Chamberlain, Master Sloan—I'm well aware it can't be comfortable to have a stranger come up from the south and stick his nose into what was only your business. I do it for two reasons. First, what happens to Middle Kingdom in this war will determine what happens to North Map-Mexico. And second, I have found no one better qualified for the work. I am, if you'll permit me, not 'Extraordinary' in anything but battle. There, though no Toghrul Khan, I am very competent."

"And better be." General Bailey shifted in his seat. "Joan, these damn chairs . . ."

"Want a cushion?" The Queen seemed concerned. "You being so old and frail."

"I see *you* have cushions. . . ."

"Peter, I'm the Queen. Of course I have cushions. Now, do

you have anything to contribute here beyond complaints about your backside?"

"What I have to contribute, is congratulations to our young commander on the performance of his army, since he is apparently too modest to announce it. Word, likely from creek fishermen out of Map–El Dorado, was pigeoned from one of Her Majesty's ships off Greenville, and received here a little more than a glass-hour ago. It appears his man, Voss, *has* brought their cavalry divisions east to join North Mexico's army near Bossier City. That force is moving north as we speak, and will soon be within striking distance of the Khan's only lines of supply and reinforcement."

"Good news," DeVane said, "if it's followed by more good news."

"My army will be where it's supposed to be—and without delay," Sam said. "Losing St. Louis leaves us little time."

"You have great confidence in your people." The smaller admiral, Hopkins, had lost the tip of his nose in some engagement.

"I have the same, Admiral, that you must have in your veteran captains. But my army can only *threaten* from the south, until both the Fleet and East-bank army are on the ice below St. Louis. . . . Then, as the Kipchaks face a fresh force attacking in the north, across the river, so they will also face an advance severing their lines of supply in the south. The Khan will have to divide his army and fight both of us at once, unless he chooses an harassed retreat of almost a thousand Warm-time miles to West Map-Texas . . . likely never to return."

"From your lips, to Weather's wind." General Lenihan frowned. "But the Fleet seems to me to be in question. East-bank army will move; Aiken already has skirmishers out on the ice. But no pigeon has mentioned ships of the line sailing up to meet him. And unless there are warships skating through those *tumans* with scorpions and pitch-throwers, the East-bank army will be swamped just as the West-bankers were."

"It will be news to the army, I'm sure," Admiral Hopkins said, "that warships must be careened to fit with runners. This can be done by the crews, but cannot be done properly in *less* than a day."

"If this had been planned . . . had been started earlier—"

"Lenihan,"—the larger admiral, Pearce, seemed to swell in his seat—"if the Fleet had been *advised* earlier, you would have seen ships rigged earlier. We can do only what we're told to do at the time. We hadn't expected West-bank army to lose St. Louis!"

"And where were their *reinforcements?* Where was the fucking Fleet—down in the Gulf playing grab-ass with some rowboat pirates!"

"Am I to take that as personal, Lenihan? As a personal remark?"

"You are *not*, Admiral!" Sam had thought the Queen would interfere, then saw she was watching him, waiting. "There will *be* nothing personal in these discussions. We have no time for it. If any officer feels offended, he is free to come complain to me . . . then regret it."

Silence.

"Admirals, at least sixty warships are to be ice-rigged within the next five days, or there will be more *energetic* admirals commanding them. . . . And general officers will keep their mouths shut about Fleet matters—of which they are largely ignorant—and prepare to support Aiken's East-bank army with any and all personnel and supplies they require."

"Sir, we do not commingle—"

"I understand, Parker, that it hasn't been the custom to transfer troops and equipment from one bank army to the other, though it appears that General Lenihan has been making an *attempt* at coordination. Still, I know that complete separation of the bank armies has been the rule—and when we win this war, if Middle Kingdom is more comfortable with that situation, it may be reinstated. Now, however, it no longer holds."

There was a little stir around the table. Muttering.

"I will have any supply or maintenance officer, or officer commanding, who withholds troops or equipment or rations from any engaged unit of *either* bank army, court-martialed, convicted, and hanged. . . . To which end, from this meeting onward, the generals provost-marshal in both armies are united into one command—to be armored in red—under whichever officer is senior, to enforce this order without hesitation. . . . There will be no appeals from his judgment."

There were soft scratching sounds back from the table as notes were made. "No. Absolutely not!" DeVane shoved his chair back and stood. "I won't—"

"General," Sam said, speaking quietly, "I'd hate to lose you; I understand you're a *fighting* officer. But the Queen and I will have obedience. Unless you sit down, sir, you will command nothing in this war but a labor battalion."

"Floating *Jesus* . . ." DeVane hesitated, then sat down.

"Thank you, General, for yielding to necessity."

"And what . . . necessity, Monroe, do you find for us?" Lords Sayre and Cooper both looked only politely interested.

"Contribution of those goods and household fighting-men you and the other river lords can spare, short of ruin."

"Plain speaking." Michael Cooper looked at Sam as pleasantly as an old uncle might. "I do wonder, though—your pardon, Majesty—I do wonder whether this apparent emergency might be being used to take our rights away, and leave us helpless before the future's crown."

"Milord," Sam said, "I'm sure that any ruler, except Her Majesty, would find you too formidable to attempt any such thing."

Lord Cooper smiled. "Nicely said. But why am I not comforted?"

"Why, because you are alert to your interest, sir."

"As I am, Monroe," Sayre said.

"Yes—both alert to your interests, as all river lords will be. Which is why I have no doubt at all that the units of East-bank army—now concentrating above Girardeau—will receive drafts of five hundred men-at-arms from every major estate on the river. And have no doubt also that six hundred barrels of barley grain, six hundred crates of dug potatoes, and two hundred crates of iced chicken-birds or fish will be delivered immediately from each estate—or proof *positive* shown why that cannot be done. . . . The estate that withholds, will be fined in acres forfeit to the Crown—and those acres never returned."

Silence.

"—And this, milords, not punitive, but absolutely in your families' interests, since, should he win, the Khan will take care to destroy you and yours. Despite, by the way, any secret assurances his . . . emissaries . . . may have made to the contrary. Unlike Her Majesty, Toghrul will never allow the existence of *any* independence."

"So," Sayre said, "you grant us this . . . benefit."

"Yes, milord. And in addition—since the river lords are to be so generous—neither the Crown nor the armies, nor the Fleet, nor the people-Ordinary, will demand their heads for treason."

". . . Such favors," Lord Cooper said. "How will we ever repay them?"

"I dread discovering *that*, sir," Sam said, to some amusement around the table. "And now, gentlemen, if Her Majesty and Princess Rachel will bear with us, we have the tedious professional questions of Warm-times' *logistics*—timing, transport, and supply." A stir of staff officers and aides, rustling paper turned to fresh pages. "Leaving aside my army, since supplies, remounts, and reserves should already be coming behind it, how can we get onto the river ice south of Lemay 'fustest with the mostest'?"

Smiles at that around the table. No soldier, no sailor, but knew that fine Warm-time phrase.

. . . Three hours later, a stack of written orders in various scribbles—dire and demanding news to executive officers, supply officers, field commanders, ships' captains, civilian sutlers, shipyard owners, and the accomplished of many guilds—stood before the Queen.

She put her hand on top of the stack, riffled through the pages with her thumb. "Well-enough. Not too much nonsense here." Then she stood, and everyone stood with her. "But drive your people, *drive* them, gentlemen—otherwise the Kipchaks will use this paper to wipe their asses."

The Queen turned to go, but the Princess stood waiting until Sam came to her and offered his arm.

". . . Thank you, Rachel."

"For yielding," the Princess said, "to necessity?" And they followed the Queen and her ax-girl out of the Room of Conference.

. . . Lord Cooper walked back to the small stove, stood warming his hands as Sayre came to join him while their people were at the table, making certain of hand-copies.

"Cold. . . ."

"Yes. She won't have this chamber heated."

"And your opinion, Cooper?"

"My opinion . . . My opinion is that we have no choice but to give our men and our goods, while giving is in fashion."

"Obviously. I meant, your *opinion.*"

"Oh. Well, we certainly have a king in all but future's crowning. Then—unless he dies before—it will be . . . bend."

"We're bending already," said Lord Sayre.

* * *

"I'm sick of walls."

"Mother—"

"Sick of them!" The Queen was examining short spears, two assags, peering close at the grain of their hickory shafts, flicking their gleaming heads' razor-edged steel to hear it ring.

Martha, on orders, was packing leather duffels with warm woolens and boots, harsh furs . . . and, in a separate case, two light, nasaled pot-helms—one with gold fluting at its crown— and two long, heavy, chain-mail burnies, both very fine, custom-fitted, and with each of their thousands of tiny rivets welded, not simply hammered home.

"Mother . . ." Princess Rachel, upset as Martha'd never seen her, reached out to touch the Queen's hand—and had hers impatiently batted away. "Mother, listen to me. You have men whose business is going to battles, and seeing, and reporting back. You are needed here, not up on the ice."

"Oh, the boy-Monroe is busy enough, here. And Brady, pompous old fool."

"You're going because you *want* to, Mother—and no thought to the Kingdom or anyone else!"

"And you care for the Kingdom?"

"I do, and I care for you."

"And showed it never!"

"Mother, that's not so. . . . You are not easy to deal with."

"Then stop dealing with me.—Martha, what the fuck are you doing over there? Get us *packed.*"

"Taking your old knife, Majesty?"

"I'm *carrying* my old knife, yes. That's Trapper steel—best steel. I only wish I could take my bow, but this draw-shoulder won't bear it anymore." The Queen struck her shoulder with her fist, as punishment.

"Mother—"

"Rachel, if you don't stop bothering me over this, I'll lose my temper."

"Then *lose* your fucking temper, you selfish old bitch!" Princess Rachel's face was flushed red. "You don't know who loves you, who *cares* for you!"

Martha stopped packing and stood still. She sensed, throughout the tower chambers, others standing still. There was silence enough for the wind to be heard very clearly, hissing round the tower's stone.

"Now . . ." the Queen said. "Now, Daughter, you begin to please me—and don't spoil it with crying. I'd better not see a single tear."

"You won't," the Princess said, though it sounded to Martha as if tears were waiting.

"Comb-honey," the Queen said, and set her spears aside, "you should know I loved your father, and mourn him every day. And love you the same. . . . But this is no season for a queen to hide in her tower. Our people need to *see* me on the ice."

"But not fighting."

"Certainly won't, if I can help it. I don't care to make a spectacle of myself. A silly old woman, stiff in the joints."

"You are not." Princess Rachel went to her mother like a child. The Queen seemed startled, then opened her arms. A hand, strong and long-fingered, scarred from battles long ago, stroked her daughter's hair.

Martha left the packing and left the room. She was certainly allowed tears, if the Queen didn't see them.

22

"May I congratulate you, Great Lord?" General Shapilov—tall, a lean rack of bones—knelt on thick carpet in a camp yurt fairly large, and well-warmed by a folding stove. "After my fumbling, you plucked this St. Louis like a ripe blueberry."

Shapilov had a habit of admitting blame at once—apparently thought that protection. Toghrul found the habit was becoming tiresome.

"I plucked it by using my head, General, instead of wasting men and horses fighting through these unpleasantly crowded streets and structures. Surely . . . *surely*, Shapilov, it occurred to you that a river port would find survival difficult if its waterfront were taken and blockaded. All that was required was a thrust from the north down along the riverbank, then a single *tuman* dismounted to hold it."

"Now, I see it, lord."

. "Hide your face from me." Toghrul said it pleasantly, with no bluster, no bullying. "I am not pleased with you."

General Shapilov fell forward and pressed his face to the blue carpet—a really fine many-knot imperial. He said something, a muffled something. A mumbled offer of suicide?

Toghrul sighed. "It's a notion. Perhaps another time."

Were those sobs? Certainly sounded like sobs. And perfectly, perfectly illustrative of the difficulties in absolute rule. Here was a fairly competent senior officer—but he could only *be* fairly competent, or he might become dangerous . . . well, troublesome. Yuri Chimuc's grandson, the so-brilliant young Manu Ek-Tam, would have had this dirty and unpleasant city in three days. He would have gone to their river-front at once, like a wolf leaping. More than competent. Too much so. Soon he would have to suffer a hero's death down in South Map-Texas, and be wasted.

General Shapilov now lay silent, slack as if fucked—which in a way, of course, he had been.

"Get up. And get out."

A sort of bony scurrying then, as he backed out on all fours. Surprising he hadn't backed into the stove. Amusing, of course, but also deadly serious. To be a khan meant that no else must be found *also* fit to be a khan—which left only limited servants, limited generals, so the ruler must do every truly important thing himself.

An odd and potentially disastrous structure, really. And, considering oddness—though not yet disaster—what in the Blue Sky's world was happening with the idiots of Supply? Surely it was simple enough to haul a very-important hundred sledded wagons east through the wilds of North Map-Arkansas and up into Map-Missouri to the army. Then what explanation for them not yet arriving? Unlikely they'd been attacked by crows or coyotes. . . .

Pigeons from Chang-doctor say Ladu keeps the child safe in her belly, and is well, no damned complications.—What did it mean when a Kipchak khan, campaigning, found his wife's unremarkable face, her remarkable bright black eyes, in every inked map, every diagrammed plan of attack . . . ?

* * *

Margaret had left General Lenihan's office—they dealt surprisingly well with each other, at least on the subject of possible supply runs to the west bank, *if* needed by North Map-Mexico's army. They'd dealt with each other on that subject by Lenihan saying, "Never." and "No chance." and Margaret saying, "Horseshit, sir." Then gone on from there.

The general, a widower, had seemed slightly bemused by a

fighting officer with breasts. It was an advantage Margaret had been happy to take advantage of.

Sergeant Mays, massive and still, stood waiting for her in the corridor. "Princess," he said to her.

Fresh from Lenihan's ambivalence—wonderful Warm-time word—Margaret thought for an antic instant that the sergeant was declaring affection, then followed his glance down the hall to see Princess Rachel, an older Boxcar lady, and a large sergeant in green armor.

Margaret went to them, managed an awkward bow—looking, she thought, a little ridiculous with a long, sheathed rapier poking out behind her—and said, "May I be of help?"

Princess Rachel—ordinarily pale, very composed—was flushed and restless, her hands finding no place to be still. "I'm looking—Captain, I would like to speak with Lord Monroe."

"I believe he's on the wall, Princess. On the west wall, perhaps below the tower there."

"Very well. Very well." The Princess turned, hesitated—and Margaret lied and said, "I'm going to him now. May I escort you?"

"Yes, please. Lady Claire, I won't need you."

"But Rachel, you can't—you have no cloak, for one thing."

"She has mine," Margaret said, swung off her cloak, and draped it over the Princess's shoulders. A tall young woman—taller than Margaret by two or three inches.

"Still," the lady said, "you shouldn't—"

"I have—what's your name, Sergeant?"

"Ralph, ma'am."

"I have Ralph-sergeant here—and after all, Claire, I am *engaged* to the Captain-General; I think I'll be safe enough with him."

The older lady made a little clucking sound. "*Claire* . . ."

It seemed to Margaret that that 'Claire' had sounded almost in the Queen's voice. Lady Claire, apparently feeling so as well, ducked into a curtsy and left them.

. . . The cold struck with ice-knives as they stepped from a stone embrasure onto the broad, paved crest of west wall. Its massive tower rose high above them as they went leaning into the river wind. Margaret's face and hands went quickly numb, so she unbuttoned her jerkin and tucked her sword-hand in against her belly to stay useful.

"You must go back." The Princess's voice was snatched from her by a whining gust. "No cloak. . . ."

"Refreshing!" Margaret had to almost shout, and the Princess smiled, so they might have been friends on an adventure.

They bent to the wind, the big sergeant trudging behind them, and passed great springals and catapults, all covered in waxed cotton canvas and squatting in their redoubts like patient beasts. It seemed to Margaret a hard wall to take, so massive and high above the river. Only Light Infantry, up from small boats on a dark night, would have any chance at all. And with the garrison alerted, might expect half those people lost, even winning, and with the rest of west-fortifications still to seize. . . . Not that it couldn't be done. Not that the Kipchaks couldn't do it, once the river froze down to Island. But the doing would kill thousands of them.

Margaret began to think they'd come up for nothing but frozen fingers and toes, then saw Sam standing with another man by the wall's granite crenellations a bow-shot away, their cloaks billowing in the wind. Seeing Margaret's party, the men came to meet them, Sam in leather and mail, the other in blued-steel breast-and-back. Margaret saw the Boxcar was the West-bank general, Parker, tall, handsome, coldly adamant as the wall he walked on.

"Princess. . . ." Both men bowed.

It seemed to Margaret that Sam was doing the bowing thing better, less stiff at it. But he was looking older. Grown older in just these last weeks.

Sam raised his voice; the freezing wind was buffeting them like the greeting of a large, friendly dog. "The general and I were judging drift ice."

"I see." The wind had struck Princess Rachel's face white and mottled red, drawn tears to her eyes. "The Queen . . . my mother has left Island!"

"This morning. Yes, I know." Sam glanced at Margaret. "Get under cover."

"I'm fine. Not frozen yet." They were all almost shouting over the wind's moan and whuffle.

"She's sailing north." Perhaps wind-tears in the Princess's eyes, perhaps not. "And for no good reason! No good reason at all."

"Well, perhaps to be with her people," Sam said, "when they fight."

"It's ridiculous! It's ridiculous . . . she's needed here."

"Rachel." Sam put his arm around her—the first time Margaret had seen him do that. "Rachel, I know you're afraid for her. And so am I. But she's doing what she must." He smiled. "I won't say she isn't also enjoying herself."

"That is what's so . . . *stupid.*"

"No doubt." Sam held her a moment longer, then took his arm away.

Done perfectly, it seemed to Margaret. . . . The cold was making the bones in her face ache.

"—And while we're here turning to iced cream, Rachel, I must tell you I'll be leaving soon also. For the west bank, and inland to my army. The Khan will know by now that something's wrong in North Map-Arkansas. He'll be bringing part of his army down to deal with it."

"You're going. . . ."

"Yes." A harder gust shoved at them. "You'll rule at Island for your mother, Rachel. You'll rule as she would,"—he smiled—"but perhaps with an easier temper."

"I'm . . . I can't."

"Tell me, General," Sam almost shouting over the wind, "can she rule—and the armies behind her?"

"On my honor," Parker said, handsome even with iced eyebrows.

"Sergeant?"

The big sergeant seemed surprised to be asked. ". . . Yes, sir!"

"There, Rachel," Sam said. "What more could you ask? And in any case, both the Queen and I will be back very soon to embarrass you."

"You don't . . . embarrass me."

"Very kind. . . . Captain Mosten, you'll be staying with the Princess. You'll be her right arm—do you understand?"

"But I should be with you."

"Every time, Margaret—except this time. I'll miss you, but your most important work is here, with Rachel. If more muscle should be needed in Island, you'll have Pedro, Noel Purse and the tower guards, and Mays, Carey, and Burke. I'll be taking Wilkey with me. . . . And listen to Ansel Carey, Margaret; he has a nose for trouble."

Margaret was going to argue, but Sam seemed too tired to argue with.

"Yes, sir."

"But what . . . my lord, what do I need to *do?*"

"Rachel, do what seems sensible to help in this war—and to maintain your power so that you *can* help in this war. Do what seems sensible, do it quickly, and let no one stand in your way."

The wind had slackened so that 'no one . . . stand in your way' echoed a little from the stone.

. . . Warmer at last—at least not freezing—Margaret breathed on her fingers as the sergeant led them back down the battlement's covered steps . . . the narrow stairway winding down with a wall to its left, to leave invaders unshielded as they came.

"Your cloak," the Princess said.

"—Is where it belongs," Margaret said. "We don't need you chilled and sick."

The Princess said nothing down another flight of steps, until they reached a landing. "You would rather have gone with him."

"It's shocking, how little all armies care for 'rathers.' "

"A lesson for me?"

"I didn't intend that, Princess."

"No, but a lesson all the same. And since we will be together, please call me Rachel."

"Margaret," said Margaret.

23

Dearborn was regarded in the service as a soft captain. Was nicknamed 'Daisy' because of it. Daisy Dearborn.

But—rowers sent south—a day and night of sleepless effort by captain, officers, and crew to haul the skate-rigged Queen's ship *Mischief* up onto the river ice, had worn away Dearborn's softness. A man he'd noticed slacking at the forward winch, now lay manacled in the bilge, whipped, and discussing the matter with the rats.

A day and a night of brutal labor—all in a near-blizzard of wind and hard-driven snow. But at last this morning, with winches working block and tackle fore and aft, *and* men up on the ice with grapnels (thank Jesus-Floating for Bosun Hiram Cate), she was up and skating, sails slatting in quartering winds as the deck-crew stowed pulleys, winch bars, and two miles of ice-crusted cable, rope, and cord.

The cost had been the whipping, a broken arm, four various broken fingers, and a thumb pinched off. Sprains, aches, bruises, and fingernails torn away—uncounted.

Not for the first time—though more and more, lately—Captain Dearborn was considering himself old for active service. And while considering it, stepping down the narrow starboard ladder from a poop deck crowded by two big scorpions and their stacks of massive steel-tipped javelins, he found some confirmation in the lookout's yodel from a raven's-nest barely visible itself, high in swirling snow.

"*Deck there! Somethin' off to the southwest.*"

"Horse-riders?"

"*. . . Sir?*"

"Horse-riders?"

"*A sled . . . sir.*"

A sled? Dearborn and Jim Neal, his first officer—who should

have been trimming sail—both went to the starboard rail. Peering through ice-rimed boarder netting, they saw, sliding out of clouds of blowing snow, a sight that confirmed the Fleet's oldest tradition. Comes always something worse.

"Mother of God," said Neal, appealing to the most ancient Great.

It was a huge sled—gilded, painted blood-red, and drawn by a blanketed six-horse team shod with spiked iron. Furred and fur-hooded, a bulky groom rode postilion on the left lead. And a red banner, ranked with twelve gold dots, curled and spanked in the wind.

Captain Dearborn said, "Oh, no. Oh, *no.*"

A trumpet spoke up from the sled as if the 'no' had been noted. Then a woman's voice, just as loud. "Is this the fucking *Ill News?*"

"No! No, ma'am!" Dearborn shouted in relief. "We're *Mischief* . . . Your Majesty?"

There was conversation down on the sled, hard to hear over the wind. Then, something easy to hear.

"We'll board this one! You—you up there! Lower some fucking ladder or whatever. I'm coming up!"

"Oh, my God. . . ." Lieutenant Neal's second prayer. Apparently too little, and too late.

* * *

At four glass-hours after the center of the night, the river below the Bronze Gate was black as running ground-oil, and brought a black wind with it.

Sam, with Sergeant Wilkey nimbler after him, managed from the dock-finger into a narrow sailing boat, then past a low cabin to the bow. He found it an advantage, in that sort of scramble, having his sword strapped down his back, rather than tangling and tripping him. . . . The boat shifted, as even within a stone harbor, ice came nudging, scraping against its hull.

The two crewmen—both River-men—loosed the lines, came aboard neatly, and sheeted in the single sail.

General DeVane, standing beside Lenihan and two other officers high on the wharf—and seeming even plumper, cloak-wrapped in torchlight—called out softly, "Good hunting, milord."

Already seized by the current, the boat was swinging out into the harbor pool, rocking a little as a crewman took the tiller. It drifted . . . then, caught by the wind, its sail bellied taut, bucked into low waves and tapping ice-shards as it carved away west, out onto the river.

Island—a dark mountain except where specks of lamplight shone through granite casemates and arrow-slits—loomed behind them for nearly a glass-hour, till swallowed by the night.

For glass-hours after, Sam sat at the boat's bow, enjoying freezing spray and wind gusts. He would have been pleased by anything taking him from the Boxcars' palace. Taking him from inescapable scheming, persuading, and threatening. Taking him from admirals, generals, and river lords. . . . He rode the river's sinuous courses, taking deep breaths of night air, no matter that it bit his lungs and made them ache. He yearned for his army like a lover—an army, and a home to him—and knew he would lose that simplicity, whether the coming battle was lost or won.

A secret, of course, that Queen Joan already knew. That the Khan already knew. "Victories," Sam said aloud, "but triumph never."

"Sir?" The sergeant barely visible by the small cabin behind him.

"I was talking to the river, Wilkey."

"Sir."

Behind them . . . dawn's first light.

* * *

Martha had always thought battles, however frightening, must at least be interesting. It was disappointing to discover that wasn't so, at least wasn't so yet.

Certainly not as interesting as Ralph-sergeant—after saying no special word to her since he'd come—suddenly stepping from his post on the tower stairs as Martha and the Queen were leaving, taking Martha by the arm, then hugging her as if she'd given him leave. His armor and her mail had been pressed hard between them when, though startled, she'd hugged him back.

Then he'd taken his helmet off, and kissed her.

The Queen, a few steps lower, had looked back and said, "Martha, for Christ's *sake*,"—referring to the first Jesus—"this is not the time for it!"

Though it had seemed to Martha the perfect time for it. . . .

The battle had been going on—the Queen had been assured by Captain Dearborn—for a day and a night, as reported by little ice-boats hissing along fast as birds. But a battle scattered over miles and miles of river ice, so only faint formations—looking, it seemed to Martha, like spilled ground pepper on a glittering field—appeared and disappeared, and left no trace. Except once, when the *Mischief*, rumbling along fast as a fast horse could gallop, its great skates leaving plumes of ice-powder behind, sliced its way over sheets of frozen blood and frosted slaughtered Kipchak men and horses that crunched and thumped beneath the ship's blades as its tons sailed over them.

"Well done!" the Queen had shouted, and danced on the narrow poop. She'd hit Captain Dearborn on the arm with her fist. "Well fucking done!" as if the *Mischief* had killed those horse-riders.

The captain had said, "So far, ma'am, matters do seem to go our way." He appeared to be a cautious man.

Too cautious. By the next morning, the Queen had noticed.

Martha followed her up from breakfast—oat cakes and hot

apple juice brought to the captain's cabin. The main deck was ice-slippery, but the Queen, wrapped in a lynx cloak, a slender circlet of gold at her brow, stomped over it sure-footed, past coiled lines and awkward devices. Ship's officers bowed as she went past; crewmen stood aside. She climbed the narrow ladder up through the poop-deck's railing, to where the captain was standing, observing the set of the sails.

"*Captain.* . . ." The frost clouding from Queen Joan's breath seemed like smoke from a story dragon's.

"Ma'am?"

"Don't you 'ma'am' me! I want to know what messages, what orders you and your yellow dogs have been passing back and forth to those packets. Have you—have you *dared* to keep me back from my soldiers? Keep this fucking boat—ship, whatever—back from the fighting?"

"I do . . . I do as I'm ordered, Your Majesty."

Martha thought Captain Dearborn looked pale. The *Mischief* hit a low ice-reef, and he had to reach to the rail for balance, but the Queen stood as if she were nailed to the deck.

"Give me a better answer," she said, no longer shouting, and put her hand on her knife.

"It was felt . . . Admiral Hopkins feels that Your Majesty, while viewing aspects of—"

"I'm losing patience," the Queen said, in a very pleasant way.

"He felt . . . you should not be put in danger."

"And ordered so?"

"Yes, ma'am—Your Majesty. Lord Monroe had also asked special care for you."

Then the story dragon *was* on the poop, roaring, and a steel fang out and brandished. Martha stepped away. The captain clutched the rail.

Below, the *Mischief's* main deck seemed frozen as the river, and all the men stood as still, until slowly . . . slowly the Queen grew calm and quiet, took a deep breath, and sheathed her knife.

"Now you listen to me," she said to Captain Dearborn. "You turn this fucking boat in whatever direction is needful to get to my soldiers—and my *brave* sailors—who are *fighting*."

"Yes, ma'am. As you command." Captain Dearborn ran down the poop's steep ladder quickly as a boy, shouting orders as he went, so sailors raced to do this or that, and climbed to shift the sails. . . . It seemed to Martha as if the ship, that had been drowsing, now sprang awake. The *Mischief* leaned and leaned with its swollen canvas, until the great port-side steering skate lifted from the frozen river. And in a long, curving reach, the great ship took course to the northwest, running angled to the wind.

It was the fastest that Martha had gone anywhere.

And remained the fastest into a sunny middle of the day. The Queen, leaning on the port rail, was eating a cold sausage and one of the ship's brittle biscuits—Martha had already finished hers—when the lookout called, *"Deck there! More dead'ns!"* And a moment later: *"Nothin' she can't run over."*

The *Mischief* skated from perfect ice, bright as snow-dusted mirrors, onto a field of the dead . . . its massive blades cracking shallow sheets of frozen blood, rumbling, jolting first over heaps of fallen fur-cloaked men, and horses—then one . . . then another rank of East-bank infantry slain, their burnished green armor beautiful in sunshine. This armor bent and broke as the ship sped over.

The Queen stared out over the rail. "My boys," she said—then turned and called, "Stop! *Stop!* One moved! Captain, stop, there are wounded there still alive!"

"No, ma'am," Dearborn said. "We cannot. Those men are frozen already—stuck hard in blood and ice. We'd be hours getting any aboard, and very few to live."

"My boys . . . my boys." The Queen was weeping, tears odd down a furious face. *"Del . . ."* she said, a name Martha didn't know.

The *Mischief*, which knew no regrets, no losses, sailed on over the dead and dying at great speed, only shrugging where they'd fallen thick.

Though no officer, no sailor, said so, there was relief as the ship left that field, and sketched its way again over ice bare of anything.

The Queen turned from the rail, wiping her eyes with her sleeve. "Martha, we'll go below, and you'll arm me."

"Majesty," Dearborn said, "I swear not necessary!"

"Then," the Queen said, "I will be disappointed."

. . . They ran and ran into afternoon, the sails handled for the wind, and saw dead here and there. The Queen, cloaked in her lynx, the ends of a blood-red scarf flowing with the wind, stood on the *Mischief*'s high poop full-armed in mail, leather, and boots, her light steel helmet hanging by its laces down her back. She watched near the scorpions with two assags in her hand, her long Trapper knife at her belt. And though standing at the ship's stern, she seemed a figurehead of war.

They heard the battle before the raven's-nest saw it. There was a sound as if distant different songs, sung by many people, were echoing over the ice.

Dearborn called an order, and sailors climbed fast to set a triangular canvas. "Staysail," he said to Martha as they watched the sailors work above them, the winter sun blazing over their shoulders.

"*Ship!*" the lookout called, and as they sailed into those battle sounds—coming clearer, harsher now on a bitter wind—a ship appeared on the ice horizon. *Mischief* approached fast off what Martha had learned was starboard, and soon they could see that the ship was not a ship any longer. Once, judging from the massive side-skates and smaller steering blades still boomed out for a turn, it had been *Mischief*'s size. Now it lay burned to the ice, stuck in a lake melted by fire then frozen again, its charred timbers and charcoaled masts absolutely black against a world so white. Many smaller things, the size of persons, had burned with the ship. And others, dead men and dead horses, unburned, sprinkled the ice around it.

First Officer Neal stared as they passed. "It's the *Chancy*."

"Perhaps not, Jim," the captain said.

"I know the ship. Steer-skates always rigged elbow off the beams. . . ." Neal turned away and went down the ladder to the main deck.

"Has a brother on her," Dearborn said. ". . . *Had* a brother on her. Younger brother."

Now, as if the burned *Chancy* had been an introduction, they could see the battle.

It stretched, like a great shifting black-and-gray serpent, as far as could be seen from the *Mischief*'s decks. More than a mile . . . almost two miles away, huge rectangles of bannered infantry in East-bank's green armor formed and reformed on the ice—nine, ten of them, and each, it seemed to Martha, made of maybe a thousand men. These formations stood offset, some slowly turning, wheeling ponderous as barges—but barges in a flood of horsemen that shifted and flowed about them as if to wear their ranks away as fast water wore stone. The distant infantry seemed coated by a sort of glittering fur, that Martha thought must be bristling pikes—and long, swift shadows fleeted away from them over the ice.

"What are the shadows?" Martha said.

"Bolts volleyed from their crossbows." The Queen set one of her assags against the rail, and stretched to ease her muscles. "If you have to pee, dear, do it now."

"I don't have to."

"A lot of Kipchaks," Dearborn said, looking out over the ice. "Thousands."

"But not thirty thousand," said the Queen. "The fucking Khan *has* gone south, and taken half his savages with him!"

Martha heard a trumpet, and saw another great ship skating,

sailing fast enough to port to draw even with the *Mischief*. Though far across the ice, the men aboard her must have seen the Queen's banner at the mast-head. Tiny figures waved from her rigging. Martha heard them cheering.

"The *Ill Wind*." Captain Dearborn smiled. "Old Teddy Pelham. . . ."

The Queen stood clear at the poop's port rail, raised an assag's gleaming head, and waved the weapon in great sweeping strokes. The cheers came even clearer then. And Martha saw, past that ship, another . . . then a third came skating to run side by side across miles of ice. And more ships, and more distant, came sailing up and abreast, port and starboard, until there were warships skating in a massive line of stripe-painted hulls and hard-bellied white heights of sails, sun-flashing skates and bright banners. Drums, drums were thundering along the line of great ships stretching so far to the left and right that they diminished into distant, seeming-toys, bright as jewelry.

"My darlings," the Queen said—the first time Martha'd heard that copybook word used. "My Fleet!"

Captain Dearborn said, "Ladies, step away," and called, "Fighting stands! . . . *Fighting stands!*"

That cry was taken up by officers, bosuns, and rattling shaman drums—and the *Mischief*'s decks, which had looked to Martha busy enough before, suddenly stirred as ground wasps stirred in summer's last week. Sailors snatched pole-arms and axes from chain-loops at the masts, as marines, in band armor enameled half-blue, half-green, marched to their places along the rail, or climbed rope ladders to the fighting tops, and the huge crossbows waiting there.

Sailors came jostling up the two narrow ladders to the poop, saying, "Pardon . . . pardon," as they shouldered Martha and the Queen aside, then bent to winches and began to wind the two scorpions' giant steel bows slowly back . . . and back, the machines' captains calling, "Faster—*faster!*"

Two men unfolded tall, hinged mantelets—stood the heavy rectangles of linden-wood in four places to shield the scorpions' crews—then fastened them by thick steel hooks to thicker steel rings set into *Mischief*'s deck.

"Back from these bows!" One of the machine captains hustled Martha and the Queen forward, past the mantelets and against the poop's railing, paying no attention to majesty. Martha saw the Queen enjoyed it, and went where she was told, perhaps pleased by moments of not being a queen at all.

She and Martha stood watching as the great steel arcs were drawn back to a final solid *clack,* so the machines lay fully cocked—both already loaded with five slender steel javelins, each a little longer than a man was tall.

Now the noise of battle, no longer odd and distant, sounded near, hammered from shouts and screaming.

Martha was looking down the line of ships, racing, trailing long plumes of powdered ice behind their runners—and saw men galloping small horses right between *Mischief* and the nearest ship, the *Ill News*, but going in the other direction. Twenty, perhaps thirty horsemen, galloping over the ice.

"Look!" Martha called—and the Queen and one of the sailors looked—but the riders were gone, and no one seemed to have noticed, or shot at them.

"Kipchaks," Martha said. "I saw them."

"More where those came from," the sailor said, and pointed forward along the port rail. The Queen and Martha leaned out to see along the ship's side. The ice lying a distance before the *Mischief*'s bow was not white, but as deep a stirring gray as storm clouds.

Horsemen.

The ship jolted, then ran on, and Martha saw a great ball of blazing pitch heave up from the *Mischief*'s bow catapult, and rise . . . rise into the air.

"Bow chaser," a sailor said, and his machine's captain said, "Be silent for orders."

Martha watched through tangles of rigging as the burning thing went. It seemed to arc away like a rainbow, though with no color but hot fire. Then, very slowly, it fell . . . and fell out of sight. Men were cheering at the *Mischief's* bow.

The Queen unfastened her long lynx cloak, and spun the fur away, out over the ice as the *Mischief* skated. "To Floating Jesus," she said, then loosened her long Trapper knife in its sheath, and twirled the shaft of an assag over her fingers.

"Ma'am." Martha was breathless as if she'd been running. "Please . . . you should go below."

The Queen just looked at her, and smiled.

Martha sighed, unfastened her cloak, draped it over the poop's low railing, and reached over her right shoulder to lift her ax from its scabbard.

"You're a good girl." The Queen looked comfortable in her chain-mail. Comfortable leaning on a spear's shaft. Her blue eyes, narrowed in the wind, seemed to Martha a tribesman's, some warrior down from the ice-wall. Which, of course, was really so. "—A good girl," the Queen said. "I'm . . . fond of you."

"*And so you should be! She's a wonder with that ax.*" Master Butter, his cloak's fur hood thrown back, climbed the last ladder rungs to the poop, and bowed. ". . . Just your humble postilion, Majesty—with a flatter purse after paying boatmen to follow your galley north, *and* a sore ass from that damn sled horse's back." Butter stood squatly massive in heavy mail, belting two straight swords, one long, one short. The wind had reddened his round cheeks.

"*You. . . .*" The Queen turned a cold look. "You have no business here. You were ordered—"

"I know. You said to keep away for a year, my dear." Master

Butter glanced around the poop's deck, narrowed by the great scorpions and their warding mantelets. "But this year has proven exceptionally short, so I came to keep you company."

"Company I don't want. Stay away as you were fucking *told* to stay. At least . . . at least go elsewhere on the boat!"

"Of course, Majesty, as soon as possible." Master Butter went to the rail, leaned over, and looked toward the bow. "Dearborn's going to ram them!"

"I won't tell you again—" But the Queen said no more as Master Butter turned, caught her and Martha in his arms—left and right—lifted them, and drove them back behind a mantelet as a snake-hiss of arrows came. One cracked into the mantelet's linden, humming, its bright head just peeping through.

"A sort of punctuation," Master Butter said of the arrow, and let the Queen and Martha go as the *Mischief's* crew roared a cheer. The great ship seemed to leap ahead, borne by hard-gusting wind—then crashed, shuddering, driving up and into a low hill of impacts, horse screams and men's screams, the multiplied faint crackle of breaking bones.

Blood jetted onto the snow along *Mischief's* hull as she drove on and over, huge skate-runners slicing packed cavalry that then was knifed aside, fanning in a fur-lumped blood-red skirt as the ship sailed through them.

And as the *Mischief*—so every other warship of the racing line.

The scorpions began their slow-paced slamming from the poop—noise loud enough to hurt Martha's ears—and at each release of those mighty bows, five steel javelins whipped whining away over the ice, to flash like magic through drifts of mounted Kipchaks the battle-ships had shrugged aside.

The mast-head's smaller scorpions, the heavier machines along the main-deck rails, the chasers at the bow—all hurled steel, clustered stone, or molten pitch as the ship skated on, its massive blades brisk on bloody ice, then muffled, crunching where they met men and horses.

The Queen shoved clear of Master Butter and went to the rail for a better view. Kipchak arrows still came, but sighing, failing with distance.

Butter stepped to the Queen's left. Martha to her right.

"Joan—" Master Butter leaned to shield her.

"Edward, I have to see." The Queen pushed at Martha. "Girl, get behind those things." Meaning the mantelets, apparently.

"No, ma'am," Martha said, and stayed close to keep the Queen's right side safe.

A single horseman galloped past the other way, just beneath their rail. He looked up—showing a young face and black hair in several braids—drew a short bow, and shot it as Master Butter reached to hold his hand in front of the Queen's throat. But wherever that boy's arrow went, it came not to them.

"Oh, for my *bow*," the Queen said.

Orders were shouted amid other shouts, and the *Mischief* leaned, skating . . . leaned more, and took a wide curving course north and easterly. The long line of warships to port and starboard, each fluttering bright little signal flags, leaned as she'd leaned, and raced with her into the turn.

"Ah, my Fleet, my dear ones. . . ." The Queen turned almost a girl's face, beaming. "Martha, do you see them?"

"Yes, ma'am," Martha said, though she winced as a crushed horse shrieked beneath them. She'd wondered about battle, found it dull . . . then found it dreadful. Now, she hated it— hated more than anything the slaughter of horses, who never meant harm to anyone.

"We're cutting the Khan's people off from West-bank." First Officer Neal stood just behind them; Martha hadn't noticed him come up. An arrow, or falling tackle, had cut Neal across the forehead, and blood had run down into his left eye. "These seem to be their right-wing regiments." He pointed out across the ice, where drifts of gray maneuvered in bright afternoon light. "Another pass—and they'll have to run *farther* east."

"And the army?" The Queen shaded her eyes to look north. "Where's Aiken—where *is* he?"

"West, ma'am." Neal pointed almost behind them. "West— and from the signals we're passed, doing very well."

"Then Lady Weather bless that man!—And we chase?"

"We chase," Neal said, and smiled. His left eye-socket was full of blood.

A wind gust suddenly thudded into the sails above them, rattled the tackle and gear aloft so Martha was startled, and ducked a little.

"And you," the Queen said to Neal, and raised her voice to be heard above the wind, the harsh swift sliding of the *Mischief's* skates, "—you've lost your young brother on that *Chancy* ship?"

"Yes, ma'am."

"Officer Neal," the Queen said, and seemed to Martha to become even more a queen, "I will see that boy is remembered . . . as I will see you and all your family remembered, and favored by the Crown."

Neal bowed, and when he straightened, Martha saw tears of blood run from his eye.

A trumpet called from forward, and Neal was gone and down the ladder to the deck.

"If we can win this day," the Queen said, her breath frosting, "and Small-Sam ruins the Khan in the south, then, *dear* Floating Jesus, I will let the bishop come to Island and stay."

"Don't offer *too* much," Master Butter said, and the Queen laughed and hit his shoulder with her fist.

The *Mischief* lifted slightly off its starboard skates, buoyed by richer wind—and racing where distant Kipchak divisions labored to work west, passed nearly a regiment of horsemen scattered in ragged squadrons here and there, fugitives on the field of ice as the battle-line sailed on.

The scorpion crews practiced at those, cutting a number down as *Mischief* passed them swiftly by. But still, arrows followed, coming . . . then falling like weary birds to rest in deck or rigging, and sometimes in a sailor.

The ship ran quieter now, no shouts, only a single scream by someone wounded. Orders were given quietly, in speaking voices, so *Mischief*, though sailing so fast, seemed to Martha to be resting, taking long breaths of the cold west wind that sang in its rigging.

Marines, here and there, fired their heavy crossbows out into the air—*crack-twang*—to ease them from cocked tension, the bolts vanishing at an horizon of ice beneath gray sky.

"Your Majesty," Captain Dearborn called up from the wheel, "no one injured there?"

Master Butter glanced back at the scorpion-crews; their captains shook their heads. "No one hurt up here!" Butter called, and Martha heard the captain say, "*Lucky.*"

Then, with hardly a pause, as if that 'Lucky' had called bad luck, the man high in the raven's-nest screamed, "*Lead! LEAD!*" The Queen stretched out over the rail to see, Master Butter holding one of her arms, Martha the other, to keep her on the ship.

"Water," the Queen said, looking forward along the hull. "A stretch of lead water."

Martha heard Captain Dearborn shout, "*Way starboard! Strike those fucking sails!*" And the ship leaned to the right . . . tilting farther and farther, its main deck foaming with crewmen like a pot of soup boiled over. Men ran like squirrels in the rigging. Others worked with knives along the belaying rail, so lines whipped free—and heavy crosstrees, their stays sliced, fell smashing, the great sails collapsed.

Awkward on the tilting deck, Martha leaned out beside the

Queen. She could just see a widening crack in the river's ice—black, and spidering across the *Mischief*'s course.

The ship ground and bucked into its steep turn, swinging hard . . . hard to starboard, long clouds of powdered iced streaming away from its steering blades on the wind. Master Butter shouted, "Get hold!" Behind them, one of the scorpions' great bows broke its tackle and swung free to smash the right-side rail.

The *Mischief* seemed to balance for a moment, like a person running the top of rough fencing. It felt strange to Martha, as if she were balancing, she and the ship together. Then the warship fell.

Water thundered up along the port side in a spray that fanned away and as high as the raven's-nest, and the *Mischief* splintered itself along the open edge of the ice—then struck and stopped still.

All else kept flying. The tops of the masts split loose and sailed forward. Weapons, gear, and men sailed also . . . flew through the crowded air like birds, and broke when they struck.

Every grip was lost. The Queen, Master Butter, and Martha were pitched together into the poop's cross-deck rail—and would have been injured, but that rolled hammocks had been packed there to shelter the helmsmen, just beneath, from arrows. Only the fat canvas, and their mail, saved them broken bones.

24

There were a few moments of silence, except for crashes and clatter as things came to rest. And a sort of sobbing as *Mischief's* great timbers twisted out of true.

"*Up!*" Master Butter stood, then heaved the women onto their feet.

"My assags . . ." The Queen bent to retrieve one spear from coils of fallen rough brown rope. Martha found her ax still gripped in her hand.

The ship rested once more on the ice. But—her back broken as she'd struck the lead, then crashed across it—she lay with her great stern tilted high in the air, like a sleeping child's bottom, her bow fallen, collapsed.

An officer was shouting orders—Neal, not the captain—and men began to stir, but many didn't.

"The pinnace!"

"*Sir. . . . Somebody help—*"

"Shut up and die, Weather damn you!" Neal. "Hiram-bosun, rig the pinnace out! Cut that crap away and get her *out*. Her Majesty—"

"Oh, Jesus! Sir, sir, Master Cate is dead!"

"I'm not leaving here," the Queen said, then called down to the ruined deck, "I'm not leaving!"

"Ma'am," Neal called back, "you'll do as you're damn well *told!*"

Other officers, petty officers, were calling orders. Martha had never heard such cursing, not even from horse dealers or teamsters at Stoneville Fair.

"Edward," the Queen said to Master Butter, "go down there and tell that young fool I'm staying with them. No need to go skating away nowhere because there's been an accident!"

"My dear," Master Butter said, "those stray Kipchaks we

passed—and butchered some, passing? I believe they'll now be coming to call. So yes, you are leaving—and quickly."

"How bad?" First Officer Neal had spoken quietly, well down the steep-sloping deck and through the sounds of men at desperate work, but Martha heard him. It was the only question being asked.

A person said, "Sprung and split."

"—But she'll skate!"

"No, sir," the person said. "Wouldn' make not a mile. Fall all to kindlin'."

The Queen—her second spear found under a fallen spar's fold of sail—stood, seeming to listen to other than the *Mischief*'s voices. Then she said, "So, no pinnace and scurrying away.— *Neal!"*

They heard his "Ma'am . . ." as he half-climbed the main deck's rise, stepping over wreckage his men labored on.

He came up the narrow port-side ladder, his left eye still plugged with blood. "Ma'am?"

"The captain?"

"Captain's dead, ma'am. Skull broken when we struck."

"And no pinnace."

"No, ma'am. Launch also smashed—I knew that, soon as I stood up."

"I see. . . . And the chances of another ship coming?"

"Oh, another ship will come, ma'am; a lookout certainly saw us wreck." Neal paused, stared out over the ice, one-eyed, where the Fleet had gone. "But the line was sweeping east on the wind. Ships'll have to tack and tack again to get back to us."

"How long?" Master Butter said.

"Sir . . . ma'am, I believe a glass-hour at least."

"And probably more?"

"Yes, ma'am. Probably more." Neal glanced at the scorpions' crews. "You people get down on main deck. Your pieces won't depress at this angle to do any good at all."

"Leave 'em?" A sailor put his hand on a massive machine as if it were a family dog.

"Yes, Freddy," Neal said, "leave 'em. All of you go on down, now."

Below, an officer called, "I said, rig out more boarding net, Carson! Are you fucking deaf? . . . Leave that. Leave it! The man's dead."

"Company coming?" Master Butter said.

". . . Why yes," Neal said, "I believe so, sir. Ma'am, you'd do better below, where the marines might hold the hatches."

"Might?" The Queen smiled at him. "No. I like it here. Now, get back to your people, *Captain* Neal."

Neal bowed, then turned for the ladder to follow the scorpion crews down—looking, it seemed to Martha, pleased as if the *Mischief* still sailed and was sound under his promotion.

"Captain Neal," the Queen called after him, "I expect this ship, though ruined, still to kill the Kingdom's enemies."

"Oh, we will do that, ma'am," Neal said, and was gone to the deck.

". . . Children," the Queen said. "They're all children." She looked at Martha and Master Butter. "And my doing, that both of you are here." She reached a cold strong hand to Martha's cheek. "Another child. . . . And you, Edward, you foolish man."

"Only an old friend, my dear—who would be no place else on earth."

. . . There was no longer a raven's-nest, so it was from some lower perch a sailor shouted. *"The fuckers is comin'! Comin' west by west!"*

Martha went to the back of the poop—edging past the mantelets, then between the scorpions—to look out from the stern, now reared so high. She saw only ice behind them at first, then darker places that seemed to move from side to side as much as forward through late afternoon's sun-shadows. She stood watching until, as if her watching made it so, those darker places became groups of riders. . . . Soon, she could make out single horsemen among them, coming swarming like late-summer bees. Dozens. A hundred . . . perhaps two hundred, skirting the end of the water lead as they rode. Then, many more. Their right arms were moving oddly, and Martha saw they were whipping their horses on. She heard a war horn's mournful note.

Battle whistles shrilled down the *Mischief*'s sloping deck. A drum rattled. Sailors and marines—those with no bones broken in the wreck, or at least no crippling injury—took up their battle-standings.

Martha went back to the Queen, and said, "They're coming," feeling foolish, since of course they were coming.

But the Queen only nodded, and said, "Infuriating, the things I have left undone . . ."

"Not a bad place to fight, though." Master Butter paced the poop deck. "Considerable slope, and fairly narrow . . . crowded with machinery. They can't climb to us up the hull, stuck this high in the air, so our backsides will be safe enough. May take arrows, of course, once they have the main deck, if they get up into the rigging . . ."

"If there were only one ladder coming up here . . ."

"Yes, dear, but there are two, and twenty feet apart. When they come up both, we won't be able to hold them." Butter stepped out a space . . . backing between the tall mantelets, the two scorpions. "Just here, I think."

The Queen walked up the tilted deck. "Yes. Wide enough," she said, "but not too wide."

It seemed to Martha they were only interested, not frightened as she was frightened.

The Queen said, "Shit," and the back of her left hand was bleeding. Arrows murmured past them and snapped into timber. Two thumped into rolled hammocks, and men shouted below. The Queen looked at her hand. "Nothing," she said, and flicked the blood away. "Most of the fools are shooting blind up to this deck."

Hoofbeats clattered down the ice along the ship's side. Shouts and orders along the main deck below. Deep twanging music from crossbows, heavier crashes from the *Mischief's* machinery still able to bear.

"So, our company's come." Master Butter rubbed his hands together. "Three can stand here, though no room for more—a space, what, ten . . . eleven feet across? Just over three feet for each of us to hold." He nodded. "Mantelets forward on both sides to funnel them onto our blades, while—let's hope—catching their shafts. . . . *And* these scorpions, beside and behind us, each a mess of gears and cable, timbers and steel." He smiled at Martha. "Could it be better, my student?"

"Better not to be here," Martha said. An arrow hummed high over her head.

"Sensible Martha," the Queen said. "But really, this place is so high, so good, we might *hold* it a glass-hour."

Martha saw many Kipchaks out on the ice . . . riding, circling in like hearth smoke swirling to an opened door.

"Would that we could," Master Butter said, and was difficult to hear over rising noise. Shouts, and the ship's crashing war-machinery. "Martha, you will fight at the Queen's right side; I'll be on her left. Keep two things in mind. It's cold, and will grow colder, so consider your grip on your ax—might want to thong the handle to your wrist. *And*, remember you have a dagger as well. I don't want to see that knife sleeping in its sheath."

"Yes, sir."

"Orders for me, also, Edward?"

"No, my dear. You need no one to tell you how to fight. But knot that scarf tighter; don't leave the ends loose for someone to seize."

Men bayed like hounds along the *Mischief's* slanted hull, and

Martha looked over the poop-deck rail and saw gray-furred Kip-chaks in the boarder nettings down at the bow. They'd climbed to that lowest place . . . were slashing at the netting with short, curved swords. As she watched, ranks of marines turned from the ship's rails, and their crossbow bolts—fired almost to-gether—emptied the nets of nearly all those men, as if with magic.

But then the nets were full again—being sliced apart by more horsemen, by many more, climbing up shouting.

It seemed to Martha like a dream—so odd and wild and un-expected—unreal as a dream, so she might simply fly away into the air and dream of something else.

"If," the Queen said, "if I'm down, disarmed, and it seems I'll be taken—"

"Kill you?" Butter smiled. "I won't do it—and Martha won't do it. So, Queen, don't *go* down, don't fumble. I've understood Trappers were dire fighters, and I expect to see a sample of it."

"You had better hope, Edward," the Queen said, knotting her scarf tight around her throat, "with this fucking impudence of yours, you had better *hope* these savages kill us."

"I rely on it, sweetheart," Master Butter said, and seemed to Martha happier than she'd ever seen him.

The marines fired another volley—and again almost cleared the nets. Martha could hear a ripple of *smack-smack-smack* as the bolts struck. It had grown very cold; she saw her breath frosting in the air. Her hands were cold; her left hand was shak-ing. She put it on her dagger's hilt and held on hard.

"Soon, now," Master Butter said. "And there'll be blood freezing on this decking, ladies. So mind your footing; let's have no comic pratfalls."

Martha'd never heard 'pratfalls,' but she knew what he meant.

The marines fired another volley—but arrows had been kill-ing them, and their fewer bolts didn't sweep the netting clear.

It hung in tangles along both sides of the *Mischief*'s bow, and Kipchaks were coming through it, howling war cries.

Someone called an order, the marines drew short swords all together, and that same person—it wasn't Captain Neal—called another order. Then the marines marched down to the bow as if there was no hurry, and struck the tribesmen all together. Martha heard the musical sounds she and Master Butter made, practicing with steel—but this was much louder and many more, and there were screams.

Sailors shouted and went running down with axes and pikes, following the marines. The whole forward part of the ship seemed to Martha to become like the river's wind-waves and whirlpools, but made of fighting men, with the marines in ranks like sand-bars in the current, flooded with furred fighters. There was terrible noise over the ringing steel, as if animals were killing children.

Martha turned away to look at anything else, and saw herds of horses wandering out on the ice, with only a few Kipchaks to keep them. Their riders had come to the *Mischief*.

"Gauntlets and helms," Master Butter said. He sounded just as he had at their lessons. "Draw, and guard." He drew his long sword from its sheath. A heavy sword, Martha saw—only a few inches of its top edge sharpened.

The Queen, standing between them, settled her helmet, pulled on her mail gauntlets. "Rachel," she said, as if her daughter were with them, "—how will you do?" Then, driving the point of one assag into the deck to rest within reach, she spun the shaft of the other in her right hand for a comfortable grip, and drew her Trapper knife with her left. Ready, she stood relaxed—so at ease, it seemed to Martha she looked younger.

Martha pulled her gauntlets from her belt, let her ax hang from its thong as she tugged them on, then fitted her helmet. She could feel her heart thumping . . . thumping.

"And what are you to remember, Martha?"

"My knife, sir."

"That's right," said Master Butter. There was a change in the noise below them; it had come closer, risen up the slanting main deck.

"What *I* will remember," the Queen said, "while I remember, are my dear friends beside me."

Martha stepped forward and could see, over the poop's rail, more Kipchaks swarming, fighting with sailors up the sloping deck. She saw no marines still standing.

The horsemen, smaller, stockier than the sailors, yelped to each other as they came. They reached the helm's wheel, just below and out of sight from where she stood.

Martha heard sounds that drove her back to her place beside the Queen. She drew her dagger so as not to forget it, held it low at her left side. . . . It still startled her, after such fearful waiting, when one of the Kipchaks—an older man with a gray mustache, his round wind-burned face framed in a dark fur hood—stepped up off the port-side ladder, and started toward them. He looked serious, but not angry, and was holding a short, curved sword running bright drops of blood.

It seemed to Martha that this man intended to say some-thing—another tribesman had come up the ladder behind him—but the Queen stepped out in two long strides and stuck her assag's blade into the man's belly. He looked amazed, turned as if to walk away . . . then seemed to melt down to the deck.

"First blood," said the Queen—and the second Kipchak came howling.

Martha was sure Master Butter killed that one, though she didn't see it. She was sure because she'd heard the sudden *thrum* of a sword-blade whipped through air, and the man's shout stop. Then two . . . and a third horseman came running from the starboard ladder and her ax met one before she even thought about it. She stuck the other with her dagger and didn't know what happened to him, because the third man was on her, shoving, and swinging a sword.

She was surprised he wasn't stronger than she was—and perhaps he was surprised, too, since he guarded against the ax but forgot the dagger. Master Butter had been right about the knife.

Something hit her left side, and Martha thought she was hurt—more Kipchaks were coming up both ladders—but she glanced over and it was the Queen, wrestling, cutting a man's throat. He hit Martha, trying to dodge away, and left warm stuff on her neck and shoulder. Blood. *Don't slip . . . don't slip!* Two more men came and ran into her, tried to knock her down, struggling to get sword-points in.

Then she used the ax—second time she'd used it. She'd lost her temper. Another man—or one of those two, maybe, was still standing in front of her. His jaw was hacked and hanging down so his tongue was out in squirting blood. Martha supposed she'd done it. A very strong man edged past a mantelet, cut her hard at her right hip, and drove her, drove her back into a scorpion. This man was much stronger than she was. She smelled his breath, fresh as a child's, as he grappled with her, working to get his sword's edge across her throat. Martha crouched suddenly, so he'd think she'd fallen down—then stuck her dagger hard as she could into his nuts, and wrenched, *wrenched* at the blade with all her might to draw it up into his belly. The dagger blade was caught—then sliced its way free and ran up into him.

The man made a terrible noise, and she was able to pull away from him. He'd been very strong. Martha was standing against the curve of a scorpion's bow; couldn't remember how she got there. She hacked her ax's spike into another man's shoulder as he struck at her—used that to haul him off-balance—then turned the ax's handle to chop its blade into his eyes, and was surprised at how easily she'd done it. He made a mewing sound, like a kitten, and stumbled away. Blinded, he bumped into a mantelet's edge.

Someone limped across and thrust a spear into the blind man's back, so he screamed and fell down. Martha smelled shit, and supposed it was from him. She saw it was the Queen who'd done it. Her beautiful helmet was off—its lacing broken—and strands of her long hair, red and gray and red again with blood, were down past her shoulders.

Martha looked around as if she were waking up, and saw no more horsemen coming at them, though several—they had the oddest slanting eyes—still stood down the narrow way, at the head of the ladders. There were six . . . seven men lying still on the deck, one man sitting up, and two men crawling. The wind was making bright red puddles stream and run along the deck. The blood crinkled, freezing as it ran.

There were noises from below . . . shouts and cheering. Martha saw things thrown high in the air from the main deck. She thought they were hats, then saw they were heads.

"So far, so good," Master Butter said—a copybook phrase so perfect it sounded just made up. He was leaning on his long sword's point, his short-sword in his left hand. Three of the men lay before him, two piled across each other, looking like killed animals with their furs rumpled and soaked with blood. "Well enough, so far, since it seems we're only an afterthought, up here."

Martha saw they'd all had been pushed back against the scorpions' rigs and timbers. The Kipchaks had forced them back there, fighting.

There was stinging in Martha's left arm. She looked down and saw the mail sleeve had been sliced open, and her forearm, too. She didn't remember that happening at all. Blood was running dripping, and she could see a piece of polished bone deep in there. . . . It looked dreadful, but only stung her as if wasps were at it, didn't hurt as much as her hip. But that hand hung empty and white, and her dagger was gone.

"Floating *Jesus*." The Queen tugged her long scarf off, bound it around Martha's arm, and knotted it tight.

The few Kipchaks at the ladders only stood watching. It seemed to Martha they were all—the tribesmen, too—very tired already, though only sudden time had passed.

Then, one of the horsemen shouted something to the others, and they came running—so the Queen had to snatch her second assag from where it stood on the deck, her other apparently lost, stuck in some man's bones. . . .

Everything seemed to go slowly and strangely, so Martha felt she almost knew the name of the next man who attacked her— slashing, slashing—he became so closely familiar, his face almost a friend's, though twisted with effort, fear, and rage. She guarded and struck with her ax, missing her left arm and her dagger. Then that man went away or was down, which was just as well, since she was feeling sick. A fever's dream-sickness, it felt like. Tribesmen were standing by the ladders, blood on their furs.

She heard the Queen say, "Probably better on their horses. Cree would have chopped these people to pieces."

"No doubt." Master Butter, at the Queen's other side, sounded out of breath. "Embarrassing . . . but I've been taken in the belly, dear. I thought the son of a bitch was dead . . . *Martha?*"

"Yes?" Martha saw Master Butter was standing hunched as an old man.

"My . . . last lesson. Man worth killing once . . . is worth killing twice."

"Yes," Martha said, "I will."

She heard Master Butter catch his breath and say, "And how do you, my dear?"

"Still standing, Edward." The Queen sounded oddly pleased,

though Martha saw she was trembling, and had been cut hard across the side of her face. Strands of her long hair, come down, were stiff with freezing blood. "—Still standing, though bleeding like a pig . . . and my knee cut by some fucker so it flops." She turned to look at Martha, and smiled. "Dear girl?"

"I'm with you." Martha looked down to be sure she still held her ax. "I'm with you." Then, though feeling so sick, she footed a corpse away for room to fight as the Kipchaks shouted and came again, now more of them pouring up the ladderways from left and right, all steel and fur, frost trailing from their mouths like smoke.

Martha called, "Ralph," as if her sergeant might come to her, his armor green as spring leaves.

25

"Good? . . . Sufficient?"

The Khan Toghrul, lying at cushioned ease in his camp yurt by lamplight, scattered a few more grains of feed down the front of his yellow over-robe, and watched a small blue-and-white pigeon strut on his chest, pecking. He felt the little steps the bird took as it fed.

Apparently sufficient feed for this bird of best luck—a pigeon to live, from now on, a life of reward and no message flights where birds of prey might strike it down, the Sky's winter storms freeze it in flight. A lucky bird, a bird that had *brought* luck, the news of a baby boy. A boy . . . and an end to uneasiness in certain Uighur and Russian chieftains. Men who, so mistakenly, thought the succession their business.

But politics—wonderful Warm-time word—the usual political triumph didn't occasion joy. Not the joy that had a Khan lying cooing to a pigeon, sprinkling pinches of seed for it on his breast. A boy—Bajazet, for the old Khan—and reported healthy as his mother was healthy. There was no pretending the wife's life wasn't dear as the child's, or nearly. This fondness for her a weakness, no question, and as a weakness, best admitted to.

Toghrul blew gently to ruffle the bird's feathers, and the pigeon glanced at him, startled.

"Only fondness," the Khan said to it, cupped the pigeon gently in both hands . . . then got up, crossed piled carpets to a small cage-roost, and ushered the bird in. "Soon, once we're finished here, a silver cage for you. A silver cage, but big, with room to fly."

Toghrul closed the roost's little wooden door. Happiness a danger in itself, a sort of drunkenness, so that everyone seemed a friend and all seemed possible.

As, of course, it seemed *im*possible that an experienced commander—granted Shapilov had not been a vital intellect—still it seemed impossible that an experienced commander, left with his dispositions in the north carefully ordered, and careful warnings given of the River's ice-ships, their strengths and limitations . . . that the man would still prove fool enough to keep *tumans* in mass formations, unwieldy, and perfect prey for those vessels.

Fortunately for him, the ass had died in his own disaster—where, supposedly and by third-hand information come just this evening, the Kingdom's so-rude Queen had also died. That news, as copybooks had it, likely 'too good to be true.'

So, even the happiest of men, of fathers, was left with work to do. A catastrophe—with truly catastrophic losses—to be balanced now by victory. . . . Toghrul went to his yurt's entrance, paged heavy felt hangings aside, and stepped into darkness and a freezing wind that made the guard-mount's torch flames flutter.

"Senior officers," he said.

"Great Lord." The officer stationed there went to only one knee in the snow—the Guard Regiment's privilege—then rose and ran for the commanders' camp.

The other sentries stood still, eyes front.

"Uncomfortable," Toghrul said to them. "This damp cold, here. Not like our prairie air." And it *was* uncomfortably dank amid deep-snowed stands of hardwood trees and thorn-bush thickets, on ground that always sloped away down tangled draws.

The guards seemed to have stopped breathing, apparently frightened by being spoken to. And, of course, they didn't answer him. Stupid creatures. . . . Toghrul stepped back through the curtains, went to the near brazier to warm his hands, then bent to warm his face. He opened his eyes to the coals' bright blazing till they watered as though he wept.

Bajazet. A name chosen before the boy was conceived. A

name both ancient and noble. . . . What lessons must the boy be taught? Weapons and war, of course. And should be given treacherous ponies, difficult horses as he grew older, so distrust became natural to him, despite his father's love. He must be given young companions, as well—of good blood, but none quite his equal. One boy might be stronger, another more clever, a third luckier or more handsome. But none as strong *and* clever *and* lucky. . . . The best of virtues must be his: endurance, unswerving purpose, patience—and cruelty, of course, that tedious necessity. He would have to be taken from his mother early—by four, perhaps by five—or Ladu's gentleness would suit him only for defeat.

So, treacherous ponies for the boy, and difficult horses. But not dangerous. . . .

"As you commanded, lord."

The four trooped in, breathless, bowing. Murad Dur—and three competent nonentities, interchangeable brutes with at least veteran notions of giving and obeying orders.

"Oh, Lord of Grass, and now—father," Dur led the others in more bowing.

"So," Toghrul said, foolishly pleased, "good fortune follows ill."

"Still," Murad said, and bent his head so his face—harsh, hook-nosed, very like a red-tailed hawk's—was shadowed by a hanging lamp. "Still . . . some illness lingers."

The other three said nothing, stood dripping melting snow onto the carpets.

"So?"

"Sled savages, lord."

"*Sleds?*"

"As reported, Great Lord. Savages—though only a very few. Archers from North Map-Texas, driving dog-sleds over deep snow, attacked a remount herd. Eight hundred horses."

"Go on."

"The remounts were dispersed and lost, Great Khan. Herders were killed, and the Lord Chimuk was . . . also killed. An arrow struck his throat."

It was surprising what a shock that was. For a moment, Toghrul couldn't catch his breath. . . . Old Chimuk, killed by some Sky-cursed savage. Yuri had seemed one of those men who couldn't be killed by any enemy. In how many battles had that old man fought? From Siber Gate, across and down to Map–New Juneau . . . Map-Portland. *Years* of battles. And now, an arrow through his throat in this stupid wilderness.

"Were all the herd-guards killed?"

"Most, Great Lord."

"Kill the rest of them," Toghrul said. "Their throats to be cut for the cowards they are."

"As you order, lord."

Not caring to be stared at after such news, Toghrul turned back to the brazier and stood holding his hands to the warmth, thinking. What was that wonderful copybook saying? *It's an ill wind that blows no good.* Yes, really a perfect old saying, since now, with his grandfather gone, there would be no powerful person troubled by the unfortunate death of that so-brilliant young commander Manu Ek-Tam—presently demonstrating his talent by chasing sheep in North Map-Mexico.

An ill wind . . . Certainly including the clever North Map-Mexican rabbit—that had run, jinking here and there as the hawk went stooping—but was now revealed to be a wolf. Wolf enough, at least, to have snarled some sense into the Kingdom's cannibals, so they'd actually concentrated for battle in the north. . . .

Silence from the four commanders. It occurred to Toghrul that those silences—so usual, so proper—might occasionally have deprived him of useful information.

"Very well." He went to his couch, sat, and settled amid cushions, booted legs crossed, his sheathed sword across his lap.

"Very well. As put so perfectly by the ancients: 'To business.' We have a lost battle in the north—but not a lost war. It requires only to finish the clever young Captain-General in these hills—I think of him as younger, though apparently we're close to the same age." Toghrul considered having his generals sit, then decided not.

"—If this Lord Monroe is beaten quickly enough, then we have time left to march east to the cannibals' river, and campaign north *up* the ice—instead of south, *down* it. The result would be the same, and Shapilov's defeat only incidental."

Murad Dur nodded, apparently understood. The other three generals—perhaps only careful to *appear* stupid—stood stolid as posts.

Toghrul paused, considered reviewing good news—beside the birth of his son—pigeoned from Caravanserai, then decided not. It might be considered weakness, an attempt to obscure the disaster below St. Louis. Good news from Map–Los Angeles; payments in silver now perfectly acceptable to the Empire. . . . Good news from Map–Fort Stockton; herds being replaced through bitter snows. Good news, but not good enough.

"It's an interesting problem, really." Toghrul smiled. "An interesting problem. By day after tomorow, Third Tuman will have joined us. And certainly by that time, the Captain-General will have joined his army. We will have a competent—say, very competent—commander, whose army has taken a defensive position just south of us, in broken hills. His intention will be to hold those draws, slopes, and wooded ridges against our tumans. Hold the slopes with his Light Infantry, of course, the crests with his Heavy Infantry, the ridges, with his cavalry. Short charges through deep snow, brush, and so forth, to keep us off the heights."

"Great Lord . . ."

"Yes, Murad?"

"Isn't it possible that Monroe is already with his army?"

"Murad . . . *Murad*. Have your scouts reported yet that the soldiers of that army—usually proud of silence—have begun to sing, to strike their cooking kettles, to joke while performing sentry duties? Any such welcoming celebration?"

"Ah . . . of course," said Murad Dur.

Toghrul waited for any additional comment, response. The three wooden generals seemed less worried, now, perhaps even interested. . . . But was it, perhaps, not the best notion to have Manu Four-Horsetails killed? Should even dangerous talent be allowed for its usefulness? No question, that officer would have been valuable here, if his arrogance could have been borne. . . .

"—So, certainly the enemy will have made those dispositions. *Object?* To bleed our people in country they don't care for, and in which it's difficult to maneuver to effect. Monroe will assume we're much too subtle to simply go slaughtering in direct attack at his center. He'll expect something of our steppe and prairie way—sudden sweeps, brisk flanking, and staggered assaults into the resultant confusion. I believe he'll expect those maneuvers—or at least as near them as this rough country allows."

Nods. The wooden three were capable of nods, at least. Not entirely simple.

"—Since, however, I'm not inclined to do as an opponent expects, we will do the opposite. His object is to bleed us. My solution, since flanking would find the same country east and west, with no advantage . . . my solution *is* to bleed—and win, bleeding. The last thing this North Mexican will expect from us is a stupid and direct frontal assault on foot, heedless of losses." Toghrul tried another smile. "After all, long winters in warm yurts breed replacements soon enough."

And, by the Sky, at last one smile in return. Murad, of course. Intelligent, and not afraid—sad to consider that these very virtues might, in time, make him dangerous.

"To continue. We dismount the tumans, so our clever

Captain-General fights, not horse archers, but archers as woods' hunters first, then infantry in assault. And, of course, we'll have to mount a very convincing—though necessarily shallow—attack on . . . the western flank, to persuade Monroe to weaken his center to oppose it. This false attack is to be driven home as if all the army came behind it. Officers are to spend their men for that effect—and, if necessary, spend themselves."

Toghrul clapped his hands. "A solution certainly not perfect, but probably sufficient."

And no general said otherwise.

At the handclap, a guard had come through the yurt's entrance. "My lord wishes?"

"Your lord wishes roast lamb with the Empire's golden raisins, dishes of soft cheese and dried plums, kumiss and vodka for himself and his generals."

The guard bowed.

"Oh, and music. Is Arpad in the camp?"

"His squadron's in, lord." Murad Dur.

"Then we'll have the captain and his oud—and any decent drummer."

The guard bowed and went away.

"Sit." Toghrul gestured the generals to the carpet. "I'll draw our dispositions in lamb gravy, while we enjoy an evening's pleasure—before *tomorrow's* pleasure." And got smiles at last from all of them, properly, since they were being honored by his presence at a meal.

The commanders sat carefully cross-legged, their boots tucked under so no dirty sole was exposed as Toghrul joined them. They leaned a little back and away from him as he sat opposite, since no honor was without peril.

. . . A reminder that Bajazet would need to know more than how to frighten such fools. More than knowledge of horses and archery. There must be a tutor for the boy. But who? Would it be possible, once the North Mexicans were broken, would it be

possible to forgive an old man his treachery? And if Neckless
Peter Wilson *were* forgiven, and became the boy's teacher, what
lessons would be taught? An aging man's cautious consideration
of every point of view, so decisions came slowly, if at all? Bajazet—while certain to be a delight—might not be gifted with
sight so perfectly clear that argument evolved swiftly into action. . . .

The commanders were sitting silent until spoken to, as was
proper, eyes lowered so as not to offend.

. . . So, a tutor for Bajazet, certainly. But an old man who'd
insulted his master by refusing service? Worse, who'd taken
service with an enemy. A dilemma. It was a tremendous responsibility, raising a boy. And all the more, raising him to be
lord of everything he saw, everything his horse rode over. . . .

The yurt's thick entrance-curtain was paged aside, and four
servants filed in. They carried a tray of silver cups, a pitcher
of warm kumiss, and polished brass bowls of dried fruit,
scented herbs, and rose-water. Toghrul could only hope his op-
posites might wash hands undoubtedly dirty, before the lamb
arrived.

* * *

Sam came ashore in bitter dark before dawn, from a freezing
river already streaked and stiffening with ice, so the boatmen,
as they'd done off and on for two days and nights, had had to
batter and break thin shelves of it, sailing, then rowing, to reach
the appointed West-bank beach.

Sam, then Wilkey, despite their protests, were lifted and carried ashore like cargo bales, the rivermen splashing, cursing,
stomping crackling edge-ice. Carried, deposited . . . and left.

Wilkey held a boatman's woolen smock as he started away.
"Is this the fucking place?"

"An' how would you know if it wasn'?" the boatman said, and pulled loose—but managed a bow to Sam. "Sir, here's North Map-Arkansas, an' jus' the spot away to your people. We didn' fail you."

"I never thought you would," Sam said, gave the man silver . . . then stood with Wilkey to watch the boat pull away.

'The fucking place' looked to be just that, as much as a fading moon, cloud-buried, could show. A narrow, frozen bar of beach, then a steep bank with dark trees and tangle thick along its top, all bending to the river's wind.

"We'll get off this shelf." Sam led the way up sliding sand, gripping frozen roots and brittle vines to climb. . . . At the top, he got a good grip, hauled himself up and over onto all fours—and found six pairs of shaggy moccasins waiting. The savages, pale as the dead in dark-gray light, were tall, thin men. Five were carrying steel-blade tomahawks, and one, the tallest, a long-handled, stone-headed club.

Sam heard Wilkey, coming up behind him, say, *"Shit,"* and was considering a lunge to one side to clear his sword, when someone laughed.

"Not the most dignified entrance, for a Captain-General! And . . . bride-groom?"

"Ned—you son-of-a-bitch." A perfect use of the copybook phrase.

Ned slid down from a dappled horse, and walked out into the last of moonlight to offer Sam a hand to stand. "You're in one piece, anyway. They didn't kill you.—Sergeant."

"Sir." Wilkey stood watching the savages.

"Don't be troubled by my Bluebird friends. I'm a favorite of theirs, for some reason I'd rather not know."

The tallest of his friends, the man with the stone-headed club, smiled and said in fair book-English, "Ned man, is a merry man." The Bluebird's teeth were filed.

"Very merry, now," Ned said, smiling. "Our song-birds,

here, came from their camps last evening with wonderful news. News, I suppose, drummed all the way down the river, from tribe to tribe."

"Wonderful?"

"We—well, the Kingdom's people—have *won*, Sam! A victory in the north, fighting all day yesterday—and according to Toothy, here, right on through the night. He says the drums say, 'A so-cold dying on the ice for the horse riders.'"

"If it's true . . . if it's *true*." Sam felt relief rise in his throat, painful as sickness.

"Oh, my friends here don't lie, Sam. Don't think they know how, actually.—Great thieves, of course, steal anything not chained to a tree. Understand they like to bake children in pits in the ground. . . . Reason I haven't accepted invitations to dine." Ned went back into the brush, came out with four more horses on lead. "Didn't know if more might be coming with you. Sure you recognize your favorite."

The imperial charger, Difficult, night-black and looking big as a house, tried to bite Ned's shoulder.

"Behave yourself." Sam took the halter. "So Toghrul is coming down with only half an army, Ned—thanks to the Boxcars. Lady Weather bless Hopkins and Aiken!"

"Friends?"

"Well, a winning admiral, and a winning general—which *makes* them our friends."

"And Toghrul is not 'coming,' Sam. He's here. Arrived with his first elements yesterday. Man seems to be in a great hurry."

"But he hasn't attacked?" Sam went to Difficult's left side, tugged the stirrup strap down, hopped in the snow to get his boot up, and swung into the saddle. The charger sidled, began a buck, and blew noisy flatulent breaths.

"What a brute," Ned said, and was on his horse simply as taking a step. "—No. Still settling in just north of us when I rode out to meet you. Fourth day I've ridden up and down the bank, hoping to their Floating Jesus this was the place meant. No real notion when you'd be coming, only word sent over from a Kingdom ketch."

"Supposed to be a one-day sail here. Became more than two, with the ice."

"Yes. A possibility Toothy mentioned. Not much the Blue-birds don't follow on the river. Have to—the Boxcars hunt them, now and then. . . . Sergeant, mount up."

. . . Then, a long morning's ride through deepening snow. They climbed slow-rising slopes west of the river, horses buck-eting through deep drifts—the white lap of Lord Winter—as the Bluebirds paced them, drifting in and out of sight through bare-limb trees and snow-drifted bramble, jogging along, never seeming to tire.

"Good men," Sam said.

"Yes,"—Ned smiled, riding beside him—"but risky at din-ner."

"I see that. What news from home, Ned?"

"One piece of very bad news, Sam, pigeoned up a couple of weeks ago."

"Yes?"

"Elvin . . . The old brigadier's dead, back home. Died in his sleep of that fucking disease."

"Elvin dead. . . ."

"Yes, sir. Jaime's still doing organizational work down there."

"Mountain *Jesus*."

"Does seem wrong, doesn't it, Sam? Old man was meant to die fighting."

A dusting of new snow was falling. Nothing much. It barely sifted in Sam's sight, then vanished. "Jaime won't live long, now Elvin's gone."

"I suppose that's right," Ned said. "So there was that mes-

364 { M I T C H E L L   S M I T H

sage, a while ago—then, last few days, three separate gallopers come all the way up from the Bravo—killed a couple of horses doing it."

"Saying?"

"First one was from Charles: 'All going to copybook hell-in-a-handbasket. Trouble with the provinces. Trouble with money. There *isn't* any money. Imperative you return soon as possible!' . . . Then, the second, from Eric: 'Enemy agents cropping up, possible rebellion planned in Sonora, paid for by the empire. Imperative you return as soon as possible!' "

"And the third?"

"Oh, the third—and last—was from the little librarian. Four words: 'Nothing important happening here.' "

Sam smiled, still thinking of Elvin. Remembering him throwing the dinner roll.

"A sensible old librarian," Ned said, "Neckless Peter."

"Yes. A sensible man."

As they climbed a steep slope through cold clear light—come far enough that the river, when it could be seen those miles behind them, was only patches of bright glitter in the rising sun—Sam heard bird calls, but calls from the birds of the *Sierra*. The tall savages trotting alongside laughed, imitated those calls perfectly . . . and Light Infantry—from Kearn's Company, by their bandannas—stepped out to meet them.

 . . . Sam had said to the Princess, 'My farm will be the camps; my flock, soldiers.' Saying it, of course, as a measure of loss—which now was proved a lie, since he found himself truly happy in dark, wooded hill-country, deep-snowed and freezing. Happy that a ferocious and brilliant war-lord had come south to oppose him. Happy in the warmth, the trust of more than ten thousand soldiers, men and women who greeted him now from regiment to regiment with stew-kettle drums and singing. They enclosed him like a warm cloak of fur . . . fur with fine steel mail woven through it. 'My flock . . . soldiers.' He prayed to the Lady, riding through them, for those who would die by his decisions.

. . . Most of the rest of the day was spent learning the ground—riding rounds down deep, snowed gullies, then up their wooded, steep reverses—and in greetings, embraces by officers and their scarred sergeants, shy as girls. Wilkey had gone back to his company, reluctant to leave Sam guarded by only a half-dozen.

From one height, Howell pointing, Sam could see over bare treetops to the Kipchak camp—sprawled, as his army was sprawled, across country too rough for regularity. An imperial far-looking glass cold against his eye, he thought he made out the Khan's yurt, bulky and bannered in a town of lesser shelters. By fire smokes, by men's movements across white snow, by horse lines that could be seen, the camp looked to hold perhaps twelve, perhaps fifteen thousand men.

"All Greats," Sam said, his breath frost-clouding, "bless the Boxcars and their Queen."

"Yes." Howell took the glass. He began, by old habit, to put it to his black-patched socket, then held it to his right eye and peered out across the hills. "Or we'd have thirty thousand of the fuckers to fight."

Sam had been . . . not startled, perhaps saddened to have noticed Howell, Ned, Phil Butler, and the others seeming older now than when he'd left them only weeks before. He supposed that he looked older, too, the price of large matters being dealt with.

Howell slid the glass shut into itself and handed it back. "How do you want to go about this, Sam?"

"To begin with, let's get warmer."

. . . Sitting on his locker, Sam envied Toghrul the big yurt. His canvas tent was cramped, packed with commanders sitting on his cot or camp-stools, with their silent second-in-commands: Carlo Petersen, Horacio Duran, Teddy Baker and Michael Elman, standing or kneeling behind them. And all

smelling of sweat, leather, horse, and oiled steel. It was not a
restful space, though warm enough now, with crowding.

"First, I want to thank Phil, and the army, for a brilliant
march up through Map-Louisiana, Map-Arkansas."

"I had to hurry, Sam." Butler had brought only one dog on
campaign; rat-sized, brown-spotted, it peered from his parka's
pocket. "—That Boston girl was *impossible*. One more week,
I'd have hanged her."

"No," Howell said, "*I'd* have hanged her."

"A wonderful march of infantry," Sam said, "and, Howell, a
perfect move east. Not a trooper lost coming over from Map–
Fort Stockton."

"Luck, Sam."

"No. Not luck. Charmian, how was the Bend border when
you pulled your people out?"

"Busy." Charmian Loomis had a rich, sweet singer's voice,
sounding oddly from someone so lean, dark, and grim. "They
had a very good commander come down with them—not Crusan; better than Crusan. If he'd had a couple of thousand more
people, it would have been a problem."

"But as it was?"

Colonel Loomis considered. "As it was, it was . . . busy, but
not a problem. We killed them at night, usually. And left . . .
oh, perhaps eleven, twelve hundred still riding that whole territory, trampling farmers' starting-frames. Just good practice for
our people down there."

" 'Good practice,' " Ned said. "You terrifying creature."

Colonel Loomis smiled at him—a rare event for her. She'd
always seemed to like Ned, so much her opposite in every way
but soldiering. Sam had wondered, as had others, if there might
be a match there, someday. An odd match, to be sure. Lightness
and darkness.

"This is my first day back. Tell me about the Khan."

"Sir, his dispositions—"

"I know how his army lies, Charmian; I've seen it, seen your map. I meant . . . what do your people *feel* about that army."

"They're careless," Charmian said.

"Careless?"

"Yes, sir—as if they have no doubt they'll win. Their patrolling is alert, but not aggressive."

"Right," Ned said. "They don't push. Just run regular patrols, keep in touch with our people."

"And on our flanks?"

"Nothing much. More . . . a little more activity at the base of our main ridge, Sam."

"Just a little more," Charmian said. "We've got high ground here, running up to all five ridges, though the west ridge is lowest. They seem interested in Main Ridge, and the rise to the left of it, but they're still willing to let my people hold those slopes. No contesting."

"No contesting . . . And nothing much on the flanks at all."

"That's right, Sam," Howell said. "And it's strange, because he brought those people south like a rock slide. Came down through Map-Missouri very fast."

"They overran two of my patrols." Ned tapped the curve of his steel hook against the tent's pole. "Killed them."

"So," Sam said, "in a hurry, then; but now . . . not in such a hurry."

"I'd say,"—Butler had his little dog out on his lap, was stroking it—"I'd say he intends to move very decisively. Whatever feints he may or may not use, he'll drive his main attack all the way. Don't think he means to toy with us at all, no two or three days counter-marching for advantage."

Howell nodded. "I agree."

"Flanking," Sam said, "has always been their way."

"A good reason for him not to do it," Ned said. "Good reason for him to go for the center."

"He already lost," Butler scratching his little dog's belly,

"—or his general lost, that battle in the north. First really serious defeat for them. Bound to take that into account, dealing with us."

"Yes," Sam said. "So, a decisive move, not a drawn-out piecemeal battle that might leave some of our army intact, even losing. It's a temptation to attack *him*—last thing he'd expect, an attack tonight."

Some apprehension in his officers' faces.

"—But this position is *so* perfect for defense." Sam smiled at their relief. "Now, if he goes for our flank, it will be a hook to our left. Attacking to our right, he takes a chance of being caught between us and a possible sortie by Kingdom troops from the river. So, if it's flanking, it will be to the west."

"Country over there's not much different, Sam." Ned shook his head. "No advantage for horsemen."

"But less chance of a disaster for him, than in a direct engagement up the middle."

"Less chance of a decisive victory for him, too," Howell said. "I think he intends to wipe us out, then go for the river down here and ride north into the Kingdom. Bluebirds say it's freezing fast."

"Yes," Sam said, "—it is. But win *or* lose, we won't leave him enough men alive to do Jack Shit."

"I've read that one," Ned said. "That's a good one. 'Jack Shit.' That's very good."

"So . . ." Butler put his dog back into his parka pocket, and stood. "How do you want us?"

Sam sat silent, eyes closed, picturing the army as it lay across wooded hills and hollows. Picturing the draws, wooded and deep in snow, stretching away north to the Kipchak army. . . . For Toghrul to attack there, to come directly at him that way, was to sacrifice his men in the hope of swift and overwhelming victory. Taking a great, almost desperate, chance.

In 'his mind's eye'—wonderful old phrase—Sam saw them

coming. Dismounted, of course. At least, he would dismount them. Thousands of short, tough men with hard-hitting bows and curved *yataghans*. But not trained infantry, not really comfortable off their horses. . . . And all remembering that half their *tumans* now lay dead, north on the river's ice.

"I think . . . a flank attack to the west is more likely. He can always regain his balance, if he's beaten trying that."

"My people stay in the center?"

"Yes, Phil, Heavy Infantry stays on the center ridges. And no reserves. Bring everything up on the line."

"I disapprove of that."

"And very sensibly. But do as you're told."

Butler sighed, and strolled out into the snow, Duran behind him. They could hear him shouting for a dispatch-rider to take orders. *"Is there a fucking man on a horse?!"*

"Speaking of men on horses," Ned said, "where do you want the cavalry?"

"I want them—want you—to do two things at once."

"Nothing new."

"I want the Heavies high on the west ridges, ready to oppose any flanking attack successful enough to threaten our center. I want the Lights positioned, in company and squadron strength, as reaction forces to charge any breach that forms elsewhere along our line—and also prepared to chase when we win. Then, as many Kipchaks as possible are to be ridden down and killed. The Khan is to be hunted and killed."

"Toghrul killed . . ." Ned breathed on his hook, polished it with his bandanna. "Right."

"Sam," Howell said, "who opposes his flank attack directly?"

"I do," Charmian said, and got up and left, Teddy Baker following.

"I wish she wouldn't do that," Howell said. "Damn woman always just walks out. No fucking further planning . . . no coordination."

"I know," Sam said. "It's annoying."

"But, Sam—only light infantry?"

"Yes."

"That's . . . You're sacrificing them."

"Yes."

"Best we have!"

Sam sat looking at him.

"Howell," Ned said, "it's *because* they're the best we have."

Howell stood, seemed to wish to pace, but found no room for it. "Still wrong, to sacrifice Charmian like that. If her people go under, she'll go under with them. . . . Hard to forgive, Sam."

"Howell," Sam said, "these things are *impossible* to forgive. I thought you understood that."

". . . Alright. Alright, where do you want me?"

"Highest hill, back of Butler. Best place to command from, if something happens to me."

"And you'll be where?"

"He'll be with *Charmian*, Howell." Ned stood and stretched. "Now, let's get out of here, and leave him in peace."

Sam stood—his back feeling better, standing—and put his hands on their shoulders as he walked them out into falling snow, Petersen and Elman trailing after. "Listen, both of you; there is another order. *Live.*"

"That's it?" Ned smiled. "I'd already decided to."

"It may be too much trouble." Howell reached up to rest his hand over Sam's for a moment.

Their boots crunched in the snow. "Once the people are in place," Sam said, "which is going to take time, with the Light Infantry completing a march to the west—once they're in place, no fires, no noise. I'll be along to review dispositions, make any adjustments to our lines." Ned and Howell swung up onto their horses. "—Feed the people at least a little hot food, as much Brunswick as Oswald-cook can send up from the field kitchens, then give them a few hours' sleep. But they're to be *in position* at least two glass-hours before dawn. . . . I'd come with the last of night—and so will he."

"Good to have you back," Ned said, saluted with his bright hook, then turned his horse and rode away, Elman spurring after him.

"Sam . . ." Howell held his big charger still, Petersen just mounted beside him. "Don't do anything stupid. We've got ten thousand swords on these hills—we don't need yours."

"And won't have it, if I have the choice."

"I hold you to that," Howell said, "on your honor."

"On my honor."

Sam walked back into his tent, past a smiling Corporal Fass, on guard—a tent, now he was alone in it, no warmer than the evening. 'On my honor,' he'd said. Certainly the least of his concerns—to strike or be struck at with sharpened steel. It would be . . . such a relief to have only that to consider, and not his thousands of soldiers here, not the hundreds of thousands of men and women in North Map-Mexico, waiting to hear whether they would live free and at peace—or in a desperate resistance of several generations against the Kipchak *tumans*.

And would be such a relief, also, not to have to consider Rachel—and those hundreds of thousands more—waiting along the river for him to win their war, or lose it.

Sam sat on a camp-stool, spread Charmian's map on the cot, and bent in yellow lamplight to study neat notes inked at its edges, fine lines drawn curving with hills' slopes and rises.

"Corporal."

"Sir?"

"If they carry up stew, please bring me a bowl."

"Yes, sir. I can go back to the kettles and get it."

"No. But if they bring it up to the lines, I'll have some."

"Yes, sir."

Sam leaned closer, saw the pen's crosshatching of indicated forest thicken to the west, showing awkward country . . . then much more awkward. And if the Khan did flank to the right, instead, taking the chance of being trapped against the river? The country east *was* a little more open . . . bore thinner forest. But the snow had drifted that much deeper there—slow traveling when he'd come that way, and by tomorrow, even more difficult. It didn't seem a likely line of attack, with all their nice maneuvers slowed to lumbering.

Also, the east flank offered no surprise. The army, camped higher, would see the Kipchaks coming miles away, and all the better as they came over snow, in daylight *or* moonlight.

Charmian's fine map made the Khan's choice for *any* flanking clear. 'She'll go under,' Howell had said. 'If her people go under, she'll go under with them.'

And so, of course, she would. How old was Charmian? Twenty-eight? No, certainly thirty, at least. There was gray in her hair—as in all their hair. They were all dyed a beginning gray by blunders, however rare, grim enough to stain anything.

. . . This was a time, if Margaret were here, that she'd nudge the vodka flask out of sight. Wasted effort. There wasn't vodka enough on earth to drown *this* difficulty.

Did fine Warm-time Caesar, did fine Napoleon or Lee dream of leaving their tents before battle, of walking away into the night, free of any expectations? So their armies and their people and the future would no longer know of them at all, leaving only a fading mystery to their puzzled, aging soldiers.

Howell had done a very good job, settled like the banner's scorpion on several rough hills, claws and stinger poised and ready. But was there another way than flanking to shift this ten-thousand-soldier scorpion, send it scuttling sideways, then back . . . and back, until the Kipchak boot came finally down?

Assault to the front. Possible, though not Toghrul's style at all—which, as Ned had said, argued for it. And would have made some sense if he still had a whole army, instead of only half. Here—with, probably, neither force withholding reserves—

to lose in a frontal assault would be to lose utterly. It seemed unlikely Toghrul would accept that gamble. Seemed unlikely . . .

Sam folded Charmian's map—really fine paper, imperial stuff—stood, and tucked it into his belt's wide pouch. To arm, or not yet? . . . Not yet.

He turned down the lamp's wick, unslung his sword, and lay down on the cot with the weapon beside him. The cot seemed more comfortable than Island's feather bed had been. Probably spoiled for comfort, by soldiering . . .

Sam dreamed of Rachel, tall, dark-eyed, her father in her face. They were in her solar tower. Sergeant Burke was there with them, sitting reading a copybook, tracing the words with his finger, moving his lips as he read. Sam was explaining to Rachel the difference between the Ancient American Civil War—*Red Badge of Courage*—and the wars he'd fought in North Map-Mexico. "In those ancient battles," he said to her, "few screams were heard, because of the noise of tremendous bangs of black powder. Cannon. Muskets. So those were the noises heard during their battles. Very few screams, until the fighting was over."

Rachel agreed it was probably so, but Burke said, "Sir."

Sam said, "What?" both in the dream and waking.

"Sir . . ." Corporal Fass. "Lady to see you, sir. Told her you were asleep."

"Alright . . . alright." Sam rolled off the cot, turned the lamp's wick up.

"I've brought stew," the Boston girl said, the shoulders of her blue coat dusted with snow, "—and news. Wasn't that kind?"

"Very kind." Sam took the bowl from her. "Please . . . sit." Standing to one side of the hanging lamp, he dipped a horn spoon into the steaming Brunswick, took a sip.

Patience settled onto the cot, her scimitar across her lap, and smiled up at him. She seemed as she always seemed, rested, lively, interested. "You don't think I might have poisoned it?"

"I don't care," Sam said, and took another spoonful.

"Poor old Louis, in Map-McAllen, would have wanted me to poison it. Boston would have said, 'Well done.' "

"If the Khan wins, you won't need the poison." The stew was very hot. Some solder must have run from back of the hill, run through the dark with the yoked buckets slopping.

"If the Khan wins," Patience thoughtful, "I do think he will fall in love with me. He can't be used to someone as pretty *and* clever."

"Probably not." Sam blew on his spoonful. "You said, 'stew—and news.' "

"Yes, and you're the first to hear it. I came to you first of all. A Mailman flew here just a little while ago; he must have hunted the camp like a night-jar to find me—I heard him calling. A really nasty thing; I asked his name, and he said, 'Fuck you.' Webster hates him and tried to bite, but still, he's the first to ever bring me news."

The Brunswick had cooled enough to eat. "And that is?"

"The battle north—on the river ice?"

"Yes. Won, thank Lady Weather."

"And will you thank her that there the Queen was killed? The nasty Mailman brought the note—news down from Baton Rouge by pigeon, then up from Map-McAllen to here."

". . . *Killed?*"

"Yes, killed. Her ship broke, and the Kipchaks swarmed over."

. . . Then, sitting puzzled on the cot, Patience reached up to take the stew bowl from him, and said, "Weeping. . . . How does that feel to do?"

26

As clouds sailed over a setting semi-moon, the regiment called Dear-to-the-Wind filtered through trees and frozen underbrush. Stocky men in fur cloaks, felt trousers, and felt boots, they managed fairly quietly through deep snow, carrying strung bows. The bow-staves were short and curved as *yataghan* blades were curved, both, some said, to honor that same crescent moon that rode through Great Sky above them.

. . . Lieutenant Francisco Doyle, always insubordinate, didn't hesitate to lean close to his colonel and whisper in her ear. "Get back out of here, ma'am. Get up the hill."

It was not a suggestion most would have cared to make to Colonel Loomis. Charmian shrugged him away and ignored it. One of the Kipchaks, scouting, stepping shuffling through a drift, was coming close to the evergreen overhang where she and Doyle stood in darkness.

Doyle, really a brave young man, was considering another whisper when his colonel strode suddenly out into the snow, her moon-shadow stretching lean and swift beside her. She flicked her rapier's bright blade to set the startled tribesman's half-drawn bow aside, then thrust him through the throat.

The man convulsed, dropped his bow, and clawed at the blade's razor edges, arching back and back to get a breath for screaming. But the blade point stayed in him. The colonel, as if dancing, accompanied him as he lurched away, still slicing frantic fingers along the steel.

Their shadows pranced over the snow while the bowman managed a sound at last, a soft squealing that ended as he fell, in liquid fart and stink.

Arrows—one, then another, whistled past into the woods, and Doyle saw hundreds of Kipchaks now coming on foot through the trees downslope, kicking through the snow in ragged ranks. Some shooting as they came, but most with *yata-ghans* out, steel flashing in moonlight. There were no war cries, yet, or shouted orders.

A second rank of many more hundreds was emerging from the trees behind them.

Colonel Loomis, wiping her blade, paced across the hillside a little higher, with Doyle hurrying behind, arrows flirting past them through moonlight and shadow. As they went, a thousand of her men and women—waiting buried or half-buried in fallen-branch rambles, in clearing drifts, on snowy slopes—stirred slightly, so she could mark their places as she passed.

At the line's west, anchor end, more than half around the hill, Colonel Loomis stopped and looked back across the moonlit breast of the slope. To Doyle, she seemed—in a shifting wind that blew snow-powder swirling—a copybook witch, so tall, angle-faced, and fierce, her long black hair sailing free . . . her sword's sharp, slender yard the brightest part of her.

She stood waiting and watching, until soon the first screams were heard with the *snap* of light crossbows, the harder *twang* of the tribesmen's weapons. Then, like anticipated music, the clash of steel rang through the night, and Kipchak war horns sounded their deep, bellowing notes.

. . . Sam spurred Difficult up the main-ridge rise, through wet snowflakes barely visible in the dimness before dawn. His trumpeter, Kenneth, followed, and six horse archers, at Howell's insistence, paced along. Arrows nocked to the strings of their odd longbows, they trotted guard in shifting order beside, be-fore, and behind him. To the west, the uneven voices of battle sounded, softened by falling snow.

Both regiments of heavy cavalry were standing dismounted, each trooper by his horse, in long ghost rows along the ridges, their armor dimly lit to gleaming here and there by wind-blown torches. Two thousand big men—with a number of big women—waited in silence, but for the stamping of impatient chargers.

Sam found Howell, torch-lit, beneath the scorpion banner—and stayed mounted so the people near enough could see him.

"It's slippery, Sam." Howell looked up at him, squinting snowflakes away from his good eye. "Falling footing."

Sam leaned from the saddle to answer. "Footing enough for down-slope charges. If men and horses fall then, they fall into the enemy."

"True."

"Where's Carlo?"

"Down the line."

"He knows to move without your order?"

A nod. "If the Kipchaks get through."

"Right. If the Light Infantry breaks on our left flank, Howell, they'll fall back up these slopes. If that happens, if you see it's happening—"

"Charge as they clear."

"No. If Charmian's people *start* breaking, *start* backing up the ridges, you and Carlo are to take both regiments—at the charge—down those slopes and into the Kipchaks. That's my order, and that's what you will do."

"We'd be riding our own people down!"

"Yes, Howell, you would. You'd have to go over them to strike the Kipchaks as soon as possible, as hard as possible, to give Phil time to pull out of the center and march his people west."

"Dear Jesus . . ."

"Howell, am I right in this—or wrong?"

". . . You're right."

"Then be sure Carlo also understands that order."

Howell nodded, and they both listened to the battle sounds, west. No cheering, of course, from their people, only shouted commands, shouts of warning. The Kipchaks were noisier fighters, calling battle cries, war horns sounding their mournful notes. . . . Still, there was in that dull, shifting roar, a sort of music to commanders, and they heard in it no advantage yet, either way.

"Holding," Howell said.

"And probably will." Sam reached down, shook Howell's hand, and found reassurance in that grinding grip.

. . . Beside being a painful trotter, and uncertain in response, Difficult almost always lunged out a start—did so now, only touched by the spurs, so Sam had a moment's vision of being dumped into the snow in front of his soldiers, the battle's loss beginning with that comic humiliation. But he found his balance, settled the beast smartly between the ears with the butt of his quirt, and managed to ride along ranks of cavalry . . . then down the far-western slopes in a reasonable way, with Kenneth following. Three of the horse archers rode before them, three behind.

As if they'd entered a different country deep in the draw, dawn-light darkened almost to night again, and the battle's sound grew louder, so that screams of dying men and women, grunts of effort for savage blows, and officers' shouted orders all became individual under countless strokes of steel on steel.

Sam rode to angle across the hillsides, and soon, high in a rise's deep shadow, he looked down and saw a roiling motion beneath him, as if the dark forest below the hillsides had come alive, writhing like one of the great far-southern serpents, coiling up and up to reach the dawn's light. The noise rose terrific with clashing steel, shouts, the Kipchaks' yelping battle cries. Sam could hear the tribesmen's bowstrings twang—and as if hearing made fact, one of his flanking guards grunted and fell, white fletching at the side of his chest.

Another dismounted to him, as the four still mounted bent their longbows, shooting down into shadow. Kipchak arrows hummed around them, and the escort's sergeant, a man named

McGee, rode to crack Difficult across the hindquarters with his bow-stave. The charger leaped forward and bounded across the slope like a deer, Sam only a bundle hanging on.

He'd found nothing more unusual in battle than laughter. On campaign, of course, and even in maneuver under threat. But rarely in the heart of slaughter. Now, Sam was treated to that sound as he saw, in dawn's light, Charmian Loomis—with two officers, and blood down her side—leaning on the staff of a battle pennant and laughing at him amid a flickering sleet of arrows.

"Never saw a man so eager!" she called to him. "Damn near *flew* down the line!"

Sam wrestled Difficult to a skidding halt, swung down—and resisted temptation to draw and take off the animal's head. McGee'd followed, and Sam tossed him the charger's reins as the other bowmen rode up.

"And what are *you* doing on the line?" He had to shout. "You're the fucking *commander* here!"

"Came down to listen to the fighting."

"You get your ass up on the ridge!" And to the officers standing by, both crouching a little as if arrow flights were pressing them down: "Get her *out* of here!"

Charmian grinned. "Listen. . . ." An arrow passed almost between them, a slight disturbance in the air.

"Your wound—"

"I've had worse." Still smiling, a happy woman in battle. "*Listen,* something's wrong with the fighting here." Supporting herself a little on her rapier's springing blade, she turned, slightly stiffly, to look back down the slope. The light was good enough, now, for Sam to see clearly the tide of Kipchaks coming against the supple, almost silent formations of Light Infantry all along this hillside and another beyond it. The dismounted tribesmen attacking in a surf of slaughter . . . then slowly, slowly easing back down the slopes to gather and come again.

Between these advances and withdrawals, men and women fought stranded on the snow in sudden knots, wrestling at knife-point, slashing with swords and *yataghans*. But Sam saw it was the short Kipchak bows that were hurting his people most. The Light Infantry crossbowmen were overmatched.

"See?" Charmian pointed with her rapier's blade. "We need to keep *close!*" As if to prove it, an arrow came whisking past her throat, touched her long hair like a lover fleeting past. "And we *can* keep close, and hold them. They hit us, and hit us hard—"

"But they're not pushing your people back."

"Right. There's no *weight* to this attack."

A surprising smacking sound, and the younger officer—Sam hadn't known his name—pitched down into the snow with an arrow in the side of his neck, just beneath his helmet's edge. The officer grunted, kicked at the snow, and died.

"Oh . . . Bobby." Charmian bent to stroke the dead man's back, then straightened. "They're coming at us as if they meant it—"

"—But with no army coming behind them." Now, listening, Sam could hear a fragility in the Kipchaks' shouts and war cries, their lowing battle horns. Two thousand men, perhaps more, attacking along the slopes. But not with ten thousand coming behind them. . . . *Mistake . . . mistake. I've made a very bad mistake.*

He turned and shouted to his trumpeter. *"Kenneth!* Ride to the center! Tell Phil Butler they're coming at him after all!— And he's to refuse! Refuse and fall back slowly, in order!"

"Comin' at him . . . to refuse an' fall back slow, in order."

"Ride! *Ride!"*

As the trumpeter spurred away, Sam pointed at the bowman sergeant. "McGee—to General Voss and Colonel Flores! The Khan's main attack *is* to the center! They're to withdraw cavalry formations as his people come in—we'll let them push us back.

Light Infantry will then attack his right flank from here. All cavalry—*all* cavalry to move east *now*, into position to attack his left flank as it exposes!"

"Voss an' Flores." The sergeant already reining his horse away. "Comin' at the center—we're lettin' 'em push in so their flanks get bare—then Lights hit his right, Cav goes east, gets set to hit his left!" And he was off, his horse spurning snow across the slope.

As the man rode, Sam gripped Charmian by an arm he hoped unwounded, and tugged her up-hill. "Come on—come on! Get out of this! And put your fucking *helmet* on!"

"I can't *see* with the thing." She looked back, called down-slope, "*Manuel! . . . To your left!*"

Sam thought he saw an officer there look up.

"Shit!" Charmian yanked her arm free and was off, limping awkwardly down the hillside as twenty or thirty Kipchaks hacked their way up into the Infantry's line—then broke it.

"Charmian . . . !" She was gone and at them. Sam drew and ran down after her . . . heard his bowmen yelling, "*No!*" He saw more Lights coming along the slope to reinforce as he galloped down the hill, snow flying.

Charmian had gone for the nearest, a big Kipchak in black furs. Sam saw the man's face, a mask of rage and effort as he struck at her.

Then it was not fighting, but killing.

Charmian caught his curved blade coming across—picked it out of the air with her rapier's tip, guided it sliding to the right, and thrust the long, slim blade of her left-hand dagger into his belly.

Two more stomped up through the snow at her, and Sam yelled, "On the left!" ducked low and swung a two-handed cut across the first man's leg. He felt the sword's grip kick as the blade hacked through boot-top and bone—then yanked the steel free to spin the other way and thrust, one-handed, into the second man's armpit as he raised his *yataghan* to strike.

The crippled one slashed at Sam from the snow and caught him lightly at the thigh—a touch below his hauberk—with the so-familiar icy stroke of steel, then burning.

Sam drove his point into that man's mouth—felt his blade break teeth, then slide through delicate stuff in a spurt of blood to split the spine.

Joy came to him as he freed his blade, joy at the wonderful simplicity of action, and he and Charmian, on guard for any others, shared an instant's glance of pleasure.

Then his mounted bowmen, and a storm of Light Infantry from above, struck the two of them and the advancing Kipchaks together, knocking Charmian down and sending Sam sprawling. Furious officers and men stood over them—"*Stupid . . . stupid fuckers!*"—picked them up, and listening to no orders, showing no respect for rank, hauled them up the hill.

Loosed near the ridge, his sword wiped and sheathed, Sam looked back and saw the Kipchaks once more in shallow retreat . . . then gathering to charge up the slope again. The base of the hill was thick with their formations—by squadrons, as if they were mounted. The dead and dying lay scattered across the snowy slope, streaks and pools of bright red gleaming under the rising sun. The hillside breeze brought the coppery smell of spilled blood, the stink of the dyings' shit. . . . There were great concentrations of tribesmen, and driving activity along the base of the hills. But no massive movement coming on through the forest beyond. No trembling of tangled foliage, no glimpses of columns followed by more columns marching toward them through the snow.

"Busy," Charmian said, catching her breath beside him. She staggered a step. "Busy . . ."

"Now, you stay the fuck out of that line!"

"Yes, sir."

Sam glanced down, saw where his leather trousers were slit

a few inches at his right thigh, and felt a little blood sliding warm to his knee.

"Sir," a bowman said, "you're hurt."

Sam waved him to silence as flights of arrows whistled up the slopes, and the Kipchaks shouted and came again, charging higher . . . higher on the hillsides, their battle lines extending half a Warm-time mile.

"Charmian, can you hold them?" He had to lean close, almost shout in her ear; the noise was terrific.

"Yes, I can hold them—unless we're wrong, and they're strongly reinforced."

"They won't be. I've *made* my mistake for the day."

"I can hold them. And if they bleed a little more, *and* I commit every man and woman—and the wounded still walking—I can drive them!"

"Not yet." Sam ducked—thought an arrow had come near him. "Not yet. Wait for a galloper with the word. We need him to come deep into the center, uncover both his flanks while he thinks we're breaking."

"Understood." Charmian turned to yell across the slope. "*Catherine!* What the fuck are you waiting for? Crossbows *front*, for Christ's sake!" The last, a phrase once forbidden. "Stupid bitch," Charmian muttered, standing bent a little to the right to favor her wounded side, "—looking around with her thumb up her ass! Made her a fucking captain and I can damn well *un*make her. I could have used Margaret here. . . ."

She turned back. "Sam—I know what you want. Now please go away; I don't have time for you." She limped off over the snow, calling, "*Where is Second Battalion? We're replacing in echelon here. We're supposed to be replacing in echelon along the fucking line! Where are they?*"

"Can I help you, sir?" The bowman had brought Difficult to mount.

"No." Though Sam wished he had the help, struggling aboard

the beast. His leg held the stinging tingle of injury . . . and the fucking horse kept sidling away. "Will you hold this animal *still?*" A Kipchak arrow moaned past. They were fighting higher on the slope, now. Sam could hear the sword blows, like camp-axes chopping soft wood. But screams followed these.

* * *

He heard trumpets as he rode fast, east along the ridges, four bowmen riding behind him. He saw, in morning sunlight, the armored columns of Heavy Cavalry, the spaced squadrons of Lights, already slowly shifting along the heights, beginning to shake out into line of march, their banners leading east.

"Thank you, Howell, for getting them *moving.*"

"Sir?" A bowman spurred up alongside.

"Nothing. . . ." As if a deck of pasteboard playing cards—but these for fortune-telling—cascaded in his mind, Sam saw on each, as it flashed by, a different problem, or an opportunity already lost to him. Great or small, it made no difference as they dealt. . . . Lieutenant Gerald Kyle carried vodka with him, and lied about it—what now, to keep him from misjudging and killing his company? Man should have been replaced. . . . Thousands of crossbow bolts needed to be greased for this wet winter weather. Had that been done? Company officers' responsibility. Had it been *done?* . . . Fodder clean? No mold or mildew to sicken the horses. Might have spoken to Ned, might have checked to be sure. . . . When the cavalry swung in to flank the Kipchaks to the east, had it been made clear they were to hook in—hook in after, to hold the tribesmen while the infantry marched back from their false retreat to finish them? Fucking cavalry always galloping off into nowhere, and full of excuses afterward. Had that hooking-in been made clear?

Difficult—not so bad a horse. Stupid, stubborn, but strong

for this kind of uneven going. Steep going. . . . And for Weather's sake, promote Jack Parilla! Poor man a captain for years—always a hard fighter, always took care of his men. No fool, and ready for more rank. Overlooked, a good man overlooked, and no complaint about it, either. . . . Sonora—what was it about those people? Where the fuck did they think those taxes *went?* Having to build that son-of-a-bitch Stewart a bridge! . . . Should have at least shown Rachel how much he liked her, that he thought her an interesting woman. And good-looking, really. Should have told her that. . . .

Some of the cavalry saw Sam riding by, shouted and raised their lances in salute. As he passed a second column of Heavies, three horsemen broke through their formation and came galloping after him. One carried the army's banner on a stirrup-staff—the great black scorpion on a field of gold—cloth rippling in the wind of his riding so the creature seemed to crawl and threaten. All three were coming fast through a light snowfall.

"Sir! *Sir!*" One of them was a captain Sam knew. Collins—Roberto Collins. "Sir,"—Collins rode up beside him—"General Voss's compliments." The captain a little breathless. "He says you are to keep the fucking banner with you, sir! So people can find you, sir! And you are to have me and Lieutenant Miranda with you. Also additional escort, sir!"

From the captain's mouth, to fact. As they rode up a rough draw to the Middle Ridge, the horses slowing with the climb, a half-dozen more mounted bowmen—Sam saw Sergeant McGee leading them—came riding to join. So, it was with a thundering tail of twelve men and one woman, the large Lieutenant Miranda, that Sam kicked Difficult through a last deep drift to lunge out along the iron ranks of Butler's Heavy Infantry.

As they heard Sam's party coming, every second man of the nearest company's rear file had reverse-stepped together, lowering fourteen-foot pikes.

"Platoon, put . . . *up!*" The pikes rose all together. The men stepped back into ranks.

"Phil—or Horacio!" Sam called to their officer.

"General's down-slope, sir! One rise over!"

Sam was reining Difficult in when the charger suddenly shied away, sidestepping through frozen crust. Sam steadied him, looked for the cause, and saw something high in the filtered sunlight . . . a shadow coming down with the snow. Someone behind him called out.

Sam blinked snowflakes away, and the Boston girl sailed down and down to him out of sunlight and snow flurry, her open dark-blue coat spread like wings.

"Over there!" She pointed north with her drawn scimitar, struck the snow, stumbled, and went to a knee. "Short walkings. . . ." She got to her feet. "They make me weary."

Sam saw blood on her blade.

"The savages shot arrows at me!" Her pale, perfect face twisted in fury, and she stomped a little circle in the snow. Sam was reminded, for a moment, of the Queen's raging at Island. . . . Patience flourished her sword; little crimson drops flew from its curved edge. "I took one's hand—then backstroked to his throat!"

"Be quiet," Sam said. "Now, take a breath . . . and tell me what you saw."

"Oh, those fools are coming."

"Here—*here*, to our center?"

"Yes." Patience nodded. "I saw them in the forest. All of them—well, almost all. I think there are a few over there,"—the scimitar swung west. "And even fewer over there,"—her blade flashed toward the river.

"Sir. . . ." Horacio Duran, shoving the escorts' mounts aside. "Colonel."

Duran, blocky as a tree stump in dull steel-strap armor, came to Sam's stirrup with his helmet under his arm. "General's received your orders, sir. Resist as we retire—not making it *too* easy for them."

"Right, Colonel, and have your rear ranks guide."

"We'll keep in formation, sir." Duran smiled, though he had a face unfitted for it. "—But with occasional cries of panic and despair."

Sam leaned down to thump Duran's armored shoulder with his fist. "Perfect. They'll be coming soon."

"Coming now, sir. We've seen birds and deer clearing out of those woods."

"*Good,*" Sam said. "I'll want some daylight left, to finish them." At which vainglory, he was slightly saddened to see Lieutenant-Colonel Duran smile again . . . hear pleased murmurs from his escort.

Birds were flying almost over them—a doom of crows, cawing. Sam supposed it would be crows, in these hills—not ravens—who would come to take the eyes of the dead.

He saluted Duran—it had become, after all, the army's habit—was briskly saluted in return, and reined Difficult around. It was time for the Captain-General to get out of his soldiers' way.

"Wait! Take me up!" Patience sheathed her scimitar and came floundering through the snow. "I'm tired of walking." Meaning, apparently, traveling in the air.

Sam reined in, seeing himself parading before his troops with this odd creature riding pillion behind him. Then Patience, with a boost from Duran, was on the charger's rump and settled. Seemed almost no shift of weight at all . . . and as he kicked Difficult through falling snow along the ridge, no odor either. No lady's perfume, no woman's warm scent. He might have had a doll behind him, or a child's snow-person.

Patience gripped his waist, leaned her head against his cloaked and chain-mailed back. "I have a headache," she said, as they went bounding. Difficult's only virtue, strength.

As they rode, the banner-bearer and escort spurring after, a sound like distant storm-wind, like a change in Lady Weather's wishes, seemed to come rising the long wooded slopes behind them. Barely heard . . . then slowly, slowly heard more clearly . . . until, in a rolling thunderclap—with flights of winter birds across the sky—the storm became the voice of an attacking army, its war horns a chorus, as if wild bulls bellowed from the woods.

"Oh-oh." A child's exclamation in almost a child's soprano, and Sam felt Patience turning back to look—though nothing would be seen but the backs of serried ranks of Phil Butler's two thousand pikemen and crossbowmen, draped like a segmented steel-link chain across the ridges and hollows. . . . Sam closed his eyes as he rode, seeing them standing ready to receive, as ten thousand Kipchaks came boiling out of the forest, surging up the slopes in tides of steel and arrows.

Difficult tripped on a branch in the snow, and Sam hauled him up on the reins. Along the ridge-line, the snow grew thinner, and he urged the charger to a gallop, heard his escort coming up behind. Troops were cheering as he passed—squadrons of Light Cavalry riding east. He saw a pennon through falling snow. Second Regiment, Elman's people. Good officer, but mad for fighting, and perhaps not the best second-in-command for Ned. Two madmen. . . .

There was a sound like a great steel door slamming. The falling snow seemed to swirl with the impact of it. The center was being hit with everything that Toghrul had. Thank God— that oldest thanks of all—thank God for Charmian's sharp ears and battle sense, her call to him to *listen.* It had given him just time enough. *May* have given him just time enough. . . .

The smash and roar of engagement sounding behind him, Sam rode along Main Ridge to be certain all the cavalry had shifted east. So difficult, to leave commanders alone in a battle, to depend on them to do what had to be done. It was hard to see how the Khan managed without a Howell Voss, a Ned Flores. Without a Phil Butler, a Charmian, and all their officers. Toghrul must be an extraordinary man to depend, really, only on himself. Must be lonely. . . .

Sam reined up, reached behind him to give Patience an arm to dismount. "Now, go down that south slope. Stay with Portia-doctor and her people."

"I will," Patience said, "but only to rest to go back again. They shot arrows at me!" And she trudged off into the snow.

"Comin' up!" One of the mounted bowmen.

An officer galloping, chasing the banner . . . then drew up in a spray of snow, and saluted. A lieutenant, very young—what was his name? Carlton . . . Carter? Boy was crying, or snow was melting down his face.

"Sir—Colonel Duran regrets to report . . ." Tears, they were tears. "General Butler has been killed, sir. At the very first engagement. An arrow struck him."

Carter. Boy's name was Carter. ". . . Thank the colonel for his report, Lieutenant. He assumes command, of course—and is to retreat his regiments as previously ordered."

"Sir."

"—The dog," Sam said. "His little dog."

"We have the dog safe, sir." A weeping lieutenant—nothing new in war.

Sam saluted, and the boy turned his horse and was gone north, back to the center of the line, where companies, battalions, regiments of Heavy Infantry stood killing with long needle-pointed pikes, killing with hissing crossbow volleys—as ten thousand grim shepherds with slanting eyes came swarming up the hillsides.

Phil Butler would be out of all that, lying safe behind the ranks in a warm woolen army blanket, his imperial spectacles folded and tucked into his parka pocket. . . . Horacio Duran would now be wearing the yoke of responsibility. He'd be here and there and everywhere, shouting orders, watching for the time to begin to back away. Then more orders, and galloping back and forth to keep the formations steady as the Kipchaks yelped their battle cries and came on, certain they were winning.

Sam spurred Difficult south, imagining Phil had only been wounded, and Carter had said, 'Injured, sir. Seems not too serious.' If Carter had only said that, then Phil would be alive, fondly cursing his soldiers as they hustled him to the rear. Odd that a single arrow could carry a friend so suddenly away, that there was no time for good-bye.... Unfair. Unfair.

Sam saw Heavy Cavalry where there should have been none. Saw two troops ... three, through the light snowfall. Three troops standing in a defile. *Standing!* He spurred that way, down a steep dip, then rode up the column with his people behind him—took an officer by the cloak and hauled him half out of his saddle. "What are you people *doing?*"

Startled face behind a helmet's basket visor. "Cover reserve, sir! In case of retreat."

Sam shook him hard. "There *is* no fucking reserve held today, you jackass! No retreat! We lose, they'll follow and kill us all!"

"Orders, sir!" Fool almost shouting, as if Sam were deaf. "—Orders."

"*Whose* orders?" Shake, shake. The man's cloak tore a little.

Lieutenant Miranda, very large, had heeled her horse alongside. Her saber was drawn.

"Major d'Angelo's orders."

Major d'Angelo ... decent officer. "The major was mistaken. Orders are *no* reserves. Everyone to the line!"

Nods from Torn-cloak.

"Now, you get your ass and these troopers east at a fucking gallop! You understand me? Join General Voss's people to attack on that flank."

More nods. Sam shoved the man upright in his saddle. "—*Move!*"

Sam stayed to watch them go—go galloping, as Lieutenant Miranda sheathed her saber, backed her big horse. . . . Three troops of Heavy Cavalry almost lost to the attack. Have to speak to d'Angelo. A little less attention to the usual ways of doing things; a little more attention to fucking immediate orders!

"Who was that officer?" A question asked of the snowy air.

"Captain Hooper, sir," said Captain Collins, behind him.

"—Good man." Which recommendation, in the face of his commander's anger, also recommended Roberto Collins.

Sam felt tired as if he'd stayed with the Lights to the west, been fighting all this time. . . . He turned Difficult's head, kicked him back up onto the ridge, and looked for a place to stand on the hilltop. Now, unless disaster came, he would be only a watcher, avoiding the dangerous confusions of casual interference. Separate from his soldiers as if he were sleeping far south in Better-Weather, or eating roast pork at the high tables in Island's hall.

Now, he would be a ghost of war, all a commander's directions given. As the Boston girl had done, he could only hover over, his sword blooded once, and watch below him for a battle won. A battlefield ghost, perhaps to be joined by Phil Butler, and many more.

It seemed to Sam he already heard a different music sung from the northern slopes, the higher-pitched chorus of fighting men seeing a triumph before them. Duran would be beginning to coax his men back . . . back. But slowly, Horacio, and in *formation* for the love of Mountain Jesus.

Sam found a sensible place, high enough to see all the center below and before him, and at least some of the distant hillsides left and right. Difficult seemed pleased to be rested from snow-galloping. He and the other horses stood blowing and farting. Comical beasts, really. . . .

"*McGee.*"

"Sir?" The sergeant kicked his mount alongside.

"Sergeant, take your bowmen off to the east. Join Colonel Flores, or any Light squadron you come to, and go in with them. They'll be moving now, need every archer they can get."

A sudden roar from the northern slopes, as if snow-tigers had come to fight. Sam saw the first ranks of Heavy Infantry retreating . . . falling back toward him, some men running this way, over the first ridge.

"*Runnin'!*" McGee said.

But as they watched, the scatter of running men slowed as retreating formations overtook them. They stepped back into ranks, waited . . . and broke to run again, making another show of flight.

"That's okay," said Sergeant McGee.

"Sergeant—take your people and move off."

"Musn' leave you, sir." Then, more definitely: "Won't do it."

"Yes, you will, Jim." How had he remembered this man's first name?

After a silent moment, the sergeant said, "Shit. . . ." Then turned and called, "We're goin' east. So kick it!"

As the bowmen rode away, Captain Collins drew his saber and came up on Sam's left side, Lieutenant Miranda did the same on his right. The three of them—with the banner-bearer stoic behind—sat their horses and watched the Heavy Infantry of North Map-Mexico, never before defeated, slowly driven crumbling back along the ridgelines, seeming just short of desperate flight.

Sitting his horse in safety, Sam closed his eyes, imagining every sword slash, every hissing arrow come by merciful magic to strike him instead of a soldier. So that he, who commanded suffering, received it.

Lieutenant Miranda murmured beside him, and he opened his eyes to see the Kipchak horse-tails rising on the ridge, hear the war horns' dark music triumphant.

"Come on . . . come *on*." Sam felt the oddest flash of sympathy, of sadness for Toghrul, as if he were a friend. The Khan's looming defeat would have been a victory instead, if Sam had held to his blunder only a little longer. Now, the *tumans* lunging deeper into disaster, the Heavy Infantry stepping back and back to draw them in, Toghrul—like Sam, a young man chained to authority—would likely end the day destroyed.

* * *

It was remarkably like riding up a shallow river in rapids, though these currents were tumultuous with gray fur, drawn bows, and steel. Mounted, of course, with only his hundred of the Guard mounted with him, Toghrul spurred Lively on in the midst of the tumans' assault.

An oddity, this attack on foot, but an oddity that was succeeding. They had already struck the first of North Mexico's lines of heavy infantry, and despite desperate—if fairly ineffective—resistance, were driving them back up their slopes to destruction. . . . Future use of infantry was perhaps something to be considered, with the forests, hills, all the broken country to be encountered east of Kingdom's river, should the New Englanders continue arrogant. Infantry . . .

A roar of cheering up ahead. Through fading snowfall, Toghrul saw the horse-tails of First and Third Tumans on the ridge. He and his Guards rode among the second—which began to run. More than five thousand men racing, flooding up snow-drifted slopes to join the thousands driving into the enemy's center.

Toghrul spurred on, his Guardsmen swinging whips to win a way through rushing ranks of soldiers, the *nagaikas'* cracking lashes heard even over war cries, over the sounds of battle as the North Mexican infantry fell back into the hills in retreat.

Once on the heights, the tumans would divide, strike east and west along the ridge-lines to complete the victory. Then, Shapilov's foolish loss in the north forgotten, the subjugation of Middle Kingdom would become inevitable.

His center destroyed—in only Warm-time minutes, now—Monroe would, of course, dream of flanking movements. But dream too late . . . too late to reposition troops, to reorganize his army. There would be no time for it.

There was a sound to the east. . . . Toghrul rose in his stirrups to hear better over the noise of the advance. Something there at the left flank—*from* the left flank.

There was . . . something. A trembling in the air. A sound from the eastern slopes as if a great barrel of stones were rolling. . . . Cavalry.

Toghrul shouted, *"Cavalry!"* Sul Niluk, at the head of the escort, heard him as other Guardsmen heard him—and all turned to stare east.

Out of a fading curtain of falling snow, blowing, drifting with the wind . . . movement. Shifting movement on the hillsides' snow-draped brush and bramble. Gray gleams of steel, and the rumbling noise louder and louder.

Then a grand choir of trumpets—and horsemen, banners, a host of three . . . four thousand riding in an armored tide a half-mile wide across the slopes, thundering down on tumans dismounted. The men scrambling—so slow on foot—crowding, surging away to avoid that avalanche of cavalry, its trumpets blaring like the cries of monstrous beasts.

Then bugles answering from the west. Toghrul looked to the right, saw nothing yet, but heard the bugles. That would be their Light Infantry coming, of course. And commanded by a *woman*, of all absurdities.

There . . . *there*. The first formations coming at the run to swing the western gate shut upon him . . . some sunshine coming with them, shining on their steel. His Guardsmen were shouting . . . the dismounted men, thousands of them, also slowing their advance on the hillsides, calling, crying out as they saw death come riding from the east . . . running from the west.

"Rally!" Toghrul howled it, and hurt his throat. *"Rally and fall back!"* Hopeless . . . hopeless.

Monroe had dreamed of flanking after all, and dreamed in time. His Heavy Infantry's so-convincing retreat would now end as a blocking wall of pikes and crossbows at the last high ridge, to hold the dismounted Kipchak army as it was flanked, slaughtered, then hunted as those still alive fled north. . . . Really fine generalship. An interesting man.

Toghrul's Guardsmen had reined to face the cavalry attack, to hold it for the instants he would need to gallop free. Everything was perfectly clear, went very slowly, could be seen in each detail. Sound, though, seemed muffled, so that trumpet calls, men's screams, and the rumbling shock of hoofbeats were like distant music. He saw the pennants' colors perfectly . . . noticed an officer in the first rank of those horsemen, brown uniform, black cloak streaming as he rode, a shining steel hook for a hand.

Toghrul reined Lively around, blessing the animal, and spurred away as his escort of one hundred wheeled to guard. His standard-bearer had turned to stay with him—but reined his horse left, rather than right, so Lively lunged shouldering into it. Caught off-balance, the man's horse stumbled in the rush and went down as if it had taken an arrow.

Lively, stepping over the fallen horse, was kicked and his left fore broken.

Toghrul picked him up on the reins and heeled him stagger-

ing away, three-legged, as the hundred of the Guard—tangled
by fugitive soldiers into disarray—were struck at a gallop by a
surf of cavalry. The Guards and their mounts were hurled aside,
ridden down, driven back and back in a tumble of flesh, bone,
and steel.

This great breaking wave of frantic thrashing beasts, of dead
and dying men, caught Lively and drove him under.

Toghrul had an instant to try to kick free of the stirrups—
leap for his life in a desperate scramble, then run, *run*. . . . And,
of course, look ridiculous in the attempt.

He stayed in his saddle, called only, *"My son . . ."*

* * *

Sam had noticed before, that the near silence at a battle's end
seemed loud as the fighting had been. This end of the day
sounded only with distant trumpets calling the chase, with orders spoken nearby, with conversations and the rasp of grave-
digging, the hollow *chock* of axes cutting campfire wood. And
an occasional muffled scream as the parade of wounded was
carried on plank hurdles over snowy slopes, then down the
main-ridge reverse to the medical tents, and Portia-doctor's people.

The remnant Kipchaks were scattering north, pursued by
Light Cavalry. They would ride, killing those people, until their
horses foundered.

Poor savages. Only shepherd tribesmen now, without their
brilliant Lord of Grass—and hunted by every people they'd conquered before. It would be years before the Kipchaks were an
army again—if ever.

Victory. Its first taste, chilled imperial wine—its second, rotting blood.

"General Voss comin', sir." Corporal Fass—alive and on tent-guard as usual. . . . More than could be said for Sergeant Wilkey, that quietly dangerous young man. Assuming Sam might have some special affection for him, Charmian had sent a word of regret that he'd been killed.

A people whose bravest men and women died in wars to defend them . . . after years and years of such losses, might a country of mountain lions became a country of sheep?

Howell was riding a strange horse—his charger must have been killed in the fighting. A tired horse, and a tired man climbing off it.

"Thank you,"—Sam took his hand—"for Map–Fort Stockton, and for here."

"Sam, don't thank me for giving orders, and I won't thank you for it. Our people did the dying, enough so Lady Weather let us win." Voss—left eye already lost, its socket hidden under his black patch—had nearly lost the right. A blade-point had struck his cheek just beneath; a run of blood was clotted down his face. . . . But it seemed one eye was enough to reveal sorrow.

"Tell me, Howell."

"Phil . . ."

"I know Phil's dead. Dead in the first engagement. Horacio sent a runner when it happened. He's got Phil's little dog. . . ."

Howell made a face like a punished child's. "And Carlo."

"Carlo. . . . All right. Go on."

"Teddy Baker, Fred Halloway, Michelle Serrano, Willard Reese . . . and a number of junior officers."

"A number . . ."

"Two hundred and eleven, Sam."

"By the dear *Lady*. . . . Certain?"

"As reported. Still could be more—or less. A few may turn up, might only have been wounded."

"Soldiers?"

"Sam, it's too soon to say; still calling rolls. Likely at *least* three thousand killed or wounded. A number of companies don't seem to exist, now. Fourth Battalion of Lights is gone, but for twenty or thirty people.—And Oswald-cook is dead. Apparently heard 'No reserves,' and brought his people up on the line as the center fell back. Fought with cleavers and kitchen knives, some of them."

"Kitchen knives. . . . Elvin would have been relieved. No more experiments for dinner."

"Southern peppers stuck in everything . . ." Howell tried a smile.

"Who else?"

Howell stopped smiling.

"Who *else?*"

"Ned."

"You're—you don't *know* that. He could be anywhere out there!"

"Sam, they found him. Sword cuts. Elman saw him fighting in the charge, surrounded by those people. . . . Found the Kip-chak Khan a little farther on. Fucker had been trampled—his own people rode over him."

"Yes. . . . One of Horacio's officers, Frank Clay, told me they'd found Toghrul dead."

"Ned was maybe a bow-shot away from him. Going to kill the son-of-a-bitch, I suppose, and there were just too many to ride through."

". . . Howell, I gave him that order. I said, 'The Khan is to be killed.' "

"A proper order, Sam—and Ned and his people drove the Kipchaks over their own commander."

For a while, they stood and said nothing. It had become a beautiful day, no snowflakes falling. The evening sun shone warm as egg-yolk through clear, cold air. The blood in Sam's right boot had turned to icy slush.

By the greatest effort, he managed not to recall a single day of the numberless days he and Ned had spent together in the

Sierra. Laughing—always laughing about something . . . usually mischief, sheep stealing, trying to lure ranchers' lean, tough daughters out into the moonlight. Always some . . . nonsense.

"There'd better be two worlds," he said to Howell. "There'd *better* be a place with open gates, for all the ones we've lost."

"If not,"—Howell managed a smile—"we'll take the army and break those gates down." He saluted, and went to mount his tired horse. A lucky man, not to have been blinded by that wound. . . .

* * *

At dark, by a campfire built high of hardwood—as, Sam supposed, a sort of victory beacon—his commanders, senior officers surviving, many limping and bloodied in battered armor, stood around him on the high-ridge hilltop like monuments to war's triumphs and disasters. Some were drawing deep, exhausted breaths, as if still uncertain of their next.

The Boston girl, Patience—no longer looking quite so young—knelt in the fire's light, polishing her scimitar's slender steel.

"Sam . . ." Howell had cleaned the dried blood from his face, and looked only weary. "Sam, what do we do now?"

The campfire roared softly, its smoke rising into deeper night.

"We bury our dead," Sam said, looking into the flames. He held Phil's little dog, trembling in a fold of his cloak. "Then ride to the river, to celebrate a wedding."

* * *

The elderly Bishop of the Presence of Floating Jesus—a man habitually bulky and full in flesh—stood a little shrunken in his Shades-of-water robe, on which many little jeweled fish were sewn, mouths open to sing adoration of the Lord.

Old Queen Joan had been the bishop's casual enemy for years—supposedly he'd bored her; she'd certainly refused him residence at Island. But her death, nevertheless, had struck him such a surprising blow that these new matters, these over-settings of what had once been so, had worn him severely, and made what was real seem unreal.

True, the sun shone into the eight-week summer; true, the river's wind blew richly through the stone of Island—he felt his robe-hem ruffle to it—and true, men and women wed.

But standing on the wide balcony of North Tower, he faced not only the familiar—he'd known the Princess Rachel since she'd been a child—but the unfamiliar as well, a stocky North Mexican war-chief, supposedly soon to be the *King*. . . . His officers, still battle-lame, crowded the chamber beyond, alongside great river lords—and one of the Boston creatures as well.

The sun shone, and the river's wind blew, but all else seemed a dream, and his reading of the marriage vows—'fidelity to flow,' and so forth—unreal as the rest.

But he ended at last, and the Princess was gathered—cream lace crushed, diadem tilted awry—into her husband's arms and kissed with rather coarse energy, and apparent affection. Then a great rolling roar, an avalanche of shouts, welled from the crowds packing the wide landings, staircases, and distant broad, paved squares of Island—though many still wore blood-red in mourning for the Queen they'd loved. The granite rang, hundreds of hanging, ribboned decorations swung to that thunder, and the banners, pennants, and flags flying from every tower, flying from every ship in the near gate-harbor, seemed to ripple out also in celebration, as if with the river's blessing.

Still, the bishop felt he dreamed . . . until the bridegroom, smiling like a boy, reached out to take his hand—and woke him with an iron grip, eased to gentleness.